The
Lost Daughter
of India

The Lost Daughter of India

SHARON MAAS

bookouture

Published by Bookouture
An imprint of StoryFire Ltd.
23 Sussex Road, Ickenham, UB10 8PN
United Kingdom
www.bookouture.com

ISBN: 978-1-78681-119-6
eBook ISBN: 978-1-78681-118-9

For Miro

Chapter One

Caroline snuggled deeper into Meenakshi's lap, her favourite place in all the world. Meena's whole body was a cushion, soft and yielding, and when you cuddled into her it moulded around you and held you safe. It was the best place for a five-year-old to spend a summer evening, swaying gently in the rocking chair on the back porch, Meena's arms around her as she held the book.

The backyard smelt of summer: of sun and moist earth from the water sprinkler gently waving to and fro. The sounds were of summer too. Birds twittered in the chestnut tree in the centre of the backyard, squirrels scampered across the branches, chattering among themselves. The sights and sounds and fragrances of a leafy neighbourhood in Massachusetts, America surrounded them. Meena didn't smell of America. Meena had her own distinctive smell, and Caroline breathed her in. She smelt of India, sweet and spicy all at once, a thousand secret aromas all mingled together. It was in the fabric of her saris, in her hair, in her very skin, dark as a hazelnut and shiny as silk. It wafted, too from the pages of that book, which Meena had brought with her from India when *she* was a little girl, the same age as Caroline was now.

It was a big book, the biggest book on Caroline's shelf, with over a thousand pages. They had been reading it for months now, every day a chapter, and it might be a year before it was finished, and that was fine with Caroline. She hoped it would last for ever. It was that sort of a book, the kind that took you off on journeys

with different characters to different places but sooner or later
brought you back to the main story; and you would understand
the main story a little bit better because of that little excursion. It
was the sort of book that took you on a voyage far, far away and
made you live in another place and another time and become
another person while you were away. It was the sort of book that
created vivid pictures in your mind so that you were actually
there and *then* and *among* those people and even *turned you into*
those people so that they weren't foreign any more because you
became them.

Meena's voice was perfect for the story. It was languid but
strong; Meena was never in a hurry to get to the end of a story
and close the book. She read as if she had all the time in the
world, and probably she did; and she could put on a man's voice
or a girl's voice or a demon's voice or the voice of a god and make
you believe that very person was speaking. She could give you
goosebumps, and make you quake in fear. She could transport
you into that person's soul.

Right now, Caroline was in India, a young prince disguised
as a simple priest, and he was about to win the hand of the most
beautiful princess in the world, Draupadi.

'*"Arjuna strode over to the bow, head held high,"*' Meena read,
in her strongest book-voice – her royal voice, Caroline called it.
'"*As effortlessly as Karna had done before him, he raised it; the kings
gasped. He picked up one of the glittering arrows, took aim at the fish
spinning high above, released the arrow. With a silver streak almost
invisible to the eye it pierced the eye of the fish, which tumbled to
the ground. A roar as thunder filled the arena; furious, fuming, the
assembled kings waved their fists and screamed insults into the arena;
but Arjuna was unmoved.*

"*With three wide springs he leapt onto the royal dais and stood
before Draupadi, holding out his hand. Dhrishtadyumna helped his
sister to her feet and placed her hand in Arjuna's. Conch moaned and*

trumpet blared as Arjuna led his bride away: like a young celestial with a heavenly apsara…"' ('What's an *apsara?*' asked Caroline, and Meena replied in her normal Meena voice: 'a heavenly dancing maiden.') '"…*like god Vishnu with his consort, the goddess Lakshmi, like the sun with the moon by his side, the two left the arena, flowers raining down on them from heaven. Brahmins cheered, kings raged. Karna fell to the ground. The four remaining Pandavas looked at each other and they, too, left.*"'

Meena closed the book. 'And that, my sweet, is enough for today.'

'No!' cried Caroline. 'I want to know what happened next! Do the Pandavas get their kingdom back? Do they come out of hiding? Does Draupadi have to go and live with them in the forest? What happens, Meena?'

'Well, you will just have to be a bit more patient, because tomorrow I will read to you some more. Your mommy and daddy will be home from work any time now and they will want to see you and hear what you have been doing all day.'

Caroline pouted. 'I want you to read some more! I want—'

'What! What are you telling me! What happens to little children who say *I want* all the time?'

'"I want never gets,"' replied Caroline, her bottom lip stuck out. 'I know. But still. It's not fair.'

'Life isn't fair,' Meena said as she lifted her up and placed her on the ground. Laying the book on the porch table, she tilted the chair forward and slowly, with much effort, pushed her cushiony body to her feet, grasped Caroline's hand and led her indoors, through the kitchen where Lucia was cooking the evening meal, into the hall and up the stairs to Caroline's bedroom to get her ready for her parents' homecoming. Her three older brothers were still outside, at friends' homes, playing baseball on the street, climbing trees; the things boys do after school. They'd be in soon, too.

Caroline's father was a lawyer; he worked very hard and sometimes he didn't make it home for dinner. But her mother, a doctor, always did; and it was her mother who, after dinner, would give her her bath and put her to bed and read her a story. But those stories were never as real as the ones Meenakshi told from memory, or read from books: stories of Indian kings and queens, heroes and villains and gods disguised as animals or beggars; cows who could fulfil desires and deer who could speak and monsters who could change shape at will.

If you asked Caroline what she wanted to be when she grew up, she'd say, like many an American little girl, a princess. But Caroline would be no Disney princess. She'd marry a prince like Arjuna, and ride to her wedding in a howdah on an elephant's back wearing a fabulous sari adorned with real jewels; and her palace would be in India.

Caroline was in love with India before she could even write the word. She could point to it on the globe, and she'd tell anyone who asked that *that* was where she'd live when she grew up. Adults would laugh indulgently, and pat her on the head, and tell her she was dreaming; but Caroline knew it was destiny. She *would* grow up to marry an Indian prince.

Chapter Two

Asha. Mumbai, 2000

I am forever lost. No one can save me. Not one of my three mothers is here to rescue me from this hell. Not one of my two fathers.

The mother who gave birth to me? I have no memory of her. I know her only through the letters she wrote to me over the years, the photographs of herself; she has yellow hair and pale skin, because she is a foreigner. She signs her letters Mom. She is so far away in a country called America, and does not even care. She can never save me.

Amma is my other mother, the one who raised me. Mom gave me to her because she had no milk. She is the one who nourished me at her breast, the one I love. But she is dead.

Janiki is my third mother, my chinna-amma, my little mother. She isn't really my mother. She isn't even really my sister. Janiki was thirteen when I was born and she has told me the story over and over again. How Amma placed me in her arms after the one called Mom left, and said to her, 'Janiki, I have been given this little waif to look after but my hands are full with Kanaan and the next one to come. I give her to you; you care for her. She is yours. I will feed her, but everything else, you must do. You must be her chinna-amma.'

And so, though I shared Amma's milk with Kanaan, and later with Ramesh, Janiki became my little mother. But she too is far away now, in another country, another world, and she will never find me in this hell.

Three mothers, and two fathers. The man I called Appa, Father, was Amma's husband. He is also dead. Appa was headmaster of the English Medium School and so he was highly respected, and so were his children. He wore large thick glasses and he would peer at you over the top of them and smile. He was kind but distant, and could also be strict. As a headmaster you have to be very strict. Sometimes he even flogged some of the naughtiest children, but only the boys, never the girls. But then girls are never naughty. Why then is it always the girls who get the worst punishments? I would rather have been flogged a million times than endure the punishments I had to take later, because of being a girl.

A father should find his lost daughter. But Appa is not my real father.

There is only Him. The man I am supposed to call Daddy, but I cannot. Daddy is too ordinary. He is not ordinary.

I've always known about Him. Always, as far back as I can remember, there he was, the man who was supposed to be my real father, but who for me was more like a god, up in the heavens somewhere along with Indra and all the other celestial beings, occasionally deigning to descend to us and bless me with his presence. He came seldom; the last time I was only about eight, and I never forgot that last visit.

By then, Amma had told me he is really a prince. And that makes me a princess. Amma used to call me Little Princess. But I am not a princess. A princess does not live in such wretchedness.

Whenever he came I was truly tongue-tied – I could hardly speak a word to him, and answered his questions with a yes or a no or even just a shrug of my shoulders, turning my face away so as not to meet his eyes, for I could not bear the way they seemed to see all the way through me, right down to the bottom of my being, and I would tingle with happiness. And when he left again the tingling would stay with me for a long time so I hardly felt like a human child until normal life seeped through me once again and called me back to earth. What I am saying is I really worshipped that man, and I didn't think of him as a father but as my saviour, even as a small child. Yes, I worshipped him. But he never came again, and so I know he has forgotten me. Amma told me he lives far away, in another country, a country that is all desert. So he, too, cannot save me.

I want to go home!

I used to live in a big house in Gingee, with Amma and Appa and Janiki and our five brothers. At least, for me it was a big house, though I have since seen really grand homes and ours was a hovel in comparison. But compared to other Gingee homes it was certainly large. I had seen the homes of other children in my school class and ours seemed so much grander – though now I can only laugh at such innocence. I mean, I *would* laugh if I could, had I not forgotten how to laugh.

Our home, in fact, was just a gathering of rooms, and mats laid out where we slept – inside in winter, outside in summer – and some shelves where we kept our clothes and utensils. That's all, though we did have electric lights and a radio that blared *filmi* music all day long; Amma liked this music, and she sang along with the radio.

So we had comforts, and our home in Gingee was no hovel either – for now I live in a real hovel. The very worst kind of place, a hole in hell. The only escape is in sleep. I sleep as much as I can. But when I open my eyes again and remember where I am my heart beats faster and I feel the panic rising in me like vomit, panic that is trapped inside me and can never leave the body, like vomit that lurches up but falls back down again. I would give anything to be able to vomit but I cannot. It is trapped in me for ever and when I pray it is for healing from that sickness in me.

Looking back, I think of my Gingee home as paradise. And I would exchange all the palaces in the world and all of paradise to go back there – or better yet, never to have left. But my destiny said otherwise.

We were all so happy, but didn't know it. We lived in a quiet part of Gingee. When we finished our schoolwork and our household chores we children could play in the street outside our door as much as we wanted, because there was not much traffic, not like in the busier areas of town where the whole street would be filled with all kinds of vehicles with stinking exhaust fumes, as well as rickshaws that would appear out of nowhere and pounce on you if you tried to cross the street. I used to be terrified of streets like that and always grabbed Janiki's hand when we went anywhere in the town. Janiki was always there for me.

But of course now I know that that those terrifying Gingee streets were really nothing more than quiet lanes; because now I have seen the world and I know the terrors the world holds are worse than any terror on the main streets of Gingee.

I have read about hell, and the demons that live there, but I can assure you, this hell I am in now is a million times worse. That is the truth. And because I was happy with Amma and Appa and Janiki and my brothers I can compare, and so I can say my childhood was pure heaven. That is how it seems to me now.

Looking back, I cannot see much of the details. I see our home, a house with a large veranda at the front, where Amma used to sit cleaning rice or stringing beans and things like that, because she liked to see who was passing by and sometimes have a little chat with the other ladies who lived on that street.

I cannot believe I was fortunate enough to have parents like them, even though they weren't my real parents. And Janiki. How I long for Little Amma! When I think of them and that time before my twelfth birthday tears come to my eyes because a good family is so rare. I know that now, and when I close my eyes I can see Janiki's beautiful face and those eyes brimming with love.

I am sure there were unpleasant things in Gingee as well, but I don't remember them because they are nothing. I only remember the good things. It is as if my life back then, the life I lived from day to day, was nothing more than a film passing before my eyes, insubstantial pictures of no lasting value, so there's no use at all in describing them to you. The important thing was the feeling I had, the feeling of being embedded in this wonderful cushion of love where nothing could touch you and nothing could ever hurt you. I suppose that is the essence of my childhood, not the individual events that followed each other in a chain – because those things pass away, passing pictures in a cinema. What remains at all times is the thing behind it – the screen of my being, you could say, over which those pictures passed; a backdrop of goodness. Because that is what has stayed with me, what keeps me alive: the remembrance of goodness. Of what goodness was like. That memory is what really keeps me alive when everything else is dying, crumbling into a dark abyss and swallowing up my soul. That is what has sustained me in my journey through hell.

Because I am able to say to myself, if the events of my childhood are nothing more than passing pictures, then so is this horror. Everything else is a passing picture.

That is the secret of my survival. I don't mean my physical survival, for my body, though often injured, was never even near death – though often it felt that way, and often I prayed it could be dead, and I know that one day it will be dead. I mean the survival of my soul, which has been so much in jeopardy these past weeks or months or even years. I have lost count of time. I have stopped counting the days. My life now is from breath to breath. The only one who can save me now is Bhagavan, God. He could but he won't. My prayers go unanswered.

I said I don't remember the unpleasant things of my past life; well, that's not quite true. I do remember the day when Amma and Appa never came home.

That was the beginning of the end. Now I am in this monstrous city, a single grain on a beach full of sand. No one can find that single grain. That is what it means to be lost. But my name is Asha. It means hope. In her last message my sister Janiki said never give up hope, Janiki. Hope, and faith, will keep you safe. Even just a spark of it. And so, though I know I am forever lost, I cling to that one spark of hope.

Chapter Three

Kamal. Moti Khodayal, Gujarat, India, 1972

Kamal tried not to breathe; he was sure they'd hear him if he did. He could hear his own breathing and the drumming of his heart, loud and erratic, and it seemed to him the whole world must be listening, watching for him. He crouched lower in the hamper, hugging his knees, curled into a ball with his head tucked in, exactly fitting the circular shape of the basket. For the first time in his life he was glad that he was so small, so supple, like a cat, they said, loose and limber and able to crawl into the smallest spaces and jump from the highest windows, landing like a coiled spring and sprinting off before they could blink twice.

That's why they never caught him; that's why when Rani Abishta, his grandmother, Daadi, sent them for him he was able to wriggle loose and run, and that's why Daadi tried all the more to bind him to herself. But bondage, for Kamal, had the effect of a whiplash, urging him to escape, stimulating his ingenuity so that, short of winding him in thick chains, Daadi remained the loser. He smiled to himself, thinking of Daadi's rage, and then her panic, when he turned up missing.

He had placed a cloth over himself so that if someone did happen to open the hamper, they wouldn't notice he was there; they'd be deceived into thinking the hamper had been sent back with its contents intact, rejected by the caretaker. At first he squeezed his eyelids together as if, by shutting out the world, the world would also shut him out – at least the little world of Moti

Khodayal which he knew so well, every tiny corner and crevice so that he could find his way blindfolded through the labyrinthine passages and staircases; led on by the pungent smells, the sounds, the shape of the cobbles, the smoothness of the stones beneath his bare feet, the texture of tapestries and curtains, the senses of touch and hearing and smelling refined to such perfection he could almost abstain from the sense of sight.

With the passing of each second his excitement grew, but also his anxiety. The more time it took to load the cart and coax the bullocks into movement, the more dangerous it would become for him; he had to make sure everything outside was *normal*. Cautiously he opened his eyes to a slit. It was dark inside the hamper but not fully dark: slabs of daylight glinted between the strands of wicker. Curiosity won over caution: carefully he adjusted his position, pushing his face right up to the hamper's side, aligning his right eye with one of those daylight cracks, and peered out.

Everything seemed normal. In the greyness of the first morning light there was the usual courtyard bustle. Punraj, wearing only his loincloth and a turban, trotted across Kamal's limited line of vision, bent slightly forward under the weight of the rice sack he carried on his back. Punraj's body, black as ebony, glistened with sweat although the sun was not yet out; it was a long way to the storeroom at the back of the complex and this was certainly not his first sack. Kamal smiled to himself. He wished he could call out to Punraj, and share his secret; Punraj wouldn't mind and Punraj wouldn't talk. Punraj was a friend, a forbidden friend, one of the many forbidden friends Kamal had made among the palace subordinates.

He couldn't see much through the slit, and after Punraj there were a few seconds when all he could see was the red-brick building at the back of the courtyard. But he could hear the familiar morning noises and knew therefore that he had not yet been missed, that everything was as it should be.

A goat ran across the fine strip of courtyard revealed to Kamal, the white nanny goat that Kamal had named Wendy. Wendy was being chased by six-year-old Bibi, Punraj's daughter, another of Kamal's forbidden friends. Bibi wore a long red skirt and she raced zigzagging behind Wendy, thrusting out grasping arms that the little goat neatly evaded, before she, too, disappeared from sight.

Kamal smelt the smoke from fires lit in the kitchen at his back, and his mouth watered as he heard the sizzling of ghee as the cooks began to fry the breakfast puris. He heard the clang of buckets being let into the well to his side, the creaking of the pulley, the gush of water poured into clay vessels. The chatter of a hundred servants; the strident calling of a peacock on a faraway roof.

He felt another prick of impatience; it was time to get going. Else they would… there! The bell for breakfast rang out and Kamal bit his lip in nervousness: he should be long gone because if he didn't come for breakfast it would certainly be noticed. And they would start the search for him while he was still within the palace and would certainly find him. He felt his spirits sink – had everything been in vain? Every day for the past week he had watched and waited and every day the bullock cart had left well before breakfast began.

The empty hampers were loaded in the blackness of pre-dawn, which was why it had been easy to slink through the empty corridors, mount the cart and climb into one of them, covering himself carefully before reaching out, groping for the propped-up lid and closing it over himself. Once hidden all he had to do was wait. Today, though, driver-*wallah* was taking his time. Kamal knew that on every other day he had sat on the freshly swept earth outside the kitchen drinking tea and sharing gossip with some of the male servants who breakfasted at this time, before the day's work began. They sat in a circle around a small brazier, wrapped in layers of cloth for warmth since the mornings were chilly at this time of year, murmuring to each other, pouring their tea from curved-lip cup to cup to cool it, raising their chins and opening their mouths to receive the milky brew. On previous days Kamal had watched, hidden, and on every day well before now the men had stood up and shaken out their clothes and dusted themselves off before separating to go about their various tasks.

Driver-*wallah* would return to the cart, settle himself on the wooden perch between the rumps of the two bullocks, call out *hey-hey,* prod the slothful animals several times on their backsides, and the cart would rumble off long before the bell for breakfast began its rigorous, joyous pealing. The bullocks would pause at the huge grid of gates let into the palace walls. Watchmen swathed in heavy wraps would draw back the many bolts and turn the many keys and unwind the many chains before heaving the heavy gates slowly inward, letting the bullocks and the cart pass through. The gates would close again, be bolted, chained and locked. The bullocks, the cart, the hampers were Outside.

Kamal, in all of his nine years, had never once been Outside.

He had a cramp in his right foot, bent awkwardly into the curve of the hamper. He adjusted his position slightly, wriggled his toes, and tried to move his foot but couldn't; it seemed stuck into position. Everything was aching by now. And he was cold, and hungry. And worried about being found. Everything was going wrong. Driver-*wallah* had disappeared from the face of the earth. Today of all days, the day of his escape. That was the worst of it.

Kamal knew that things only worked out if they were supposed to. You could plan and plot and arrange circumstances as much as you liked but if your plan was not simultaneously destiny's plan it would definitely go wrong: for, as Teacher always said, man proposes but God disposes. So if today of all days driver-*wallah*'s schedule had changed, then destiny was saying a loud clear unmistakable *no*. And now there was an unfamiliar commotion somewhere up in the West Wing, and Kamal couldn't see but he knew that Lakshmi who was Rani Abishta's right hand was up on the balcony outside the servants' room shouting down to somebody in the courtyard. He could hear every word clearly, and he knew his time was almost up; if driver-*wallah* did not turn up in the next few minutes they'd start a serious search for him.

'Ramanath, have you seen Kamal?'

'Kamal? No, he's not here, why?'

'Well, he's missing, he didn't go to breakfast and the Mistress is frightfully angry, in fact she's furious. He's not in his room either.'

'He's probably in the stables, have you looked there? That dog must have had her pups, you know he watches for them every day. I'm sure he's there.'

'That's a good idea. I'll go and check.'

And then Kamal breathed out in gratitude, for the cart swayed to one side with the weight of driver-*wallah*'s ascent, and the bullocks shifted, the cart creaked, and he heard the familiar cry of *hey-hey*, and they were off. He heard the grating of gates opening, and then they were Outside.

Chapter Four

Kamal

Near the *chowk,* the marketplace, the cart came to a halt and Kamal climbed out unseen. He jumped to the ground and, following his senses, drawn by the noise and smells and whirls of colour, made his way to the bazaar. What a world! A world teeming with fruit and vegetables, some of which Kamal had never seen, much less tasted. His nostrils absorbed a thousand different aromas at once, some so sweet he stopped simply to look, and because he was hungry and had had no breakfast his mouth began to water as he stared at a man cutting open a big round fruit and pulling it apart into soft, slippery, translucent sections, bright yellow and luscious.

'What's that?' he asked the vendor, who laughed out loud.

'You don't know what a jackfruit is? Where are you living, little boy?'

'In the palace,' said Kamal truthfully and immediately clapped his hand to his mouth and gazed at the man with petrified eyes; then he ran down the row of fruit stalls till he came to the flower vendors. Here the fragrance was intoxicating. Kamal looked right and left and all he saw were flowers, piles of garlands and baskets of roses; a girl his age sitting on the ground before a basket of tuberose blossoms threading them expertly with quick, nimble fingers; vendors coming with full baskets and going with empty ones, for it was still early, the stalls were still being replenished, and Kamal alone had nothing to do but stare.

Having seen all there was to see in the bazaar, he wandered up and down the surrounding lanes, the hunger in his stomach gnawing more and more insistently. He found himself in a narrow alley where the road's tarmac crumbled and the shops on either side all seemed to sell nothing but rusty nails. Another lane was unbearable because here every building was a tea-shop and outside every shop pans of oil sizzled on open fires and golden puris swelled up into crisp balloons, emitting the aroma of breakfast that invaded his nostrils and sank into his belly and screamed there for succour.

Kamal's pockets were empty. He had not thought to bring money; even had he thought of it, he would not have known where to get it. He had never handled money; he'd had no need to. And now, though his clothes were of silk and the chain around his neck and the ring on his finger were of pure gold, he was as poor as the poorest beggar – *those* he had seen everywhere – because he could not eat silk or gold. At this thought something clicked in his mind and boldly he approached the boy – not much older than himself – frying puris outside the next shop. He eased the ring from his finger and held it out.

'Would you accept this ring as payment for breakfast?' he asked hesitantly.

The boy stared at the ring and then at Kamal and called to someone in the black interior of the shop. A man came out, wiping his hands on a grubby cloth, and, looking Kamal up and down, said, 'Where did you get that ring, boy? Did you steal it?'

'No, of course not,' said Kamal angrily, and then remembered that no one knew who he was and so added in a milder tone, 'My grandmother gave it to me. It is mine. I would like to eat but I have no money. Would you accept this ring as payment?'

'Yes, yes, of course,' said the man then and showed Kamal a bench at a long table where three other men were sitting eating. Kamal slid in and waited to be served.

One of the men, dressed in white pyjamas and a white cap, looked keenly at him and said, 'Are you a fool, or what?'

'Why should I be a fool?'

'To pay for your breakfast with that valuable ring. Look, don't do it. Come with me afterwards and I will show you where you can sell it for a good price. I will pay for your breakfast. You can pay me back when you have sold the ring.'

'Very well,' said Kamal gratefully and ate with more appetite than he had ever done in the palace, for the simple food tasted more delicious than the most sumptuous feast Rani Abishta had had prepared for him alone.

The shopkeeper was not happy with this new arrangement. When Kamal and the man got up to go he spoke some sharp words, but the man simply left the money on the table and strode off, Kamal running behind him, thanking him profusely.

'It was only my duty,' said the man, brushing off Kamal's gratitude. 'A boy like you must be careful in this town: there are wicked people just waiting to rob you. Look at your fine clothes, your jewellery! Why do you walk around looking like a prince in his palace? Where do you come from? What are you doing on the streets at this time; shouldn't you be at school?'

Kamal felt he could trust this man and told him his name and his story. The man laughed and wished him luck. 'I hope you enjoy your day,' he said. 'Goodbye. It was interesting meeting you.'

'But aren't you going to show me the jeweller's shop? I have to sell my ring and give you back the money!'

'Don't worry about the money,' said the man. 'It was my pleasure to buy you breakfast. Just be careful!'

Kamal found the jeweller's shop anyway. It was on a street with several such shops. He sold his ring for thirty rupees and felt delirious with joy at possessing so much money of his own. When it was time for lunch he paid for his own meal in a dark restaurant where boys younger than himself ran around with pails of water, collecting the dirty plates and wiping the tables after the customers left. He ate with joy and he paid with pride.

After lunch he wandered up and down more streets at random. He found himself in a part of town where the colours were reduced to black and grey, the streets teeming with human and animal life. There were beggars sitting at the roadside, their clothes black and caked with grime. There were children, infants, with limbs bent backwards and eyes oozing pus and swarming with flies. There was a dog with half its head missing, walking around with its brain hanging out. Pigs in the gutters, eating human waste. A stench of offal pervaded these lanes; Kamal felt on the verge of vomiting yet still he walked on, observing, wondering, asking himself questions that could not be answered.

He had never in his life seen sights such as these; he had not imagined such misery could exist in the same world as the palace of Moti Khodayal where he had grown up.

It was mid-afternoon when he found himself in a potholed street, wider than the others, lined by ramshackle buildings. The strange thing about this street was that there were so many women on it. The women sat or stood outside the open doorways; they sat in the dust or on mats or on *charpais,* or they leaned against the doorframes, laughing, chatting with each other. They combed and plaited each other's hair; they gathered around an open tap and walked home carrying full buckets in their hands or on their heads. Some of them held plates of food in their hands and ate; others nursed babies; a few crouched on the ground cooking over an open fire, or washed pots and infants over stinking gutters. They glanced at him as he walked past but quickly went back to whatever they were doing. There were one or two girls among them, some not much older than he himself. There were several small children. But there were no men.

He was mistaken: there was one man. He stormed out of one of the doorways, chasing a screaming girl with long dishevelled hair, a girl about the size and age of Nirmala, Punraj's other daughter, Bibi's big sister, who had married last year when she was fourteen.

Just before she reached the street the man caught hold of the girl's arm and pulled her towards him, shouting words Kamal did not understand. A few of the women nearby looked up for a moment but quickly returned to their tasks. The man turned back to the house and shouted one sharp word; an older woman emerged with what looked like a piece of broomstick, which she handed to him. To Kamal's utmost horror the man began to rain blows on the girl's back. The girl screamed pitifully, begging for mercy, but still he beat on, shouting all the time, his face almost black with rage.

For two seconds Kamal stood petrified with outrage; then he ran up to the man and began pulling at the beating hand. 'Stop it! Stop it! You're hurting her! Leave her alone!'

For one frozen moment the man stopped, his hand raised. Kamal grabbed the girl and tried to pull her away. The girl looked up at Kamal.

Those eyes! He would never forget them, not in all his life. The look in them! Such terror, such agony, such abject despair! The wretchedness in those eyes wrenched at Kamal's heart, for he had never seen such inner pain nor even a shadow of it; he had not known such anguish could exist on earth, for earth for him was a happy place where people smiled, and even if they felt pain, they hid it behind that smile, unless they were babies and could not yet tuck away their hurt. This girl's pain lay naked in her eyes, in the mouth pulled down at the corners. Her wretchedness was in the wet smudged cheeks, the lacklustre hair; it was in the body twitching away from Kamal's grasp, the shrill scream she now let out as the moment unfroze and the man's hand whisked down. The stick met her arching, writhing back with a dull thud.

Fury grabbed Kamal. He pummelled the man's forearm, sank his teeth into it, but the man was tall and strong and Kamal slight, and with only a flick of annoyance the man flung him away. Kamal landed on hands and knees in the middle of the street, like a cat, and scrambled to his feet again. He was about to hurl himself once more at the man but he felt strong hands on his arms pulling him back. He looked up; a woman, obviously a neighbour, was holding him back and speaking.

'Don't interfere, boy, that's her uncle and she's been a bad girl. She has to be punished.'

'But he's hurting her!'

'He's only hurting her so she'll obey him next time. We all have to learn to obey; that's life. You have to obey your mother too, don't you? And your father? So she has to obey her uncle.' She cackled with foul laughter.

Another woman approached them. 'What are you doing here? You're only a child; go away. You have no business on this street.'

'I only want to—'

'Go away. Don't come back here. You must be mad, to mix yourself up in what does not concern you.'

'But that girl…' Kamal turned back to the man and the girl but they were gone.

'She'll be fine, don't worry about her. Her uncle will take care of her. Now you go away and don't come back here.'

'Not till you're grown up,' added the first woman, and laughed again. Kamal stared at her; she was not like any of the palace servants. Her face was small and pockmarked. There were loose black-ringed holes in the sides of her nose and in the lobes of her ears but she wore no jewellery save a cluster of plastic bangles rattling on a bony wrist. Her teeth, those that remained, were yellow. She wore a threadbare faded sari of an indistinguishable colour. She smelt of rancid coconut oil and stale sweat and perfume gone sour.

'Yes; *then* you can come back,' said the other woman. 'With all your silks and your fine jewellery!'

Both the women roared with laughter at a joke Kamal could not understand. What he *did* understand was that they were right: he had to go. He did not like this street; he did not like these women; he could not help the girl. Instinct told him he was out of his depth. It was time to go home. The women were still chatting about him.

'Where do you live, boy?'

'In Moti Khodayal.'

At that, they all burst out in raucous laughter.

'In that big palace? With the fake queen? Are you a prince, then? Is that why you are dressed in fine silks?'

'Ah, little prince! You grace us with your presence! Should we bow before you? How can we serve you?'

'Ay, little prince, do you have a job for me in the palace?'

'Will you make me a patola-silk sari, boy?'

'Only royals wear patola silk, girl – you think you are a royal?'

'Ay, maybe I will marry a royal and then I too will get to wear patola silk!'

'Go home to your fine palace, boy, and your patola silk. This is not the place for you.'

'Yes, go home. Shoo! You need to be saved from the likes of us. We will only lead you astray. We are bad women.'

They all laughed again, and in the space where they stopped talking Kamal found his voice.

'I don't know the way home.'

'Ah. The little prince is lost. No worries, boy. We will make sure you reach home safely. Hey, you! Baldev, come!'

Baldev was a boy of about twelve, sweeping a doorway across the street. He came immediately.

'Take this boy back to the palace. He is a fine prince; got lost and stepped into a cowpat. He doesn't know the way home.'

'But don't steal from him on the way back, hey! He will give you some baksheesh when you get him home. He is so rich.'

And indeed, the boy called Baldev led him home through the labyrinth of streets, and Kamal gave him the rest of his money. And so, in the early evening, Kamal found himself outside the gates and the sentries called out in relieved astonishment, and, it seemed to him, the entire palace household came running out into the courtyard, calling out to him how much he had been missed and where had he been, and what a naughty boy he was, and how angry Daadi would be.

'She's angry with me, too, Kamal,' his friend Hanoman, Teacher's son, whispered. 'She thinks I helped you out. Look!'

He opened his hands and showed Kamal the thick red welts across his palms. 'She beat me to tell her the truth. But I didn't know! I didn't know anything!'

Kamal's filthy clothes were peeled from him by clucking servants. He was bathed and perfumed and bedded for the night.

'Rani Abishta says she will see you tomorrow,' came the message just before he fell asleep.

Chapter Five

A few weeks before I turned twelve the terrible thing happened and that was the beginning of the end of my life.

Amma and Appa were on their way home from the market, walking along the side of the street with their baskets slung over their arms, when a strange black car swerved off the road, rammed straight into them and, without even stopping to check the damage, raced off again. Amma died instantly, Appa a few hours later, in hospital. The police wrote it off as a hit-and-run accident – the driver must have been drunk, they said, and there was no chance of tracing him. They had too many serious crimes to solve to bother themselves with this.

Their deaths put an abrupt end to my happy childhood. The death itself was terrible enough and we were all plunged into the blackest grief; if you can imagine a dark mist where you cannot even see your hand in front of you, well, that is how we all felt.

Janiki, my little mother, came back from America where she was now working, her face pale with shock. We cried and comforted each other.

'What now, Janiki?' I wept. 'What will become of us?'

By this time Appa's younger brother Paruthy Uncle had already moved into our big house, along with his family. He said it was because his own house was too small for all of us, my four elder brothers and one younger one, and his three little daughters.

I had never liked Paruthy Uncle. He was not like Appa at all. He was not kind. And he did not like me. That is why I wept to Janiki, 'What will become of us?'

'Don't worry, Asha,' Janiki said, wiping away my tears. 'You have another amma and appa and surely they will come and get you now. Your white amma lives in America – I am sure she will come and get you, and then you'll be near me. Or else your appa in Dubai. You are a very lucky girl. You must write them and ask them to come and get you. I am going back to California now – I only got one week of compassionate leave – but you will continue to write me and let me know how you are doing. And wherever you are, I will come and visit you one day.'

Those words were a great comfort to me. It is true that I did not remember the people I called Mom and Daddy very well. I had only seen Mom once, when I was five: I remember her pale face and amber eyes and yellow hair, and I remember I was scared of her. But she had written me letters over the years and sent photographs of her and a tall pale man and I knew that Mom means Amma in American. Sometimes I wrote back. Amma told me to. And Amma dictated the letters and then she posted them for me.

I remembered Daddy better. They told me to call him Daddy because I only had one appa and could not call him that. Daddy came once a year to visit me. But I never knew what to say to him and he didn't know what to say to me. He sent me postcards of mountains and famous places in India. I never wrote him back because I did not know what to say.

But now I had to write to them both, because it was an emergency. So I wrote them both and told them what had happened, two letters. I did not tell them to come and get me because that sounded rude. I just told them that Amma and Appa had died and that we were now living with Paruthy Uncle and that I did not like him.

I did not have their addresses so I gave the letters to Paruthy Uncle and asked him to find the addresses and post the letters. And then I waited for a reply, or for them to come and pick me up and take me to America, or to Dubai. I did not care where, just that they would come for me, one of them at least. Or at least write back to tell me what to do. But they didn't. I wrote them again but still they didn't come, and didn't write. It was plain they did not want to be bothered with me.

I wanted to write Janiki emails every day because it hurt so much, but I couldn't, because Paruthy Uncle took away my computer and sold it.

'What is a small girl like you doing with this newfangled stuff? You don't need it,' he said.

'Janiki! I write to Janiki on it!' I wailed.

'You can write normal letters like everybody else. I cannot believe how spoilt you are. If you have a letter for Janiki just give it to me and I will post it.'

So I did that. But Janiki never replied.

Chapter Six

Kamal. Moti Khodayal, 1972

Rani Abishta was having a foot massage, reclining on her cloud-cushion of puffed purple velvet, exclusively designed to enclose her enormous bulk, its invisible steel skeleton taking over the work of her atrophied muscles, buried as they were in mounds of flesh.

Her legs were spread open before her, her sari drawn up beyond her knees and bunched up between them. Her feet rested on matching purple pouffes while two crouching sylphine maidens kneaded her puffy soles and massaged her swollen toes.

Her right hand lay languidly on a plate of milk-sweets, occasionally conveying one to her mouth. Her other hand loosely held a fan of peacock feathers that now lay on her extensive bosom. Her eyes were heavy-lidded, half-closed, and a less knowledgeable visitor might think she was asleep. Kamal knew better.

He knew that behind those sluggishly drooping eyelids lurked a mind as sharp as a two-edged sword, and that Daadi's outward appearance of sloth, the inertia of her fat, indolent body, was his grandmother's best disguise, one that only a mind of her cunning could have divined. And Kamal had not the slightest doubt that she wore this disguise not of necessity but of design.

Obesity had not crept up on Rani Abishta from behind; she had seen the advantages of wrapping keenness of wit in layers of fleshy languor, and concealing daggers of guile within a mound of innocuous jelly.

It was part of her master plan.

He approached from the garden. The white floor-to-ceiling louvred door-flaps were folded back, opening onto the terrace and the cupid-fountain (imported from France), so that the Surya Hall, where Rani Abishta spent the greater part of her life, extended in one unbroken expanse of grey marbled flagstones to the emerald-green lawn. Rani Abishta sat in a shadowed recess at the back of the hall, for she could not bear the sunshine, yet liked to look out on her domain, occasionally dozing off, usually just sitting, watching, waiting, motionless except for the one hand moving from plate to mouth and the other hand now and then rising, fanning and sinking again.

Beyond the reach of sunlight lay a scattering of plush carpets. Kamal felt Rani Abishta's concentrated perusal as he drew nearer; he saw the instant's pause as her hand drew near to her lips; he knew that the eyes had narrowed to slits barely visible between folds of fat, and that the very air surrounding her vibrated with venom.

With a barely perceptible motion of her fingers Rani Abishta dismissed the two maidens. They stood up, *namasted* and bowed with a graceful bend of the knee, stepped backwards and vanished on silently tripping feet. They left in their stead a vague perfume of jasmine and rose, which Rani Abishta briskly eliminated with a sonorous passing of wind, slightly raising one side of her body to allow the pungent wind to escape, falling back into position with a thud and a wobble of flesh. Kamal held his breath, *namasted*, smiled and lowered himself to the carpet before her, sitting back on his heels.

Her lips moved. 'Come nearer!' she commanded, and Kamal edged his knees forward a fraction.

Rani Abishta grunted and shifted position again, and Kamal feared another blast of exhaust fumes, but all she did was lean forward to bring her face slightly nearer to his.

'Yesterday you left the palace,' she said.

Kamal shrugged.

It was done, it was over, he was back, and there was no way Rani Abishta could erase what had happened. No punishment would make the day undone; it was there, impressed upon his consciousness, senses stirred awake and fed but not nourished, doors and windows opened that would never again be closed. Yesterday could never be unmade, and he regretted nothing, no matter what the punishment.

'I have forbidden you to leave the palace, and yet you left,' Rani Abishta continued. She spoke slowly, her voice low and without emotion: simply stating a fact. It was the voice she used when the anger was boiling within her, boiling with such violence that all her strength was involved in holding it back. Those who were in daily contact with Rani Abishta knew that voice well, for a thousand little things drove her to anger: a carpet with an untidy fringe, a stray dove relieving itself on the terrace, a sesame seed lodged in a back tooth. Summoned into Rani Abishta's presence, the evil-doer (the maid who had not brushed the carpet fringe, the gardener who had not chased away the dove, the cook who had made the sesame sweet) would stand quaking before her while first she stated the bare facts in this voice, crouching low like a leopard before a deadly lunge.

Kamal, ever since he was a small child, had marvelled at Rani Abishta's ability to inspire fear. He had seen countless hand-wringing servants stand or kneel before her, sweating with terror, their eyes pleading for pity, sometimes clasping their hands, kneeling and begging for mercy. What was it about Rani Abishta that evoked such naked terror? Even when Rani Abishta's inner dam burst and she shouted at someone, it might not be pleasant, but she didn't actually *hurt* anyone with her noise. Why didn't they just shout back? Kamal used to think. Or simply turn their backs and walk away, the way he did when she yelled too long or too loud?

Kamal himself had never known fear. Neither fear of Rani Abishta, nor fear of any living thing within the walls of the palace. He had *heard* the word fear, of course, and had feared vicariously with many of the heroes in the adventure books he loved to read, so that he did have second-hand knowledge of what it was to sense danger, but here there was nothing to fear. Here he was safe. Here there was nothing to hurt him.

Rani Abishta had made it so. Rani Abishta had created this safe soft perfect world, this world of golden platters overflowing with ambrosial eatables, of silk garments and emerald lawns and bowls filled with jewels you could plunge your hands into, hold them in the cup of your palms and raise up, letting them ripple through your fingers like water. A world where peacocks strutted across brilliant lawns, their tails fanned out in glory. Rani Abishta had created this world and kept it perfect for him, which was why he did not, could not, fear her. Rani Abishta, who reigned with absolute jurisdiction within the high walls of her empire.

'This is the only world you need to know,' she had told Kamal when he was a little boy. He had come to live with Rani Abishta before memory, at a time before he could think; all he knew was that his mother had died in childbirth and his father, Rani Abishta's only son, had brought him here and then left again, to rebel against Indira Gandhi and her Emergency. Thrown into prison, where death had met him. Nobody was allowed to mention his name in Moti Khodayal. 'I am your mother and your father,' said Rani Abishta. 'Moti Khodayal is your world.'

And he knew there was a world outside those walls, a bigger world, but he had no idea of what big meant; how big was big, and how much bigger could it be than the palace of Moti Khodayal?

Moti Khodayal was enormous.

'I have created this world for you,' Rani Abishta had told him again and again. 'It contains all that you will ever need. It is enough for you. I have provided for you; here there is everything you want; and if you want more, you only have to ask.'

'But what is outside the wall?' Kamal had asked, for he had walked all around the perimeter of Moti Khodayal and looked up along the high stone wall, topped by bits of spiky broken glass set in concrete.

'Bad things. There is poverty and dirt and bad people who will hurt you and who will want to take away the things you have. Do not even think about the world out there; you do not need it. It is bad and ugly.'

She had smiled then, and held out her arms, and Kamal, not knowing better, for Rani Abishta was mother and father and all people for him, ran into her arms and she lifted him onto her knee. She pointed out beyond the terrace.

'Look! Look at that beautiful lawn! See how it gently slopes away to the garden! Look at that peacock, strutting across! Soon he will lift his tail and open his wheel, and then he will dance for the peahens, and for me! The peacock dances because he is aware of his beauty; only beauty must exist in the world. I want you to know only beauty, Kamal. I am sorry I have lost the use of my legs, else I would take you by the hand and walk with you through those beautiful flower groves and tell you the names of all the roses. When I was a young girl, Kamal, I loved the roses and tended them myself. Now it is all done by gardeners. But they are the best gardeners in all of India. I have instructed them to make of Moti Khodayal a paradise; and this paradise is for you. For you, Kamal, are a prince and you must have the best. Never forget that you are a prince.'

And she told him for the billionth time the story of the family, a line of kings dating back further than it was possible to think.

'Moti Khodayal was bigger then. Bigger than what you know now; a real kingdom. There were no walls around it, for its lands reached out among the rolling hills. It contained villages, towns

even, and all the people worshipped us and paid us tribute. I was
just a girl, but I remember well my grandfather, not yet a maharaja but a prince. I remember when we went to the royal palace
at Jaipur, for the wedding of Princess Gayatri Devi, the Jaipur
Princess, to Maharaj Jai. I am second cousin thrice removed to
her. I remember Prince Jai raising me up, Princess Gayatri placing
me on her lap feeding me with *gulab jamun.* I remember playing
with the Princess's jewels. She was wearing a patola-silk sari; we
had given it to her as a present. What a fabulous present! But,
Kamal – and this was the fate of all the great kingdoms of Bharat,
not just Moti Khodayal – there came conquerors from abroad,
white men with weapons, white men who wanted it all for themselves, and those white men reduced us to what we are now. So
we built the wall to keep what we had, and this is what you see
today. It is smaller than it was, true, but it is still big enough to
call a kingdom, and one day it will all be yours.'

'And we owe it all to the worms!' Kamal declared.

'The worms?'

'Yes. The silkworms. The silkworms that work for us.'

'Who told you about the silkworms?'

'Hanoman did. He says we have an army of silkworms in the
hill district working for us. And that is how patola silk is made,
which is the best silk in India and only royals wear it. And it takes
a whole year to make a single patola-silk sari. And he told me that
if it weren't for the silkworms you and me would be poor like the
rats in the bazaar.'

'Hanoman told you that? Hanoman knows nothing. Worms!
Pah.'

'Hanoman is my friend. He knows a lot and he tells me a lot.'

'Hanoman cannot be your friend. Hanoman is only Teacher's
son and you are a prince.'

'No, I'm not. Hanoman says the English conquered the kings
and there is no royalty in India any more so I'm not really a

prince. And Hanoman has been Outside. He knows about all the things Outside and he tells me.'

'Then I forbid you to talk to Hanoman!'

'You cannot, Daadi! He is my friend, the only friend I have! Hanoman and me, we are like brothers even—'

'You are of royal blood, Kamal! You are a Ksatriya, you cannot be the brother of a teacher's son.'

'Oh, but I can, we are! He tells me so much and I need to know about everything, about Outside and the silkworms and everything.'

'You do not need to know about the silkworms. That is not your business. They do their work, you do yours – every creature on earth has its allotted place. I have paid servants who care about the silkworms and look after them and make sure they are doing their work. I have servants to collect the silk and turn it into wealth so that you may live like the prince you were born to be. Because one day India will return to her former glory and you will sit in the Surya Hall and rule. It is destiny. Nobody, least of all the English, can outsmart destiny. The Wheel of Time turns slowly but one day she returns to recapture all that was lost; and all that was lost returns to its rightful owner. That is you. That is why I am preserving everything for when that time comes. I am the only one left who believes in the old ways, who knows that the old ways were good and that the old ways must return.

'I am the guardian of your fate, Kamal. Do not sully your mind with matters that do not concern you. You must have the attitude of a king: you must rule, and command, and delegate, and demand obedience. You must show your subordinates that you are their head, that your word is the word of God. And not even Swami Naadiyaananda—'

She suddenly stopped speaking, and sent him away.

Kamal was seven when Rani Abishta told him this. His mind was sharp as a razor and picked up details the adults slid over, which is why, at the next opportunity, he had run to Teacher and asked, 'Teacher, who is Swami Naadiyaananda?'

Teacher had looked down at him and raised his brows and said, 'Where did you hear that name?'

'Oh, I just heard someone say it.'

'Well, forget it. It means nothing.'

His curiosity piqued, Kamal asked others.

'Who is Swami Naadiyaananda?' he asked his favourite counsellor, Jairam, who only shrugged and raised his shoulders and shook his head. Teacher had smiled secretly and turned away.

Only Gaindha Dwarka, Rani Abishta's Chief Counsellor, had hinted at more. 'You must not speak that name,' he whispered to Kamal. 'Never mention it again. It is better for you.'

'But why?' Kamal insisted.

Gaindha Dwarka had looked right and left before whispering, 'He is the one who knows who you really are, and what will become of you if you leave Moti Khodayal. More I cannot say.' And he had placed a finger on his lips and slid behind the curtain leading to the Indra Hall, and Kamal had never been able to unseal his lips again.

So Kamal had been left to smoulder, not understanding. All he knew was this: Moti Khodayal was Rani Abishta's creation, and she had tried to make it perfect, for him. Rani Abishta was queen here; Rani Abishta ruled with an iron hand; Rani Abishta's word was law. And for some reason known only to herself, Rani Abishta would not allow Kamal, her only grandson, her only relative, the only living human she cared about, to pass beyond those walls. And a mysterious Swami Naadiyaananda had something to do with it. And now he had left the palace without her permission, and there would be trouble.

So now he knelt in silence before her and watched her and waited for her to speak. She would have him locked in his room for the evening, perhaps. Or for several evenings in a row. It had not been fear of punishment that had kept Kamal from escaping a long time ago, but lack of opportunity: the walls were so high, the sentries so diligent, that it had been near impossible to find a way out. But despite all this, and the inevitable punishment that now awaited him, he would escape again in a heartbeat; he knew that with certainty.

'How did you get out?' Rani Abishta's voice was now little more than a whisper, and the lower her voice, the more dangerous her mood. Kamal kept quiet.

'You will not speak? You won't tell me how you got out? Very well, then I will take my own appropriate measures. Obviously the sentries were negligent. You must have bribed one or other of them – there is no way out without the help of a sentry. If you will not tell me which one then I will have all of them punished. Every one of them.'

Kamal froze at those words; he had never expected this. His eyes opened wide in horror, for now he understood why her last words had been so soft as to be almost indiscernible, hardly stirring the heavy space between them.

'Tell me.'

But Kamal could not speak. His tongue seemed stuck to the bottom of his mouth, his jaw locked, and for the first time in his life he knew fear.

He knew then that he was not invulnerable. He knew that Rani Abishta, with a word, with a nod of her head even, could punish him by punishing others. He knew now that Rani Abishta knew him better than he had assumed; she knew that he *cared*.

He had never even tried to hide from her that he cared. Rani Abishta's instructions, to treat the servants with contempt, he ignored, and blatantly did the opposite: he courted them as his equals. His only friend his own age was Hanoman, who had his own duties to attend to, and so he had found other friends among the servants: Munsami, Gangadin, Ali Yusuf; he knew them all by name. He knew their children's names, and their children's ages. He knew when their wives were ailing and the children were sent to an aunt. He knew when an eldest son won a place in a better school, and when a daughter's betrothal turned a father's hair grey. It was easy to make friends with the servants, for Rani Abishta was immobile and her eyes could not see around corners. Confined as she was to the Surya Hall, what did it matter what she ordered? True, she had her spies. Kamal knew whom he could trust, and whom not.

Soondath was a snake, and Ramsaywack was a rat. They and their underdogs: Kamal avoided them; those were the ones sent to catch him when he disappeared, who clawed his upper arm and dragged him through the corridors and into Rani Abishta's presence, where they immediately turned slimy as snails and released their grip – for Kamal was not to be hurt – and pasted simpering smirks of deference on their faces. They were the ones who would betray him in the wink of an eye, whenever there was something to betray. But up to now there had been no transgression so serious that the blame could be placed on anyone but himself. Up to now it had been fun and games: a little boy being a boy. But now, since he'd left the palace, things were different...

Kamal knew that servants who transgressed were whipped. He knew, but avoided the matter neatly by making himself absent during such times, removing himself to the farthest point of the Surya Hall. Once he had seen a fellow afterwards, bent and broken, dragged across the courtyard, the gates flung open and the man kicked out, never to be seen again. Kamal had turned and fled and pushed the incident to the back of his mind. Today there was no avoidance. Kamal was made to sit beside his grandmother as one by one the guards were brought forward, stripped to the waist, flogged across the backs until they were unable to stand, and booted out of the presence.

Kamal tried to plead with Rani Abishta. He begged and coaxed and swore on his life that not one of them had helped him escape. He told her the whole story of his escape, in all its details; he beseeched her not to hurt the guards, to whip *him* instead, for *he* was at fault and no one else. He wept his apologies; he knelt before her imploring her to accept his remorse; he promised on his life never to do it again: all to no avail.

Rani Abishta made Soondath and Ramsaywack hold Kamal, one on each side, and though he writhed and wriggled he could not escape their iron grip. Soondath grasped him under his chin and held it up so he was forced to watch, and he cried aloud and squeezed his eyes shut but the tears escaped and flowed down his cheeks, and still he could hear the buzz of the whip as it slashed the air and the dull thwack as it cut across a bare back, and the agonised cries of the guards. He heard them beg for mercy and he recognised their voices: Mahadai and Challu and Basdeo were among them, men who had smiled and joked and laughed with him, men who were his friends, and punished without guilt for his foolishness.

Even before it was over Kamal fainted, for he could not bear the pain; it was as if every whiplash landed on his own back. His cries were louder than those of the guards, for he cried not only for them but for the girl in the street of women, and Ramsaywack tied a cloth through his mouth to gag him. That was when he mercifully fainted.

When he came to, he found himself lying on the carpet at Rani Abishta's feet, the hall emptied except for Hiraman, sitting naked to the waist in a far corner and playing on his tabla. The hollow rattling of the tabla had replaced the screams. A soft tranquillity now filled the hall, the reverent hush that heralded the evening.

Rani Abishta sat in her usual position, eating. At first Kamal simply watched her out of half-closed eyes, without moving, and knew that she watched him too. He moved then, and so did she, signalling for Hiraman to leave.

When they were alone, Rani Abishta gestured for him to come nearer.

'The next time the punishment will be worse,' said Rani Abishta. 'So I am hoping for your peace of mind there will not be a next time. I have not dismissed those guards. They have been returned to their positions with their backs stinging and bleeding, and now they will be more vigilant than ever.'

Kamal never tried to go Outside again. He accepted his confinement, knowing that one day it would come to an end. Somehow, he no longer minded. Outside, he knew now, was too much for him to bear.

Chapter Seven

Caroline. Cambridge, Mass., 1982–1985

As Caroline grew into womanhood her childish dreams faded, along with the comforting memory of soft-bosomed Meena with her never-ending tales of swarthy kings and queens and the eternal battle between Good and Evil. Swept up in the dramas and emotional roller-coaster rides that greet every American girl on entering her teens, Caroline learned that the world stood open to her; that she already was a princess of sorts. Indulged by wealthy parents, spoiled by older brothers, folded in the safe and cosy arms of Cambridge high society, she wanted for nothing. She dated boys, fell in and out of love, dressed up for Halloween parties. Visits with Grandma and Grandpa Mitchell on Cape Cod, family gatherings around the Christmas table, weddings and christenings, vacations in the Caribbean, trips down to Florida every now and then to see Great-Aunt Janey: that was Caroline's life, and she loved it.

Yet as the years passed something happened, something changed. It started with a boyfriend, Samuel, who didn't quite pass muster with her parents: Sam had an untidy beard and he came from less than prime stock. She was seventeen when she met him, he nineteen, in his first year at college, and not at Harvard either, but at Boston U, and studying politics; and his parents were one-time hippies. He had been born on a farm in Ecuador while his father was on the run from the Vietnam draft, had grown up on a series of alternative-lifestyle farms and communes in South America and, later, in Vermont, California and Arizona. She liked him a lot; she didn't love him. But she loved his mind. Sam put new, revolutionary ideas into her head.

Sam told her about the world Out There: about the Amazonian Indians whose habitat was being eroded by greedy corporations tearing down the rainforest. He told her about the rape of Africa: about apartheid. He opened her eyes to the plight of blacks on their own continent; right next door, in fact, in Boston's South End and Roxbury. About the Boston busing crisis of 1974, about racism and oppression and crime caused by poverty and lack of opportunity.

'You're a white princess,' Sam scoffed, 'living in dreamland in your pretty Queen Anne mansion!' He made her feel guilty; it was a good and healthy feeling, so she listened. Feeling guilty made her feel, incongruously, noble.

He told her about the oppression of women in the Middle East, and Pakistan, and India—

'India!' interrupted Caroline. 'I used to have an Indian nanny – Meena was her name. She practically raised me when I was a little girl – like a second mother. Oh, I loved her so much! I love India so much! It's so *romantic*!'

'India, romantic?' scoffed Sam. 'I've been to India. My parents took me when I was just a kid. They took me along the Hippie Trail: through Europe and Turkey and Iran, Afghanistan, Nepal. We lived in India for a year. India is a basket case, Caroline. Millions of people in abject poverty, hardly scraping together enough to survive. They are exploited and downtrodden. The women are nothing but chattels. India is anything *but* romantic.'

And so Sam opened her eyes to the misery of millions, billions of human beings who shared the planet with her, but did not have the almost random – it seemed to her – good fortune of being born to privileged white parents in America. Caroline began to think, to explore. And even when the relationship with Sam broke down – deep down, he resented her privilege, and mocked it just a little too much – she continued on the trajectory he had launched her on.

The seed Meena had planted so long ago, hidden in the depths of Caroline's soul, stirred, and yearned for nourishment. India called. And though she was not ready to go there yet, she decided to flout her parents' will and, instead of studying law at Harvard so as to join her father in his practice, or becoming a doctor like her mother, Caroline chose a different path altogether: anthropology, at Boston University, specialising in South Indian tribes and family structure. Because India still fascinated her. *One day,* she swore to herself, *I will go there and see for myself.*

Chapter Eight

Asha, 2000

Paruthy Uncle was a schoolteacher, just like Appa, but that was where the similarity between them ended, because Appa's brother was not kind but very cruel. That's how it seemed to me, anyway. Paruthy Uncle lived on the other side of Gingee. His was a much smaller house than ours, and we could not possibly all move there, so that is why he brought his whole family and moved into our big house. He did that the day after Amma and Appa died, because there were children in the house he had to look after. Even though my big brothers were looking after us quite well and said they could carry on doing so.

I think he would have liked the house very much if it weren't for its contents, which were us; but he had to take both the house and its contents. I think there was some law about that, or some duty he had to fulfil towards his brother. So now we all lived together with Paruthy Uncle, Paruthy Uncle's wife, Udhaya Aunty, Paruthy Uncle's three daughters and Paruthy Uncle's old mother. And all of a sudden our big house seemed much smaller, though it was the same size, just much fuller now, especially because Paruthy Uncle's three daughters were all quite young and very noisy and took up a lot of space for themselves. In fact, Paruthy Uncle and his family took over most of the house for themselves, and left the five of us – four brothers and me – to live all in one room, all together.

I never liked Paruthy Uncle. Not even before all the terrible things happened I'm going to tell you about. I suppose that's only natural, because he also did not like me. He didn't like any of us but he didn't like me most of all, because he said I was an extra mouth to feed, and not his flesh and blood, and a useless girl, and such things. There was a lot of talk about money in those days, but I didn't understand it. How could I? I was so innocent. Only now I understand the meaning of money, and how a human life and human happiness weigh nothing against money. I only remember things that were repeated often, like the two words 'ten mouths', which seemed to my eleven-year-old mind to be the axis upon which our whole life turned: 'ten mouths to feed,' Paruthy Uncle would complain all of the time.

'I have to cook for ten mouths!' Udhaya Aunty nagged. Or almost as often as the 'ten mouths' there were the 'five extra mouths', meaning us: my four brothers and me. Janiki and my eldest brother Rohan had moved out by now; Janiki lived in America and Rohan was studying in Madras. So that left four brothers and me as the five extra mouths. I even used to dream about those five extra mouths, gaping open and floating by without heads and bodies while Udhaya Aunty placed a tiny spoonful of food in each one, after which the mouth would snap shut. That is what we were for them: open mouths they were supposed to fill.

Janiki flew back from America the moment she heard of the accident and stayed for a week. She was very angry when she saw that we were all in one room, and they lived in all the other rooms, each daughter with her own room. I didn't really listen to all the quarrels on the matter; all I remember is that Janiki was both angry and sad, sometimes weeping, and often when we were supposed to be asleep I would hear her shouting at Uncle and Aunty, and they shouting back. And Janiki took me in her arms often and held me close and wept, but still I did not know what was going to happen.

'You must write to her parents! Give me their addresses and I will write them! Let her go to them at least!'

And my heart raced and I grew excited, because it sounded as if Janiki was trying to get me away from Aunty and Uncle, who hated me the most of all of us, and sometimes struck me if I was bad. They said I was only a girl. The boys were useful because they had no sons of their own and one day the boys would look after them, when they were old. But a girl is only a burden and how would they ever find a husband for me? If I had had even an inkling of what was to come, you can be sure I would have run away, though where could I have gone, eleven years of age and no knowledge of the world? That was when I wrote letters to Mom in America and Daddy in Dubai, and gave Paruthy Uncle the letters to post, but they never came for me. While I was waiting for them to reply, though, Janiki said I should move out and live somewhere else. So Janiki tried to rescue me.

One night she woke me up and pressed a finger to my lips, wrapped me in a blanket and guided me through the darkness of the garden and out into the street. It must have been very late at night because the street was quite empty. Janiki had both hands on my shoulders and almost pushed me along, and though I was not fully awake and though she did not speak I felt the urgency in her manner and hurried as best I could, sometimes tripping on the edge of the blanket dangling around my hastening feet, sometimes stumbling on one of the many potholes we crossed.

We walked for a long time but soon I had an idea where we were going to, and I was right – she was taking me to Amma's sister's home. Saasna Aunty. Saasna Aunty seemed to know we were coming because the moment Janiki touched her shoulder – she was sleeping on the back veranda – she sprang to her feet like an uncoiling spring, and ushered me into the house. It was all so stealthy, so secret!

'You are safe here,' Janiki whispered to me and kissed me on my forehead. 'I will find your daddy and he will come and get you. Saasna Aunty will be kind to you. I have to go back to

America now but I will find your daddy for you. Paruthy Uncle is not telling me his address but I will find it.'

I felt so scared because I knew that Janiki was scared, though I couldn't tell what of. Nobody had yet told me anything of what was really going on, though I knew it was all about money. Now that I am older I know that Janiki should not have taken me to Saasna Aunty, because of course that was the first place Paruthy Uncle looked for me next day when he found I was gone. And early in the morning he appeared, and there was a big quarrel. I didn't know what it was really about at the time, I was so confused, but I heard bits and pieces of the things they shouted at each other: Saasna Aunty pleading with Appa's brother to let me stay with her, it wouldn't cost anything, and then Paruthy Uncle's nasty remark, that neither would I earn anything. That last remark I remember most of all because of the nasty way he said it. Nasty things stay in a person's mind as well as kind things; they are like thorns sticking in there and even if you try to pull them out they edge themselves in deeper. So I never forgot those words of Paruthy Uncle, that I would not earn anything, and that was the first time I realised that I had to earn my living from now on. And Paruthy Uncle took me back home, but not for long. And Janiki could not help because she had already gone back to America.

Chapter Nine

Kamal. Moti Khodayal, 1974

Kamal was now twelve, tall for his age and handsome. But he was ill. He was dying. Rani Abishta sent for the best doctors; doctors from Bombay and Delhi, and they all said the same: Kamal was dying.

'What does he have?' Rani Abishta cried. She would have had the doctors whipped for incompetence. She almost wept in frustration, if only she could weep.

The doctors shrugged and packed their bags. 'We don't know. We can't help him. He has decided to die and he will die.'

Rani Abishta sent for doctors from abroad but they could not cure Kamal either. 'The disease is mental. He needs a psychiatrist,' these foreign doctors said, so Rani Abishta sent for a psychiatrist, the best available in all the country. The psychiatrist sat next to Kamal's bed with a notepad in his hands and tried to talk to Kamal but Kamal did not answer. He stared at him with vacant eyes, or turned his head away.

Finally – and Kamal heard the words clearly through the mists that veiled his mind – Rani Abishta spoke the magic formula that would lead to healing.

'Send for Swami Naadiyaananda!!'

Though his eyes were closed, Kamal knew the moment Swami Naadiyaananda entered his room. He felt a cool hand on his scalding forehead and light filter through his soul. He heard the soft words whispered: 'Come out of the night, Kamal. Come out of the night. Come into the sunshine. All will be well.'

He opened his eyes.

Swami Naadiyaananda had a shaven head, shining like honey, and eyes that saw through him and knew him. When Kamal looked into those eyes he no longer wanted to die. He felt life stir within him and he felt the certain knowledge that it was not his time to die. He felt grace like a glorious dawn within him, and he returned the swami's smile.

'All will be well, my son,' said Swami again. 'You will leave the palace.'

To Rani Abishta, Swami said: 'The disease is spiritual. He is suffering from asphyxiation of the soul. You must let him go. A bird in a cage has no option but to lie down and die, even if that cage is golden. This boy must spread his wings, and fly.'

From that day on Kamal recovered rapidly, but he never saw Swami again to thank him. There was so much to thank him for: soon, very soon, he was leaving, going to board at the Kodaikanal International School in the Palini Hills of Tamil Nadu. Rani Abishta herself had given the order, it was said – it had to be so – and she had done so on Swami's advice.

It was Kamal's friend, the counsellor Jairam, who told him the truth. 'He said if you remain here you will surely die. He told Rani Abishta she had abused his words; that she had lived against his injunctions; that she herself was killing you. Only for your sake he returned: to save you, he said. It is her one last chance.'

'Swami Naadiyaananda,' Kamal mused. 'I have heard that name before, when I was a boy. There was some mystery surrounding it, some kind of taboo attached to it. Do you know...?'

Jairam laughed. 'Everybody knows,' he said. 'Everybody knows except you. We were forbidden to tell you when you were a boy. Now, what does it matter? Now, you are leaving anyway. So I'll tell you. When you were a baby – you were not a year old, and your father had just been killed in prison – Swami was in the palace. Rani Abishta had sent for him in her grief and her anguish, not knowing which way to turn, alone with you, the only heir. She needed his guidance in that situation. He was Rani Abishta's guru, you know, who came from his hermitage in the Himalayas once a year until he spoke the words that made her send him away – for ever.'

'What did he say?'

'Well, your Rani Abishta had great plans for you. You would become a great statesman and businessman. You would grow wealthy in the silk industry. You would receive the best education the world has to offer. You would be rich, famous, powerful – you would be India's leader, bringing back royalty, restoring all the kingdoms to their rightful heirs. You would turn back time. Oh, she had so many ideas, so many plans, some of them far-fetched, impossible, and you were at the centre of them. Swami took one look at you and said: "This is a child of God. He is not made for worldly matters. He will renounce women and gold – he will be a monk."

'Rani Abishta flew into a rage, tried to make him take back those words – she believed whatever Swami said would inevitably come true – but he refused to recant. That's when she banned him from ever setting foot in the palace again. She ordained that his name should never again be spoken. She went so far as to banish our religion from being practised anywhere in the palace – she turned against God himself, as if that could prevent what God himself had ordained! She hardened her heart. You were to be trained by worldly, private teachers, and reared expressly for the role she had set for you. You were not to go outside – she knew the story of the Buddha, she knew how the sight of poverty and suffering could inspire a man to seek the highest goals of the spirit, turn him away from worldly gains. So you were not to know poverty and suffering. You were to be kept a prisoner in a golden cage – like the Prince Gautama. But Prince Gautama escaped, and became the Buddha, and you, too, escaped, in your own way.

'When you were dying Rani Abishta knew she had lost the battle – for the time being. She would never have sent for Swami had she not truly feared for your life, and known that her rejection of her guru was responsible for your illness, and that only he could heal you. She genuinely loves you, you see.'

'So now she will let me go?'

'Yes. Swami said you should go out into the world and get an education. Rani Abishta is still Rani Abishta – ambitious as ever, and she will never give up on her dreams for you, the only heir. But she has modified them somewhat; and besides, she may be a dreamer, but she is a realistic dreamer. She knows to be a statesman you will need an education; the best India can offer. She also now believes that in letting you go she can hold you all the better. When you see the suffering outside, she believes, you will want to take up the reins of power. She's sending you to a Christian school: the Christian ethic, she believes, is kinder and more tolerant towards worldly ambitions and temporal affairs than the Hindu. So now it's up to you.'

Kamal shrugged. 'What do I know about power? What do I care? I'm glad I didn't die, and I'm glad I'm leaving the palace. I look forward to Kodaikanal. But what the future holds – what is written in my destiny – who knows?'

'Possibly only Swami.'

Chapter Ten

Kamal 1978–1985

Kamal's years at Kodaikanal flew by, as happy times always do. He found friends and freedom. He found hobbies; he discovered a talent for both music and acting. He learned to play the piano tolerably well, and the guitar, and sing along. He joined a theatre group and discovered he was particularly good at playing dastardly villains. He was the brightest student in his class, and could take his pick of the best universities in the world. He wanted to go as far away from Rani Abishta as possible. He chose the Massachusetts Institute of Technology, in the USA.

Rani Abishta, of course, had been strictly against his going abroad. There had been a hot discussion, with her extolling the virtues of the Indian universities in Calcutta and Bombay and Delhi. But since his illness a subtle change in the balance of power had taken place, and Rani Abishta knew now that there was nothing she or anyone in the world could do when Kamal had made up his mind. She accepted defeat on this issue with something very much like grace.

Besides, she told Jairam, there was absolutely no sign of Kamal fulfilling Swami's prophecy. Kamal might be intense and strong-willed, but definitely not religious: there was no danger of him taking *sannyas,* becoming a monk. He had chosen to study engineering for his degree – what could be more worldly than that? She had pleaded with him to take up economics, business studies, law, degrees that would fit into her plans for him, but he

had refused. She pleaded with him to at least let it be *textile* engineering, which would come in useful when he took over the silk
business, but no, stubborn as usual, Kamal had set his mind on
civil engineering. And, he told her, he had absolutely no intention
of going into the silk business.

Rani Abishta shrugged and accepted defeat. It was a pity;
but, after all, the family business ran itself. She had placed good
and trustworthy men in charge, and with only a minimum of
supervision the profits were good. The market for patola silk was
still thriving – patola silk was royal silk, and although there were
no more royals in India, there were plenty of millionaires who
behaved and dressed like royalty. They had also expanded, in-
vested, purchased a struggling silk company in Tamil Nadu, built
it up. Moved on to a lesser, but still exquisite, quality for their
top range, and more commercial qualities for the export market,
and profits had only increased in the last few years. People would
always want silk; women would always want to wrap themselves
in fine garments. The future was rosy.

In his third year at MIT, Kamal received a bulging envelope
from Rani Abishta that made his blood boil.

'Soon your studies will be over, my son,' she wrote, 'and no
doubt the offers of work will be flooding in. It is time to start
looking for a bride for you and I have initiated the process. In the
envelope you will find five possibilities: all beautiful ladies with
good connections. I have already negotiated with their parents.
I have decided we will not demand a dowry as we are modern
people, but the connections are important. My favourite is Miss
Battacharya – a lovely girl and her father owns a chain of retail
fabric outlets all over the North. They are from Delhi. She is having an excellent education, which she will complete at the end of
this year. She is perfect for you but if you prefer one of the others
I am quite understanding. All of them are extremely suitable, just
that Miss Bhattacharya is the best.'

Kamal threw away the entire packet of colour photographs and marriage proposals, and wrote Rani Abishta a curt reply: 'None of them are right for me, Daadi. Please do not send any more marriage proposals, and please do not search for anyone else.'

* * *

Kamal met Caroline Mitchell in his fourth year at MIT. He first came across her at a Thanksgiving party in the home of a friend, and he spent that first evening answering all her avid questions about India.

As Caroline had spent her early years in the care of an Indian nanny, Meena, she had been nourished for years on the stories of the great epics *Mahabharata* and *Ramayana*. Meena had created a paradisical India in her mind, a place of flowers and birdsong and fabulous palaces and magical landscapes, snow-capped majestic mountains and sparkling lakes. As she reached adulthood and became involved with liberal politics she of course came to understand that this India was a clichéd, one-sided version of a very complex country; that the real India was far more multifaceted; that great misery and ugliness existed there side by side with the beauty and sublime ideas. But she remained fascinated. Against her parents' advice she chose anthropology as her major, and for the theme of her thesis, the Language and Culture of the Dravidian People of South India.

She would be going to India! In a year's time, she told Kamal; to do the fieldwork in Tamil family traditions necessary for her thesis. She hoped he could give her some tips, maybe some addresses?

She looked up at him with warm amber eyes that somehow touched him with their cool blend of naivety and intelligence. That naivety came from a pre-knowledge of India that was entirely idealistic and totally clichéd, established by a homesick nanny in whose lap she had dreamed her first Indian dreams, and later modified by a thousand books and articles written by Western-ers, brimful of Western prejudices and Western condescension. Kamal was able to set her straight on a number of issues.

They were so thoroughly engaged in the discussion that they did not notice the passing of time, and had to be gently levered out of their wicker chairs on the wraparound porch at two in the morning. Caroline lived with her parents in Cambridge, just a ten-minute walk from the friend's home. Kamal walked her home.

They talked all the way. Then Kamal felt her hand in his, and stopped speaking in mid-sentence. They walked the next few pac-es in silence. Then Caroline said, 'There's my house,' and pointed with her other hand, and Kamal squeezed the hand in his.

'I hope—'

'Kamal, it was—'

They spoke simultaneously; both stopped and looked at each other and laughed. Then Kamal said, 'Go ahead, you first.'

Caroline took his other hand and clasped them both between her smaller ones. 'I just wanted to say, I haven't had such a stimu-lating evening for… oh, my God. I don't think I've *ever* had such a stimulating evening in my whole life! It was awesome, talking with you, Kamal, and I think we're going to be great friends.'

Caroline's words were prophetic. They not only became the best of friends, they became lovers. From that first evening Kamal had known that this was the woman he was going to marry. She was so different from him, and not only physically, with her long blonde hair and pale heart-shaped face. She was the stranger he longed to embrace because she represented the half of him he did not yet know, that missing part of him that, once united with him, would make him whole. She was intellectual and warm at the same time; genuinely interested – no, interested was too weak – *enchanted* by India and all things Indian; touchingly ingenuous;

sometimes brittle, but the brittleness was only superficial and easy to melt. They could talk for hours, and be silent for hours; when the first snow fell she drove him out to the countryside and they walked through the whiteness without speaking a single word, arms slung around each other in a silent intimacy overflowing with warmth, and though the bitter cold stung his bare cheeks Kamal felt the winter must melt before them, like the snowflakes melting on his lashes. He opened his lips and caught the snow on his tongue and laughed out loud. Caroline, her face small and white in the soft maroon shawl wrapped around her head, glowed with inner joy. She pressed an icy-cold, snow-encrusted glove against his cheek and said, 'Kamal Bhandari, if you don't promise to marry me I swear I'm going to lie down right there in that snowbank and let the snow drift over me and cover me till I look like the Abominable Snowman and just wait there until you do!'

Kamal chuckled and moved her hand from his cheek. He pulled off her glove and flung it away onto the snow, and replaced the warm hand on his warm cheek.

'That's more like it. Now, Caroline Mitchell, what do you want me to do? Go down on one knee and propose officially?'

'No. Just say it. Say it. Say you want to marry me. Say you want to be mine for ever and ever.'

'You know it already.'

'But I want to hear it. I want you to say it out loud. I can't stand this deep Indian silent communication. Go on, just say it.'

'You don't know me properly yet, you know. Wait till I get you back to India. I will turn into the tyrannical Indian patriarch of your worst nightmares! I will ravish you as my wife and keep another four in my harem just for good measure. I will keep you well under my foot, forbid you to step outside the walls of our marital abode unless you walk four paces behind me. You will occupy yourself with raising five fine sons to follow in my revered footsteps. You will refer to me exclusively as "Father of my Sons" and bow your head, hiding your face in the folds of your sari, when I enter the room. You will humbly serve me delicious meals you have cooked with devotion on golden platters and only take food yourself when I and all our sons have been sated. When I die you will—'

'I'll stuff this snow down your damned *throat* if you don't look out!' cried Caroline, then made good on her threat. Kamal wrenched himself out of her grasp and ran stumbling through the snow. Caroline bent down and picked up a handful of snow, pressed it into a huge snowball and pelted him with it, screaming, 'You asked for it! You *jerk*!' It hit him square on the back of his head.

'OK, it's WAR!' cried Kamal, and bent over for his own snowball.

They fought fiercely, hysterically, for a good half-hour and then, suddenly, Kamal threw up his arms and said, 'OK, OK, you win. I admit my defeat. I surrender unequivocally. I will fulfil each and every one of your demands.'

She flung herself at him so that they both lay in the snow. 'Marry me. That's all I want. Say it out loud.'

'Marry me,' he whispered, and the words came out on a breath like smoke, fading into the crisp cold air.

'Louder. I can't hear you.'

'Marry me, Caroline.'

'Sorry? What was that?'

'I refuse to shout. I'm not going to shout. Come here.' He drew her head close to his, her ear to his lips, and there he spoke the words again, clearly and gently. 'Will you be my wife? To have and to hold, till death do us part?'

She smiled, put her arms around him and rested her cheek on his. 'Yes,' she sighed 'I will.'

* * *

The path to marriage was, for Kamal and Caroline, rough. Caroline took Kamal to meet her parents and they received him with a civil but icy reserve that caused him to fear the worst.

'You see, they belong to the old Boston aristocracy. Old money, real old. Very Anglo-Saxon, very white, very Protestant. They have a precise idea of the kind of man they want me to marry and – well, Kamal, you just don't fit the cookie-cutter.'

'They haven't even *tried* to get to know me.'

'Getting to know you isn't the issue. *Who* you are doesn't count; it's *what* you are.'

'What I am? Come on, I'm not exactly the plumber! I'm a MIT student, for goodness' sake. All right, I realise a medical or a law student might be more up their street but—'

Caroline cut in. 'That's not the point, Kamal. Even if you were going to be a doctor they'd be against you. It's where you come, from, how you look.'

'In other words, they're racist.'

Caroline hung her head. 'I'm sorry, Kamal. That's just the way they are. They can't jump over their shadows. I *warned* you they'd be this way.'

'Look, I don't give a damn about *them*. The question for me is, can *you* jump over their shadows?'

'Oh Kamal, why do you even ask!'

'So you'll go against them? Marry me, even if they don't agree? Come with me to India?'

'Kamal, I've always known I'd end up in India. Ever since I read *The Jungle Book* as a child I've known it – it's a pull I can't explain and for me it's only logical that I should marry an Indian and go there with him and there's nothing in the world my parents can do about it. They can't hold me back. But anyway' – she smiled – 'sooner or later they'll have to give in because they love me. And when they hold my first baby in their arms, they'll be just like grandparents anywhere. They'll go completely gaga.'

Of course, Kamal told Caroline all about his childhood in the golden cage. Caroline was beyond excited.

'So you're a real Indian prince! Wow! I can't believe I'm going to marry a prince! Does that make me a princess? I can't believe it! Kamal, I used to dream of becoming an Indian princess but no one would believe me, and now it's going to be true! I can't wait to see the palace! Shall we have a big wedding in the palace? Shall I arrive riding on an elephant? Just kidding, don't give me that look! But you know, knowing you're a prince might be just the thing to win over my parents. You should have told me earlier!'

But Kamal frowned, and his eyes clouded over.

'No,' he said. 'You're not a princess, and I am not a prince. I'm not taking you to that place. I don't want to see Daadi ever again.'

Caroline was persistent. 'But why, Kamal, why? She's your grandmother; your only relative. Surely she'll want to meet your wife, and when we have kids—'

'I don't want to discuss it, Caroline, OK? She wouldn't approve of you anyway, so you can forget about a big royal wedding. It's not going to happen.'

That was the only time they ever came near to a quarrel, and Caroline thought it was wiser to leave well enough alone. She understood: Kamal wanted to be loved for himself, not for his blue blood. And she did love him for himself.

Chapter Eleven

Caroline. Gingee, South India, 1988

Kamal took Caroline to India and married her there at a small, private Hindu ceremony, against her parents' wishes. For Caroline's thesis on Tamil family structure, she wanted actually to *live* in a Tamil family, in a traditional village far away from modern influences. So the newly-weds travelled around Tamil Nadu for a while, looking for just the right village, just the right family; the plan was for Kamal to help her get settled, and then decide on an engineering job not too far away – he had in mind a hydroelectric dam project somewhere in South India, and had sent off several applications. Invitations for interviews were already coming in.

It would mean separating during the week and only seeing each other at the weekends but it would only be for a while – their love was strong enough; it would only be nourished by the pain of parting.

Caroline found her place. The Iyengars lived in a village on the outskirts of Gingee, a small town a few hours' drive from Madras. It was perfect: a traditional Hindu family, mother, father, five children, the eldest a girl of eleven. But best of all, the parents were both well educated, with degrees, and spoke English; the father, Viram, was headmaster at a private secondary school, and took a personal interest in Caroline's thesis. He was able to explain to her everything she wanted to know, and for an hour a day he taught her Tamil. His wife, Sundari, had a bachelor's degree in

English, and loved reading; she and Caroline hit it off immediately, especially because they shared many favourite books.

The house itself was a little cramped, what with five children and another on the way, but they had a large back garden and it was an easy and quick thing to add a double room and a bathroom at the back where Caroline could live, and Kamal could visit at weekends.

Kamal got the job he wanted, at the Aliyar reservoir in the Coimbatore District. The dam had been built in the seventies for irrigation purposes, and had just been commissioned to generate hydroelectric power; the project consisted of a series of dams interconnected by tunnels and canals for harnessing the waters of several nearby rivers, all flowing at various elevations, for irrigation and power generation. It was exactly what Kamal wanted, for it not only challenged his engineering skill but was also of immense use to the farmers. A wonderful start to his career.

* * *

They hadn't planned a baby just yet – but these things happen, and six months later Caroline found she was pregnant.

They were delighted. They made plans to build a nice house near the dam. She would finish her thesis and have the baby: perfect.

Who needed the Mitchells of Cambridge, who needed Kamal's Daadi of Moti Khodayal? Not Kamal and Caroline Bhandari.

But they were forced to delay their plans for a while. They hadn't built their house yet, for there wasn't enough money, and both refused, for obvious reasons, to ask their families for help. Then Kamal received a lucrative offer to go and work on another dam project in North India, on a two-year contract. He'd earn well and improve the family finances; they could have their home sooner. It was a magnificent offer. 'That's the benefit of a MIT degree,' he said, laughing. 'It's an offer I can't refuse.'

After the two years he'd come home, get back his old job but with a better salary – his present employers certainly didn't want to lose him – and build their home.

The set-up with the Iyengars was so ideal it would have been nonsensical for Caroline to accompany Kamal to North India. She was happy with her Tamil family; Sundari and she were now close friends, and she was learning Tamil; moving to the north would mean a new language, a new environment, disruptive for all. Sundari was eager to help and advise Caroline in all matters concerning pregnancy and childbirth; with five, soon to be six children, she was an expert. Yes, it would be foolish for Caroline to move.

Caroline's baby was a girl. Kamal could not come down for the birth, which was sad for both of them, but, after all, Caroline was in good hands and the future lay before them, round and glowing. Soon they'd have their own home and watch their daughter grow.

They named her Asha. Caroline took hundreds of photographs of her and sent them to Kamal accompanied by expansive, euphoric letters. What she didn't tell Kamal, though, was that she was finding the adjustment to motherhood difficult, especially breast-feeding. But it was not a problem, since Sundari was there and her breasts seldom ran dry; she was still feeding her youngest, Kanaan, and the next baby was due in four months' time.

'I have enough milk for all,' she said with a laugh, and took the squalling Asha confidently from Caroline's arms and laid her at her breast. Asha's lips closed around the nipple; the screaming stopped. Caroline breathed a sigh of relief and tucked her own breast away.

'But what will happen when your baby comes?' she asked. 'You won't have time for two little ones – three, counting Kanaan!'

'Janiki will help. I will continue to feed her, but Janiki will do all the rest. Won't you, Janiki?'

Janiki nodded eagerly. She was thirteen years old, the eldest child and the only girl, already her mother's right hand in the home, helping to care for her youngest brother, Kanaan. She loved babies.

'Of course, Amma!' she said. 'I will be her chinna-amma, her little mother.'

Chapter Twelve

Kamal. Gingee, 1988

From afar, Kamal adored his daughter. He was working six days a week and it just wasn't practical to fly down and back in the space of a day and a half – and it was expensive, of course. And as for Caroline visiting him with the baby, or even coming up and their renting a home nearby so they could live together for that year – they simply decided to save the money. It was so convenient, her living with the Iyengars. She had two built-in babysitters as well as a companion in Sundari, and could continue to work on her thesis.

Then, at Christmas, at Caroline's insistence, Kamal finally came home. Asha was six months old.

At Madras airport he saw her right away, behind the wall of dark Indians waving their signs behind the barrier. Caroline stood aloof, beyond the fray, just as she was in that sacred place where he held her in his mind. She wore sparkling white cotton trousers and a long, soft blouse batiked in various shades of blue. Her blonde hair, cut short now, was like a sleek, polished cap framing a tanned face, glinting in the midday sunlight; she held one hand as a visor above her eyes as she scanned the line of passengers pushing their rusty brown trolleys out of the airport building. At the moment of recognition her face lit up, as at the sudden emergence of the sun from behind a cloud; her hand shot upwards, waving furiously. She ran forward and into his arms.

When they separated again Caroline took his hand and led him to a waiting taxi.

'You didn't bring her?' Kamal said, peering into the back window of the taxi. He felt a twinge of disappointment. Time was so short; their minutes together were precious. She should have brought Asha.

'Oh, no, I left her with Janiki,' said Caroline. 'It's a three-hour drive in this hot sun; it would just have been a hassle. You know, with nursing and all that.'

'So you had to leave her for six hours? Is that all right? I mean – doesn't she have to be fed?'

Caroline hesitated. She had not yet told him about the feeding arrangement. She'd have to confess; better to do it now.

'Kamal – my milk dried up. It happens often with first-time mothers, you know. But thank goodness Sundari had so much and so she has been feeding her. She gave birth two months ago and she still has so much milk – it's practically pouring out! Enough for three babies.'

Kamal's face fell. 'So you haven't been feeding her at all?'

'Oh, sure!' said Caroline. 'Sundari expresses the milk sometimes and puts it into a bottle, so I can feed her. You can too – you'll love it!'

She squeezed his hand and he squeezed hers back.

'Kamal – you're the father of the most beautiful little girl in the world and you don't know it! I can't wait for you to meet her!'

The drive home was interminable. But then they were there, the taxi bouncing slowly down the unpaved street to the big white house at the end, meandering around the potholes. Children swarmed around the car – for motor vehicles were rarities in this village – running backwards before it or skipping along beside it, slapping its bonnet, grinning in through the open window, calling out to Caroline and Kamal. One little boy in ragged blue shorts threw himself across the bonnet and sprawled there waving; another hooked his elbow in through the open window; two others jumped onto the back bumper and clung to the hind parts of the car like stick insects glued to a window.

Kamal, with wise prescience, had brought several packets of wrapped sweets. He opened one with his teeth and held it out of the window, emptying the lemon and orange sweets onto the dusty road. Immediately the children dropped away from the car and fell on them, scrambling on the ground and grappling frantically. Kamal looked out of the rear window, then turned to Caroline.

'Some things never change!' he said.

'And some things do,' she replied. 'Look in front of you!'

Kamal turned around. They had arrived at the Iyengar home; the taxi halted. Janiki, who had either heard the commotion or the hum of the car or been warned of their coming through the swifter-than-light grapevine, stood in front of the door, a broad smile on her lips and a bundle of Asha in her arms. Sundari came out behind her, wiping her hands on a towel and smiling broadly.

A tiny hand waved clumsily above the bundle. Two small legs hung below it. The rest of Asha was concealed by a thin cotton cloth, but now Janiki changed the position of her arms and held the baby upright in the crook of her arms, one hand bracing her, so that the cloth dropped away from the little bare chest and the child sat as in a comfortable chair, facing her father.

Kamal stared, suddenly silent. Slowly he left the car, not bothering to close the door, and crossed the short stretch of sand to approach his daughter, coming to a stop immediately in front of Sundari. He wanted to speak, to reach for the child, but the words caught in his throat and his arms felt crippled – he could not move them. Even his breath stopped, it seemed, and his mouth was dry, and his ears had lost their hearing for all the world was silent around him, and even his thoughts had raced headlong into a wall and ceased. But then his eyes were suddenly involuntarily moist, his arms moving upwards to receive the child who in the same moment Janiki was holding out towards him. He took Asha as if he had held her a thousand times before, clasped her to his chest and covered her with his crossed forearms and moved away, walking towards the fence and away from the others so that no one could see his face – or his tears.

* * *

Caroline had tried her best. She had bought a plastic Christmas tree and decorations in Madras. She had arranged cotton wool around the base of the tree for snow, and hung the cheap plastic baubles in glaring red and gold along its branches, and draped long strips of glittering tinsel around it, all in an attempt to reproduce the spirit of Christmas as she remembered it. It didn't work. Not even the fat candle glowing on its polished brass stand could make her believe it was truly Christmas.

'Look at this angel,' she said, handing him a tinny white thing that had fallen from one of the branches. 'Isn't she unbelievably tacky? But I couldn't find anything else. And believe me, I really scoured the stores. I guess Christmas isn't a big thing here.'

'It isn't,' Kamal said. He looked down at Asha, who was wearing a bright red dress, which set off perfectly the jet black of her hair and her sparkling eyes, now fixed on the bright angel. Kamal, as he had done so often, marvelled at the perfect little features.

'Christmas is something we read about in books. I'm sorry.'

'Well, could we at least sing some carols?'

'I'm not so good at carols,' Kamal admitted. 'Remember, I never even heard "Jingle Bells" till I got to America. So I don't know if... Hey, what's the matter? Caro, Caro, why're you crying?'

Caroline wiped away a tear with her bare forearm. 'It's nothing, I guess. Well, no. It's just that... it's just that... that...'

Kamal gently laid Asha on her blanket on the floor, and leaned towards his wife. Her face was turned away from him, and huge tears rolled down her cheeks. He placed his hand on her chin and gently turned her face up towards him.

'Tell me. Please tell me what's bothering you. You know you can tell me everything. Here.'

He gave her a clean square of cloth, one of several they used for Asha to burp on, and wiped her cheeks with it. 'Can't you tell me what's the matter?'

'I… I suppose it's just Christmas,' Caroline admitted. 'A bit of homesickness. Nostalgia and all that. I feel so… so sentimental… I sort of miss my parents and stuff. And snow. And church. Santa Claus. All that soppy stuff. Family stuff, I guess. And Christmas dinner. The turkey! Oh, Kamal, what I wouldn't give for a turkey! And apple pie. When… when I was a kid I used to be in the church choir and we used to walk around town singing carols and collecting for charity. I had this muff and a coat with a furry bonnet and it was all so warm and snuggly and I would so love to offer all of that to Asha and I can't – she'll never know Christmas! She'll grow up without snow and Santa! And Thanksgiving. I adore Thanksgiving, everyone around the table and Mom basting the turkey! And fall – the golden leaves! And oh, Kamal, it's just so damned *hot* here! All year round! And all my friends and everything. I miss them. The time difference makes it impossible to even call them to wish them a merry Christmas. And presents – books! I had to leave all my favourite books behind and I miss them so. And music. I should have brought my violin. Why didn't I think of that? And…'

But she couldn't speak any more because her face was buried in Kamal's warm shoulder. Kamal patted her back and held her close. She let the sobs come and they broke from her in stifled, breathless gulps. Finally she moved so that her lips were free and she could speak.

'I want to go home! I want to go home, Kamal, I can't stand it here a day longer. I haven't done any work on my thesis since

Asha was born. Sundari and Janiki are angels, looking after Asha so well. I'm a terrible mother, Kamal. Sometimes I can't even stand to see Asha. Sometimes I wish she'd never been born. I shouldn't be telling you this. I hate myself. Sometimes I even hate you, but you're all I have. I wrote to Mom and Dad and they didn't write back! I don't have anybody but you... and... and Asha. I'm so alone here! Asha doesn't even like me very much, she prefers Sundari and Janiki. I don't know how to love her. I'm such a bad mother and I'm so ashamed to admit it. I thought it would all be perfect but it isn't!'

Kamal held her all the time, rubbing her back.

'I can't even finish my thesis!' Caroline wailed. She spoke on and on, repeating herself, sometimes breaking down and crying, sometimes falling silent for a length of time only to start again. She was bored, she was restless, she was a bad mother, she couldn't write her thesis, she missed Thanksgiving, she missed her friends, she missed her family.

When it was over Kamal spoke.

'Caro, Caro, what have I done to you? I shouldn't have brought you here. I shouldn't have left you here all by yourself. I can't bear to see you unhappy. Listen – it doesn't have to be for ever. I don't really mind where I live. It doesn't have to be India. It was *you* who wanted to come here. It was you who had work to do here. I tell you what. We'll go back. Back to America, get a job there. Just try to be patient. Let me work out my contract. Can you hang on that long? Just one more Christmas, and the following summer we'll go back. Asha will be two. You'll make it up with your parents; they'll adore Asha. And even if they still don't like me it doesn't matter. I don't have to visit them. You can spend every Christmas with them. I don't mind – Christmas means nothing to me, you see, so I won't feel left out. Anything you want. I can work anywhere. You can do what you want to do. You can go to work. We'll find a way.'

'But – what about Asha? She loves Sundari so much! And Janiki!'

'She'll learn to love us, her parents,' Kamal said. 'It'll happen, just you wait and see. I know you've had a hard time as a mother but that's normal at first and I bet it changes over the next year. You just have to make a tiny bit more effort, win her over, make sure she knows that you are Mom. If you go to work in America I'll look after her so you can work, or study, do anything, or we'll find another solution. Whatever you want.'

'Oh, Kamal.' Caroline's voice broke, because she was laughing. 'What did I ever do to deserve someone like you? I swear, I'm the luckiest girl in the whole world. My girlfriends should be green with envy. I'm sorry I broke down, truly. I'm so lucky. So very lucky. I think we must be the happiest family in the world.'

'Even if things aren't so perfect right now. But they will be, I promise. We'll make them perfect.'

'As long as we love each other, Kamal, everything *is* perfect.'

'Then let's hold onto this perfect moment. If we can just remember how it is now, nothing can ever go wrong.' He chuckled. 'Even if the Christmas tree is, well, to put it tactfully, best Indian quality.'

Caroline laughed with him. 'And even if you can't sing "Silent Night" with me and my family.'

'And even if I've got to leave you again, the day after tomorrow. But now at least I know *her.*'

They both gazed in silent wonder at Asha, who had fallen asleep on her blanket. In the steady light of the candle's flame her skin glowed softly golden. Long black lashes touched her cheek. Her chest rose and sank to the rhythm of her breathing.

'She's so, so, so…' Caroline whispered, and paused, searching for the right word.

'Sssh,' said Kamal, and placed a finger on her lips. 'I know.'

Chapter Thirteen

Caroline

Perfect moments come and go, and not long after Kamal returned to the north, Caroline's homesickness returned with a vengeance. She missed everything. Her music, her books, her friends, her parents, the winter, the trees, the springtime, the food. A little nagging voice within her began to moan and groan. About everything.

She had been so willing to adapt to local mores at first; now, they began to vex and even outrage her. Why, when the sun was so hot, was she required to wear a long skirt and keep her shoulders covered, whereas men could walk about with naked upper bodies? Why did the women do all the housework, while the men went out to work and just relaxed on the veranda with the newspaper when they came home? Viram was truly lovely, but he left the running of the household entirely to Sundari. When questioned about this, Sundari only smiled and said, 'He works hard outside the home, I work hard inside the home. It's a division of labour. Out there, he is boss. In here, I am boss. It's a very fair set-up.' But Caroline did not, could not agree. She said no more, but it rankled within her.

She tried to suppress her unkind thoughts – after all, she was not only a guest here, but a liberal, and must be accepting and even approving of other cultures – but suppression could only go so far and she thought them nevertheless.

The things about India, about Gingee, that had charmed her at first began to irritate and annoy her. Sitting on the floor to eat, for instance; she longed for a chair and table. Eating with her hands; she longed for a knife and fork. How *primitive* it all was! And surely unhygienic! She longed for folded napkins and her mother's apple pie. *Anyone's* apple pie. She tried baking an apple pie herself but it was a flop.

And then the toilet business. Using your left hand and water to clean your butt after a crap. Disgusting! Squatting over the Indian toilet, really just a ceramic surround of a hole in the ground. How she had enthused about this method in the beginning! So much better, from a physiological point of view, than sitting on a toilet, she wrote to her best friend Deb, 'because squatting provides a massaging effect for the abdominal organs and stimulates the nervous action of the bowels to give a good motion. It's simply the most natural position,' she lectured. 'My landlord, Viram, showed me an article in the *Hindu* that said squatting is scientifically proven to be better. Sitting on a toilet chokes the rectum, and that's why bowel-related diseases like haemorrhoids, appendicitis, constipation and irritable bowel syndrome are so prevalent with us in the West.'

That was then. Now, she would give her all for a Western toilet with a roll of puppy-dog soft paper on the wall next to it.

And there was no one she could talk to about these things. Kamal, certainly not. She couldn't criticise his country and culture to him; of course not. But who then? She couldn't write long letters of complaint to her liberal friends at home as they were so approving of her, applauding her for choosing to live in a Third World country (although one wasn't supposed to use that label any more, and anyway, India was supposed to be in a different category, one of the economically emerging nations). Her friends would be shocked should she betray them by letting slip even a word of complaint.

So at most, she complained of the heat. *You wouldn't believe how hot it gets here in April! I swear you could fry an egg on the street!*

she wrote jovially to her best friend Deb. *We all now sleep on the veranda – it's just too hot to sleep indoors. And no air-conditioning at all! At least it's good for the environment!*

She couldn't, of course, complain to her parents and siblings, who would only say *I told you so.*

She could only complain to herself. The nagging voice grew louder; horrible, mean, ugly. Try as she did, she could not shut it up. She was beginning to hate India.

* * *

Most of all, the food. The food seemed to stand for everything that was inherently wrong about her present life. Not that it was bad – Sundari was a superb cook, and the meals she prepared were invariably elaborately prepared, and delicious. But they weren't *American.* Caroline simply missed good home cooking. It became almost an obsession for her. She had always been quite particular about what she ate, something of a health-food fanatic. She liked fresh vegetables, salads, seafood, home-made casseroles and never, ever ate out of a tin.

She'd been an on-and-off vegetarian back at home, and moving in with a vegetarian family had not been a problem. But during her pregnancy she had developed a craving for meat, which had not receded since the baby was born. Especially at Thanksgiving, and Christmas. Turkey! Roast chicken! Salami pizza! Even – disgraceful! – a hamburger. What she wouldn't give for a hot dog, with all the trimmings! But you couldn't get meat here – or not much of it. There were one or two butchers in Gingee, but just seeing the conditions in those shops – the meat lying in the open, the flies, the blood, the unwashed knives, the dirt – put her off.

Sometimes she had a chicken specially slaughtered, and she watched over it and made sure it was all done quickly, no flies, clean knives, everything. However, cooking a chicken was a bit difficult in the Iyengar household – Sundari wouldn't touch it, and she didn't really even like Caroline doing it herself, and sully-ing her cooking utensils with the carcass.

But she struggled on, and the months creaked past. Another Christmas, with Asha now a toddler, and Kamal home again for only his third visit (he had managed to come for a week in June, for Asha's birthday). A resignation of sorts laid itself upon her soul. It was just a question of time, and time would pass. Slowly, for sure, but it would pass, and she would make it, and they would return to America. And Asha would learn to love her. Though that didn't seem to be happening much. Asha was as ever attached mostly to Sundari, and to Janiki. Caroline felt like the visiting childless aunt, awkward and bumbling, and Asha treated her with something verging on boredom. She just didn't have the knack, the warmth. *Bad mother!* said the little nagging voice within her.

* * *

Shortly after Asha's second birthday – Kamal had managed to get leave, to come and visit for a week – Caroline discovered a supermarket in Gingee hidden away in a back street, where one could actually buy food from the city – butter, cheese, spaghet-ti, soy sauce and so on. She asked the shopkeeper if they could get tinned corned beef, sausages and spam. They could. She ate all the things she bought and enjoyed them. She went back and asked for more. The shopkeeper was delighted to oblige. The next time she went there he showed her a real treasure: tinned ravioli! The tin was old, dusty and slightly dented, but Caroline couldn't care less. She couldn't wait to get home, open it, warm it up and eat it. Delicious!

The next morning, though, she felt sick, and vomited up her breakfast. Other symptoms followed quickly – a dry mouth and throat, and then she had difficulty swallowing. Her eyelids drooped; she felt dizzy, light-headed. She went to see a doctor, and his verdict was: botulism, food poisoning, caused by eating infected food from a damaged can.

That was the straw that broke the camel's back. Casting pride aside, Caroline rang her parents.

'I want to come home!' she wailed.

'Come, darling, come!' they said. 'We will arrange your flight. Don't worry about a thing. Just come home!'

It wasn't possible to contact Kamal – he was out on location – before her flight so she sent a telegram. SERIOUS FOOD POISONING FLYING AMERICA TOMORROW STOP LEAVING ASHA WITH SUNDARI STOP.

Chapter Fourteen

Kamal

Kamal held the bottle to Asha's lips but she pushed angrily against it with her little clenched fist. She kicked and wriggled, and twisted around so that her head was bent almost backwards. Kamal tried to put his arms around her, hold her in the crook of his arm to try again with the bottle, but she lashed it away again and frowned, squawking in fury. She twisted around again; she had heard sounds in the kitchen and she knew who was making them. Kamal gave up and put her on the floor. Immediately Asha was running at full speed towards the source of the sound. She disappeared into the kitchen. A moment later Sundari appeared from there, Asha in her arms.

'She ran away again,' she said smilingly, and held the child out to her father. Kamal reached for her but Asha kicked his hands away, squirming and struggling, refusing to be handed over.

Sundari smiled. 'The Terrible Twos, they call it in America. Caroline told me. Besides, she just doesn't know you well enough. It will come.'

'And her mom's gone,' Kamal reminded her.

'Yes, that is true. But to tell you the truth, I don't know if she even noticed that. Caroline has always had problems bonding with her, and it hasn't changed. Asha thinks I am her mother, and Janiki is a close second.'

'I noticed that,' said Kamal.

'Well, what was I to do? Whenever the child cried Caroline panicked. She gave her to me and Asha was quiet. Should I have refused to take her? And then Janiki took over after Ramesh was born. And now it's the same thing. She doesn't know you're her father. She won't even let you feed her.'

Sundari bent over and picked up the bottle that was lying on the ground, wiped the teat with a corner of her sari and handed the bottle to Asha, who was already reaching for it, gurgling with anticipation.

'The thing is,' Kamal said slowly, 'I don't know how long Caroline will be gone. You don't mind carrying on as before?'

'Of course not. Nothing will change.' Sundari changed Asha from one arm to the other, away from Kamal. Asha lay luxuriantly in the curve of her arm, sucking at her bottle with eyes half-closed in bliss. She looked as if she belonged there, would always belong there.

'I'll keep on paying you, of course, even though Caroline isn't with you. I'll keep paying as if nothing has changed. Room and board, till she comes back.'

'*If* she comes back.'

'What do you mean, if? Of course she'll come back!'

'Well, the way she was carrying on, I actually doubt that. Your wife hates India, Kamal, hadn't you noticed? Well, I had, even if she tried to hide it. She hates India and she won't be back. Trust me.'

'Well, we planned on moving to America later this year anyway.'

'Not with Asha, I assume? You will leave Asha with me.'

'No! The plan is for all three of us to move to America as soon as my contract expires. We told you this, Sundari! Of course we'll take Asha! We want to be a proper family at last.'

Sundari turned her back.

'Well, good luck with that. Of course you have every right to take Asha. But you understand you will be tearing her life apart? She does not know you at all and she has a very poor relationship with her mother. I don't know how you can even *consider* taking her out of the family she knows and loves. In my eyes that is child abuse.'

'Sundari, don't exaggerate! She will get used to us and to life in America. She's so small! Children adapt very quickly and easily.'

'And what do you know about children? Just because you're a big-shot foreign-educated engineer doesn't mean you know everything, you know. You should listen to me – I'm a mother. *Her* mother, she thinks. I know this child, and I know you cannot tear her from the family she knows and loves without doing her terrible damage. If you want to take that responsibility, then go ahead. But don't blame me when the damage is done. It's your child.'

Kamal turned and walked away. He had to think. Sundari, of course, was basically right – it was just the *way* she said it that bothered him. So bossy! It was true what they said, that women might have a socially inferior position in Indian society, but in the home they were the undisputed head of everything, and men the inferior. He'd known it from his own upbringing, of course –Daadi was the boss. And he saw it here, with Sundari. Sundari's husband submitted to her without a murmur, and now she expected such submission from him, too, regarding his own child.

He wanted to protest, to argue, to shout, even, and yet he couldn't, because at the heart of it she was right. It's not biology that makes a parent, but love, bonding, care. And Asha loved Sundari more than she loved her biological parents; Sundari had cared for her more than her parents; and the bond between the Iyengars and Asha was deep and lasting, whereas the bond between Asha and her parents was loose and weak and one-sided and complicated. Yes, she was loved with a passion by both parents – but that love had never found expression in everyday life. The last thing he wanted was to cause Asha damage – would he, by taking her away, to America, in a few months' time? But how could he – they – leave her here? Would Caroline return, once she had recovered, to help him fight for Asha, to make a renewed effort to win her affection? Somehow, he doubted it.

In the end he returned to the north. Sundari had won. Of course Asha's needs must come first. He couldn't tear her out of her familiar surroundings, her home, away from her amma and chinna-amma.

* * *

He wrote to Caroline, who agreed that he had done the right thing and wrote back:

'We must do what's right for her. I mean, yes, I do feel guilt about not being a good mother and leaving her behind. But, Kamal, I was truly desperate! The botulism was simply the last straw – I had to come home. It was the right thing to do, and I could only do it with the knowledge that Asha is truly happy and well cared for. She couldn't have a better mother than Sundari, and I say that as her real mother. One day, hopefully soon, we will all be together. Until then, I am trying to put my life together here in Cambridge, get back on my feet, build a foundation for us all.

What I really need to do, Kamal, is think about my own future, my own career. I've been able to finish my thesis but it was a bit of a rushed job – the fire had gone out of me and I was unable to reignite it. I need to do something else, something more relevant. I want to go back to college, get a more practical degree. I'm torn in two directions. Law, which would be the sensible thing. My parents are urging me in that direction. But I'm tired of being sensible. I want to do something I truly love, and I'm really pulled towards the Creative Arts Therapy course at Lesley College in Cambridge. That's something I'd love to do, and the good thing is, I can live with my parents. So that's the direction I'm going in. I probably will choose what I love.

I've reconciled completely with Mom and Dad. They are happy to have me stay with them, and even if I don't study law, they'll be happy just to have me here. I don't think they're yet accepting of you, my darling, but we can live with that, can't we? You won't have to see them. They'll adore Asha, and maybe in time they will learn to reconcile with you as her father. I'll do my best to bring that about. I love all of you and I want us to be one big happy family. I'm sure it will happen eventually.'

Reconciled to Caroline's decision – which he agreed with, in principle, though it would mean a delay in the grand plan for them all to come together in America – Kamal returned with renewed vigour to his job in North India. It was for the family, for the future. For the time being, he was glad that Caroline was happy.

* * *

But in the end she became too happy. Their phone calls – always difficult because of the time difference – grew more and more rare. And at the end of the year Kamal received a Dear John letter.

Dear Kamal,

This is the hardest letter I've ever written in my life, and believe me, the pain of writing it is equal to the pain I know it will cause you. I do apologise for taking so long to reply to your last letters. That I haven't called you in months. The truth is, I didn't know what to say; I had no words. How could I put into a letter all the changes I have been going through in the last six months? It was just too much, and I chose to keep silent until the turbulence calmed down and I could arrive at some sort of a resolution, some sort of a conclusion, some sort of a confirmation that I have made the right decision.

Kamal, it truly breaks my heart to tell you this but I have met someone else, someone with whom I am completely comfort-

able, in all areas of life. His name is Wayne Richmond. It is as if all the loose ends of my life are tied up with Wayne. He is an up-and-coming attorney at Dad's firm and – well, we just clicked. These things happen – the chemistry was there from the beginning and I did try hard to fight it off; I did, Kamal! I do take my marriage vows seriously but you have to admit that the hurdles for the two of us have simply been too high to overcome. The physical separation, the cultural differences, the geographical problems: all of these have contributed to the distance that has grown between us.

The physical separation is just a metaphor for the spiritual distance, Kamal. I need a husband who is at my side, and apart from the honeymoon phase of our marriage this has just not been the case. It's just not working, Kamal. I'm sure you must have felt it too? I'm sure you must have, but your loyalty and sense of duty – those very Indian qualities that I admire so much – have kept you bound to me. I think we should both be free, Kamal. Free to explore our lives and to find other, better alternatives for our paths forward. I know you will be hurt by this letter but one day you will see it as a blessing: I am setting you free! Free to find the right path for you. I am sure there is a beautiful Indian woman out there, near your workplace, someone who is just perfect for you.

It's not that I don't love you – I do, but in a very quiet, passionless way. It's not enough, Kamal. It's not what I imagine I should feel for my husband. I don't feel the butterflies! It's not good enough for you. You will surely find someone who loves you as much as you deserve. You are such a good man; you are wasted on me. And we will always be bound together because we have Asha.

Asha! My darling Asha. My one consolation is that she is in the best hands possible, in a family that loves her. A child needs a stable family, with both parents; brothers and sisters, a stable home, a nest where she can grow and thrive. We have never offered her that. The Iyengars have. Sundari writes often and sends photographs and I am confident enough to say that I think we have made the best choice, the unselfish choice: we have chosen what is best for her, and not what we want. I often felt guilty about not being a good mother but Sundari is just that. Mothers have such a high status in India – they are next to God, and I could never live up to that. I no longer feel that guilt. Just knowing she is in good hands is enough for me, and that makes me a good mother, comfortable with my decision. There are many ways to be a good mother.

I will always write her letters, send her photos, so she will always know she has a second mother – a third mother, because isn't Janiki her little mother too, her chinna-amma! And I will visit her as soon as I can. But I cannot tear her away from her home, from the people she regards as her parents, from her family, from her culture. She would not feel at home in America, as was our original plan. Yes, it does break my heart a little not to see her growing up, but so be it. It's for her sake. When she is grown up she will understand.

I'm hoping that you feel the same way, Kamal. That when you find the right woman for you – and you will! – you will resist the urge to tear her away from the family she regards as her own. You will have other children, as will I, and you will always be her father, but I hope that as a father you will always choose what is best for her and however much you want her, I am hoping you will do the right thing.

I'm not asking for a divorce as yet. I have three more years of study and we're not planning to marry before I graduate. We're doing this the proper, traditional way! I guess I was always a daddy's girl at heart and it's good to be back in the heart of my family. I hope you, too will find peace, and soon.

On that note, Kamal, I embrace you as a sister, not as a wife, and hope you read these words in the right spirit and know that my decision is the right one – for both of us. I know you will be hurt at first but trust me, in time you will know that it is best, for all of us.

All my love, Caroline.

Kamal was devastated. He had not been expecting this, not at all. For him, fidelity and trust were at the heart of a marriage, and he had not at all, as Caroline hinted, felt that it wasn't working. The difficulties they faced – well, they were challenges to what was basically a strong marriage, he'd thought, and would make that marriage stronger yet. Challenges, after all, were at the heart of strength; anything that was too easy just wasn't worth having. Challenges gave muscle to a relationship, because you had to work all the harder to keep it alive. A relationship was like a muscle, and needed to be worked in order to be strong, for otherwise it would grow slack and useless. Kamal had worked his own muscle; Caroline, it seemed, hadn't. For how else could she do this thing?

As for Caroline's suggestion, that he find another woman, another wife – it floored him. Did she think a wife was like a shirt that you just changed when you felt the old one didn't suit you any more? Was this really the woman he had married? Was her outlook so very shallow? Or was this just the American way? Perhaps he really was too Indian for her. That must be it. It was the only explanation he could think of. And now he had no choice in the matter, but must live with Caroline's choice. In his heart he would always be married to her. But one thing was certain: Asha's well-being must come first. And in this one thing Caroline was right: thank goodness for the Iyengars.

But what about *him*? What about the turmoil, the sense of abandonment, the disappointment, the pain, of his loss? He had built his life on the hope of a new beginning with Caroline and Asha, in America. What now? His job seemed futile; and unlike Caroline, he had no one in the world except Asha.

Chapter Fifteen

Kamal

Broken-hearted, Kamal took three months' unpaid leave and went to stay with Swami Naadiyaananda in his Himalayan retreat. There, in the serenity and stillness of nature, living in a hut beside a rushing brook, his desolation melted and he found the strength to carry on; a different man, more silent, less gregarious than before.

For the last two weeks of his leave he travelled down to Tamil Nadu to visit Asha. She was all he had left; he would now build his world around her. Take her up to Uttarkund with him, find a home for the two of them, a carer for her during his working hours.

But she did not know him, did not want to know him. She stood there with her hands behind her back, shrinking away from his open arms, crying when he hugged her, resisting Sundari's gentle coaxing: 'Go to Daddy, Asha, go to Daddy like a good girl!' But Asha wasn't a good girl; she obviously didn't care for him.

'You see how she is wary of you,' Sundari said, taking the child into her arms and handing her a bottle of water. 'That is normal at this age; to her you are a stranger. The first three years are most crucial in the life of a child. A child needs stability. Familiar faces. A steady home. You cannot just tear a child from one home and put it in another. That would be most selfish. And apart from that, what do you know about small children? What is your experience with them?'

Kamal rubbed his temples tiredly. He had asked himself this question several times in the last two days. So Sundari answered for him.

'Nothing whatsoever. And anyway, you are at work all day so you would be obliged to give her into strange hands. You would pay someone to keep your daughter! Why go to all that trouble when she has a good home here already?'

'Sundari, I've thought of all this myself. I've asked myself if it wouldn't be better to leave her here, with you—'

'Better? Of course it's better. How could there be any other alternative? I love this child as much as any of my own children. Janiki adores her. You must see that.'

'But just until my contract runs out. Then I'll move here and try to get to know her, and be a proper father.'

'Still the child will need a mother. You realise that, don't you?'

Kamal nodded. 'I know I can never be father *and* mother to her.'

'So you will have to marry again, once Caroline and you are divorced. Very quickly.'

Kamal shook his head vigorously. 'No. I won't marry again. Caroline was the love of my life. I can never replace her.'

Sundari smiled knowingly. Asha smiled too, gazing up at Sundari and hooking her forefinger into the woman's bottom lip. She threw her empty bottle to the ground, where it rolled into a corner. Startled by the noise, Asha twisted around in Sundari's arms, saw the bottle and struggled to be put down. Sundari placed her on the floor and she darted off to retrieve the bottle.

'Ah, that's what you say now. However, once the sadness has faded, you will start searching once more – you will try to fill the emptiness.'

Caroline had once laughingly told her the story of how Rani Abishta had tried to find a bride for Kamal. Sundari had not laughed; she had found it rude of Kamal to reject the potential brides, after Kamal's Daadi had gone to so much trouble; it was her *duty*, she had told Caroline sternly. It wasn't a joke. Marriage was an important step; it should not be left to chance meetings. Kamal had been wrong to reject them all out of hand. 'But then,' Sundari said, with a smile of reconciliation, 'he found you and now I have met you and we are such good friends. Everything happens for a reason; even when we make mistakes, the outcome is what had to happen. You and I, we had to meet. And Asha had to be born.'

Sundari had been curious about Rani Abishta, as Kamal himself never mentioned her, never spoke of his childhood. Caroline herself had known little, but what she knew, she had told Sundari.

'He doesn't tell me much either,' Caroline had said. 'It's like a taboo subject for him – I've no idea why. He just has issues with her, I guess. She's very possessive, very domineering, I think, and I guess he just wants to assert his independence. He likes to think of himself as an ordinary person, not a prince. He's so modest. It's what I love about him.'

'It is not good to be estranged from family,' said Sundari sternly. 'Family is everything. It is the foundation of society. One must respect one's elders.'

Caroline shrugged. 'I agree, and I'd love to meet her and go to that palace and meet my grandmother-in-law!' she said, and, laughing, added: 'It's not every American girl gets to go into a real old Indian palace and meet a real old Indian ex-queen! I wish we could have married there. My parents would have adored it – their daughter, a princess!'

'So Asha is really a princess,' Sundari said in awe. And from then on she called Asha Little Princess. Now, she said to Kamal:

'You must start looking for a new bride. A new mother for Asha. Why not ask that grandmother of yours, that woman who thinks she is a queen? I'm sure she would be eager to find a good match for you. Or if you like, I will help. My husband has some excellent connections, you know. It is always better to have a go-between in these marriage matters.'

Kamal shook his head, held out his open palm as if to repel the very suggestion. 'No, no, I won't remarry. I'm certain of that.'

'How will you look after Asha, then? It's not as if you have a mother who would take her.'

'Other men have raised children alone.'

'Maybe in those foreign countries. Not here, not in India. Perhaps when she is older, but as long as she is young she should stay with us. Here she has two mothers, Janiki and me. We'll be happy to have her. In fact, Janiki would be heartbroken if you took Asha away. She already feels all the love of a mother for her, even though she is so young. We would both be so very happy. And Asha too.'

Asha, meanwhile, had clenched the rubber teat expertly between four tiny teeth and, the bottle swinging gaily before her, returned to Sundari's feet where she pulled herself upright and made the appropriate noises. Sundari bent over and picked her up. Asha pulled the *palu* of Sundari's sari over her face and tried to engage her in a game of hide-and-seek. She ignored Kamal completely.

Kamal felt despair wash over him like a cold and final wave. All the peace he had gained in the mountains fled him; once again his soul reeled at the thought of Caroline's betrayal; he felt incapable of making a single decision. He wanted Caroline! He ached for her. Where she had been there was a huge black gaping hole inside him, and he stood precariously at its edge, tottering, tottering, bracing himself against a fall. It was the thought of Asha that held him back.

He looked at the child in Sundari's arms in despair; Asha was now twirling a curl of her thick mop of silky hair around a fat finger, gazing up adoringly at the woman she called Amma.

She will never call me Daddy, Kamal thought, *even though I can love her enough for that love to fill the emptiness in me. She is all I have in the world, now. But where do I begin? What can I do? To provide for her is my greatest duty. But she must be cared for, mothered. I cannot do both. To take her away would be heartless, egoistic; it would be serving my own purpose, using her. She is happiest here. Caroline and Sundari are right – her happiness must come first. I must love her enough to lose her. True love is letting go. I can love her as well from a distance as by her side, with a love not bound by time or space.*

Two days later Kamal left Gingee. Reconciled to Asha's place as a daughter of the Iyengar household, he went back to work a week earlier than planned, after making arrangements with the Iyengars for the continued payments for Asha's maintenance. He plunged into his work, and that became the focus of his life. A few years later he found an extremely lucrative position in Dubai, bringing water to the desert. He would save every penny for when Asha grew up and became an independent woman. He lived a quiet life. He was an introvert, a recluse, doing his job well but with no social life to speak of.

He was doing it all for Asha. He would save up for her, so that one day the world would be open to her. And so the years flipped past, turning like the pages of a book.

Chapter Sixteen

Janiki

When Asha was six Janiki went away to Madras to study, having persuaded her parents that she was not yet ready for marriage. Sundari, who had been keeping her eyes open for a suitable groom since Janiki was a child, had been sorely disappointed, as she was keen to send out feelers to the parents of several eligible bachelors; but Janiki was adamant. She wanted to continue her education.

'There are so many other fish in the sea,' she said, 'and I will meet so many nice boys when I am a student. I am sure these boys you found for me will find nice brides! Don't worry about it, Amma. I am only eighteen and if I meet someone I like I will let you know and you can have great fun chatting to his amma about marriage. Just a few years more.'

And so Sundari, trying to be modern and liberal, had agreed. Appa, being compliant to all of Sundari's decisions, and anyway in favour of women's education, also agreed; he was willing to maintain his daughter for a further four years, and so Janiki went off to Madras. Asha wept bitterly when Janiki left. Janiki embraced her and comforted her.

'See, little sweetheart, I am not far away. Just a few hours. I will come as often as I can and visit you. And when you are a bit bigger you can visit me too. I will show you Madras. I will show you the sea! I will take you to Higginbothams Bookstore and buy you lots of English books. You'd like that, wouldn't you?'

Asha was an avid reader and that last suggestion comforted her somewhat, because Gingee did not have an English language bookshop, and she loved the stories of English children eating strawberries and cream and drinking ginger beer, and looking for treasure or going off to boarding school. Still, though, she was not satisfied.

'Why you have to go, Janiki? Why you have to leave me?'

'I am going to learn all about computers,' Janiki said. 'I am going to study at the Indian Institute of Technology Madras. It's a great honour to study there and I am so happy I got a place. And if you work hard at school you too can study there or somewhere else in Madras or Bangalore, or even in Bombay or Delhi.'

'The Indian Institute of Technology!' repeated Asha slowly. 'It sounds scary!'

'It's not at all scary, baby.' Janiki laughed. 'It's one of the best technology universities in all of India. It's a wonderful opportunity, especially for a girl. Now come on, give me a nice long hug and a kiss and let me go – I have to finish packing. Run along now and remember Higginbothams! So many books. You will be in paradise!'

And Asha had to be content with that. Janiki would go off into the big wide world, and one day she, Asha, would follow.

* * *

Janiki kept her promise and came back as often as she could – after all, Madras wasn't that far away from Gingee. And one day she even kept her promise and took Asha to see the sea. Asha frolicked in delight in the surf and went back home having made the firm decision that one day she, too would go to Madras to study. Asha showed her the Indian Institute of Technology Madras and the little room where she lived in a hostel for female students, which she shared with a girl called Naadiya.

'It's just a small room but it's my home, and I love it!' Asha told her.

Naadiya became Janiki's best friend. And just as she had predicted, Janiki met some nice young men and it wasn't long before she met someone she could love. He was an aeronautical engineering student at the same university, and his name was Gridihar. Gridihar's and Janiki's parents wrote to each other and eventually the marriage was arranged, to take place a year after Janiki's graduation.

For Asha's eighth birthday, which fell on a Saturday, Janiki came with a huge cardboard box.

'Guess what's in here, baby!' she said with twinkling eyes. But Asha could not even begin to guess. 'Just let me open it,' she begged, dancing around the box in excitement. So Janiki gave her a pair of scissors and Asha cut through the tape holding the cardboard flaps together, and opened the box. There was a lot of paper padding, but underneath that there was…

'Oh! A television! My very own television!'

'No, sweetheart, it's not a TV set. It's something else that looks like a TV. It's a computer! Look, let me lift it out, carefully. See, there you go. And there are some more parts to it. This is the hard drive, and this is the keyboard, see? And his little thing is called a mouse. See?'

'A mouse? That's funny! But it's not a real mouse!'

'No, thank heavens! We don't want a real mouse in the house. But let me set it up for you. It's not a new computer, darling, but it's not very old either. You remember my friend Naadiya? You met her when you came to Madras. Well, her family is very rich, and her daddy bought her a brand new computer, the very latest model called Apple Mac, and so she gave me her old one. She just gave it to me, like that! Because she's my friend. But I thought I'd give it to you, because after all, I can use the university computers. Naadiya didn't mind.'

'But what's it *for*, Janiki? What can I do with it? Can I watch TV on it?'

'No, Asha, it's not for TV watching. It's for something very special and very amazing, called email. I will show you how to use email. When you have email you can write me every day and tell me what you are doing and I get your messages that very same day, imagine! Now that you can write so well you must write me every single day. Then you won't miss me so much.'

And Janiki set up the computer for Asha in a corner of the living room, and connected it to the telephone line, and set up an email address, which was ashabhandari@yahoo.in.

'So, now let me show you how to send an email. It's very simple. See, you just put in my address – mine is jiyeng@yahoo. in – and then you write something right here. Go on, write something!'

'What shall I write?'

'Anything at all. Just a simple message.'

So Asha wrote *I love you, Janiki!*

Janiki laughed, and kissed Asha on the cheek. 'Thank you, dear, and I love you too! Now let me connect it to the Internet, which is an amazing thing just like a spiderweb in space.'

Janiki pressed some buttons and the computer began to buzz wildly, and then Janiki said: 'So now it's connected – see that little sign? That means it's in the World Wide Web. Now all you have to do is press this button on the keyboard – *Enter* – and see! It's gone, and it will be in my account and I can read it. If I were in Madras right now I could read it immediately, and here I can read it too, I just have to go out of your account and into mine, and hey presto!'

'It's like magic!' said Asha. 'So no more letters?'

'You can still write me letters, of course you can. But it's such fun to send emails!'

'I'll send you an email every day. I promise!'

And she did, though after the initial wonder wore off she tended not to write every day any more, but maybe once a week, or once every two weeks, and Janiki would write back and tell her what she was up to. She enjoyed her studies, she said, and was doing very well, and she had ideas and plans.

* * *

After her last year of university Janiki applied for, and won, a paid internship at a big company called Grant Reed IT in Silicon Valley, in California, and in great excitement she packed her bags and flew off to America.

'But it doesn't matter, baby. I won't see you for a year but we have email, don't we? We're never very far away from each other. This is a great opportunity for me. America! Who knows: perhaps Gridihar and I will move to America later, when we are married, and you can come and live with us then – you will be near your mom!'

And so it happened that Janiki was in America when the terrible thing happened that ruined Asha's life. Janiki hurried home in shock.

Chapter Seventeen

Asha. Gingee, 2000

The next day, the day after I came home from Saasna Aunty's, Paruthy Uncle took me on a bus to Madras. I don't remember much of the bus drive because I was so terrified about leaving my brothers, and of course my home, which was now actually Paruthy Uncle's home. But still I missed it so badly I cried all the way to Madras, which is why I didn't look out the window much. And I didn't want to go to Madras at all, though of course everybody wants to go to Madras; the way people always used to talk about Madras, I used to think it must be a kind of paradise, and if somebody had been to Madras it was a very special thing. That's why when Janiki took me to Madras that one time I had been so excited. I had friends at my school who had been to Madras and everybody treated them like kings and queens afterwards, and they strutted around telling about all the marvellous things in Madras, things the rest of us had never seen and never would see. And when Janiki took me there I thought it was a trip to paradise. But now? I didn't want to go there with Paruthy Uncle because all I could remember was Janiki's scared face when she took me to Saasna Aunty's place, and I knew that I would not come back home. Don't ask me how I knew this. I just knew it. And this time there was no Janiki to save me because she had already gone back to America.

I told you already that I was to see bigger houses than our own house in Gingee. Well, the place he took me to was the first of those big houses. It seemed to me then to be a palace, though now I have seen yet bigger ones. So you see, everything in life is relative. Happiness is relative and so is suffering. People complain about this and that, and they think their sorrows insurmountable and unbearable, yet if I could have exchanged just one little moment of my own burdens for a whole lifetime of those little trivial things some people call problems, oh, I would have rushed to do so! But that was to come later. Reaching this big house, which was also very beautiful inside, was the beginning.

I still don't know how Paruthy Uncle heard about these people and that they wanted a maid, and I don't know why they took me and not a girl from Madras; perhaps they knew I would have nowhere to run, if running ever came into my head? Anyway, Paruthy Uncle handed me over to them and I heard some talk about wages, and how Appa was to have them sent to him every week. All that was not my business, it seemed.

Living with those people I began for the first time to wonder about the nature of cruelty. Why do some people choose to be cruel, when they could just as well be kind, and happier? I can tell by their faces that cruel people are not happy. Have you ever looked into the eyes of a cruel person? I have, and they are all muddy and twisted inside, and their mouths are ugly slits, and when they are being cruel I can see so clearly how terrible will be their fate. Cruelty is like a heavy ball thrown up into the sky: once it reaches a certain height, it changes course and falls with terrible speed and will hit the very thrower – perhaps not in this life, but in the next. Was I, then, a cruel person in my last life, that I should be the recipient in this? I do not know. Only God has his eye on such matters, and who are we to question him?

But I am straying away from my story. I will return. Paruthy Uncle left me with those cruel people. It was a man and his wife. Their names were Sri and Srimati Ramcharran. And I was to be their servant.

But instead I was their slave. You may think that now I was living in this grand house it can't have been so bad, but you know, even if you live in the grandest of places, if you are treated like a beast of burden the pain is unbearable. That lady beat me for the slightest misdemeanour, or what in her eyes was a misdemeanour.

For instance, if I polished a mirror, and she found one fingerprint on it, she would beat me with the leather belt she kept hanging on a hook especially for this purpose. The house was certainly magnificent and well furnished – they had real tables and chairs, Western-style, and it was the first time I had ever seen a home furnished this way. And carpets everywhere, and beds, and several electrical machines. I didn't know how to operate these machines at first; as a matter of fact they terrified me. That mixer for instance. The first time I used it Srimati had given me a bowl with some kind of mixture in it and she only told me to place the bowl under the beaters of the mixer and switch on the button but when I did so the bowl woke up and started dancing in wild circles, and when I grabbed it in panic the yellow slop inside started to dance and flew out all over the kitchen. She whipped me for that, of course. The vacuum cleaner wasn't much better; it was much stronger than me and pulled me in several directions at once, it seemed. But I won't complain about those machines – they can't help being what they are; they do not have a soul and they were not trying deliberately to hurt me. Srimati was.

In Appa's English school Teacher taught us that rhyme 'Sticks and stones can break my bones but words can never hurt me.'

Well, it's not true. I may not be very old but in my whole life it's always been the feeling of being worthless to other people that hurts most of all. Yes, I have had my share of blows, but it is the words, and even the unspoken things, the looks of people who think of me as nothing and less than nothing; that is the worst kind of hurt in the world. I was hurt this way by Appa's brother and then by that lady and that man. But they hurt my body too, each one in a different way.

Look at my legs, and excuse me for lifting my skirt this way, but I must show you: do you see these marks on my upper thighs, like the rungs of a ladder marching up and down? Those are from her. When I had done something wrong – it was always little things, so little I can't even remember – she would stick a fork into the flame on the gas stove, leave it there till the prongs were red hot. And then she would lift the hem of my skirt and press them against my thigh. And the more I screamed the more prongs I got. Now I mention forks, I remember the first of my crimes, which was not knowing how to use knives and forks, for of course at home we always ate with our fingers. But when I started to do so there – well. They gave me a bowl of rice with some thin *sambar* on it, that first evening, and I took it into a corner and sat on the floor to eat, a far corner where I wouldn't disturb anybody – that's when she scolded me the first time, calling me a stupid pig. She said I had to learn proper manners and must sit at the kitchen table like civilised people, so I did, but then I put my fingers in the rice and made a ball of it and that's when she laughed that horrible mocking laugh, which she always laughs before getting really angry, and she said to him, *Just look at this nasty little pig, how she eats!* So I had to use a knife and fork, which I had never done before. I didn't know how to use them and by mistake I put the rice on the knife and lifted it to my mouth and she lashed out and slapped it away, scattering the rice on the floor. *That's not how we eat in this house!* she screamed. So I had to put the rice on a fork, which seemed silly – surely the grains would fall through the prongs? Seeing the fork must have given her the idea of torturing me this way, because that was the first time it happened.

It is hard to believe that people can treat others this way but it is true; here are the marks to prove it.

But I am not complaining, I'm just telling you because you asked. I was locked up in that house. I was not allowed to leave. They had other servants, a cook, and a man who went shopping and came back from the market with bags of food that he gave to the cook, and a gardener. I was the only maid and I was not allowed to leave the house, not even for a moment.

So with that lady I had to do all sorts of things in a different way, and I learned a lot about Western ways, though of course they were Indian. But they said Western ways were better and I had to do things so and not so.

I haven't told you about the children yet. She had two and though I have always loved small children I must say that those two were hard to love, for they were as nasty as their parents. They took such great pleasure in hurting me whenever they could; but in sneaky sly ways, especially that little girl. She was even worse than the little boy, if you can believe that. She would walk behind me quite innocently, but in passing kick me from behind, or pull my hair, or pinch me. Little things, to be sure, but still they hurt.

The man hurt me in a different way but excuse me for not talking about that, not telling you the details. Even after all this time and much worse things I am filled with shame at the very thought. I'll just tell you that it started soon after I came to live with them and it always happened when she was not at home. Perhaps she had taken her children to her sister's or some such thing; she went visiting often, leaving me at home, locked up in the house, which had heavy padlocks at the doors and bars at all the windows. That man would come home now and then and do dirty things to me. That's when I learned about the demon that lives in every man. But as I said before, it is all relative. Now I can almost laugh at the things that man did. But back then they were no laughing matter. But I won't tell you. I don't want you to feel shame for me. The details don't matter.

The woman spoke only Tamil but the man spoke English too and he spoke to me in English, and he tried to force me to speak back to him in English. But I would not speak, and he could not force me. It was the one power I had, not to speak. Sometimes he got angry when I did not speak and threatened to beat me, but he never did.

One day they both came to me and made me take off all my clothes and then they put a red sari on me. I don't know why. They took off my worn old sari and threw it in a corner and then wrapped me in this shiny red sari. And then the woman put jewels on me. And put funny creams on my face and black around my eyes and on my eyelashes and styled my hair in a fancy style like I saw in the magazines she liked to read, just like a grown-up woman. And put jewels in my hair and around my neck, but I don't think they were real jewels, and bangles on my arms. And they made me sit on a chair. And then a man with a camera came into the room and took photos of me sitting on a chair. And they told me to move this way and that and I did.

But still I refused to speak English. Not to that man. It was the one way I could defy him.

Chapter Eighteen

Caroline. 2000

Email from Caroline to Kamal:

Dear Kamal, thanks so much for sending me your email address, it will make communicating a lot easier. Because no matter what we are still Asha's parents and nothing can change that. It's a bond that will remain for ever, and I'm so glad we were able to remain friends – well, pen-pals, I guess – even after the divorce. Though I would feel much better if you too married – I still feel so guilty about being the one to bail out on our marriage! I hope you have your eyes and heart open for someone new – it would make me feel so much better to know that you are in good hands with a wonderful wife!

Kamal, I'm writing today because I'm so very worried about Asha, and I wondered – have you heard from Sundari at all in the last two months? Because I haven't.

You know that I send Sundari some money to buy a birthday present for Asha every year. I kept my HSBC account in India open, and I just wire money into that account and then to Sundari's – Internet banking is a godsend, isn't it! Whatever did we do before? Anyway: after her birthday she always writes me a short thank-you message. I'm sure Sundari forces her to write it but at least it's her own writing. And Sundari sends a photo so I can see how much she's grown in the past year.

They are always studio photos so a bit stiff and serious – I understand that the Iyengars don't have a camera, but I long for a photo of her at play, natural, laughing! – I treasure them. I also send photos of myself regularly, so she won't forget what I look like.

But this year, nothing. I wrote Sundari to ask if everything is OK but no reply. It's been weeks now since her twelfth birthday. I called the house and a strange woman answered the phone, and she didn't speak English. I sent a telegram last week and again asking for confirmation that all is well and again – no response.

I am so worried that I have decided to close down my therapy practice for a month and go to India. It's going to be a huge hassle and my patients will be upset and you know how I hate India but I don't care – I have to do it.

I'm telling you this because my one hope is that for some reason it's just me – that for you contact is as usual, that you got a thank-you for your birthday money etc.

If not I expect you are as worried as I am. I'm wondering if it would be possible for you too to take leave and we meet in Madras and travel up to Gingee together? I do feel such a stranger in India and it would be great to have you at my side as co-parent and to help me out if there is truly some problem. Of course I don't know how easy it is for you to get leave at such short notice but my fingers are crossed. I haven't booked a flight yet but I'd like to travel ASAP – next week hopefully. How about you? If you can come we should coordinate our bookings.

No other news really. Wayne and I are fine. I'm doing my best to be the perfect wife to an up-and-coming junior partner at a prestigious law firm but I have to admit that sometimes I feel I'm just playing a role – that this perfectly groomed hostess in a perfect home leading a perfect life isn't really me, she's just a character in a movie! But Wayne is a good man at home – ruthless at work, I've heard! – and I suppose I'm happy.

As for children – he desperately wants a few but while I was building up my career it just wasn't feasible and in the last few years, well, it just hasn't happened. So Asha is still my one and only. My precious. I sometimes wonder what would have happened if I'd been a better mother, or if I had liked India more, or if we had moved back to America soon after she had been born, after I'd realised I was having problems? What kind of life would we have had, Kamal? And most of all, would Asha have been happier, growing up as an American kid? We'll never know the answers I guess and it's wrong to speculate, but I just hope she is still as happy as she was and nothing is wrong. I have to admit I have a bad feeling inside but I keep telling myself it's just my own fears speaking.

By the way, do you have Janiki's email? She's sure to have one as an IT student. Last year Sundari told me she was coming to California on an internship and hoping we'd meet – she didn't realise just how enormous America is, and that Cambridge is on the other side of it to California! But Janiki would know more, if only we could get in touch. I wish now I had asked Sundari for Janiki's email – I just didn't think of it at the time. And after that the letters stopped.

So this turned out to be a very long email – hope to hear from you soon.

Kamal's head hurt. He'd been planning on writing to Caroline himself – had she heard from Sundari? It wasn't like her not to respond to letters, not to send a thank-you letter from Asha after her birthday gift arrived. That is, the money for her birthday gift – not knowing what Asha liked, he always sent extra money and Sundari chose the gift; usually books, which Janiki would buy in Madras and either send or bring for Asha. Asha, he knew, devoured detective stories by Enid Blyton; ever since Janiki had given her the first she had craved more and more, and luckily Janiki had been able to supply them. Though that was likely to have changed – in her last letter, about six months ago, Sundari had said that Janiki was now in America, working as an intern at an IT company. Janiki, it occurred to him, would know what the problem was – but how to contact her?

Yes, Caroline was right – he was worried, very worried. The worry was compounded by guilt. He hadn't seen his daughter since she was eight years old, and she had been so non-communicative then that he had lost all confidence in himself and his role as father. All he could do was send money, transferred from his Bank of India account to Sundari's. He knew very well that money wasn't enough. He knew very well he was a bad father. *Bad father, bad father* went the mantra in his head, impossible to silence by positive thinking. Because it was true.

And because he knew it was true, and because the worry had escalated to a nebulous panic, he knew he had to do something, Something drastic. It was time to be a good father. Good fathers acted. They didn't just sit back, hoping and praying. Good fathers were on the front line for their children. His return mail to Caroline, unlike hers, was succinct:

I haven't heard from Sundari either. I've been very worried. I'm not taking leave – I quit my job. I've got so much overtime due I can actually leave without notice, which is good. Planning on flying to India next week, so great minds do think alike. My flight arrives in Madras next Tuesday, so book to arrive then. I'll meet you in Madras.

Chapter Nineteen

Asha

There was one thing, and one thing only, that gave me hope in that house. The man had a home office full of bookshelves and a big desk and chair and cabinets. And he had another desk, a smaller one, and on that desk stood a computer, and the man would get up early in the morning and sit at the computer and do things on it for hours and hours, before breakfast. I would watch that computer with such longing! I can't tell you how much I loved that machine. We are not supposed to love things, but I loved it and it was the only thing I loved in that whole house, because it gave me hope.

One day, I promised myself, I would sneak into the office and switch on that computer and write Janiki an email. But it was difficult, because the man went off to work after breakfast and the woman would be in the house all day watching me and telling me what to do, so that I did not get lazy. And so I did not get a chance to get to the computer. I thought maybe I could sneak out at night and use it, when they were asleep, but when I tried I found the room was locked. He had the key on his keychain with his other keys, door key and car key and the key to his business premises – I watched him carefully when he thought I wasn't watching, and that's how I knew this.

But there was a spare key, and I knew where it was kept: with all the other household keys on a board in their bedroom. I knew this because once a day Srimati would take the office key and open the office for me so I could clean in there. I had to dust the desk and wipe down the computer, and I can't tell you with how much love I wiped that computer, because one day I would use it to write Janiki. I promised myself this. But Srimati watched me like a hawk, and while I was cleaning the room there was no chance to do anything. And then one day in my third week my luck changed, because Srimati complained of a headache all morning. It's because she was having her period because I saw the bloody things in the bathroom rubbish bin.

After lunch she said, 'I am going to lie down for an hour. You have been here long enough – you know which rooms need cleaning. Do the office and the children's bedrooms. Don't be slack – I will control everything when I wake up.'

And so I actually had the office key in my hand!

'Yes, ma'am!' I said and went off to do my work while she lay down in her bed.

I cannot describe my joy the moment I sat down on that desk chair and switched on the computer and saw it lighting up, leaping into life, just for me! I was a bundle of nerves. And then something strange happened. Across the screen, a little box, and it said, 'Enter Password'. I did not understand. On my own computer I did not have this. I switched it on and I could go straight to my email. I knew what a password was because I had one for my email, though Janiki had explained to me that it was 'saved' so I didn't have to enter it every single time. 'Only on a different computer,' she said, and 'Never tell anyone your password. It's your secret.' I thought it was strange that this computer was asking for my password so soon, so I entered it, and it said, 'Wrong Password. Try Again.'

I didn't know what to do. I was afraid to try again. I was afraid of what might happen. Probably it was asking for the man's password, not mine. So I switched the computer off and in utmost dejection cleaned the room. My plan had failed.

* * *

I would not have believed things could get any worse but of course they did, as you know. But before they got worse they got better, much better, and for a while I believed I was saved – that God had answered my prayers. It's no consolation to say that that man and his wife got their just punishment. Because that is what happened next. And at first I thought my luck had changed because all of a sudden the sun came out and I got what I wanted. That is Lady Karma. She always wins in the end.

Chapter Twenty

Caroline. Madras, 2000

Caroline stepped off the plane at Madras International into what felt a soup of sweat. She had all but forgotten the heat, the humidity, the closeness of climate that clasped you the moment you set foot in India. And then the endless waiting in an endless queue while they checked your passport. And then another endless wait for her suitcase among a milling crowd of Indians and Westerners, all pushing themselves forward to be near the moving luggage band, grabbing suitcases and lugging them away, piling them onto rusty creaking trolleys. Remembering how long it usually took before the luggage started to be disgorged, she went to the State Bank of India counter to change her dollars into rupees. That done, she returned to luggage claim and was relieved to see movement: people, mostly Indians, wheeling or dragging or lifting their baggage out of the milling crowd.

Some people seemed to have mountains of luggage, piles of suitcases and boxes. Caroline had only one suitcase. She knew the value of travelling light, especially in India. And after all, what would she need? She wouldn't be doing any sightseeing or going on any pleasure outings where she would need nice new clothes. She was looking for Asha. She had brought practical things, light cotton trousers and T-shirts and loose blouses: comfortable clothes, suitable for the heat, but nothing armless or skimpy, a concession to Indian modesty.

There it was, her small green suitcase leaning against a huge one wrapped up in pale cotton and tied with several bands of rope, an address scrawled in large letters across one side of it. A burly man barged forward, grabbed the large suitcase and lugged it off the band and, by the time he had dragged it away, Caroline's suitcase was several metres away, chugging around the bend in the band and making its way back to the bowels of the airport. There was no way to push her way through the crowds to grab it; she would have to wait till it came around again.

At last, suitcase rolling smoothly along behind her, she was ready to exit the airport. Two uniformed agents checked her documents, wrote something on chalk on her case, and then she was walking along a corridor outside the airport with a metal barrier to her right and crowds and crowds of Indians behind it, many of them waving signs with names on them, names of passengers or hotels or companies, leaning forward over the railing, scanning the emerging passengers for the one they had come to meet.

Oh, it was all so familiar! India opening its arms and folding them around her, possessively, stealthily and yet blatantly, brazenly. Two-faced India, gentle and brutal, gloriously beautiful, hideously ugly. The India that kissed you on one cheek and slapped you on the other. The India that soothed your soul one day and ripped it to shreds the next. The India that nourished your senses and starved your ego, kicking it into the ground. The India she had embraced so eagerly the first time she had walked this very path, emerging from the sanctuary of the airport into the heart and the bowels of a culture she would never understand. That first time, so many years ago, her beloved Kamal had been at her side, and she had been in love not only with him but with his country, sight unseen. India. The India she had rejected so thoroughly, fled from in the throes of a debilitating illness, and then reluctantly returned to when Asha was five.

Now, the third time, this time almost senseless with worry. This time, to find her daughter and secure her well-being. This time, too, to meet Kamal again.

And there he was. Kamal. Waiting for her at the very end of the walkway. No sign in his hands; he didn't need one. She saw him and all the building emotions she had been holding back so bravely for the last few weeks and days and hours, the mounting fears, all the worries and the guilt and now, on seeing him, the release and the relief burst forth from her and she flung himself into his open arms. They closed around her and she was at home.

Kamal's taxi driver grabbed hold of the trolley and she and Kamal walked behind him. Suddenly, she felt shy. Kamal's welcome had been – well, not as warm as she had expected. He had embraced her, yes – he could hardly not embrace her, seeing as she had flung herself at him. He had been forced to open his arms to receive her, but let her go just as quickly. And now he walked beside her, not touching her – really, they could have held hands, thought Caroline. They were still friends, after all – what's wrong with a perfectly platonic holding of hands? But perhaps, as an Indian, Kamal was inhibited about touching her, a female, his ex-wife? *Well,* she thought, *I'll have to do something about that.*

Chapter Twenty-One

Asha. Madras, 2000

I never knew what really happened, I only know that one day in the early morning hours the dogs barked and the chain on the garden gate rattled and somebody shouted loud enough to wake the whole street. I jumped to my feet and ran to the kitchen and looked out of the barred window; I couldn't see much but certainly three or four people were at the gate, shouting to be admitted. I sat up on the floor, wiping my eyes. The man as usual had been working in his study as he did early every morning, before dawn, and I heard footsteps, running feet as he rushed from the room and the lady rushed from her bedroom and they stood there in the corridor whispering together. The kitchen was still dark but the door was open and I heard them whispering. It seemed they had decided not to open the gate; at least no one went out to do so, and the shouting only grew louder.

Somebody brought one of those cone-shaped things people shout into... Yes, a megaphone. And then I understood. *Police, open!* they were shouting. Still no one opened the gate, yet the next thing I knew one of them had cut through the chain – I didn't know it at the time, of course, but I saw the cut chain later – and the three policemen were marching down the drive. The dogs charged at them. They were on long chains, long enough to reach the path and jump up at any stranger coming along. The first police simply shot them. Both dogs! It was so scary I decided to hide. Well you know what big Tamil houses are like, built in a square around a central courtyard. So I ran out of the kitchen and into the courtyard and hid. I knew exactly where I would hide because that is where I hid from the man sometimes. There was a bench with a seat that clapped up and a compartment underneath with a few cushions, and room enough for a small girl like me. So I jumped in and closed the lid, which was the seat; but because the bench was made of wood slats I could still see some of what took place within the courtyard. And of course I could hear everything too.

They were at the door, banging away, and the lady must have finally let them in; I suppose she knew they'd break down the door if she didn't. They swarmed through the house. I could hear them in all the rooms and see them as they criss-crossed the courtyard searching the place. The man had disappeared, but he must not have had a good hiding place because soon they found him. There was a lot of shouting. The children were running everywhere, crying and screaming. I couldn't see very much but I could hear. Through the slats I glimpsed the man in handcuffs being marched across the courtyard to the main hallway, the woman being held at the wrists and dragged behind him, the children screaming and clinging to her clothes. She was wearing her old night sari and her hair was all loose, hanging down.

And then there was silence. They were gone.

Well, I had to see more so I climbed out of my bench and ran to a front window and watched, and my heart soared when I saw them dragging that man, handcuffed to the wrists of two policemen, up the garden path. The woman was not handcuffed. They held her at the elbow. She was shouting about the children, who were running behind her screaming *Amma! Amma*! A lady policeman was trying to grab the children's hands but they were screaming and kicking. So it was a lot of madness out there on the drive with everyone bawling and screaming, and then they were out of the gate and I couldn't see any more but heard several car doors slam and then cars driving off. But that wasn't quite all. Two policemen stayed behind and they were laying tape all around the house, you know that yellow tape you see on American TV shows after a crime. So the house was shrouded in this tape and I was inside and nobody knew. And everything was quiet and I was alone in the house.

And all I had to do was open the front door and break the tape and run. I was free to go. But I didn't go and do you know why? There are two reasons.

Because, reason one, I didn't know where to go – I couldn't go back to Gingee, of course, but where else? Madras was such a huge city. Teeming with people and buildings and vehicles, two-wheelers and four-wheelers and busses and lorries, and I was scared of that city and didn't know where to go at all.

And reason two, the office door was open and the office was empty and there stood the computer and it was on, shining brightly with bubbles flying all across the bright blue screen. And that computer was calling me. Because in the computer was Janiki.

I rushed to the computer and touched the keyboard and lo and behold, the bubbles went away and everything was open for me to use, Internet Explorer calling me. The man had been writing something but I knew enough about computers by now to click that away and look for the little *e* that would open up the World Wide Web. I knew how to do all of this because Janiki had taught me on my own computer and this was the same. And I opened up my Yahoo account and there were several messages from Janiki begging me to reply and asking how I was and if Paruthy Uncle was treating me well. And after reading those messages I replied to Janiki and this is what I wrote:

Dear Janiki

Paruthy Uncle is a very bad man. First he sold my computer and then he sent me away to Madras to work for some bad people and I have been working as a maid for a long time and they beat me. But the police came and took them away and now I am alone in the house so I am using the computer. Janiki I can go but I don't know where to go. You are so far away! Please tell me where to go and what to do love I am waiting at the computer. Asha

The house was so silent and so open. All the doors open! I was afraid – what if they came back! But then I thought, no, they are not coming back. The police took them. They will not come back. Because of course I could not go, I had to wait for a mail from Janiki.

I looked at the clock. It was almost five. I was used to thinking about Janiki and wondering what time it was where she was, so I knew it was still the previous day in California. Janiki came home every evening at about six and then she would be on her own computer and read her mails. And some evenings at eight, Janiki's time, 6:30 a.m. my time, we would both go into a chat room and chat away, and then I would go to school if it was a school day. And today when she came home she would read my message and reply and tell me where to go, and maybe even we could chat. So I could not go yet. I had to wait for Janiki's instructions. I had to wait an hour and a half in this cursed house.

But first I decided to eat some food as I was getting hungry. The kitchen was full of food. They had a fridge and it was full of nice things to eat. So I had some bread and butter and jam, but I toasted the bread first just like I had seen the lady do, and I made some eggs, and there were some *iddlies* from the day before, and some *sambar,* and I heated up the *iddlies* and the *sambar* and had that too, and some samosas that were a bit old, and then some cornflakes with milk, which was what the children always had for breakfast. And then I washed up.

For a moment I wondered where they were taking the children. The man and the lady were captured and I was sure they

would go to prison, but would the children go there too? Then
I said to myself, Asha, it is not your business. And anyway they
were horrible children. I know it's their parents' fault they were
horrible but karma does come to get horrible people, doesn't it?
Even children. So I didn't worry about them.

And then I had an apple and some grapes, and made myself
some tea. It was the biggest breakfast I had ever had in my life
but I had to eat so much because I had not eaten properly since
Amma and Appa died and all the hunger came at once so I had
to fill up.

All that cooking and eating took over an hour so when I had
finished I checked the computer again but there was still no reply.
So I went to the bathroom and had a shower. It was the first
shower I had ever had in this house, because every other day all I
got was a bucket of cold water and a rag and I had to wash myself
in the room at the back of the kitchen that the lady called a scul-
lery which was where the dhobi came to wash the clothes. But
now I had a proper shower and the water was warm and it was
lovely in the coolness of the early morning. And the soap came
out of a bottle and smelt so good! And I washed my hair with
some sweet-smelling shampoo. And then I dried myself with a big
fluffy towel from the cupboard, and rubbed some special white
cream all over my body and that felt good too.

My old clothes lay on the floor. I couldn't possibly put them
back on now that I was so clean, so I wrapped the towel around
me and went looking for some clean clothes. The lady's dressing
room was full of new clothes, saris she had not even worn yet, silk
and nylon and all kinds of sparkly ones and with fancy embroi-
dery. I did not want to wear anything fancy. So I chose a plain
cotton one, green with a simple border. The big problem was that
all the sari blouses were much too big for me. And in fact the
saris too were much too wide, as I was still growing and not yet a
woman. It was a dilemma!

But then I found a collection of *salwar kameezes* and I found at the very back some smaller ones from the time when the lady was thinner and one of them was just a bit too big for me but it was the smallest so I put it on. It was blue and yellow. The trousers were much too long but I was able to roll them up at the waist and at the ankles, then they fit better. I brushed my hair at the lady's mirror. It was still wet but I brushed out the knots and plaited it so it was all neat.

When I had finished another hour had passed and I returned to the computer but there was still no message from Janiki. I was beginning to get nervous and jumpy. I did not want to spend too much time in this house because goodness knows what was going to happen now. It seems this man was a criminal. What if he had criminal friends who would come and find me here, before Janiki replied? People like that were called accomplices, and they were dangerous. What would they do to me, for stealing the lady's clothes? I was quite nervous about that. Perhaps they would kill me! I prayed to Janiki: *Janiki Janiki please go home soon and switch on your computer, please please please!* And I prayed to Lord Ganesh who is the Remover of Obstacles and since he had removed the obstacle of my criminal captors, perhaps he would remove whatever obstacle was preventing Janiki from going home early.

But then I had an idea. You see I was a very hungry reader and I had read all the Enid Blyton books about children who caught criminals. The Famous Five and the Five Find-Outers and Dog and the Secret Seven and the Mystery books and the Adventure books. So I thought, here you are Asha in the home of a criminal, maybe you can find out some things about him and tell the police when you are free and safe?

You see, I needed to distract myself because I was growing jumpier by the minute. The waiting for Janiki to reply seemed to make every minute stretch into hours and I kept having all these thoughts about criminals and accomplices coming to the house and finding me. Every sound outside the house seemed magnified – a dog barking, a car horn. It was already light outside – morning had broken properly by now. I looked at the clock. Seven o'clock. The *dhobi* would come soon and then the lady with fruit and the milkman. For some reason I was scared of meeting them all because I would have to tell them what happened. I did not want to talk to anyone except whoever Janiki sent me to. She would tell me exactly what to do.

But in the meantime I had to do something, so I decided to calm my nerves by looking through his desk. That's what a detective would do. They search for clues. It would turn the waiting into constructive activity. I took a deep breath so as to gain courage because yes I was scared and I just wanted to go but I couldn't go just yet. So while I was waiting I searched the desk.

It was a big dark desk with a pile of files on it in one corner, some wire boxes with papers on it in another corner, the computer in the middle, and a writing pad on the top. A big diary. I decided to read the diary. You are not supposed to read people's diaries but this was a criminal so it was just detective work. The diary was full of scribbles I could not read. He seemed to be a very busy man. Some scribbles were in Tamil and some in English. They meant nothing to me.

I opened the drawers and looked through them. And I realised I was a bad detective because I didn't know what I was looking for, and the papers I found meant nothing to me. A lot of receipts and things like that. Pens and keys.

The bottom drawer was locked. But I tried the keys on the keychain and lo and behold, one of them fit. So I opened the bottom drawer and in it were two photo albums. I removed the first photo album and opened it and it was full of photos of girls. Girls my age and younger, all dressed up and wearing make-up and jewellery. In fact they were all dressed up to look like women.

I thought that was so strange! And my own photo was in there, dressed in the red sari they had made me wear that day!

Pages and pages of such girls, each one with a name beneath it and the name of a town: Madras, Bombay, Delhi, Calcutta, Bangalore, Mysore etc. I wondered what he was doing with so many girl photos. It just seemed strange to me. I shut the album and put it back and picked up the second album. I opened it – and shut it immediately. Because it was also full of photos of girls but this time the girls were naked! Stark naked! Why would he keep an album full of naked girls! I couldn't bear to even think of this but I felt so bad inside, so sick, that I closed the drawer with a bang and decided not to be a detective any more.

I went back to the computer and the screen jumped on and to my delight there was a new mail from Janiki. This is what she said:

Dearest Asha, you must go immediately to my friend Naadiya. She is a student at IITM. You remember her? You met her when I brought you to Madras that time – she is the one who gave you your computer! She is very nice and will help you. I will mail her now to explain and to expect you. This is her telephone number: 96758567. And this is her address, below, and this is her email address but you won't need it if you go right away. Do not stay in that house a moment longer. You must take a rickshaw. Do you have money? If not search the house. I'm sure you'll find s a few rupees in a drawer in the kitchen, just like Amma used to do it.

I saw that the time of sending was just five minutes ago so I quickly wrote another email:

Janiki I will go because I am so scared! I just found a photo album full of naked girls!!!!! Asha

Asha, that is horrible! It might be helpful to the police if we can find out more – but hurry! If you can use his computer perhaps

you can find out his password. Is his email account open?
See if there are any suspicious looking mails there and forward
them to me – you know how to forward a mail, don't you? Just
click 'forward' and add my address. It would be great if you can
find out his password!! For instance look under the keyboard,
or the front page of a diary, or a notebook.

I looked in all these places but there was nothing resembling a password. Then I remembered a little black book in the top drawer, which I had opened but it meant nothing to me because it was just lists of words, several crossed out. Janiki had told me I should change my password every few months so maybe that was his old passwords? I looked at the book again. Yes, all the words were crossed out but the bottom one, so maybe that was the latest password. It was cushion569.

His mail account was indeed still open. I didn't want to spend time reading his mails so I just forwarded a random one to Janiki, and then I wrote her a quick email with what I thought was the password, cushion569, and I was just getting up to go when I heard a crash and I ran out into the hallway and I saw that someone had put an axe through the door and a hand was grasping through the gash to open the door and then the door opened and four men barged in. All in uniform. Police.

But they weren't police at all.

Chapter Twenty-Two

Janiki. California, 2000

Email from Janiki to Naadiya:

Naadiya love, have you heard from Asha? I'm a bit worried as we were chatting on email and suddenly it stopped. She does have your address and phone number and should have arrived today – morning your time. I couldn't sleep a wink all night, kept checking my email and as I haven't heard from either of you I'm terribly worried. Did she come? It's 6 a.m. over here, so must be late afternoon in Madras. Please tell me she's safe and sound with you!

Janiki waited and waited for news: another mail from Asha, a mail from Naadiya confirming that Asha had safely contacted her. But: nothing. She paced her room in anxiety. Had something happened before Asha could escape? What a fool she had been, to waste Asha's time looking for a stupid password! The important thing would have been for Asha to escape. What if they had come back and found her? What if her captor had somehow bribed the police and returned home? Everything was possible in India.

The last thing she had received from Asha was the password of her captor's mail address. And an idea popped uninvited into her head. She wasn't sure if it was a brilliant one or a terrible one or just a very stupid one, but it couldn't hurt. So, to fill the time, Janiki logged in to the account. There were hundreds of mails waiting to be researched, but she hadn't time for that now, nervous as she was and waiting for Naadiya's reply. She didn't care about the past mails; those she could read later. She only cared about the present, an answer to the question: *where is Asha?* It was while checking the recipients of the mails that she had her brilliant, or stupid, idea. The mails, it seemed, were sent to several recipients. Eleven in all. Many of the replies in the email exchange were a simple *Great,* or *How many?* Or *Maybe K should go?* Or, *I agree with Kapoor.*

The arrest had not yet been mentioned. That meant the other recipients possibly did not know that one of their group had been arrested. Once they knew, perhaps they would remove his address from the cc list. So Janiki did something very naughty. She replied to the last mail with an innocuous question, from Ramcharran's mail address: *Are you sure about that?* And added her own work mail address, jiyeng@grit.com, to the list of cc recipients. They won't notice, she told herself. They won't even check. And if they don't check, they won't know who I am or who added me. But I will get all their future mails. It was a risk worth taking, and could do no harm. So she did that, and since time hung heavy on her hands, she began to scour Ramcharran's old emails.

Email from Naadiya to Janiki:

Well I stayed home all morning expecting to hear from Asha but not a word. Do you have an address? If I knew where the house was I could go and take a look.

Email from Janiki to Naadiya:

No, I don't have an address. I do have the mail account details of the asshole who was keeping her captive in Madras. I've been reading all his mails and you know what? He's not just an asshole he's a big time criminal. From what I gather from his mails he's involved in a ring of young girl prostitutes. All stolen from their homes. He's in charge of the Madras branch of the ring. I've no doubt that was the plan was for Asha too but seems he was arrested yesterday. I can't imagine what happened after that. Asha and I emailed a few times back and forth but then silence. I'm desperate with worry. There was no clue in the emails as to where the house is so no help there. I'm thinking you should just go to the police and ask. Open a FIR case. They might know something. It's terrible being so far away. If I don't hear back from Asha today I'm going to have to come myself. I'm halfway through my internship contract but Asha is more important. Let me know if you hear anything and thank you SO MUCH for your help! Xxx

Email from Naadiya to Janiki:

Anything for you, my love! I remember Asha from when you brought her that time, such a sweet little girl! I can't bear to think of what she must have gone through and I'm praying that she's still safe. Anything more I can do, just say the word. If you do come you know I'm here for you.

Email from Janiki to Naadiya:

No word at all from Asha. It's now 24 hours since I last heard from her and I just KNOW she's in danger. I'm trying to contact her biological parents but I have no idea how to find them. Paruthy Uncle will never tell me. I can't believe this is happening! Poor poor Asha. She's the last person this should happen to, such a shy, sensitive girl! Not that it should happen to anyone but you know what I mean. I'm going to move heaven and earth to find her. But I need to find her parents. They have to know.

Janiki bent over her desk, her head in her hands, trapping her skull with her fingers, which was what she did when she needed to concentrate. *Think, Janiki, think.* How can you contact Kamal

Uncle and Caroline Aunty? Caroline Aunty was in New York. She remembered Amma had sent a letter with her address and telephone number, but she, Janiki, hadn't bothered to write at the time – who wrote letters these days anyway? And she and Caroline had never been terribly close so she hadn't rung her, either. Had she written the address in her book? She checked. No. Damn it! Had she kept the letter from Amma? Probably not. Her apartment was so tiny, Janiki didn't keep paperwork she didn't need. She hadn't thought she'd ever need to visit Caroline Aunty in New York or even write to her, so she had not bothered to keep it. Damn, damn, damn.

As for Kamal Uncle – Janiki had been fourteen when she last saw him on one of his sporadic and short visits. He had been friendly enough and obviously pleased that Asha and she were so close, but after all he was an adult, living in his important engineer world, foreign-educated besides, and Janiki had been in awe of him. She thought he had moved to Dubai – hadn't Amma said he had a big-shot job there?

Think, Janiki, think.

All the information would be in the house.

Finally she shot off an email to her second eldest brother, Daav:

> *...you need to find a way to search all their papers. I know that Caroline Aunty and Kamal Uncle used to write Appa and Amma regularly. The letters must be there somewhere. I need their addresses, phone numbers, anything! Preferably email address and telephone numbers. See if you can find Appa's old phone book, the numbers must be in there.*

Email from Daav to Janiki:

> *They were both out yesterday and I searched the office. Not a single letter from Aunty and Uncle. And that old phone book*

of Appa's? You mean the one with the black cover that was falling apart? They threw it out long ago. They have a shiny new phone book. I once saw a letter with an American stamp on it in the waste paper basket, unopened. And later that day Aunty burnt all the paper in the yard. I think that's probably what she does with all their letters: burn them. Sorry I can't help. If I can do anything else let me know. When you find Asha give her a hug for me.

Damn it. Typical. There was only one option left for Janiki. She had to go there herself. Back to India. Somehow pick up Asha's trail. She had just one hope remaining, and that lay in the email trail left by Asha's captors. She'd have to read those mails, one by one; some, the ones in Hindi, she'd have to get translated. There must be a clue in there, somewhere. If there was a clue she'd have to follow it. She had to be present. But she had another idea too. Quite a brilliant one, in fact. Amma had been so impressed because Kamal Uncle was really a prince. And he came from a magical kingdom called Moti Khodayal. The name of the kingdom had stuck. There, he would have relatives. There, she would track him down.

Email from Janiki to Naadiya:

Just about to leave for the airport, see you soon; flying to Bombay. If I don't find Asha I'm going to look for her father, Kamal Uncle. He needs to know. I have no idea where he is so I am going to see his grandmother, who apparently lives in a palace in Gujarat. Amma used to tell us that Kamal Uncle is really a prince from this old kingdom called Moti Khodayal. The kingdom no longer exists but the palace does – it's where Kamal Uncle grew up. He's bound to have family there and they will know where to find him. He needs to know. The more people looking for her the better. We will probably need money too and hopefully he has some, because I am dirt poor. Used every bit of my savings and sold my beloved PC to buy my plane ticket home.

Email from Naadiya to Janiki:

By the time you get this you'll probably be here in India already but just wanted to say don't worry about money. I have enough to help as much as I can. You should have told me earlier – you didn't have to sell your PC! But no worries, I'll buy you a new one.

Chapter Twenty-Three

Janiki. Moti Khodayal, 2000

Rani Abishta pulled impatiently at the bell-rope. The big brass bell swung back and forth several times, clanging out an impatient summons.

Seconds later a servant, clad in a long gathered skirt and matching blouse of evidently the finest silk, hurried through the velvet curtain that separated the Surya Hall from the Corridor of Mirrors.

'Your Majesty?' she said, placing her palms together, lowering her eyes and bending forward from the waist.

Rani Abishta's finger traced a languid bow and pointed upward, to one of the two television screens fitted into the ornate woodwork arch at the entrance to her cubicle. On one of the screens flickered the coloured pictures of a new video film Lakshmi, her lady-in-waiting, had brought the day before. A ravishing apple-cheeked heroine mouthed the words to a soundless song: Rani Abishta had pressed the mute button on the remote control. The other screen was black and white, and it was to this screen that Rani Abishta now pointed. The girl's gaze followed the finger and she looked at the screen herself, rather nonplussed, for it showed nothing but the closed front gate and a lone figure standing outside it.

'There is a stranger at the gate,' said Rani Abishta. 'A female. Find out who it is. And summon Lakshmi.'

Rani Abishta's hand sank to the carved sandalwood table at her side, and her fingers closed around the remote control. She pressed a button, and with a thwack the television screen turned blank. The servant frowned; Rani Abishta hardly ever turned off the video. From dawn till dusk the moving pictures flickered; occasionally, during conversation or to issue a command, the film was mute for a short space of time, after which Rani Abishta would press the rewind button to replay what she had missed. Two or three times a week Lakshmi would sally forth into the town to Bisheswar Video Rentals and return with a bagful of new films, which Rani Abishta would consume without break over the next several days.

Lakshmi was now sixty-six. Her legendary beauty had matured like quality silk. Her skin, nourished with rich oils and kept resilient by daily massage, held the patina of old gold. Not a wrinkle blemished her complexion; to her demanding mistress she had managed to smile through all the years of service, and not just with her lips but with her heart, so that her outer beauty remained undistorted by the inner ugliness of a disgruntled soul: Lakshmi had kept her dignity. She had gained weight, of course, and the folds of her sari now enclosed a solid form, thickset but without flab, and still shapely, curving in and out as befitting a woman in the ripeness of years. She was sorting through Rani Abishta's saris when the personal walkie-talkie that connected her to her mistress rang. Rani was calling. Lakshi dropped everything and hurried down to the Corridor of Mirrors.

Breathless and flustered as she plunged through the bead curtain, she quickly collected her wits and approached Rani Abishta, gliding up with folded palms and a winning smile.

'You called, Majesty? Shall I change the film? Did you not like that one?'

'I want to know – who is that female visitor? What does she want?'

'She wants an audience with you, Majesty. I tried to find out what her quest is but she said it is private. She wants to speak to the head of the household but when questioned she knew nothing. She does not even know that it is just you here. She asked to see the family.'

'Bring her,' said Rani Abishta, and a few minutes later Janiki was ushered into her presence.

'Janiki Iyengar, Majesty. She says that is her name. She is from a place called Gingee in Tamil Nadu. Please take a seat, Miss Iyengar.' She gestured to a puffed cushion opposite the grande dame.

Rani Abishta rolled herself a leaf of paan, her eyes fixed on the young woman before her, not saying a word. Under that unnerving gaze, Janiki fidgeted, adjusting and readjusting her legs beneath her. She was unaccustomed to sitting on the floor after several months in the States.

Lakshmi moved a small low table into reachable distance and a serving girl placed a jug of a clouded liquid and a bowl of mixed sweets on it.

'Lime juice,' said Lakshmi, pouring her a glass. 'Very cold, very refreshing. And do have some nice sweets. Those laddus are delicious.'

Grateful for the distraction, Janiki reached for a laddu and bit into it; it was indeed melt-in-the-mouth delicious. She picked up the glass and sipped at the lime juice. Tried to avoid Rani Abishta's gaze, which was fixed unwaveringly on her.

'Well, Miss Iyengar, what brings you to me? You know I am a busy woman.'

Janiki cleared her throat, coughed, and began to speak.

'I am looking for the relatives of Kamal Bhandari.'

Rani Abishta did not so much as blink. She kept her eyes on Janiki and took another deep drag on the hookah. Water gurgled; loud in the silence in the room. Outside, in the garden, a songbird warbled and far away a dog barked, but Rani Abishta only sat there gazing at Janiki. Those who knew her well, however, might have perceived a slight raising of the eyebrows, a very slightly heightened pulsing of a blood vessel near her ear.

'So,' said Rani Abishta at last, 'and how are you acquainted with the person you mentioned?'

Janiki, so encouraged out of her discomfiture, stumbled over the words in her eagerness to explain.

'Well, you see, Mr Bhandari, he has a daughter, she's twelve now, and my mother, well, my late mother, I mean, she died a while ago, she was looking after the girl. Since birth. And I am like a big sister to her – I looked after her when she was small and we are very close. And now she is missing. Lost. I am trying to find her. And I need to inform Mr Bhandari that his daughter is lost as possibly he does not know. And I do not have his address so I was wondering, I was hoping, his family could contact him or help me find him. It's urgent you see. I think Asha, that's the girl's name, is in danger, and we have to find her quickly, and—'

'Stop! Stop, stop, stop. That is enough. Did you know, young lady, that this Mr Bhandari broke off contact with me many years ago? How many years ago was it, Lakshmi?'

'Fourteen, Your Majesty.'

'Fourteen years. Not a letter, not a card, not a phone call. That is the gratitude I have earned from my grandson. My only grandson.'

Janiki's heart clouded over.

'Oh! You mean…'

'I mean he has broken contact. Doesn't want anything to do with me. I, on the other hand…'

She cackled.

'I, on the other hand, know all about him. I have kept track. I have my methods. I have my spies. I know the date he married and the name of the white foreigner he married. I know the date the two of them flew out of America and returned to India. I know the name of the family they put up with in Gingee – you are correct, it is Iyengar. I know that he first worked at the Aliyar dam at Coimbatore and then at the Tehri in Uttarkund. I know the date of his daughter's birth and the date his wife flew back to America and the date she divorced him. I know the name of the company in Dubai who employ him to this date. And I have his phone number at that office. Why don't you just phone him and tell him what you told me. Lakshmi, bring the phone and dial Kamal's number for me. It seems it is time we used it.'

And a minute later Janiki was holding the phone to her ear and it was ringing, somewhere in Dubai.

Somebody answered, spoke in a foreign language, presumably Arabic. Janiki placed her hand over the phone and with wide-open eyes mouthed to Rani Abishta, 'I don't understand!'

'Just ask for Kamal,' said Rani Abishta.

Removing her hand, Janiki said: 'May I speak to Mr Bhandari, please.'

In perfect BBC English, the voice said, 'Mr Bhandari is unfortunately abroad. Can I help you?'

'Oh, um, no – when will he return?'

'I'm afraid I can't help you with that. Shall I take a message?'

'No – but can you please ask him to ring me when he returns – it's urgent.'

'Certainly – but may I know who's calling?'

'Oh – oh sorry, yes, of course – my name is Janiki Iyengar. I need to speak to him urgently. My number is – hold on a moment…'

Janiki fumbled in her handbag for her address book, flipped the pages until she found Naadiya's number. She spoke it into the receiver.

'Will he be back soon? Like, in a day or two? Or has he gone away for longer?'

'I'm sorry I can't tell you that, ma'am,' said the soothing, polite voice on the other end. 'However, we certainly don't expect him back this week.'

'Oh! Well, it's very urgent, a personal matter – I need to speak to him! Do you have an email address for him? Any way I can contact him urgently?'

'I'm sorry, ma'am, I cannot give out his private email address. I can gladly let you have his business address. You can write to him there.'

'Yes, but will he be checking his business mail in the near future? It's really terribly important. An emergency. A private emergency!'

'Ma'am, unfortunately I can't tell you when Mr Bhandari will be checking his business email. Can I help you further? If not perhaps you'd like to write it down. Do you have a pencil to hand?'

'Just a minute.'

Janiki made frantic writing-in-the-air signs. Instantly Lakshmi handed her a ballpoint pen and she scribbled down the address dictated by the voice.

'Is that all, ma'am?'

'Yes – no. Just, if he calls, tell him it's very urgent.'

'I will, ma'am. Thank you for calling. Goodbye, and have a nice day.'

The voice clicked off; the line began the buzz of emptiness. Janiki handed the phone back to Lakshmi and turned to Rani Abishta.

'He's gone – he's not there! Seems whoever you have stalking him isn't quite up to date.'

Rani Abishta chuckled and held out her hand for the phone. She punched it a few times and then spoke in a language Janiki did not recognise – possibly Gujarati.

'I'll have that information within the hour,' she said. 'In the meantime, shall we have a little chat?'

The words, though framed as a question, were spoken as a command, and Janiki, who did not feel in the least like chatting, found herself in the middle of an interrogation. At many points, she wanted to say 'None of your bloody business,' but couldn't. Meekly she answered Rani Abishta's questions; it was as if she were under a spell, and could no more resist than she could resist eating when hungry or drinking when thirsty.

'You are very beautiful – how old are you?'

'Twenty-six, ma'am.'

'Are you married?'

'No, ma'am.'

'You are very old to be still single.'

'That is because I want to finish my education before I marry. Actually, I am engaged to be married.'

'Where is your fiancé at this time? Did he allow you to come here on your own?'

'My fiancé is working in Delhi, ma'am, and he is a modern man – he does not control me.'

'Aha. So you are a modern couple? Arranged marriage or love marriage?'

'It's a love marriage, ma'am.'

'So not binding I assume. No contract between the parents? Your parents would not be angry if you broke it off?'

'My parents are dead, ma'am. Surely you know that, the way you keep tabs on Kamal Uncle's life.'

'Don't be rude, just answer my questions. I am asking you all this for a purpose. Why is your fiancé in Delhi and you are here?'

'Because, ma'am, I am trying to find my little sister. She's important to me.'

'Kamal's daughter?'

'Yes, ma'am.'

'But you are also trying to find Kamal, is that not true? That's why you came here?'

'That is true. Because Kamal Uncle needs to know—'

'Could it be that secretly you are planning to seduce my grandson? A beautiful young woman like you?'

Janiki jumped to her feet, hot with anger.

'What a preposterous thing to say! Of course not! How dare you insinuate—'

Rani Abishta threw back her head and laughed. She waved at Janiki, downward movements with both hands.

'Sit down, sit down, girl, and don't act so offended. You foreign-returned ladies are all the same – always taking offence. Listen to what I have to say.' As if again under a spell, some power she could not resist, Janiki fell back onto her cushion. Rani Abishta continued, in a soft, soothing voice: 'There's nothing wrong with a beautiful woman trying to seduce a man. Men are weak when it comes to that. Most men, that is. Unfortunately not my Kamal. I tried my best with so many beautiful women. Tried to arrange his marriage with the most exquisite maidens – any man would have fallen for those girls. Instead, he got angry. Finally he wrote me a rude letter and cut the connection to me. Then he married that blonde *ferengi,* that foreigner. I would never have allowed it but what say did I have? Luckily she left him, divorced him, married another. He is ripe for the plucking. I need a great-grandson – I need him to remarry. Unfortunately it seems he has taken a vow of celibacy and is hard to pluck. He lives like a monk, blind to the charms of women. So my private detective tells me. But I will crack him yet. Every man has his weak spot. It was written in his stars that he would be a monk. It never happened – but he is a half-monk. Living like a monk but holding down a job. I suppose it is all destiny but destiny can be broken. I do not believe in that mumbo-jumbo. Just as an engagement can be broken, destiny can be changed. It is all a matter of will. Your fiancé doesn't sound very attached to you. Why don't you try to marry Kamal, once you find him? All this will be his one day. He is a very good catch, if you can catch him.'

She spread her arms and waved them around, to demonstrate what 'all this' was.

Janiki, reeling from the effects of that outrageous, rambling discourse, jumped up indignantly.

'That's just – that's just – it's ridiculous! Just crazy! I'm engaged! I adore my fiancé! And Kamal Uncle – he's *old*! Why would I even – I never once thought – that's just crazy!'

'Not so crazy, not so old. Only twelve years older. That's perfectly reasonable. My husband was twenty years older than me and we were perfectly happy. The younger you are, the more likely you are to succeed. Older men like younger women. It's in their blood – it's biology. Young women to carry their seeds. They can't help it. A young, beautiful woman to wake up Kamal from this half-monk nonsense. He married once, he can marry again. It's my job to facilitate a marriage but he is not communicating with me. But if you can find him it might work, if you don't mention that I sent you. Of course you would have to be subtle about it, use your feminine wiles. All you have to do is act helpless and sweet, bat your eyelashes a bit at him. How could he resist? What do you say?'

Janiki bent down to pick up her handbag. With her absurd proposition Rani Abishta had broken the spell. The woman was out of her mind, Janiki realised; living under an obsession, an illusion, and trying to make her party to that fixation. She would have none of it. Ignoring the last preposterous suggestion, she said, 'Thank you for your information, for letting me use the phone. It was very helpful. Hopefully Kamal will contact me through my friend. Hopefully I can make some headway and find Asha. Goodbye, Mrs Bhandari.'

She turned away. Lakshmi leaned towards her ear. 'Your Majesty. You must address her as Your Majesty.'

'Well, I won't,' Janiki spat back, but under her breath. 'She's just a crazy lady.'

'Ha! I heard that!' Rani Abishta laughed. 'We will see. Goodbye, young lady, and good luck with Kamal. In *every* respect. Kamal Uncle? Ha! Very funny.'

Out in the Corridor of Mirrors, Janiki turned to Lakshmi.

'Do you think… I mean, it might sound rude after what I just said to her but I desperately need to check my email. Do you have…?'

'Oh, yes, yes of course. I will take you to the office – come with me.'

Chapter Twenty-Four

Janiki

'You must excuse my mistress,' Lakshmi said as they reached the end of the Corridor of Mirrors. She led the way into a large hall, and up a staircase at the back of that hall. 'Her bark is worse than her bite. At least, now it is. She doesn't mean to be rude. She can't help it. She has lost so much... so much.'

'Is she really royalty? I mean, there's no such thing in India any more, is there?'

'Well, we humour her. But she is related to royalty, or ex-royalty. You may have heard of Gayatri Devi, the Jaipur Princess? My mistress is second cousin thrice removed to her. She attended her wedding to Maharaja Jai – as a little girl of course, but if you ask her she can remember everything: Prince Jai raising her up, Princess Gayatri feeding her with *gulab jamun*. It was the best day in her life! And she grew up in such pomp. She remembers those days with great nostalgia. And so do I.'

'What was it like, back then?'

'What it was like? Oh, it was magnificent! Nobody alive today can imagine the glory of those days! I was just a young girl then, but I remember so well standing exactly here and looking down when Maharaj Sanjay came to visit! Sitting there on his royal cushions. We could see him so well from here! We couldn't hear a thing, of course, but why should we? We were only women; for us it was the excitement of seeing, of watching from our lofty hideaway while the men conducted their business. My mistress was not much older than me, she was a young bride, just married and so full of hope for the future. Who would ever imagine that her husband would die so young, leaving her a pregnant widow! And after that we did not realise – nobody ever told us – we could not guess—' She stopped suddenly, as if reluctant to leave that magic world and talk of things that should never have happened.

'What happened?' Janiki whispered, so as not to break the spell.

'Betrayal,' said Lakshmi, her voice raised and trembling with emotion. 'Betrayed by the British Raj, those statesmen we had always been loyal to. Sold out! We had no choice! All the royals had to merge; we were given no alternative! We had to destroy ourselves in order to survive – but how? All titles taken; no more land, no more subjects. What could the Regent Maharani do? She was only a woman, and when all over Royal India even the most powerful of kings, even the most ancient of royal families were destroying themselves and merging, what could she do? Nothing. It is all destiny. It is God's will and we have to accept it.'

'And what happened when—' Janiki began, then stopped, for a deafening peal had rung out like the phantom voice of a wrathful electronic god. Lakshmi placed a stalling hand on Janiki's arm.

'I have to go,' she said. 'She is summoning me.'

She raised a whistle, hanging on a gold chain around her neck, to her lips, and blew a shrill blast. Almost immediately, a young girl in a blue chiffon sari appeared out of nowhere.

'Sita, would you please take this young lady to the office and switch on the computer and connect it. She wants to use Internet.'

'Very well, madam.' Sita gestured to Janiki. 'Come with me, ma'am.'

Chapter Twenty-Five

Caroline. Madras, 2000

The taxi slid up to the entrance to the Connemara Hotel. A porter opened the door and Caroline stepped out from the air-conditioned back seat. The mid-morning heat wrapped itself in a tight cloak around her; stifling, suffocating heat. She could hardly breathe. *This,* she thought, *is why I dislike India so much. This, and the crowds and the noise and the stench. Why I had to leave.*

But here there were no crowds and no noise and no stench, and once she had entered the lobby, no heat either; only cool luxury.

'Just one night, so you can settle down,' said Kamal at her side. 'Tomorrow we leave early in the morning for Gingee. Do you think you can make it for 5 a.m.?'

'Of course!' said Caroline, affronted. 'I *know* how urgent it is! I could make it right away! I don't have to settle down!'

But she knew it was a lie. Already her mind was buzzing as if a thousand bees had been let loose within it – not only the lack of sleep and the disruption of her inner clock from the flight to the other side of the world, stopping here and there with never a proper rest. It was now almost midnight in Boston; she had lost not only a whole day, but her whole life. *Back in India. Back in the chaos.* The monster she had fled. But that was the price she had to pay. Greater than all the monsters in the world was her love for Asha, and that was what drove her, fired her, gave her strength.

They arrived at the reception desk.

'Mrs Caroline Richmond,' said Kamal to the receptionist. 'There's a room booked.'

The receptionist smiled and handed him a key card, which he passed to Caroline. 'Room 212,' he said. 'A porter will bring up your luggage. I imagine you need a long rest.'

Caroline took the key and smiled at him. 'Yeah, I could do with a long, long nap. But we could meet up later – which is your room? When shall we meet?'

'Oh, I'm not staying in this hotel,' said Kamal. 'I'm in mid-town. But if you like I'll come around this evening and we can talk strategy. So, here's your porter with your luggage. I'll be off.'

'Oh, but – we could have a drink first? Relax a bit before I go for my nap? There's so much to catch up on!'

'No – no. I think I'll let you rest, Caroline. See you later. I'll drop in at supper-time.'

And he was gone. Caroline stared after him, disappointed and, yes, hurt. Kamal had been nothing but polite and friendly, the perfect hospitable Indian host, picking her up at the airport and escorting her to this wonderful hotel, an icon of Madras, full of history and tradition, reeking of Empire and the Raj. Enquiring into her well-being, solicitous; gallant, even. There was nothing at all she could fault him on. Except for the distance of his demeanour. Coldness, even.

To dispel her nervousness, and her anxiety, she had chattered away in the taxi during the long drive to the hotel. Talking helped to release that pent-up emotion. Just talking, about anything, anything at all, looking at him as she talked. But apart from a few glances her way, and a nodding of his head as if he were listen-ing, Caroline felt isolated. She remembered that Kamal had never engaged in small talk – was she being pesky with her chatter? Or was he being rude? Or perhaps he felt it was inappropriate to talk about aeroplane meals and delays in Frankfurt and screaming babies on the plane when such a huge problem lay in both their hearts. But there was time enough to discuss Asha in the coming days. She couldn't, she just couldn't, plunge into the heartache right now. So what were they supposed to talk about? Or should they just sit in silence on the back seat? He hadn't even asked her how was her trip – Caroline had just told him, without invitation.

It seemed as if the cultural divide had opened so wide in the intervening years that there was nothing left between them, nothing at all. How could that be? How could two people who had once loved each other, who had shared all their thoughts and all their feelings, who had laughed and cried together and become parents together and fallen in love with a baby together, become strangers, just because – well, Caroline conceded, it was true that she had hurt Kamal deeply. Probably more than she could even guess – he had never really told her just how much the break-up had affected him. He had retreated into himself, and though they had corresponded – she had insisted that they remain friends, not only because of Asha – he had never again spoken of his feelings. Caroline had thought that it was because he didn't like writing; she had believed that seeing her again would bring back the old funny, relaxed, warm, caring Kamal she had once known. That they would fall into each other's arms and be the close friends they were meant to be. Instead she had this: a stranger.

Could it be that to this day he had not forgiven her for leaving him? Not even after so much time? But he had to see how incompatible they were. And surely it wasn't *her* fault that he had not moved on, found a new life, a new wife, founded a new family. It wasn't her fault at all.

There was so much she wanted to tell him. She had thought they were now friends: close friends even; or could be. That was the impression he had given her in his last email. Sure, it had been short, but she had yet divined a warmth beyond the words. She had so looked forward to meeting him again in person and establishing a new relationship, one that centred on Asha and their love and concern for her. All that chatter in the taxi – it was supposed to break the ice. But maybe he had found it boring? Found her shallow? Now, finally alone in her room, she blushed. She felt a fool. Something was wrong between her and Kamal, and she hadn't noticed it. Kamal had changed.

Well, she reasoned, of course he's changed! For a start, he's no longer my husband. And for another start, I haven't seen him for over ten years. We've both changed in that time. I've become more American – or, I've become American *again* after trying, and failing, to be Indian. And he is back to being the Indian he always was, without having to make concessions to me, an American wife. Maybe we were never well matched. Maybe mixed marriages – at least, marriages of such extremes – just don't work.

But we have Asha. We have a quest to find out what's going on and secure her well-being. *Christ, I hope she's all right. I hope there's a plausible explanation for Sundari's silence – that maybe she's sick or something and can't write, or maybe they moved house.* But then, surely she would have, should have, informed her and Kamal? The nagging worry that something really serious was wrong clawed at her, again. That lurking beast she could not shake off. Something bad, really bad. But she couldn't give in to negative thoughts. She was a therapist herself, for Christ's sake. She took several deep breaths to calm her mind, and closed her eyes. She would NOT give in to those lurking fears!

She took off all her clothes, had a quick shower and threw herself into the luxury of a soft sweet-scented bed. She slept for six hours straight.

* * *

As promised, Kamal returned at 6 p.m. They had supper by the poolside; curried fish for Caroline, and an omelette for Kamal. This time, Caroline decided, she'd be cautious with her speech; she would not chatter away but let him lead. And this time he did, at first. But again, he spoke of nothing personal. He seemed uninterested in her life, and her feelings; he spoke only of Asha, and their movements the next day.

'I want to leave early, by five,' he said, 'and I've ordered a taxi; I'll pick you up outside at five thirty. We should arrive at Gingee before Mr Iyengar and the kids go off to college and school; the more of the family we can meet, the better.'

'I just don't understand it,' said Caroline for the hundredth time. 'Sundari has always been so reliable.'

'I also tried writing to Janiki – nothing.'

'Well, Janiki is in America right now. Sundari sent me her address last year but I didn't make a note of it – I knew I wouldn't be visiting her in California and who writes letters these days? If she'd sent her email address it'd have been a different story – I'd have fired off a quick greeting and welcome note. Sundari seemed to think we'd be living around the corner from each other. How I wish now I'd kept that letter.'

'No phone number?'

'Well – she did send the number but you know, Janiki and I were never that close. She was just a kid! A mature kid, it's true, the way she looked after Asha, but really, it never occurred to me to call her. What would we talk about? All we ever spoke of was Asha. I suppose though I should have called to welcome her to America, asked about her work, maybe even invited her to visit me in Cambridge. Maybe she expected that? Oh Lord, Kamal, I feel like such an idiot now. Yes, I guess it was rude of me to ignore Janiki when she came but you know how it is – one is so wrapped up in the daily grind, my work, my clients, my career, that all those little niceties tend to be neglected. It's all my fault I didn't keep in touch.'

'But surely Janiki would have also had your address and number and would have contacted you if something was wrong?'

'Yes, Janiki would know and get in touch with us if there was a problem. So I'm hoping no news is good news. The only explanation I can think of is that they moved house and our letters and telegrams never arrived. But that doesn't explain why Sundari hasn't sent the birthday photo.'

'Perhaps they were moving just around that time and she forgot, or couldn't find the time.'

'Well, we'll find out tomorrow. No point in speculating.'

Talking about tomorrow's plans helped to relax Caroline and she couldn't help it – she could not maintain her reserved stance. Talking was the only thing that calmed her, that distracted her from the frantic beast worrying away inside her. Talking about anything. So Caroline told him all about her career as a creative arts therapist; what she did and how many clients she had, and how she particularly enjoyed working with children and hoped to perhaps work only with children in future. That led to even more personal admissions.

Perhaps it was insensitive to speak of such matters to your ex-husband, to the ex-husband you had dumped – to put it coarsely – but after all these years, Caroline thought, why shouldn't she speak to him as she would to a girlfriend?

'I'd have loved more children,' she said, 'and of course, so would Wayne. He does have a son from a previous relationship, but we wanted children together. But in our first years I was far too busy getting my degree and then building my career and then, well, it didn't happen as soon as we thought it would. We are still hoping, but at my age – well, the clock is ticking. I'm trying to stay relaxed about it. Using my own relaxation techniques. That's one good thing about being a therapist – I can try and heal myself. Try. It doesn't always work.'

She chuckled, a nervous chuckle because she still couldn't help feeling that something wasn't right between her and Kamal. That he wasn't responding the way a good conversationalist should. The way an American would, a girlfriend. At such intimate revelations – well, there was surely a right way to respond and Kamal wasn't doing it. Not that he was rude – looking bored, for instance. No, not at all. He listened attentively, smiled and nodded at all the right places. She couldn't fault him in any way. And yet…

It was as if an aura surrounded him. Yes, that was it. Something impenetrable, something she didn't understand. His quietness, for instance. Caroline was OK with being quiet; quiet was good. But Kamal's quietness was – weird was the word that came to mind. Not weird in a bad way, no, not that. Weird in an uncanny way. It was as if her words bounced off him, echoed off him, and created more words, and the more words she spoke the emptier they felt, and the more a sense of frustration grew within her. This wasn't the Kamal she knew.

She needed to know him better, so changed tack, using her own methods. Asked him questions about himself, to get him talking, to draw him out. She asked about his job, what it was like in Dubai, what he did in his free time, his friends and so on. (She did steer clear of asking him about girlfriends. That, she knew, was taboo.) And indeed, she did manage to get him talking in more than monosyllables. She nodded enthusiastically as he spoke of his life in Dubai.

And yet. When he left her for home ('home' being a less luxurious hotel in the heart of the city, she found) she was no nearer to knowing him than she'd been at the start. She shrugged and went to bed, and the worry about Asha, lacking further distraction, snatched her back into its claws. But jet-lag was stronger, and she fell asleep again the moment her head touched the pillow.

* * *

She was ready and waiting when the taxi arrived; though it was so early, her inner clock was still in turmoil and she'd been awake even before the alarm went off – worrying, of course, about Asha. She slid into the back seat. Kamal sat in front, in the passenger seat, and swivelled around to greet her. *He hasn't aged at all,* Caroline thought. *He's almost as young and handsome as when we first met! It's not fair!*

A thought had occurred to her in the shower this morning. *What if he's still in love with me? What if he never got over me, can't get over me, and that's why I can't seem to connect with him? What if he's wearing armour around his heart, so as not to feel pain?*

An interesting thought, one she would have loved to pursue had it not been for the situation with Asha. But hopefully they'd solve that today. As usual, she pushed away all her worry, all her dread, with positive thoughts. *Asha is fine. Everything is fine. Everything is going to be OK. There's an explanation; I just don't know it yet. Today I'm going to see my darling daughter. Hold her, kiss her, tell her how much I love her.*

Once they'd found Asha she'd tackle the Kamal problem. Find out if she was right. If Kamal's weirdness was simply due to him not being able to get over her, get over losing her. If that was the case, well, she'd get to the bottom of it. That was her job, after all; her profession as a therapist. Maybe the three of them, she, Kamal and Asha, could go off somewhere for a vacation. No, the *four* of them. Wayne would come too. Wayne was such a workaholic – it would do him good to take time off. Relax him. She would insist that he take a vacation, join them in some beautiful part of the world where Asha could get to know them all. She wondered about Asha's school vacations – when were they? Could she simply take time off to go off with her biological parents?

They should have done this long ago. *She* should have done this, with or without Kamal. Made more time for Asha, come to India more often. But yes, a vacation was necessary.

They arrived at Gingee. The taxi made its slow, horn-blaring way through the crowded streets: bicycles, two-wheelers, lorries, cars, pedestrians, cows, dogs, bullock carts all contributed to the congestion, all moving haphazardly in this direction or that so that it was a wonder that the taxi made any kind of progress at all.

'India!' thought Caroline, and she couldn't help it; a sense of fondness, or nostalgia, settled within her. This was the place she had come to with such love, such enthusiasm, so many years previously and, like it or not, it had won a little corner of her heart. And it was Asha's home.

Asha! If all went well, in a few minutes she'd be holding Asha in her arms. Caroline had made every effort to maintain a positive attitude throughout everything. Clung to the belief that all's well that ends well; that the lack of news about Asha, the lack of correspondence, had a very plausible reason and Asha would be right now – she looked at her watch –right now happily sitting in class.

Hmmm. That meant she wouldn't be at home. Very well, then; they'd drive straight to the school and take her out of class for the day. The school principal would understand. She smiled. The school principal – that was Viram, Sundari's husband, Asha's foster-father! Of course he'd understand. They'd take her out of school for a day. Do something nice with her – a day trip somewhere. And finally, she would connect with Asha. All the worry about her, the suppressed panic, had forged invisible bonds that cut through every last bit of estrangement. Asha was her daughter, her beloved; and she had finally found the deep and lasting love that had been so absent when she was a baby. All would be well.

And so, Caroline wallowing deep in positive, loving thoughts, the taxi drove up to the Iyengar abode.

Kamal and Caroline stepped out of the cool air-conditioned taxi interior and into the heat that already felt like an oven warming up, though it was not yet even mid-morning. Caroline removed the light cotton shawl she had been wearing to ward off the chill of the car's interior, but then remembered that the spaghetti straps of her summer dress might count as disrespectful, and so draped it once again across her shoulders.

They walked through the gate and approached the front door. Everything seemed the same as it had ever been. Nothing had changed. They had worried for nothing. Caroline talked the hammering of her heart into calmness. Somewhere within her fear still lurked, fear, the uncontrollable enemy that ever fought for supremacy. The enemy she forced into retreat again and again and again, tirelessly. She would beat it. She would.

Footsteps, behind the door. Sundari was coming to open it. They would fall into each other's arms, weeping, and all would be well.

But the door opened and a strange woman stood there. Not Sundari. The woman looked them both up and down without speaking.

Kamal spoke.

'Is Mrs Iyengar at home?'

The woman shrugged. 'No Eengleesh,' she said.

'Mrs Iyengar – Sundari!' said Kamal, louder now, as if No English translated to Deaf.

'Sundari, Sundari!' said Caroline, brightly, smiling, trying to peer into the dark interior of the house as if Sundari might be lurking there, right behind this strange woman with the green nylon sari and rattling bangles on both wrists.

'Sundari…' The woman lolled her head to one side, tongue hanging out, eyes rolled back. An unmistakable mime for a terrifying possibility.

'What do you mean?' said Caroline, her voice far too loud, trembling. She had never learned much Tamil during her stay, apart from a few essential words, now forgotten. She had wanted to, but then, why bother? Everyone of consequence spoke English.

Everyone except this woman here, who seemed to be – temporarily – of consequence.

'Do you speak Hindi?' said Kamal in that language. The woman shrugged again and made as if to shut the door in their faces.

'Where's Asha? Where's Viram?' Caroline tried to keep her voice low, calm, rational, but panic had already closed its cold fingers around her heart and was pressing down, and the words emerged shrill, alarmed. The woman's gesture was unambiguous. Sundari was dead.

Split-second emotions shot through Caroline, darts of conflicting reactions.

First, panic gave way to joy. Because Sundari dead was exactly the kind of plausible explanation she needed for Sundari's silence. Then joy gave way to shame – shame that she should feel joy, not grief, or shock, on learning of Sundari's death. What kind of a woman, what kind of a friend was she, not to first care about Sundari, to wonder how she died? Then the assertion: *I'm a mother, that's who I am. Asha's well-being comes first.* Then, again, worry. If Sundari was dead, where was Asha? Who looked after her? Who was this stranger at the door? This last emotion emerged as prominent. She had to know.

'Where is Asha? Who looks after her?'

'No Eengleesh,' said the woman again and this time succeeded in slamming the door in their faces.

Caroline and Kamal stared at each other in confusion. Then Kamal said the only sensible thing in the circumstances.

'Let's go to Viram's school. Ask Viram what happened. And Asha'll be there too, at school. It all makes sense. Sundari has died. There was no one to reply to our letters, send the birthday photographs. With all his grief and everything, Viram must have forgotten, or didn't even know about our correspondence. We'll go to him.'

'Oh – r-i-i-i-ght!' said Caroline, cheering up immediately. 'That must be what happened. But poor Sundari! I wonder how she died – how suddenly. She never mentioned any illness. Poor Viram. And the children, half-orphaned! I wonder if that woman is Viram's new wife?'

They were back in the car by now. Kamal shook his head. 'Probably just a housekeeper. She's uneducated. Viram wouldn't marry someone who doesn't speak English. Trust me on that.'

Quite relaxed now, Caroline chuckled. 'You're right about that. If ever there was an Indian Anglophile, it's Viram. He'd marry an English-speaking woman.'

Then she remembered again that Sundari was dead, and adjusted her voice and her conversation accordingly. *How callous and cold I am, to laugh like that! Sundari is dead! I must grieve! I must be more caring!*

'Poor, poor Sundari. Poor Viram, poor children. It must have been devastating for them. No wonder we didn't get any news about Asha. Viram probably didn't even think of contacting us in his grief.'

'Yes: that explains why Viram didn't inform us right away. It would have been the last thing on his mind. It probably didn't even occur to him that we'd need to reconsider leaving Asha with him. And with that strange woman.'

Caroline shuddered. 'I didn't like her at all. She's definitely not a fitting foster-mother for Asha. We'll have to take her away immediately. Oh, Kamal!'

They looked at each other and smiled, both knowing what the other was thinking. With Sundari's passing, Asha would be theirs. No reason any more to leave her in India. Caroline reached out, took Kamal's hand and squeezed it. She left it there, because his hand was cold. Kamal had never liked air-conditioning – he always froze. She smiled indulgently, took a deep breath and closed her eyes, her head slightly thrown back against the backseat upholstery. She knew it! That was the logical explanation that had been missing. Sundari had died, and no one had thought to inform them. Asha was so much a part of the Iyengar family that Viram, absent-minded as he was about domestic affairs, had possibly forgotten completely that she wasn't. She could easily imagine him forgetting that Asha had biological parents who'd need to be updated.

She began to dream. This meant that there was no reason on earth to leave Asha with the Iyengars any longer. Not even Janiki was still here. Sure, this was Asha's home and no doubt she loved it, loved Viram, but Caroline was in no doubt whatsoever that Asha, now twelve, would be mature enough to understand the chance now offered to her. She would go to America! Surely that was the dream of every single Indian child! She, Caroline, would pluck Asha out of India, whisk her off to Cambridge and show her a life she could until now have only dreamed about.

Of course there was the question of Kamal, who, as her father, would also perhaps want a piece of Asha. But Kamal was a single man, a single working man. In Dubai. He could not offer her a home. She could. They would find a way. Kamal could come and work in America, to be near Asha. They would work something out—

'Here we are!' said Kamal, jolting her out of her daydream. She had been visualising Asha in America, starting high school. Making new friends, pyjama parties, swimming pool parties. Christmas and Thanksgiving and Halloween – what a life waited for her! But first of all, a vacation. They all needed that.

The school was a little way outside of town, a large, functional two-storey building. The taxi drove into the grounds under an arched entrance gate and parked in front of a sign that read *Jawaharlal Nehru English Medium Academy. Secondary Co-Education.*

Once more, they stepped out into the broiling heat. Caroline was sure she'd catch a cold with all this back-and-forth between the extremes of hot and cold. They entered through the main door. The place was quiet, not a soul to be seen. Obviously everyone was at lessons; all the teachers, all the pupils. They found themselves in an open hallway with a broad staircase leading up, and a corridor leading off. A sign pointed towards the corridor that read, among other things, *Principal's Office.*

Kamal gestured and they both turned down that corridor.

There was the door. Kamal rapped on it.

'Come in!' said a voice from within, and Kamal opened the door and they both walked in, smiling in preparation for meeting Viram again.

The smile did not last long, because sitting behind the dark wood desk was a stranger.

'Oh!' said Caroline, stopping in her tracks. 'Excuse me, but...'

'Mr Iyengar? Where is Mr Iyengar?' Kamal asked.

The man at the desk half-rose, looked from one to the other. His initial smile of welcome morphed into a more appropriate expression of solemnity.

'I am sorry to inform you that Mr Iyengar has passed away.'

'Viram – dead too? But – when? How? He and his wife – both dead?'

The room was not air-conditioned and the overhead fan did little more than move the hot air around, but Caroline felt suddenly cold. All over.

The man was speaking again.

'I am the new principal – Pande is my name, Gopal Pande. My name is actually on the wall outside the door. Are you friends of Mr Iyengar? I am so sorry to break the news to you; it must be such a bad shock. He and his wife were involved in a tragic accident two months ago and neither survived.'

'Oh my God! *Both* of them! I can't – I just can't...'

So not just Sundari – Viram was also dead. Caroline grabbed Kamal's arm for support. She felt faint; she swayed, and Kamal placed his arm around her for support.

'Yes. It was extremely sad, especially for the children of course.'

'But – Asha? Asha Bhandari? Our daughter? We need to see her. She is a pupil at this school.'

'Oh! Asha! Delightful little girl – but she is no longer with us. She was taken out of school about four weeks ago.'

'Asha – not here? But – but… and the other children? The other Iyengar children? What happened? You see, we are her parents – we need to know!'

'I think, Mr and Mrs Bhandari, you should take a seat. We need to talk. Can I get you a glass of water? Coffee? Tea?'

Caroline did not bother to correct him regarding their names. She was still cold, numb inside. She needed something to shake off that numbness. 'Coffee, please,' she said as she took a seat across the desk from Mr Pande.

Kamal nodded. 'Yes. I'll have coffee too.'

Mr Pande picked up a phone on his desk, punched a button and spoke into the receiver: 'Two coffees please.' He then turned back to his visitors, shoved some papers to one side, linked his fingers on the desk in front of him, leaned forward a little and said in what was obviously meant to be a soothing voice, 'Mr and Mrs Bhandari—'

Kamal interrupted. 'I am Mr Bhandari. She is Mrs Richmond. We are divorced. We came to Gingee to find Asha because we have had no news of her for all this time – usually we hear from Mrs Iyengar punctually on her birthday and this year there was only silence. No one told us the Iyengars were dead, no one told us Asha was removed from school. Who took her out of school? Where is she now?'

Righteous anger was in his voice now, and Caroline laid a calming hand on his arm.

'We do need an explanation, Mr Pande. Who removed her from school?'

Mr Pande coughed.

'Well, it was another Mr Iyengar, I believe a younger brother to the deceased. It seems he took over the care of the children and moved into the house. He came soon after the deaths and said she would no longer attend the school. It happened very suddenly. He took all the Iyengar children out of school.'

'Where did she go to? Which school? This is ridiculous! We are paying fees for this school!'

'Well, perhaps he sent her to another school in Gingee, a free state school? I wouldn't know, I'm afraid.'

'But we pay fees! He has no right!'

Kamal looked at Caroline. 'That woman at the house must be his wife.'

He turned back to Mr Pande. 'You say he took all the children out? So all the boys have gone too?'

'Yes. The eldest boy of course has anyway graduated high school – he attends the engineering college, I believe. The eldest daughter Janiki is studying in Madras, I believe; probably married by now. There were four boys left and they were all taken out of school. I assume that Mr Iyengar the younger could not afford school fees. Although his two daughters are now pupils here – strange indeed!'

'And you don't know which school they are going to?'

He shook his head.

'I'm sorry; no, I don't. There are two or three state secondary schools in Gingee.' His face brightened. 'But we could ask one of his daughters. She would know!'

At that moment a woman knocked and entered the room bearing a tray with two mugs. She placed the tray on the desk and handed Caroline and Kamal a mug each. The coffee, of course, was already milked and sugared. Caroline had forgotten that that was the way coffee was served in South India. She liked hers black and no sugar; she sipped at the milky liquid, then put down the cup. It was horrible. Much too sweet.

'Miss Pillai, please ask Miss Sohini Iyengar to come here at once. She is in fourth standard.'

An awkward silence descended on the room once Miss Pillai had left. Kamal sipped at his coffee, and Caroline decided to give hers a second chance, simply so that she'd have something to do. Mr Pande spoke of the heat and the drought and obviously wished them gone.

Sohini Iyengar rapped on the door, Mr Pande called 'Enter!' and she did, standing before the desk with hanging head.

Mr Pande spoke to her in Tamil, and then explained,

'She and her sister don't know a word of English yet. It's hard for them – they struggle. I just asked her which school her brothers and Asha attend.'

He turned back to the girl, and gave her a sign to reply.

She said something in Tamil. He asked more questions; she gave more answers. Mr Pande said, 'She says she doesn't know what school the boys attend. And Asha has gone.'

'Asha, gone? Gone where?'

More conversation in Tamil. Mr Pande raised his voice and the girl seemed to visibly shrink. He then sent her away; she shuffled to the door and disappeared.

'I'm sorry – she doesn't know much. She just says that Asha was bad. She doesn't know any more than that. The family is living in their deceased uncle's house. She just says that Asha is a bad girl. She won't say more than that.'

Kamal stood up, his face like stone.

'Thank you for your time and your help, Mr Pande. I think we must have a little talk with this Mr Iyengar. Come, Caroline.'

Caroline nodded her thanks, turned and walked to the door, coffee hardly touched.

Chapter Twenty-Six

Caroline

Kamal and Caroline slid back into the taxi's back seat. The driver, who had been sleeping upright behind the steering wheel, sprang back into life, turning to ask for further directions.

'Same house,' said Kamal, meaning the Iyengar house, and the driver seemed to understand at once (they are so *intuitive*! thought Caroline) turned the ignition key, rolled up the windows, switched on the air-conditioning and drove off.

Caroline reached into her backpack for her water bottle. The water was now lukewarm. It didn't matter; her throat was parched. Her body was parched. She finished it off.

'Kamal, I'm scared,' she admitted. 'What's going on? Why did no one tell us that Sundari and Viram were both dead? Why did they take Asha out of school?'

'I don't know but we'll find her. Viram's brother has a lot to answer for. We're paying school fees for Asha and she should have been left in the school no matter what the circumstances.'

'Kamal – look! I'm shaking. I can't help it. I'm shaking.'

She held out both quivering hands. Though it wasn't yet cold in the car, Caroline's teeth began to chatter involuntarily.

'I'm so scared, Kamal. Where's our daughter? I want my daughter!'

She began to whimper. She placed her hands under her armpits and curled up on the back seat, into a ball. Kamal placed a comforting arm around her. She leaned against him, for courage.

'She'll be fine. Viram's brother will tell us which school she now attends. We'll drive right there, pick her up, and on to Madras. Don't worry. She'll be fine.'

But in spite of his confident words Kamal, too, could not shake off the sense of dread that gnawed at his bowels, and he too felt the cold that comes from inside and freezes the very blood. He tapped the driver on the shoulder.

'No AC!' he said, and the driver turned off the cold and they opened the windows so that the warmth from outside entered the car, but it did not help, for the ice of fear had them both in its grip.

'I have an idea,' said Kamal. 'Since she – the woman at the house – doesn't speak English let's get a translator.'

'Good idea,' said Caroline, uncurling. She stretched out her legs again, thought for a bit, and remembered a woman she had once befriended, a friend of Sundari's who spoke tolerable English as well as Tamil. 'Vasanthi! Let's go to Vasanthi. She can translate for us. And explain what happened. I hope she's home.'

She was. Vasanthi burst into smiles when she saw Caroline, but then her smile vanished, for Caroline was crying now, tears of fear and frustration – and relief; Vasanthi would surely know more?

'Cold hands!' said Vasanthi as she gripped Caroline's hands in her own. 'Come in, come in.'

She led them both into the cool dark interior of her home, and bid them take a seat, gesturing to a pile of cushions in the corner. Caroline and Kamal took a cushion each and sat down in front of a low wooden table. A small naked child was crawling on the tiled floor; Vasanthi scooped him up and in a fluid motion set him on her hip, one arm around the little bare back. The child smiled at the newcomers and waved. Caroline and Kamal waved back, but unsmilingly, and the child too stopped smiling and reached out with both hands to be put down, grunting in impatience. Vasanthi returned him to the floor, where he quickly scooted off through a doorway. Vasanthi lifted the hem of her sari and sat down cross-legged on the bare floor opposite her guests.

'Tell us what happened,' said Caroline, and Vasanthi did.

'Sundari and Viram, both accident on street, car hitting, both dead. Viram, he live three days then dead. Viram brother family move into house.'

'What happened to the children, Vasanthi? What happened to Asha?'

Vasanthi shrugged.

'Children, they go another school, secondary school in town. Asha too. My children tell me.'

'Vasanthi, we want you to come with us to help us speak to Viram's brother's wife. She speaks no English – could you translate for us?'

Vasanthi shook her head.

'Don't want speak with that woman,' she said. 'She bad woman.'

'Please, Vasanthi! Please come!'

'We need to speak to her husband too,' said Kamal. 'I think he's the one we really need to blame for this. He's stealing our money, literally! Fees for that school are high, by Indian standards. He's taken Asha out but is still pocketing the money we sent. That's theft.'

'Paruthy bad man. Bad teacher too. Beat children. He beat my son with ruler, bam! Bam!' Vasanthi held out her palm and clapped it with her other hand to demonstrate how her son had been hit.

'I'll be after him. But we have to go, Vasanthi, to find out where Asha is. And to talk to that man. We need you, Vasanthi; please! Come with us.'

'Please, Vasanthi! I'm so – so…' Caroline didn't know what she was any more: fearful, confused, desperate, guilty (because this was all her fault); yet full of hope because, after all, they were going to get Asha and nobody would ever take her away again, and she would make good for all the years of neglect. *Asha: you will be first in my life. From now on, you come first.*

Vasanthi, seeing the tears in Caroline's eyes, reached out and pulled her to her, placed her arms around her.

'I will come,' she said. 'I am mother too. I will come. I will help. One minute please.'

Vasanthi needed ten minutes to dress her child and make herself presentable, and then they all got into the taxi, Vasanthi in the front seat with her child on her lap, where he kneeled, both hands on the open windowsill. Vasanthi laughed. 'He never been in car before!' she said.

Caroline had an idea.

'Shall we just go and pick up Asha and not bother with going back to that house? Why should we even talk to those people? What can they tell us? I think we should just get a Tamil lawyer and sue the skin off them. How dare they not inform us of Sundari's death; how dare they take Asha out of school!' Her eyes blazed with indignation. Now that Vasanthi was with them she felt emboldened. 'All I want is Asha. Let's just go to the school and get her. We're her parents. We have the right.'

'Definitely, a lawyer,' said Kamal. 'But we don't know which new school Asha attends. And I need to speak to those people myself, look them in the eye. Besides, we need to pick up Asha's papers. Her passport, at least. They'll have that in the house.'

The same woman opened the door when they knocked, but this time she called into the interior, and a moment later a man, her husband no doubt, replaced her in the doorway. A man with a sickening false smile plastered across his face, his gaze wandering nervously between Caroline and Kamal.

'Tell him we want to know where Asha is and why he took her out of school,' Kamal said.

A long exchange in Tamil took place between Vasanthi and Paruthy; they seemed to be arguing.

'What's he saying?' Caroline interrupted. Vasanthi turned to her and switched language. 'He say Asha naughty girl, not good behave in school when Viram and Sundari dead, bad girl, school make her leave.'

'You mean, expelled her? That's a lie. Tell him we just came from the school and we know that he took her out and all Sundari's other children and replaced them with his own. Tell him we met his daughter. Go on, tell him.'

Caught out in the lie, Paruthy didn't even have the grace to look embarrassed. He launched into a new endless speech.

'What's he saying?' said Kamal to Vasanthi.

'He said Asha bad behave at home. Not helping in house. Rude to his wife and always fighting his daughters. Therefore he had to remove her.'

'Remove her from – where?'

'From the house, Caroline. He remove her from the house.'

'I don't understand. Remove her? She doesn't live here any more?'

'No. She gone, Caroline. He send her to Madras. Wife brother was looking for maid and he send her there to work.'

White-hot rage consumed Caroline. She sprang at the man, at his face, fingers spread, screaming, 'I'll kill him, I will! Lies, lies, lies! Where's my daughter!' The man gave her a hard shove so that she tumbled backwards to the dusty ground. The front door slammed in their faces. Kamal helped Caroline to her feet, dusted her off, put a calming arm around her. Caroline tried to fling herself at the closed door but Kamal held her back and turned to Vasanthi.

'Is it true? Is that what he said? That he sent Asha to Madras to be a maid?'

Vasanthi nodded. 'Is true. I not know. My son say Asha not in school for long time, but I not know she in Madras. That man just now telling.'

'But – but… how could he?'

Vasanthi shrugged and said nothing.

Kamal thought for a while. Then he said, 'Janiki. We need to talk to Janiki. Where is Janiki, Vasanthi? Do you have her address?'

'Janiki not here, gone America long time ago. Don't know where.'

'Damn!' said Caroline, now slightly calmed. 'Oh, how I wish I'd kept her address! Contacted her!'

'Then maybe one of the brothers? One of the elder boys? They would be at school, wouldn't they?'

'The eldest, Pandu, is at engineering college in Madras. Sundari told me that a while ago. The others must be living at home still. With those people. How could they DO this, Kamal? How can people be so horrible? So mean? Poor little Asha. How scared she must be. Kamal, I want her back! I want my daughter back? It hurts so much!'

The last words came out as a wail. They were still standing outside the Iyengar house; Caroline flung herself against the door and pummelled it with all her might, wailing and sobbing. Kamal quietly drew her away and to himself, in an embrace that seemed to quieten her; her sobbing relaxed into a silent heaving of the shoulders.

'They're obviously not going to help without pressure,' said Kamal, though Caroline wasn't listening. 'We need a lawyer. And police.'

Vasanthi nodded. 'Police!' she said. 'Bad people. Police help find Asha.'

'Right. Come on. The law it is. We'll find her, Caroline, I promise. We'll find her. Wherever she is. We'll squeeze the truth out of those people. They chose the wrong victim this time.'

An arm around a weeping Caroline, he led the way back to the car.

* * *

There followed hours and hours of the debilitating, exhausting, mind-draining bureaucracy that Caroline so hated about India. Sitting in a waiting room filled with rows of plastic chairs under a slow-rotating ceiling fan while a police officer deigned to listen to their story and file a report. Another waiting room, this time a lawyer's, this time on a wooden bench, where Caroline sat squeezed between several Indian ladies while Kamal stood in the hallway swatting away flies. Vasanthi had long gone home, not without inviting them to lunch; she had waited to file the police report in case no one spoke English. But neither of them was hungry, and the hot midday hours slipped by with hardly an inch of progress made.

The lawyer proved far more helpful than the police, and once he understood what had happened, and that these were clients who would pay well for his services, he sprang into action. He picked up a phone and spoke a Tamil diatribe into the receiver.

'Police!' he explained as he replaced the receiver and stood up, tucking his shirt into his waistband. This man did not waste time, Caroline was happy to see. He unceremoniously shooed his other waiting clients away, marched her and Kamal down to the taxi and gave sharp instructions to the driver.

Back to the Iyengar house; they arrived simultaneously with two policemen on a motorbike.

'He must have offered a bribe,' Kamal whispered to Caroline and she nodded. This lawyer meant business, and for the first time for hours hope swelled in her heart.

Reinforced with the law, it was easy to gain entry to the Iyengar house. Much talking, some shouting took place, of which she understood only the occasional word. *Asha,* and *Madras,* and *school,* and *rupees,* and *foreigners.* The man, belligerent at first, turned into a cowering mass of fear in the presence of the police and finally produced a flimsy-paged notebook, which he leafed through until he found what he was looking for. He passed the notebook to the lawyer, who smiled up at Caroline.

'It is Asha's address in Madras,' he said. 'She is working as a maid for this man's wife's cousin.'

'How dare he! How *dare* he!' Caroline quivered with rage and would have flung herself, nails bared, at the man again had not Kamal held her back.

'He will face the full force of the law,' said the lawyer. 'There will be a charge of abduction as well as perhaps other charges. He did not fully understand who he was dealing with. Seemed to think she was just some abandoned girl he could exploit to the maximum. He is in deep shit now, though!' He chuckled, and Caroline too nodded and grinned at the choice of words, so unusual coming from an Indian mouth.

'I hope he drowns in it. He deserves it.'

The lawyer finished copying the address into his own notebook, tore out a page and handed it to Caroline. 'This is the place where your daughter is staying,' he said. 'You can go there now and hold her in your arms. She is waiting for you.'

Caroline wanted to jump at him and hug him, but knew it was inappropriate in India, and maybe even in America. Instead, she hugged Kamal, who hugged her back, and as they walked towards the waiting taxi – leaving the police to deal with the man – she whirled him around and laughed out loud, her body loosened by the elixir of relief.

'Back to Madras!' she sang. 'Straight to that place to pick up Asha!'

Just as they reached the car, a boy in school uniform rushed up to them.

'Kamal Uncle! Caroline Aunty! I am so glad to see you!'

'Daav!' cried Caroline. Indeed, it was Sundari's second son, now a handsome teenager taller than herself. She had always liked Daav; he was bright and friendly and had loved her stories about life in America. 'I will go there when I am big!' he had always said, and Caroline had always promised, 'I will help you. When you apply for studies there you must ask me. I can help.' Now here he was again, twice the size and grinning in delight at seeing her.

But then the grin faded from his face.

'Oh! Aunty, Uncle, Janiki is trying to get hold of you. I have been looking for your address but could not find it. You must email her straight away. Asha is missing.'

'Yes; we know that. She's working as a maid in Madras. We have the address.' Caroline waved the notebook page at him.

'No; she's not there anymore. Janiki said she's gone. Disappeared. Janiki thinks she's been abducted. By child traffikers.'

Chapter Twenty-Seven

Asha. Madras, 2000

Two policemen came back into that house. They came to get the computer. But they heard me because when I jumped back into the bench the lid fell down and made a noise so they came looking and pulled me out. I stood there while they spoke about me. They were not expecting me. I did not know what they were talking about. One of them put handcuffs on me. I did not understand why. What had I done wrong? The other did not agree with the handcuffs. They were speaking much too quickly for me to understand. In the end they removed the handcuffs.

They began to question me. My name, where I came from, who my parents were. I answered as best I could. I said my Indian parents are dead but I have other parents who are far away. My mother is in America and my father is in Dubai. Who is looking after you, they said. Nobody, I replied. I have a sister in California. She told me to go to a certain address in Madras. It is there I want to go to. I opened my bag and took out the scrap of paper on which I had written Naadiya's address. It is here I need to go, I said. And then my sister will come and get me. The sister in America. She will come and get me. She will take care of me.

We will take you to this address, said the policeman who had put the handcuffs on. I was scared of him because of the handcuffs. I liked the other one better as he did not want me in handcuffs. He was kinder. At least that's what I thought at the time but it turned out not to be true.

They collected the computer and took it out to a police van waiting outside. And then they told me to get in the van too. And I did, and then we drove off. They drove the van to a police station and took the computer in and then the kind policeman said he was taking me to Naadiya. But he didn't. He took me to a woman and told her something I didn't understand and then I was on a train with that woman. That was the next day, after I had spent the night with her. I kept telling her that I want to go to Naadiya and she kept smiling and saying, *naligi, naligi*. Naligi means tomorrow. But tomorrow we did not go to Naadiya. Tomorrow that woman took me to the train station and made me get on the train with her. I wanted to run away at the station but she was holding onto my wrist all the time. Tightly. So I could not run. And I did not know where to run to as the policeman had taken away Naadiya's address. I was scared. There were so many crowds at the station. And then we got on a train and when I asked where we were going, she said,

'To Bombay.'

Chapter Twenty-Eight

Janiki. Mumbai, 2000

Bombay: City of gold, they called it; or city of dreams, dreams that came true or were extinguished in a puff of breath. You either love it or hate it, a friend who grew up there, and therefore loved it, had once told her. Janiki knew from the start that she would hate it. Somewhere among these twenty million people rushing here and there, living in luxury or scraping a living from the pavement, was Asha. A grain of sand on an endless beach. How would she ever find that single grain?

Bombay, or Mumbai, as it was now to be called, was the enemy. She arrived prepared to do battle, prepared to wrest from its bowels that precious jewel, her Asha. But first she had to find that jewel. Find the hiding place. She would encounter Bombay – as she would always call it – at its ugliest. Let herself be sucked into its belly, dig down to its deepest abyss of depravity. She couldn't do it. But she had to.

Janiki looked up, gazing into the distance, spiral notebook in hand.

She absent-mindedly clicked the tip of her ballpoint pen in and out, biting her lip, searching for a starting point. She had arrived by train from Baroda just the day before, having finally, with Daav's help, made email contact with Kamal and Caroline. She had found a reasonably priced hotel – though she soon discovered that 'reasonably priced' is relative, for even the cheapest Bombay hotels seemed as expensive as the best of Madras – and immediately made her way to the hellhole of Kamathipura.

She had first found mention of that place buried deep in the emails she had trawled through, seeking a clue as to where Asha might be. She had dismissed those mentions at first – they had nothing to do with Asha, obviously – she assumed Asha was safely in Madras. Though again, 'safely' was relative; relative to this monster city-within-a-city whose jaws she had voluntarily entered.

And then, in a more recent email, the chilling words: *This latest one is useless. We are sending her to Kamathipura.*

She had heard of Kamathipura before, of course. Which educated Indian hadn't? Fascinating and horrifying at once, its notoriety was known to anyone who read the newspapers. Bombay's red light district, the place where men went to satisfy their most base urges. Where women lived like sardines in dirty, rat-infested holes, or even in cages overlooking the street, beckoning in their customers in the red glow of streetlamps. Kamathipura was a city of the night, for women of the night.

Now, in daylight, as she walked through the narrow lanes she felt a mounting panic, for the atmosphere seeped deeper into her consciousness; like glue, clammy, sordid, vile, clinging to her like a hungry leech. And, she realised, these are only the *streets;* I am only an onlooker; I am safe. Behind the crumbling, grey facades that lined those streets – *there* the horror took place. Day after day after day. Night after night. A thousand wretched voices silently cried out to her: she heard them. And somewhere in the cacophony of woe she could make out a single anguished strain – Asha's voice of innocence, calling in vain.

When Naadiya first reported that Asha had not turned up, not rung her, had simply remained silent, Janiki had panicked. Something had gone terribly wrong and there was no way of finding out what. If only she herself were back in Madras – she would scour the city in search of her little sister; she could do absolutely nothing in Moti Khodayal. She would have to go there herself, now. Search for Asha herself; Naadiya meant well, but she had a job and neither the time nor the duty nor this air-sucking desperation to find Asha.

However, there was a problem. To get back to Madras from Gujarat by train would take days, but was cheap. To fly back would take only a day, but cost more than Janiki's entire budget for this trip. There was only one thing left to do; she'd do it reluctantly, for she hated to beg, but she'd do it for Asha. Rani Abishta was Asha's great-granddaughter. She would help.

And so Janiki had gone back to Rani Abishta and told her the new developments, confessed her fears to her. 'I need to find her,' she said. 'She'd there somewhere, in danger; maybe a prisoner again. I don't know. I came to you to find Kamal but only so that I can find Asha. Help me, please!'

Rani Abishta had listened with great interest. Then she had said, 'Kamal has left Dubai. After your telephone call to him I put my private investigator back on the job. It is my suspicion that he, too, is looking for Asha. She is the bait. Find her, and you will find Kamal. Find Kamal, and you will find her. You must go back to Madras. I will tell Lakshmi to give you the money. Stay the night and fly there tomorrow. Lakshmi will book the first flight out for you.'

And so Janiki had stayed the night, and to pass the time she had returned to the computer and continued in her research of Asha's captor's – his name, she discovered, was Balram Ramcharran – emails. She dug deep into them and what she found there disgusted her to the core. *How can men do this?* she screamed to herself. *How can they be so depraved, so utterly debauched? So cruel? These are young girls they are talking about – children!*

And so she had spent the night digging through the mails, starting as far back as possible. The first mails were in Hindi, which she couldn't read. Then suddenly they switched to English; as if another non-Hindi speaker had joined the group. Sometimes broken English, sometimes fluent. The occasional Hindi, once Tamil, thoroughly protested by the others. They finally settled on English.

The subject was girls. Girls were spoken of as if they were so many cattle being assessed and sent to market. Shunted here and there, priced at such-and-such. This customer would like this, and that customer would like that. Now and again there were attachments, attachments of young girls, children, really, dressed up like adult women in opulent red saris and fake jewels, their unsmiling faces giving the lie to the lavishness of their attire. Such despair, such abject hopelessness in those opaque eyes! Now and then the word Kamathipura fell, sometimes abbreviated to 'K', but that hellhole was a world away from Madras. Thank goodness.

There was no mention of Asha. And then, in a recent mail: *I have a new girl, very fair-skinned, twelve years old. Speaks English but not yet ready for trade. Virgin; I checked. Contact Sukhadan; this is one for Chaudhuri. I am keeping her as a maid in my home for the time being till we hear from Sukhadan. Problem is she does not speak at all. He likes them relaxed and chatty in English so we have to work on her. Will take photo soon and send; this one is superior, will bring a good price. She is wasted here in Madras.*

That could only be a reference to Asha: fair-skinned; a maid in Madras; speaks English. It had to be her.

Janiki's skin crawled. Nausea rose in her, and a creeping coldness that started in her stomach and spread everywhere, down to her fingertips. Everything churned within her. Why oh why had she asked Asha to search for information, for the password? That had cost Asha precious time. *Get out Asha; run. Leave that place and run. Go to Naadiya. Get out.* That's what she should have said. Because Asha's silence now could only mean trouble. Perhaps someone came back for her; obviously there was a gang involved and the very minute her captor was arrested Asha had been in jeopardy. She was 'superior, would bring a good price'; someone must have gone back for her and poor little Asha had been trapped while she was at the computer looking for a bloody password. And it was all her, Janiki's, fault.

Where are you, Asha, where are you? Call out to me and I will find you! I promise!

Janiki read on. There had been several new emails since that one, all cc'd to her due to Asha's intervention, but apart from all-round approval by the other recipients no further reference was made to 'the maid in Madras'. Other girls were discussed; sometimes photos were attached.

Then, soon after the reference to Asha, a flurry of anxious exchanges:

> URGENT. Balram arrested this morning in raid. Tried to defraud Mr K. and Mr K. of course is the wrong one to vex. Idiot. Got the police to go after him.

> Damn! What about the computer? The girl?

> Don't think they got those. My source didn't mention them.

> Need to get them. Too many big names on the computer. And the girl too valuable to lose.

> Don't worry, got someone dealing with it. Can get the computer def., most probably the girl ran away after the arrest.

> Damn!

After that last *Damn!* the language reverted to Hindi, to Janiki's frustration. *But,* she thought, *I can get Vasanthi to translate. Just when they began to talk about Asha! Damn, indeed!*

Half an hour later it was over. She knew the worst and it was worse than her worst nightmare.

'They are sending her to Bombay,' said Vasanthi. 'She is to be sold as a child prostitute to the highest bidder. At the moment it is a man called Chaudhuri.'

Asha was no longer in Madras. Asha was in Bombay. In Kamathipura.

And then, one last mail, in both Hindi and English:

Who is jiyeng@grit.com?

And then silence. Janiki, cold enough before with the tension of it all, now felt her blood turn to ice. She had been exposed, discovered, and even though the discovery was all in virtual space, in the ether, it was as if she stood there naked before a host of leering criminals. And after that, silence.

'They've found me out,' she said. 'No more emails.'

'I'm so sorry,' Vasanthi said.

'I'll have to go to Kamathipura,' Janiki said.

'Talk to Rani Abishta,' said Vasanthi. 'She can help. It's her great-granddaughter, after all. She has detectives working for her; that's how she tracks Kamal. And she has money. She will help. She will. She may appear hard but her heart is soft. She can help find Asha and Kamal and she will finance it. I know her; I am her closest confidante. You need her.'

'Yes,' said Janiki. 'I'll do that. This is too big for me alone. Thanks, Vasanthi.'

She was just about to shut down the computer when a new mail popped into her in-box.

She stared, numb, at the sender before moving a shaking finger to open it.

From: Kamal Bhandari.

She opened the mail.

Where are you, Janiki? Daav says you came back to India to look for Asha? Have you found her? Do you have any news at all? Caroline and I are both here in Madras and the place she was staying, it is empty, seems it was raided by police. But the police know nothing about her. Desperate to find her. Fingers crossed she's safely with you!

Janiki's fingers flitted over the keyboard.

Come to Bombay immediately. I'll meet you there.

And now she, Janiki, was here; Kamal and Caroline would be arriving early the next morning; and she was making her acquaintance with the snakepit that had stolen her little girl.

* * *

The moment Janiki left the security of the hotel and set foot on that pavement, the city simply gobbled her up. It roared on around her, oblivious to her presence and her shock and her call. It sucked her into the stinking, churning mess of its bowels. She wished, for a moment, that she had accepted Rani Abishta's offer to put her up in luxury in a nice area of town. But she had refused; she wanted to be as near as possible to Janiki, share her fate as much as possible. She had chosen a hotel in a run-down area near the red light district, and now here she was, in this hulking gargoyle of a neighborhood, monstrously ugly, wearing nothing but a black patina of filth. She had no idea where she was, just that it was Kamathipura, and it didn't matter. She was near Asha. She was sure of it. This mess harboured innocence and purity; she had to endure it, because Asha had to. She walked for a while, every step a new assault to her senses, an offensive medley of sound and smell and sight that made her cringe backwards, into herself, into the safety of an inner refuge. *Asha: where are you? Call to me! I will hear you, and I will come!*

Somewhere, in one of those dark buildings, cowered Asha. *Get a grip, Janiki,* she told herself sternly, and straightened her back. *Be strong. This is not the time for emotion. You are here as a detective; you cannot be judgemental. This is not the time for delicate aesthetics. Toughen up. Grow some inner muscles. You're going to need them.*

She took a deep breath and strode on, into the heart of the red light district. And so she wandered the streets, turning into this back alley and that, ignoring her own aversion, recording, memorising, making inner notes, standing back from the chaos and the scum as a neutral, dispassionate observer. The professional; interested but unaffected. Kamathipura left her no choice: it was hell on earth, but she must walk through.

There were relatively few people on the streets; this was a city of the night, and the days left it deserted. A woman in a doorway washing her long hair over a bucket; two young men hand-in-hand. Children playing in the streets, an old woman squatting on a cracked pavement sifting through rice for weevils and stones. People stared at her; nobody smiled. She was a tourist, and they didn't like tourists.

After four hours of this she returned to her hotel and threw herself onto the bed, exhausted, drained of optimism, her heart weeping. It was impossible. Even if Asha were here she'd never find her. Her only hope was a computer; perhaps there'd be information in an email: She still had Ramcharran's login details, and all the past mails. But the hotel had no computer room, and she wouldn't be able to read all of the old mails anyway, as so many were in Hindi.

But Kamal knew Hindi. She longed for Kamal. And Caroline. Someone to share this desperate and futile search.

Opposite the hotel she had noticed a small shop tucked between a sari shop and a restaurant, on which hung a sign, in English: *STD/ISD Fax International Calls Internet.*

She walked in, spoke to a young man at a desk, and a moment later her fingers were clattering over the tired, faded keys of an ancient computer.

She spent two, or maybe three, hours on the computer, searching, researching, digging. Everything that could count as a clue, she wrote down in her notebook. There wasn't much, but still.

Just as she was about to close down and go to have a bite to eat there was a ping as a new email slid into her in-box.

It was from Gridihar. She opened it, and read it. She gasped. And then she sighed and pressed the button to close down.

Indian men, she said to herself. *I might have known. So that's that. Back on the marriage market.*

Chapter Twenty-Nine

Janiki. Mumbai, 2000

The sign on the gate read *Tulasa Nilayam* in washed-out red paint. It was a crumbling grey building a stone's throw from the sea, protected from the street by a man-high hibiscus hedge. A forbidding metal gate, bars pointing skywards in rusty spikes, delayed her entry by some five minutes, as a thick chain bound the two wings together, tied in a complex knot that had to be unravelled. Janiki undid the chain, swung open the gate. She entered.

A few yards down the drive a man stepped into her path. He wore a khaki uniform.

'Good morning,' Janiki said. 'I have an appointment with Dr Ganotra.' She repeated the words in broken Hindi; she knew barely enough to get by.

Several mails had awaited her in the Internet shop she had found last night, but the news was bleak and Kamal could offer little support at present. He and Caroline could not arrive until tomorrow, he said, on the earliest available flight from Madras to Bombay.

After checking her mail Janiki, with nothing left to do, took to Yahoo to find out all she could about the industry that had trapped her little sister. Her search had led her to this Dr Ganotra, who, apparently, ran an NGO, the Bombay Safe Haven, whose main focus was underaged prostitutes in the city. She had emailed Dr Ganotra; he had replied almost immediately; he would help. She was to come to this place, this Tulasa House. 'I'll meet you there when I have time,' he'd said, and that was the last she heard from him. He was her only contact in this behemoth of a city; a starting point through a dark labyrinth that terrified her, the very thought of which caused her to shiver with anxiety for Asha, caused her mouth to dry up and her stomach to churn. This Dr Ganotra, though – he would help.

* * *

So here she was. The guard shrugged and replied in rapid Hindi.

'Dr Ganotra.' Janiki spoke louder this time, as if it was volume that prevented the guard from understanding.

He frowned, looked threateningly at her and said something that she interpreted as 'Stay here, don't move, or I'll shoot.' He turned away, walked up the steps leading to the front door and disappeared.

Taking his warning literally, Janiki waited, using the time to inspect her surroundings. The house before her was more in the category of villa – large and rambling, built of stone that must once have been red, since this was the colour that here and there showed through the layer of black mould growing up the walls, enclosing the building in a patina of neglect and dereliction. Wooden shutters hung from all the windows, awry where a hinge was broken, the paint peeling away, almost all with one or more louvres missing. Looking up, Janiki thought she saw a face at one of the windows, but she couldn't be sure – her uncertainty sent a shiver up her spine.

The guard's voice broke the chill. He was standing at the top of the entrance stairs, gesturing for her to come. She did so, stepping up the wide, crumbling stone staircase. The guard stood in an open doorway, speaking again in Hindi and emphasising his words with gestures.

Janiki followed him into the house, stepping over a threshold, a line across the floorboards where darkness sliced through the sunlight. A cloak of musty gloom closed in and wrapped itself around her, cool and dismal. After the glare she could see only blackness. Seconds later her eyes had adjusted and she made out a wooden staircase against the wall of a long, narrow lobby. Several doors left and right suggested that the lobby cut the house into two halves. The doors, the walls, the staircase, the floor: all was of unadorned wood, not a carpet under their feet, no pictures on the walls, and the paint so old it peeled. A faint background smell, pungent and familiar, told Janiki that somewhere termites were at work, building their underground tunnels, hollowing out the boards.

She gathered these impressions in a matter of seconds, following the guard along the corridor to the last door on the right. He knocked curtly, called something and gestured to her to follow, all simultaneously.

It was a large kitchen, sparsely equipped. A two-burner kerosene stove stood on a stone counter along one side, and an old green refrigerator, patched with rust in the shape of a giraffe, rattled noisily beside a dirty-paned window. There were lines of shelves with cooking utensils below and above the counter, and foodstuffs – large jars of rice and dhal, smaller jars containing spices, a battered pot of limes – stood on shelves on the other side of the refrigerator. A line of half-green tomatoes basked in the sun on a windowsill, above the dripping tap of a rusty sink. A branch of green bananas hung from the ceiling.

In the middle of the kitchen stood an oblong table with two straight-backed chairs. Against another wall was a planked bed-frame, like a long, low table. At the foot end of it sat a woman, cross-legged; she was stringing beans. She looked up as they entered, and smiled. At the other end of the bed-frame lay a heap of sundry articles: a pile of folded towels, a basket of onions, two coconuts, several chilli peppers and, somewhat incongruously, a battered alarm clock and a rusty saw.

The woman was stout, in her mid-forties. She wore a faded, threadbare red sari, and under it a blouse, which looked painfully tight, pinched in at the waist and at the sleeves, where tyres of fat bulged out. Her smile was warm, welcoming, echoed by her eyes. She spoke, but in rapid Hindi, too advanced for Janiki. She shrugged and spread her hands, showing that she didn't understand. 'Do you speak English?' she asked. The woman shrugged.

'I want to see Dr Ganotra,' Janiki said. This was ridiculous. What would she even say to this Dr Ganotra, should she be fortunate enough to meet him? She felt a fraud. 'Dr Ganotra?' she repeated, and made a questioning gesture.

The woman seemed to understand. She spoke several words, gesturing and pointing outside the house. She repeated some of the words, and Janiki guessed at their meaning.

'He's not at home?'

But the woman did not understand. Janiki could only surmise that this was the case: that Dr Ganotra was out; but when or if he would be back could not be ascertained. The woman laid down her knife beside the heap of unstrung beans and, with some effort and deep breathing, rose from the bed-frame, talking all the while.

She pulled out one of the chairs, dusted some crumbs from its seat with the end of her sari, rattled it, verified that one of the legs was loose and would fall off at the slightest weight, pointed to this flaw so as to excuse her lack of seating arrangements and cleared a place at the other end of the bed-frame: she placed the heap of towels on the floor, the onions, the peppers and the coconuts on the table, the alarm clock on a shelf next to a jar of rice and the saw on the fridge. With a damp rag she wiped once over the bare planks, dried the area with the end of her sari and gestured with her open palm for Janiki to take a seat. She did so.

All this time the guard had been standing in the doorway, picking his teeth with his fingernail and watching silently. Now, hospitality established, the woman spoke brusquely to him and shooed him away. The man shrugged, stepped backwards into the lobby and closed the door.

The woman was still on her feet. She stood in the middle of the room, looking inordinately pleased with herself. She patted herself on her voluminous breast and said, 'Subhadai, Subhadai.'

Janiki pointed to herself, saying 'Janiki'.

'Leetle English,' the woman explained. 'Koppee? Koppee?'

It took a while before Janiki could figure out that the woman was offering her coffee. She nodded and smiled. The woman busied herself with boiling water and coffee powder, which she served in a mug on a saucer with three biscuits on the side. Only then did she return to stringing beans. And all the while she talked. Janiki did not understand a word. She was impatient, eager to be out there searching for Asha; she felt that each passing minute, each second accepting the hospitality of this woman and waiting for a mysterious Dr Ganotra, was wasted. She should be wandering the streets again. Futile as such a search would be, it would at least make her feel useful, unlike sitting here with this woman.

After an hour Subhadai had finished stringing the beans and chopping the onions: she had placed a pot with rice and water on a kerosene flame; the coffee and biscuits had been digested; the morning was drawing to an end, lunchtime loomed near and Dr Ganotra had not put in an appearance. Janiki decided to find out if there was a chance of meeting the good doctor today; whether he would be returning and, if so, when. If not she might as well return to the streets.

Her carefully worded, slowly enunciated questions to this end produced only a further waterfall of words. Janiki interrupted, repeating, 'Dr Ganotra coming? Today?'

She gestured as she thought appropriate, moving her fingers like walking legs, patting the table to signify 'here'. She pointed to the alarm clock and spread her hands in an open question.

Subhadai understood.

Excitedly she began to explain; Dr Ganotra, it seemed, was indeed coming. She pointed at the clock, at the cooking food, at her own mouth, made eating gestures. Then she moved her fingers like walking legs, pointed again at the clock and held up one finger.

'Ek, ek, ek,' she said.

Janiki understood. He'd be coming at one o'clock, for lunch.

Subhadai suddenly stopped talking. She placed a finger over her lips and cocked her head, gazing into space. Janiki, too, listened; and she heard. The sound was unmistakable; somewhere in the bowels of the house somebody was crying. Subhadai nodded and stood up. At the doorway she hesitated, as if making a decision, and then she gestured for Janiki to follow her. She led her into the lobby and up the creaking stairs. The crying was louder in the lobby, and grew louder still as they walked upstairs: the forlorn lament of a soul that has lost all hope of solace and every right to happiness.

On the second floor there was another lobby, but less gloomy than the one below, for it was lit by a large window at the front of the house. Subhadai opened a door and entered a room. Janiki followed.

The cryer was a girl, sitting on a *charpai*, leaning against the wall with knees drawn up. She might have been twelve years old, or a year or two older, a year or two younger – it was hard to tell, for her body was tiny and emaciated, the body of a young child, whereas the expression on her face was ancient. Her hands lay limp, palm-up, on the mattress; her uptilted chin was half turned to one side, her lips trembled as she wept, her eyes were vacant. She sat immobile, weeping apparently not because of any specific cause but because that was all there was left to do in all the world and in all of life. She did not so much as turn her face to look at the newcomers.

Janiki felt like an intruder into some intensely intimate experience, unwelcome and inopportune. She backed towards the open doorway, but Subhadai took hold of her upper arm and stopped her.

Subhadai walked over to the *charpai*, taking Janiki with her. She was speaking to the girl, and though the words were unknown Janiki could tell they were words of comfort. The girl did not react.

Letting go of Janiki, Subhadai sat on the edge of the *charpai* in front of the girl and reached over to stroke her cheek. The girl showed no reaction, did not look at Subhadai, did not pause in her weeping. Janiki stood awkwardly watching, the urge to flee struggling with compassion and curiosity. She stayed.

She stood before an abyss of misery so deep and so dark it filled every space in that child's soul. Janiki needed no explanation – she knew it. The blankness in those dull black eyes, the downward pull of the trembling lips, the wretched whimpers: all spoke of unimaginable woe, too awful for words. This child was lost.

Is grief contagious? It had to be, for an involuntary trembling took hold of Janiki. She tried to control it, but couldn't; her hands shook, her heart raced, a feeling of dread spread through her entire being, the fear of being drowned and destroyed by whatever agony possessed this child. Again, the desire to flee – to turn her back and never return to this terrible place – took hold of her, to be immediately superseded by its opposite: compassion, love even, the need to enter into the jaws of despair, defy its power, deny its existence. The trembling stopped as suddenly as it had set in.

Subhadai stood up and gestured to Janiki, who sat down on the *charpai*, directly before the girl, and took the trembling hands in hers.

'Ratna,' Subhadai said, pointing to the girl.

Janiki looked into eyes that saw nothing. Not even a flicker of acknowledgement. It did not matter. She leaned forward. She placed both hands on the girl's shoulders, drew her away from the wall. The child did not resist. She was passive, a rag doll. There seemed not a remnant of human will left in her. Janiki spoke to her, knowing she would not be understood, but it did not matter.

'Hello, Ratna. I'm Janiki,' she said. 'I'm from Tamil Nadu and I came to look for my sister. My sister is the same age as you. I hope I can find her. Her name is Asha and I've lost her. I think she too is sad. I think she too is crying. I really want to find her.'

She instinctively lowered her voice, softened its edges; knowing the words themselves could not be understood, she filled them with feeling, with heart, knowing that somewhere, deep inside this child's being, was someone who would receive that feeling and understand it. She spoke on a level of communication beyond thought, beyond speech, and superior to both. The girl, whatever was still alive in the girl, would understand. She brushed a strand of hair away from the little face, held the little head in both her hands, centred it so that the eyes were directly in front of her. The child wept on. The eyes stared, not seeing. Empty. Dead.

She is dead, Janiki thought. Dead inside. But no. She can't be. If she were dead she would not cry. Somewhere, deep inside, there is a last spark of life. She has heard, she has understood.

Suddenly a door flew open; not the door into the corridor, which still stood open, but a second, leading to the next room. Looking up, Janiki saw another girl, this time older, perhaps fifteen or sixteen, standing on the threshold.

This new girl was entirely different. She looked first at Janiki, then at Ratna, then at Subhadai. A short exchange of words took place between her and Subhadai, and then her gaze returned to Janiki and she acknowledged her with a curt nod. She walked to the window and stood there for a while looking out before turning swiftly, walking to the connecting door and leaving the room without speaking another word, slamming the door behind her. *This* girl was angry.

The first girl had looked up at the newcomer, and then slumped back against the wall, and so she remained, her whimpering the only sign of life.

Janiki stood up, and gestured that she wanted to go. She could not bear it. She wanted to be alone, to grieve, to gather her thoughts. Subhadai indicated that she would stay, and Janiki left the room and found her own way back to the kitchen.

Meeting the girls upstairs had at the same time given her hope and plunged her into a morass of despair. It seemed fairly obvious, now, what this house was about. A sort of refuge, a safe house. The girls upstairs had been rescued from some kind of terrible fate; they were being provided for, supported; this Dr Ganotra would be involved and might, somehow, be able to help in the search for Asha.

But where was he? When would he come? She looked at the clock. The hands crept slowly forward towards one.

At twelve-thirty Subhadai finished cooking. She prepared a tray of food and took it to the girls upstairs; Janiki went with her, and helped serve it. Then she and Subhadai ate, a simple but tasty meal of rice and vegetables on a stainless steel platter in the dining room across the lobby from the kitchen, a room bare of any furniture save a long wooden table with six chairs around it.

After lunch and washing up, Subhadai spread a cloth on the kitchen floor, lay down on it and fell promptly asleep. Janiki could not dream of sleeping. The girl upstairs nagged at her; that face! Those eyes! She made her way back up to her and entered the room. The girl was now, blessedly, asleep, the tray with the empty plate on the floor beside her. Janiki bent down, stroked her cheek, took the tray and returned downstairs.

At two Dr Ganotra still had not yet arrived. Janiki waited, leafing through a pile of old magazines. Time crept forward.

Subhadai woke up, but seemed to have lost interest in her; she clattered around in the kitchen, went up and down the stairs a few times, swept the floor for the third time. The house was full of sounds; the crying had gradually subsided, but the background drone of a radio or a television set from upstairs was persistent. At one point Janiki heard the clatter of the chain on the front gate and ran to the open window, expecting to see Dr Ganotra, but it was only a very dark old man in a turban, depositing a sack of something round in the garden. The waiting continued.

Chapter Thirty

Janiki

When Janiki again heard the chain it was almost three, and she had given up any expectation of ever meeting Dr Ganotra; she decided she would return to the streets. Walking up and down the lanes of Kamathipura seemed a better use of her time than sitting here, waiting. She glanced out of the window more from boredom than for any other reason, for she had read *India Today* and the *Times of India* from beginning to end; and so she started on a local paper, *Mumbai Drums*.

A few minutes later the door opened and Dr Ganotra entered. A tall, lanky Indian with a neatly trimmed beard, he was a prepossessing figure, and Janiki felt authority radiating from him. She stood up and greeted him with a *pranaam*: hands together at her chest.

'*Namaste*,' she said. 'I'm—'

'Janiki,' said Dr Ganotra. 'Yes; I was expecting you. Sorry I'm late; my time is unfortunately not my own.'

Dr Ganotra walked across the room and filled a kettle with water; turning on the gas stove, he put the kettle on the flame.

'Coffee?' he asked. She nodded, and then began.

'As I told you, it's about my little sister—'

'Little Asha,' he finished. 'You've been able to follow her tracks to Mumbai? To Kamathipura?'

'Yes,' she said. 'But I'm not quite sure – I've been walking about in Kamathipura but it seems to me...'

'A needle in a haystack,' said Dr Ganotra, nodding. He placed
a coffee filter on a jug, filled it with ground coffee and waited for
the water to boil. Subhadai, in the meantime, had stood up and
was busy dishing out a plate of food from the pots on the stove.
She gestured to him to sit down, indicating that she would finish
the coffee, and placed the plate on the table. Dr Ganotra sat down
and began to eat; hungrily, hastily, as if eating were a waste of
time. Between mouthfuls he spoke to Janiki.

'You met the girls upstairs, I presume. Ratna? And Sita? Two
rescued girls out of so many still in hell. I can't make any promises. I don't know if we can find your Asha, if we can save her, but
I'm happy to try. I'm always happy to try. One at a time we find
these girls, and one at a time we save them, bring them here.'

Janiki nodded. Dr Ganotra's words tore at her. Asha, lost for
ever? In Kamathipura? It could not be!

'I have to find her!' she said. 'If you can help…'

'I can help, but as I said, I can't make any promises. This place
is a refuge; I do my best, but sometimes I feel it's like water on a
red-hot stone.'

'I know,' said Janiki, her voice trembling with the despair she
felt. 'I can't imagine – I can't even begin to imagine—'

'How a place like this can exist in a modern city like Mumbai,'
Dr Ganotra finished. 'How men can do this thing to young girls,
to children. Ratna is still a child. Men have ravished her. Not
men, but animals. I've been doing this work for many years now,
and I still don't understand how a human can lower himself to
such depravity. I still don't understand it.'

'What are our chances of finding Asha?'

He shrugged. 'You expect me to put a number on it? To find
one girl, and pluck her out of there? I'm sorry, but I need to
be blunt, and you need to be realistic. There are about thirty
thousand prostitutes in Kamathipura. Ten per cent are minors,
children; and you can be sure the minors are kept hidden away,

because they're illegal. Do you know what that world's like? It's an anthill – teeming with people. Brothels on top of brothels and behind brothels; stinking hellholes where you wouldn't even keep a dog. And you are looking for one single little soul in all of that. You can figure out your chances yourself.'

'But,' said Janiki, determined not to be discouraged by numbers, 'We do have clues. I've been investigating; I was able to find some information.'

She told Dr Ganotra about the emails, about the names and the hints she had been able to glean. She rummaged in her bag and brought forth the little notebook in which she had written down those names, as well as the photo of Asha she had printed out.

'Interesting,' said Dr Ganotra, 'but still – don't think you can just walk in there with a few names and find a single particular girl. I'm sorry to throw cold water on your hopes. I'll do all I can to help, but, well, one girl among thirty thousand, well, you can figure out the odds. However, miracles do happen. You're passionate about this one particular girl, and it's always good to have passion. Passion helps. And so does faith; it's true that faith can sometimes move mountains.'

Janiki nodded. 'That's what I believe too,' she said. 'And there are three of us. Kamal is coming tomorrow – that's her father – and Caroline.'

'That's good. So your father is going to be helping to look for her too? That's encouraging. You understand, in that trade especially it's better to have a man investigating. As a young woman, you—'

Janiki raised her hand in a *stop* signal. 'Kamal isn't my father,' she said.

Dr Ganotra looked up from his food – he had almost finished by now – and raised his eyebrows. 'But Asha is your sister, and his daughter – I thought…'

'Foster-sister. It's a long story. She's my cousin-sister. We aren't related. My mother was her foster-mother. Kamal is her biologi-

cal father. He's coming with Asha's mother, Caroline, his wife –
ex-wife. She's American.'

'Ah, that's why she's so fair!' said Dr Ganotra. 'A very beautiful little girl, wheatish complexion. Fair girls like her are luxury
products…'

Janiki winced. He continued. '…I know it hurts for her to be
described as a *product* but that's the reality. That's how she's seen
in the trade; superior quality, she'll be labelled, like a carpet, or a
patola-silk sari. And in a way it's a good thing, from your point of
view. Luxury products are treated with more care. They can't be
blemished; they can't be ruined. They are kept apart, for customers with high demands. Especially if they are virgins. Some men
believe that virgins can cure AIDS. So a fair-skinned virgin might
have a good chance of being kept with more care.'

'But just now you said she was just one out of thirty thousand,' said Janiki.

'Yes, and she is. And I'll help you as much as possible and
share my knowledge with you, but to me every one of those thirty
thousand girls is worth saving. For a few days I will devote myself
to this one. But that girl upstairs, and thousands like her still out
there,' – he gestured out of the window – 'they are all equally
precious. Every human life is precious. And I will save them, one
at a time. Perhaps it is your Asha's turn to be saved. I won't take
that hope from you.'

Janiki, lost for words, said nothing. Dr Ganotra shovelled the
last mouthful of food into his mouth, chewed, swallowed, and
then said, 'Asha is lucky. She is privileged. She has family looking
for her, family with the means to stop their normal lives, come
to Mumbai and spend time and money looking for her. Other
girls are not so lucky. They have no one looking for them. Their
parents back in the villages can't come here to look for them. Yet
each one is as precious as the next. I'll help you look for Asha,
but only because out of the thousands of such girls, she has the

luck to have you here working with me. See those girls upstairs?
We were able to save them but what can we do with them now?
Where can we put them? They can't tell us where they came from,
and even if they could, it's more than likely we can't send them
back. Their parents might love them but they can't go back after
Kamathipura, for their villages will reject them. There's no going
back after Kamathipura. They will carry that shame all their lives,
through no fault of their own. They have lost their homes, their
parents, their lives. That is my dilemma. And that is the only
reason I can devote some time to one particular girl: because there
is hope for her after Kamathipura. That is rare. Still: don't hope
too much. It will take nothing short of a miracle.'

Subhadai placed a bowl of some *payasan* before him, and his
eyes lit up. 'Did you try this *payasan?*' he asked Janiki. 'Subhadai
makes the best *payasan* in the world. It is the one enjoyment in my
life. I look forward to it all morning. Let me eat now in silence.'

He stopped talking as he dipped his spoon into the soft white
pudding, and closed his eyes to emphasise his delight.

'Delicious!' he said. 'Simply delicious!'

Janiki still said nothing; she found his ability to speak of the
abomination of Kamathipura in one sentence, and the next to fall
into ecstasy at the taste of *payasan*, extraordinary, callous, even.
She couldn't even think of enjoying a pudding, ever again, as long
as Asha remained lost. She supposed that years of work in the
field would force a person to grow a scab, a skin so thick the
horror remained underground, allowing one to continue with a
shallow enjoyment of life. For her, impossible. She felt as sensitive
as a mimosa, the sleepy plant whose leaves closed at the slightest
touch. Every inch of her soul ached and longed to withdraw; yet
couldn't, as long as Asha was out there, lost.

Dr Ganotra's glance fell on the *Mumbai Drums* local newspaper Janiki had laid on the table. The paper was folded back on the
page 'Mumbai News'. She could tell by the movement of his eyes

that he was scanning the news, interest in the delightful *payasan* already faded. Suddenly he stiffened, his gaze held in place. An instant later he sprang to his feet, his pudding half eaten.

'Come,' is all he said, gesturing to Janiki. 'Maybe it's a miracle. Read that.' He thrust the newspaper into Janiki's hands and strode to the door. Janiki sprang up and, infected by his sudden vigour, hurried behind him. Out of the house, out of the gate; a black car waited in the street outside, a driver asleep at the wheel. Dr Ganotra practically leapt into the passenger seat, gestured for Janiki to get into the back. The driver awoke with a start and, as the doctor fired off a few words to him, turned the ignition key. The car drove off. Dr Ganotra seemed to have forgotten her; he was talking to the driver, now, in a rapid flow of Hindi of which she understood not a word.

The newspaper was still in her hand. She scanned the headlines; what had so galvanised Dr Ganotra that he had left behind his beloved *payasan*? She immediately ruled out the strike by medical students, now in its fifth day, and an incident at the Viddalayak temple the previous day, in which a garland vendor had been injured by a pilgrim. The planned demolition of a tenement in Mumbai's outskirts seemed also unlikely. Impatiently her gaze wandered from headline to headline, rejecting, rejecting, rejecting. And then a word in a headline, two words, jumped out at her.

She read the article, and read it again – a small item, tucked away in the bottom left-hand corner.

Child Prostitute admitted to Hospital.

A twelve-year-old prostitute was admitted to B. K. Shivnandan Hospital with several knife wounds and a broken arm, sustained during a fight between a pimp and a drunken customer in Kamathipura. The girl was in a state of extreme shock yesterday and unable to speak to investigators. However, other prostitutes from the same

**brothel revealed that she had been kidnapped in Madras
and sold into prostitution about a month ago. She was
brought to the hospital bleeding from the knife wounds by
a health worker from an NGO, who later filed a charge of
trafficking with minors...**

The article made her sick and hopeful simultaneously. Could
this be Asha? The timescale was wrong. Asha had supposedly been
in Bombay not a month, but a week, ten days at the most. But
people's memories were faulty; a week could very well seem like a
month. But twelve years old, and from Madras...

The idea of Asha as a prostitute dismayed Janiki to the core.
She had lurked around that word for days now, not wanting to
even think it in connection with Asha. Refusing to admit the
likelihood, the probability, of Asha's fate. She had clung to the
idea that no, it hadn't happened yet. She had come in time. She
would save Asha. She would. She would. There was still time.
Asha had not yet been – she couldn't say that word either. Because
to say it was to imagine it, and she refused to imagine it. But her
body knew which thought she was rejecting. Her body revolted.
The nausea was too much to bear.

'Stop the car!' Janiki was able to yell, and luckily they were
driving not in the middle of a gush of traffic but at the edge, so
once Dr Ganotra had translated the driver obeyed and came to
a screeching halt next to the kerb amid a clamour of enraged car
horns and claxons, and Janiki flung open the door and leaned out
and vomited.

* * *

The door to the ward stood open. Inside, several simple cots,
about twenty in all, lined the two sides of a long room. The patients were all girls and women, plainly of low income judging
by the simplicity of the beds and the worn-out state of the sheets

and pillowcases. All of the cots were occupied; the patients lay in various conditions of apathy or illness, some alone, others surrounded by family members; some slept or sat up in bed talking with relatives, or ate from tiffin boxes, or simply wept. An elderly woman was being hand-fed by a younger woman; a middle-aged woman with oily, uncombed hair cried, alone, into a corner of her sheet. The ward, sparse and drab in its appointments, smelt of stale urine mixed with medicine and antiseptic. A slowly rotating overhead fan did little to dilute the smell with fresh air from the open window. Nausea rose up in Janiki.

There was only one girl of even nearly the right age.

But:

The girl was not Asha. Nothing like her; for a start, she was much younger, ten at the most. She lay there, curled on the sheet, her face half-hidden in the crook of her left arm, which was encased in fresh plaster of Paris. Her left shoulder was thick with the padding of an elaborate bandage, which could be seen at the short sleeve and the neck of her white hospital nightdress. A threadbare sheet covered the embryo-like curl of her body.

Her terrified eyes clung to Janiki's face. When Dr Ganotra leaned over her she shrank away, petrified, and he stepped back, nodding. 'She's afraid of men,' he said. 'And no wonder. I'll bring a female colleague.' He turned and left the room.

It was such a sad place, and all Janiki could do was try to relieve the sadness a little way by sitting on the girl's bed holding her hand. She spoke, as she had done to Ratna before, just for the sake of speaking, this time in Tamil; the girl, after all, was from Madras, according to *Mumbai Drums*.

Not knowing what else to say, she spoke of herself; told some of the stories of her own childhood, stories she had told Asha when Asha was this age, stories she had read to Asha that had delighted her. She couldn't remember them perfectly, but it didn't matter; she told them as they came; about child detectives and girls in English boarding schools, and she told them in her best storytime, bedtime voice. Her voice seemed to have a calming effect, for the little girl began to listen, the little hand she held gripped hers tightly, and the eyes still fixed on hers became moist and the lips moved, just a little, and the little body began to relax, and to uncurl, and a small sound came out, which Janiki did not understand: a single word.

Janiki smiled at her, brushed the hair off her face, pulled her slightly up so that she leaned against Janiki's side with Janiki's arm around her. Janiki adjusted herself into a more comfortable position and continued to talk.

Before long, a young woman in her mid-twenties approached wearing, rather than the usual sari or *shalwar kameez*, jeans and a T-shirt. She was light-skinned, but not European – the coffee colour of her complexion was natural, not a tan, and that thick black hair, swept back and up into a ponytail, and the bushy eyebrows over coal-black eyes were definitely Indian.

She smiled first at Janiki and then at the girl.

'*Namaste,*' she said, 'You must be Janiki – Dr Ganotra told me about you. And I see you've already made friends with our little patient here. Hello, *beti.* How are you? I see you have a friend!' The last caused the girl to curl up and hide her face in Janiki's thigh, and grip her hand yet tighter.

Janiki translated into Tamil.

'You speak Tamil!' said the woman, and her eyes lit up. 'Wonderful – she's terrified, and doesn't understand a word we say. Our Tamil nurses are far too busy to spare a moment to translate. By the way, my name's Gita. I'm a social worker in the hospital, but also a volunteer who works with Dr Ganotra's patients, in the hospital and out there in the wilds, as we call it. I need to ask her a few questions; can you translate? I take it that this is not the girl you are looking for? What's *her* name again?'

'Asha,' said Janiki, 'and no, this isn't her. Asha is a bit older.'

'But she has certainly taken a shine to you! See if you can persuade her to talk, to answer my questions. I see you've been talking to her already; she seems so much more relaxed now. Well done! You have the gift of kindness – I can tell. That comes first. And then the questions. Can you help?'

Janiki nodded. 'Of course. I'll try.'

'Tell her that we want to help her,' Gita said, 'ask her for her name and her native place, and how it happened that she ended up where she did. I'm not sure if she will answer now, but one day soon, she will. Tell her that Dr Ganotra is going to take her over to Tulasa House, probably tomorrow. She will get all the help she needs there. Dr Ganotra is dealing with the formalities. They will pass her on to him. Tell her that she is going to a good place, a safe place, a place where no one will hurt her again. Tell her she will not go back to the bad place she came from. That from now on she is in safe hands. Ask her if she has family members she'd like us to contact; a place she can return to eventually.'

Janiki spoke then, her voice calm and soothing. The girl did not respond in any way at first, but after a while began to silently weep. Janiki spoke in Tamil to her again, and a whispered word escaped her lips. Janiki looked up at Gita and smiled.

'Her name is Sakhi. It means *friend*. It is very fitting, because now she is our friend, and we are hers.'

Gita nodded, and smiled in delight. 'That's a wonderful beginning,' she said.

'I will go now. I don't think we'll get more out of her today, but it's a good start and she can go to Tulasa House tomorrow and eventually we will know more about her. Are you coming?'

Janiki nodded, and stood up to leave. She bent down and kissed the girl on her forehead, and told her goodbye, and that she'd be safe now. The girl clung to her hand, and pulled her back; Janiki spoke again, promising to see her the next day at Tulasa House. The girl shook her head, meaning yes, and released Janiki's hand.

'This is such wonderful work Dr Ganotra is doing,' said Janiki as she walked down the corridor with Gita. 'Even if it's a drop in the ocean. To save a child, even if it's just one. To return a child to her parents…'

'Unfortunately, it's not usually a happy ending,' said Gita. 'Very often we can't send a girl like this back to her parents. They won't accept her – after what she has been through, she must expect a further hurt, the hurt of rejection. These girls usually end up in an orphanage. You must ask Dr Ganotra about Tulasa, the girl he's dedicated his work to. Ask him. I have to go back to my own work now, but ask him. Goodbye, Janiki, and thank you for your help.'

* * *

Later that evening, back at Tulasa Nilayam, Janiki did ask. Subhadai had cooked an evening meal, which was waiting for them when they returned at dusk. Dr Ganotra this time seemed relaxed, and, after they had eaten, needed no prompting to tell the story of Tulasa.

'She was a twelve-year-old Nepali girl who many years ago – the early eighties – was kidnapped from her village and sold into prostitution in Bombay,' he began. 'She was systematically raped to make her fit for the trade and then forced to entertain an average of eight grown men a day. I was working at the time in a Bombay hospital and I met her there ten months later. Her tiny body was completely broken: she had all kinds of STDs as well as genital warts and brain tuberculosis, which left her disabled. She told a horrific story.'

Janiki couldn't even begin to process the story. What kind of man could do that to a child? Her voice shook as she asked:

'But after you found her, did it get better? You rescued her, so she found help, right? A happy ending?'

Dr Ganotra shook his head. 'There was a huge media rumpus when the story broke. At first there was an outpouring of public sympathy for her – offers of adoption and marriage, an invitation to Switzerland, gifts of money and medicine. None of it came to much. We managed to locate her father – her mother had died shortly after her disappearance – and sent her home. But she was sadly rejected by her father's second wife, and moved into a home. Her father avoided her to keep the family peace. She was in constant pain, but worst of all was the feeling that nobody loved her, that she had been used and abused and finally discarded like a piece of rubbish.'

Tears blistered Janiki's eyes. 'But at least the story broke, and the horror of it all was revealed. Did the police help to rescue other girls? How come it is still going on?'

Dr Ganotra shook his head again. 'Police collusion with the flesh trade was at the core of Tulasa's revelations. And not much has changed since then. The police, the politicians, the pimps – they are all in collaboration. The profit is huge.

'After the story broke, the public uproar forced the police to raise their backsides a little. In no time thirty-two persons involved were arrested, including the three brothel owners Tulasa had worked for. The police had known exactly what was going on, and only stepped in when forced to do so. Yet it took them eighteen months to find out her age and three years to file a charge. And only last January, eighteen years later, did the case finally to come to trial. The police were given a month to produce her in court. And then we found that Tulasa had died two years previously. Meanwhile, her abusers have been running free. And not everything is back to normal. There are still thousands of Tulasas out there. Sakhi is one of them, Ratna is another. We cannot save them all.'

'But we have to save Asha! We have to! We can't let…' Janiki's voice failed. She could not let her imagination run with Tulasa's story and apply it to Asha. To do that would mean despair; utter hopelessness. If not even the police could be relied upon to help, what good could she, Kamal, Caroline, three newcomers to Bombay, do? Even with the assistance of Dr Ganotra? Janiki couldn't help it – she broke down. Her body shook with sobs.

'We have to find her. Please, please, Dr Ganotra, save her! Save my little sister! She's so innocent, so young! What will become of her, out there!'

Dr Ganotra laid a hand on Janiki's trembling arm.

'I'll do my best – I promise you that. But the reality is that Asha is just one girl out of thousands. Girls abducted from villages all over India and Nepal, lured away on some pretext or the other: going to movies, cities, temples, making them film stars, lucrative job opportunities, marriage. And then every year thousands of girls are ceremoniously dedicated to the Goddess Yellamma, and must serve her as child prostitutes. Others are sold to the highest bidder and then turned over to the urban brothels. You've seen Bombay; you've seen the chaos, the crowds. I just want you to know the reality. It won't be easy. You have my help, but I can't do much. The police force isn't going to help at all. You need to brace yourself. I understand your tears, your fears, but wishing and wanting isn't going to help. Your prayers might – prayers provide strength and faith, and you will need both. You will also need a miracle. And all your wits about you. And you seem to have good wits. You got this far. You say that you were able to intercept some emails?'

Janiki wiped her tears on a corner of her *palu* and tried to steady her voice.

'Yes. I was able to contact Asha when she was still in Madras. I was able to check the emails of the people who had captured her. But I was found out and that was the end of that.' Janiki told him the details of her detective work, her communication with Asha.

'If only I hadn't tried to be so clever. If only I had told her to run, run away from that house immediately, to not go looking for passwords and things! I was trying to be clever and I just made everything worse. It's my fault this happened. All my fault.'

'Blaming yourself isn't going to get you anywhere. I think it's time you called it a day. Tomorrow I'll try to fix you up with a computer and Internet and you can maybe do some more research – you're good at that. Walking the streets of Kamathipura isn't going to help. And tomorrow her parents will be here. It's not good for you to be alone. The three of you, together, will give each other strength. Just don't give up. All right?'

Janiki sniffed. 'All right.'

'Tomorrow is a new day. You look exhausted. I'll get my driver to take you home. Where is your hotel?'

Janiki was sure she would not sleep that night. However, the moment her head touched the pillow she sank into a deep and dreamless sleep.

Chapter Thirty-One

Asha

It was my first trip on a train. It was like stepping into the belly of an enormous snake that devoured whole people, hundreds of them, thousands of them, except that we entered the snake voluntarily and weren't exactly devoured, but would leave again at the other end of the journey, exhausted, drained of all energy, limp as a thirsty vine. We were in a carriage that was called Three-Tiered Third Class. Three-Tiered meant that the bunks had three levels. There were only ladies in the carriage and some had babies. During the day there was only the seats, but at night a man came around and lowered the two top bunks and each lady slept on a separate bunk. The woman I was with – she told me to call her Sita Aunty but I never did. The words just could not leave my mouth. I did not call her anything at all, in fact. I just did not speak. Not speaking felt like the safest thing to do, but I knew I was not really safe at all. I did not want to go to Bombay but of course nobody asked me. In my heart I screamed only for Janiki. But Janiki did not come. She did not hear. Janiki was so far away, in a different country, on another continent. Janiki would just be coming home from work in her happy place, just be switching on her computer and wondering why I was not with Naadiya.

That woman – she watched me like a snake watches its prey. Especially when the train stopped – at those times she would grab my wrists and not let me go, in case I ran away. When the train started up again she would relax her grip. When the train stopped sometimes food-*wallahs* would come on board and bring meals and that was how we ate. There were four other ladies in our compartment. One of them had a baby that cried all the time. There was a mother and a daughter a bit older than me and a much older lady. They all chatted among themselves and sometimes they asked the lady called Sita Aunty questions and she replied to them but told them only lies. She said she was my aunt and she was bringing me to Bombay to get married. All the other ladies laughed and smiled at me then. But I did not smile back. I did not say a word, except when I needed to relieve myself. Then the lady called Sita Aunty would accompany me to the latrine and wait for me outside and then we would return to our compartment. The train tore through the countryside like a bullet, through the night like a comet slashing through the black sky. I slept and woke up and the scenes flitting past the windows changed and then we were in Bombay fighting through the crowds at the station.

The woman bundled us into a taxi and the taxi drove through streets so congested it felt as if we were in a metal box creeping through the streets, inching past other metal boxes full of people who were all happy and knew where they were going, and I was the only one with no inkling as to what was happening. I did not ask again where we were going because I knew the answer would mean nothing to me.

At last we came to a big house and she made me climb some stairs ahead of her. Up and up, up and up. I thought we would climb for ever and end up in the heavens but at last she made me walk down a dark dingy corridor that had not been swept for months or years, and took out a key and opened a door and pushed me through. I found myself in another hallway, darker and dingier. Then she opened another door and made me enter. The room was very small. Against one wall was a *charpai*, and that was all the furniture. She pointed under the bed and I could see a pail peeping out. The pail was for my excretions. Then she left me alone and I waited.

* * *

I waited and waited and then after what seemed like an eternity the door opened and two men entered. They made me stand up and stared at me, talking. They spoke Hindi. I had learned a little Hindi at school but they spoke so quickly I could not understand them. All I could understand was that they approved of me. They did not tell me that. They did not speak to me at all, just watched me, looked me up and down, as if I were a cow for sale in a market.

But I knew. And somehow I knew that their approval was not a good thing, but that their disapproval would be even worse. I do not know how I knew these things. I just did. It was an instinct. And then they left. Now and then the woman I had travelled with to Bombay came in and brought me meals, and water to drink. Once she removed the pail and brought me an empty one to replace it. I was so embarrassed by that. I wanted to tell her I needed another pail, one with water to clean myself. But I could not speak. It was as if a demon had clamped my throat so that no words could emerge, and all the words I wanted to say were just collecting inside me, unable to escape, jammed together in my innards where they turned into a huge quivering mass of fear, and that was all I was, fear. And all through the fear a tiny voice called for Janiki but the fear drowned out that voice. I could not even pray. Amma had taught me to pray throughout all my fears and darkness, that prayer was a lifeline I could cling to, but I was not strong enough to cling and my fear seemed to devour me from within. I was so alone, so alone in this huge strange city, and outside my walls were so many millions of people and not one of them could help me, because I was locked in this tiny room.

There was a window I could not open. And it was hot, so hot. And all I could do was lie on that *charpai* and hope that

sleep would carry me away but I could not even sleep because the
fear drove sleep away. Sometimes I tried to remember the good
times. I remembered the village streets where I had played with
my brothers and with Janiki, laughed and jumped and ran with
the other village children, not knowing that one day I would be
in hell, far away from all that I knew and loved.

How I longed for the oblivion of sleep! But it did not come
and when dawn broke the next day it was a small comfort, because at least it would be light and the light was better than the
dark.

But at least on that second day there was some change. Nothing is worse than being shut alone in a room with your fears and
your thoughts and your feelings. Nothing is worse than being
alone with all the monsters that live within, because those monsters are all you have for entertainment and entertain you they
will. If only I had something to read! Anything. Even an old dictionary or some stupid film ads, anything, anything I could latch
my mind to so that the monsters that dwell within could not rise
up; so I could not see them. This is what I learned in that little
room. That my worst companion was myself, and there was no
running away, nowhere to go and no control over those monsters.
And I longed for something, anything, to anchor myself on so I
would not have to face my own wretched self.

And so I was happy when the woman spoke a few curt words
and told me to follow her down the endless stairs again. Yes, I
said that word, happy. I was happy in my home in Gingee with
the people I loved, before Amma and Appa died. But compared
to being alone in that room, walking down the stairs with that
lady, well I felt almost bliss. And then we were on the pavement
and her hand tight around my wrist once again. A car was waiting at the kerb, not a taxi this time. A car with a driver, and she
pushed me forward and forced me to enter a car, and the car
moved off to I know not where, and even that seemed like joy

compared to being in that room. I did not know that one day I would look back on that room and long to be there again, regard that room as joy. And the car moved into that slow-moving beast of metal crawling through the streets of Bombay, became part of that beast. So many people! I could see them on the pavements, crowds of them, moving here and there, and I longed to leap from the car and throw myself on their mercy, but next to me was that woman and I knew that leaping from the car was futile as her grip was firmly closed around my wrist.

The car drove up outside a house and I was ushered through the door and into the arms of the woman who, from then on, was to be my new prison warden. She received me with what anyone would have mistaken for a welcoming smile, and welcoming words, but I knew in my heart that she was welcoming me into something so terrible I could not even imagine it. How could I know such things? I just did. And yet once again I knew something like joy, because unlike the stern silent woman who had brought me to Bombay this new woman greeted me with a big smile and chattered all the time, and better yet, she spoke English. And though her friendliness was feigned, it was better than the sheer desolation of being silent and alone.

But if I had known what was to come – oh, I would have screamed and struggled and fought like a tigercat. But I did not know. I was docile as a kitten, handed from one woman to another. I was docile because I did not know. I could not imagine. I took her smile, and her words, as a sign that better was to come.

'You are a very fortunate girl!' she said to me, and my heart leapt because I believed her.

I should not have.

Worse was to come.

Chapter Thirty-Two

Janiki

The next morning Janiki arrived at Tulasa House at the break of dawn; there was no time to be wasted. Today Kamal and Caroline would be arriving. A big day lay ahead. Dr Ganotra was there, before her; Sakhi, he said, would be arriving soon and he'd be grateful if Janiki could be there to receive her, to translate from Tamil, to make her feel welcome.

'Of course,' said Janiki. 'I'd love to help. But...'

She wanted to explain that Kamal and Caroline were due in – they had taken the first flight into Bombay – and they'd presumably be busy all day. But she stopped speaking, for the door to the kitchen had opened and Kamal stood in the doorway, Caroline right behind him. Janiki's hands dropped, and against her will she stared at them.

In her mind, up to now, Kamal had still been Kamal Uncle; a much older man, an uncle after all, a generation above her, an authority, a father figure almost, tall and prepossessing, and she the little girl who had looked up to him; the little girl who had mothered his child, but a little girl all the same, a child.

But in the intervening years she had changed. Grown up. Become a woman. And he had also changed. Almost beyond recognition; and yet he was the same, the same Kamal. It wasn't just his physical appearance. No: it was the very *substance* of him, something that could not be seen but which imparted itself to her through countless signals, imperceptible to the senses but immediately recognised by the rhythm of her soul, the drummer within, who all her life had doggedly beat a pulse of its own and who now, as if activated by the entrance of this new individual into its radius, suddenly went wild – ratatatatatatatat at a breakneck speed.

Kamal wore khaki cotton trousers and a nondescript, faded, striped cotton shirt. He wore cheap flip-flops. He was tall and straight-backed, golden-brown in colour. His face was angular, almost gaunt, his eyes under thick eyebrows deep-set and large, the look in them probing, severe even, and at the same time veiled, seeing all while revealing nothing. A short beard covered his chin, a moustache his upper lip. He was unsmiling. The overall expression was of distance and authority. He was unapproachable. Yet still she smiled. 'Hello, Kamal!' she said.

Kamal did not return her smile, and only vaguely raised his hands in a peremptory *namaste*, did not even greet her. It was Caroline who smiled, stepping forward from behind her former husband to sweep Janiki into her arms.

'Janiki!' she said. 'It's so good to see you again! I can't believe how much you've grown – you're a woman now!'

'Yes,' said Janiki, feeling shy all of a sudden. Caroline was so American; in the year she had spent in California she had grown used to the overflowing enthusiasm and friendliness of American women, but here, in Bombay, it seemed all at once alien, out of place, inappropriate, given the circumstances.

Caroline, in contrast to Kamal, was dressed in casual-but-smart attire: well-cut, obviously expensive trousers and a long floral blouse that would have been more appropriate in the lobby of a luxury hotel than here in this so shabby room. She wore shiny leather sandals with heels and a blue silk scarf around her neck. On her slender fingers she wore rings; expensive rings, one with a sparkling diamond, and a white-gold wedding band. Though still beautiful, she had aged, and bore no resemblance at all to the hippie-styled young woman in flowing skirts who had shared her home when Asha was a toddler. This woman was a stranger, and strange, incongruous here in the bowels of Bombay.

Caroline, as if recognising that her enthusiastic greeting of Janiki was somehow over the top in this sombre place, loosened her embrace and stepped back, her smile dropping away, her features falling into a grimace.

'I can't believe we're here, doing this!' she said. 'I can't believe – that Asha – my baby – is here. What a mess. Did you—'

'Have you any news?' Kamal butted in. 'Have you made any progress? You must be Dr Ganotra.'

He turned to Dr Ganotra, who now stood up from the table where he had been eating his breakfast.

'No,' said Dr Ganotra, walking to the sink to wash his hands. 'I was just telling Janiki yesterday. There won't be any miracles. This is slow, tedious, frustrating work and success is not guaranteed. You're looking for a needle in a haystack.'

'A cliché,' said Kamal impatiently. 'Asha is not a needle. She's my daughter and I will find her. I'll find her if I have to spend the rest of my life searching.'

'Right,' said Caroline. 'We're here to find her and we won't turn back. I'm not going before I hold her in my arms again.'

Dr Ganotra, wiping his hands on a towel, only shook his head, almost imperceptibly, and even Janiki, having recovered most of her equilibrium, felt that they both, Kamal and Caroline, had spoken too hastily, too confidently, too brashly. They had not yet walked the streets of Kamathipura. They seemed naive; such presumptuousness, she feared, might jinx the entire mission. She felt the need to put a dampener on their assertiveness.

'Kamal – Caroline,' she said, 'I've made a start. I went out looking yesterday, just walking around the area. And it's… well, it's a bit depressing, really. It really does seem like a needle in a haystack.'

Only after she'd spoken did she realise: she'd addressed Kamal not as Uncle, but as an equal, as her peer. She hoped he wouldn't think it rude. She wanted to make a good impression on him. But he was so austere, so grim, so brusque; she was lost as to how she would appear to him. As a little girl? As the precocious teenager he'd treated with kindness but distance in the past? As a grown woman? He seemed hardly to have acknowledged her up to now; his mind was filled with Asha. He had not even greeted her. Disappointment welled up in her, but only for an instant.

Janiki, she told herself sternly, what are you thinking? This is your Kamal Uncle, a much older man. What you are thinking is outrageous! But then she remembered Rani Abishta, and her outrageous desire to pair her off with Kamal – and Rani's suggestion at the moment didn't seem outrageous in the least. Except that obviously Kamal hardly even saw her.

All these thoughts ran through Janiki's head in the space of an instant; and then she came back to earth. In that one instant she had forgotten Asha, and the direness of her situation. She had, for that moment, forgotten what she was here for, carried away on the wings of – what? A stupid female dream. She physically pinched herself to bring herself back to the task at hand, which meant aligning herself with the desperation that fired both Kamal and Caroline.

'Look why don't you just go to Kamathipura now and look around a bit? I mean, I've only been there once myself but you should see the place to get a better idea of how to organize the search.'

'Yes – you do that,' said Dr Ganotra. 'I'm going to be busy this morning – Sakhi will be here soon.'

'Sakhi?' said Kamal.

'A girl we rescued yesterday. She's in hospital now and coming here today. A Tamil girl. Your Asha is not the only girl in trouble. She's one of thousands. I'll help as much as I can, but later today.

At four this afternoon I've scheduled a team meeting – some of the people who work for Safe Haven will be coming around to discuss some urgent matters, and they'll be able to look into the Asha problem, and you'll be able to ask for advice, help, maybe develop a strategy. But remember we're all very busy. After that, if you still have questions, we can have our talk. Now, it's best you go off with Janiki. She's been a great help.'

For the first time, Kamal looked at Janiki with something more than distraction in his eyes, as if he only now acknowledged her presence. He nodded.

'Right,' he said. 'Let's go, Janiki. Let's see this hellhole.'

'Go where?'

'To Kamathipura; where else? I want to see where my daughter might be hidden.'

Janiki looked in panic at him, and then at Dr Ganotra.

'But – is nobody going to come with us? Show us around?'

Dr Ganotra sniffed in exasperation.

'We're all much too busy to give guide-tours, sorry. Best you just go, plunge in and discover it all by yourself. Get a feel for the place. Later at the meeting you can maybe exchange a few words with someone if you have a lead or if you feel you want a closer look; maybe someone can find the time. But – well, best you just go.'

Just as they were about to leave, Gita arrived, Sakhi in tow. Sakhi was limping, but she seemed much better than yesterday, not flinching when Janiki leaned over to hug her, and even managing a half-smile. Janiki introduced Kamal and Caroline, then looked at Gita with something like desperation.

'We're off to Kamathipura,' she said. 'Yesterday you said you'd show me around a bit – do you – could you – I mean, we're supposed to be going now, and I know you're busy, but…'

Gita looked at her watch. 'I guess I could spare an hour or two,' she said. 'If Dr Ganotra doesn't mind? We've got the team meeting at four…'

She looked at Dr Ganotra, who looked at his watch.

'Subhadai will look after Sakhi,' he said. 'I've got some HIV patients at my clinic this morning – I'll be back this afternoon for the team meeting. All right, Gita, go with them. Show them the place.'

Janiki breathed out in relief; she hadn't even realised she'd been holding her breath. It had seemed, for a while, as if Kamal and Caroline were both relying on her for a guided tour of the city, as if she had been here a year instead of just a day.

The four of them stepped out onto the pavement. Gita went to hail a rickshaw, but then she stopped and turned to Caroline.

'Caroline,' she said, 'it'd be better if you remove those rings– they look so expensive! You're going to attract attention anyway as a white woman; we're going into a high crime area. Can you take them off for a while?'

'But – I always wear them – I…' Caroline sighed. 'Oh I suppose you're right. I hadn't thought of that. OK. I'll take them off.'

She did so, and then turned her back to Janiki, lifting the curtain of her blonde hair. 'Janiki – can you undo the clasp on my chain, please? I'll put the rings on it for the time being.'

Janiki opened the clasp, and Caroline hung the two rings through the gold chain on which a single simple crucifix hung. Janiki remembered that, back in the day, Caroline had worn a golden OM symbol around her neck. Marriage and respectability had obviously changed her religious affiliation. She relocked the chain for Caroline, who grinned.

'Whew,' she said, 'I feel almost naked without those rings.'

Janiki and Kamal exchanged a glance. Kamal's lips seemed to twitch slightly; but perhaps she had imagined it, as well as the slight roll of the eyes. Caroline was still dressed far too smartly for Janiki's liking, but the removal of the rings would have to do for now. Gita nodded.

'Much better,' she said, 'now come. Let's find an autorickshaw.'

As they drove towards Kamathipura, Gita said, 'It's a pity that you're going to see the worst of Mumbai. It's not all bad, you know. Mumbai is actually a wonderful city, but you have to know it. It's not a place; it's a feeling.'

Janiki nodded. 'I noticed you call it Mumbai – I'm still calling it Bombay. Is that bad?'

'Don't worry about it,' said Gita, flapping her hand in dismissal. 'The city has always been called Mumbai in Marathi, and Bombay in English, Bambai in Hindi. A powerful regional political party called Shiv Sena argued that Bombay was a corrupted English version of Mumbai and an unwanted legacy of British colonial rule and pushed for the name change. In 1995 official agencies and governments were ordered to adopt the change. It's happening gradually. In a few years it will all be Mumbai. But if you still call it Bombay nobody's going to shoot you.'

She peered out of the rickshaw. 'And,' she announced, 'here we are. Kamathipura. The sin-centre of Mumbai.'

Chapter Thirty-Three

Asha

This time we went to a house. The house was empty except for me and this lady who had brought me here, who spoke English and chattered all the time. The lady was small and round with soft flaps of flesh that wobbled between her sari blouse and skirt, wobbled as she walked and as she laughed. Her sari was green and sparkling. Her lips were painted bright red, and there was a speck of red on her tooth, which I longed to wipe away, as if that was a big problem for me, which is stupid in that situation. But I longed to nevertheless. Her eyes were outlined in thick black kajal. She had long fingernails like claws and they were bright red. On her feet she wore *chappals*, the kind where a strap goes between the biggest toes. Her feet were wide and flat with hard cracked skin, like a lizard. She laughed a lot. She seemed to think everything was hilarious, but I didn't and I did not laugh. I did not even smile. But I liked being with her because I was no longer alone with my monsters.

'I know your name is Asha but I will give you a new name, a more appropriate name,' she said to me, and I thought, why? Appropriate for what? My name Asha means hope and I could not think of anything more appropriate because hope was the only thing that could keep me breathing right now. But no.

'Asha is not a good name for you. From now on you will be called Kamini. Kamini is a beautiful name. It means you are a beautiful, sensuous woman. What a lovely name! Do you not think it is a wonderful name? It suits you so much!'

Well I did not reply to her because I was not talking at all – I could not talk – but I wished I had a dictionary so that I could look up the meaning of the word sensuous. Or that Janiki was with me so I could ask her and she would explain to me, as she explained all new words. But how futile to wish for Janiki, or even for a dictionary! But it is certainly good to know what one's own name means.

So she gave me a new name just as if she were my mother, but she wasn't. She told me to call her Devaki Aunty. But I didn't. I did not call her anything.

She gave me food in that new house. She took me into the kitchen and cooked rice for me and a little masala. She told me to sit on the floor and she handed me a bowl with the rice and masala in it. I was very hungry and I gobbled it all up at once. I was also thirsty because I had only had a single glass of water all day and it was so hot. She let me drink as much water as I wanted and so I was grateful to her and liked her better than the other woman.

After I'd had my food she took me into another room and said, 'Now Kamini, I am going to explain to you why I said that you are a very lucky girl. So that you will know what to do and what your new duties are. First of all I want you to stop looking so sulky. Sulky look is a not beautiful look. I want you to smile. Smile, dear!'

But I could not smile and so I didn't. She did not like that.

'Smile, I said! Smile!' This time her voice was sharp and she was not laughing any more.

'If you do not smile I will slap you,' she said. 'I will paddle you with a cooking spoon. You wouldn't like that. So just smile.'

And so I smiled. I stretched my lips. And she nodded and smiled herself.

'That's better. You are a good girl. I knew it! Not just beautiful but good. You see, you must be obedient and all will be well. Just do what I tell you and the most important thing is to smile. OK, you may stop smiling now.'

So I stopped smiling. I let my lips unstretch.

'Now,' she said, 'I need to explain some things to you. Mr Rajgopal is the boss. He is like an uncle. In fact he might even let you call him Krishnan Uncle in future. Mr Rajgopal is sending you to a gentleman from Calcutta, a very rich gentleman. His name is Mr Chaudhuri. Calcutta is in Bengal, so he is a Bengali, a very important Bengali. He is famous in Bombay. He wishes to make your acquaintance. He has seen your photo and likes you very much. He wants to know you better. I know you have little experience of men so I will have to teach you some things. I am sure your mother never taught you these things as you are not yet of marriageable age and it might shock you, but don't worry. It is all normal. You will see how easy it is after the first time.'

And she told me how this man wished to be entertained. And indeed I was shocked to my core and could not believe what she said. But she said it was normal to be shocked at first but once I had done it I would not mind.

'Mr Chaudhuri is a fine gentleman,' she said. 'That is why I said you are a lucky girl. He would not take just any girl. But look at your sweet fair skin! So pure! So lovely! But you cannot go to him in a sulky way. That is not good. It will make him angry. You must stop this sulking and look at him with loving eyes and smile and chat with him. That is how he wants you to be so that is how you must be. Do you understand what I am saying?'

I stared at her and said nothing.

'Do you understand?' she shouted. 'Answer me girl and stop this stupid sulking! I told you how lucky you are and still you sulk! Do you want to end up in a cage? Do you? Do you? Mr Rajgopal is a very important man. He has arranged everything with Mr Chaudhuri and will be very angry if you disappoint. He will be furious! You do not want to anger him. Mr Rajgopal will

put you in a cage if you don't behave!. Do you want to end up in
a cage?'

I did not know what she was talking about. End up in a cage?
What did that mean? And then she explained.

'That is the alternative if you are not good. The cages – that is
where the bad girls go. I will show you a picture.'

And she showed me some photographs. Indeed, they were of
girls in a window of a house, upstairs, and they were truly behind
bars, sitting there and looking out.

'These are the cages of Kamathipura,' she said. 'It is where the
bad girls go. Believe me, you do not want to end up there. But
that is where you will end up if you do not do as I say. You are
so lucky, so don't throw this opportunity away. So first you must
practise the smiling. He likes a smiling affectionate girl. It is easy
to smile. Not so easy to be affectionate. But I will teach you.'

And she tried to teach me but I would not learn. And indeed
she hit me with a wooden spoon, and shouted at me, but I would
not learn.

She showed me some films on the TV. I almost died with disgust. 'This is what a woman does when she is married,' she told
me, but I could not believe it. And the films she showed me got
worse and worse so that I had to hide my eyes but she grabbed my
wrist and pulled away my hands and screamed at me: 'Open your
eyes, girl! You must watch!'

She told me this is what she wants me to do and I must learn.
I can hardly talk about the things she forced me to watch, yes,
forced, because if I did not watch she hit me.

And then I heard her talking on the phone to someone, but
in rapid Hindi so I could not understand most of what she said,
but sometimes she spoke English words and I understood. 'She is
not compliant, Mr Rajgopal,' I heard her say, and, 'So stubborn.'

When she finished she slammed down the receiver and then
she said to me, 'I am taking you to Mr Chaudhuri now. He is

from Calcutta and very rich. You will like him. He insists on meeting you first. But you must be a good girl and do as I say. Do you understand?'

I did not understand. How could I? I did not want to meet this Mr Chaudhuri. I did not want to know the Bengali man. I did not want to do those disgusting things with the Bengali man. I am not married to him and I cannot even believe that is truly what married ladies do. Surely Amma would have told me! Or Janiki, who is to be married soon!

I only wanted to be with Janiki, but that was an impossible hope. But my name is Asha and so I still hoped. That is my name. I decided then and there that I would cling to my name. I would cling to Janiki, even though I could not see her and she was far away. I knew she was thinking of me and so I thought of her with all my might and main. And I believed too that somewhere in the invisible world where hearts and minds and souls can meet, Janiki was with me.

But I still had to meet this Bengali.

Chapter Thirty-Four

Caroline

Kamathipura.

A day ago, she had never even heard the word. And now it was a synonym for everything that was wrong with the world, and with India. All the ugliness, all the horror, all the filth, compressed into one word. Before leaving Madras she had bought a book on Bombay – an older book, so it did not refer to the city as Mumbai – and the chapter on the notorious red light district had, she thought, prepared her for the worst.

Real life, though, was worse than the worst.

I can't do this! I can't go there! screamed a high-pitched, hysterical voice within her. But then another voice, louder, sombre in tone, serious, collected, calm, replied: *Asha is there. Asha is there. You must find Asha.*

And so she walked on. Instinctively, she reached out for Kamal's hand, and his fingers closed around hers; but then Gita came in from behind them, placed her hand around both their wrists and drew them gently apart.

'Sorry,' she said. 'You two shouldn't hold hands in Kamathipura. It'll give the wrong impression. Remember where you are.'

Janiki, noticing the little incident and understanding, stepped forward on the other side of Caroline and took her hand; Caroline clasped hers as if her life depended on it. She had held Kamal's hand not for affection but for strength; and Janiki's hand was just as good. From it came both strength and comfort.

Kamal and Janiki, Caroline realised, were both Indians; somehow that explained that centred calm that she, now, was desperate for; but there it was in Janiki's hand, clasped firmly around hers. As if a current ran from Janiki to her, an anchor holding her upright when she would faint, keeping her grounded when she would run away, back to the cool luxury of the Taj Mahal hotel.

She and Kamal had arrived in the wee hours of the morning and gone straight to the Taj. She had persuaded Kamal to spend at least that one night there, instead of going out to look for a more modest hotel.

'It's past midnight,' she said. 'Come on, Kamal. It'll be an hour before you find another place. Just stay here this one night; we need to be rested tomorrow. Let me pay if it's outside your budget.'

And so he'd stayed, in a room of his own, of course, and he had insisted on paying his own way. Kamal was proud like that. But then, he had probably earned well in Dubai and since he lived so modestly... well, she could only guess at his means but no doubt he had savings enough. And so they had both slept at the Taj – though 'sleep', at least in her case, was a euphemism for tossing and turning and obsessing about Asha, and having a thousand million thoughts and fears rushing through her brain all at once. She had needed all the little calming tricks of her own trade to find some modicum of rest: breathing and meditation exercises, and some yoga.

And now here they were, walking into the den of iniquity that was Kamathipura, the place where women were nothing more than chattels, a cheap commodity, their lives bits of detritus in a drain of lost humanity. Here, you could almost smell the despair. Caroline took a deep breath; but the air was thick with misery and it did not help at all.

Janiki, walking beside her with a firm hold on her hand, did help. How Janiki had grown! In more ways than one; she was a woman now, and a lovely one at that, emitting that serene charm and calm and self-possession that came naturally to so many Indian women. Janiki seemed unperturbed by the horror of Kamathipura; she seemed physically cool and collected, in a simple but somehow stylish blue cotton *shalwar kameez,* her hair tied back in a ponytail, make-up free and smiling. So relaxed, cool.

Ahead of them walked Gita, somehow incongruous in jeans and T-shirt (though why incongruous, Caroline asked herself; why shouldn't an Indian woman wear Western clothes in India? It just went to show how ingrained the cultural clichés were), leading them confidently into a narrow lane lined with ramshackle houses. Kamal walked with Gita. Why? she thought. Why not with her? Was he avoiding her? He was so stern still, so aloof, even, at least towards her. Was it because of Asha, or did it have to do with her, Caroline, and his unresolved feelings towards her?

Front doors opened directly onto the small forecourts where people gathered. Women, leaning against the doorjambs, looked up as they walked past. One or two of them waved at Gita. Others sat on worn-out *charpais.* Many looked as if they had just rolled out of bed, though it was already almost midday.

Some, though, were heavily made-up, their perfume pungent in the congested air, adding its essence to that melange of smells that formed an olfactory assault on the senses – the tangible smells of cooking, spices, flowers, perfume, hair oil, face powder, incense, rotting fruit, drains, sewage, urine, vomit, sweat and semen, with the intangible ones of fear, loneliness, anguish, hate, hunger, malevolence, abuse, dread and horror. Mingled, coagulated, metamorphosed into that unique and pungent odour Caroline now named Bombay sweet-and-sour. It seeped out like a crawling mist through the lanes and alleys, creeping up the walls and through the windows and lying like a shroud over Kamathipura.

All of Caroline's senses were operating now on crisis frequency. She could hardly think, for the impressions they gathered pelted themselves at her and screamed for attention, a jumble of sound, sight and smell colliding with her own unsorted feelings of disgust, dread, embarrassment and sheer horror. Once again, she wanted to turn and run, but always that cool calm voice – *Asha is here!* – called her back. That, and Janiki's hand around her own.

Gita talked as she walked, sometimes waving at a woman and smiling, sometimes stopping to explain some detail. She stopped to introduce them to a friendly brothel manager, called, she said, a *gharwali*. 'But we call her Bai, like a mother, or an aunt. These women are just doing their jobs. They are not evil.'

But Caroline hardly heard, merely nodded as if she had. Gita turned a corner; they walked down another lane. And another. They were lost in a labyrinth of hell. And yet it seemed at the same time so harmless, so everyday. Just women, standing and sitting around, a few men – where was all the horror? Wasn't she being unnecessarily squeamish? She glanced up; and yes, there were the notorious cages, barred windows in the upper storeys, some shuttered, some like dark holes into the warrens of vice behind them. These homes were veritable prisons, Caroline told herself; at night, the female prisoners would sit behind those bars, all dolled up, tawdry lures for the hungry on the streets. But how desperate must a man be to come here for relief! And yet, here on the street, there was no sense of desperation. It was all so very – normal. Except for one thing: they themselves. *They* were the deviation.

Caroline felt like an involuntary tourist being led around some noteworthy cultural attraction, except that this attraction was decidedly unattractive. In fact, she felt that she herself was the great attraction. Caroline might have removed her ostentatious rings, but it turned out that they were the least of her problems. It was the white skin and light-coloured hair that drew eyes to her; that, and the tailored clothes and obviously expensive shoes. Wherever they walked, people stepped back and stared; not just the unobtrusive glances polite Westerners might throw at a conspicuous stranger, but blatant, in-your-face ogling.

Caroline, already flustered by the knowledge that they were walking through the streets of one of the most notorious red light districts in the world, grew more nervous by the minute at the attention she was attracting.

The very next thing I'll do, she said to herself, *is buy a* shalwar kameez. *I should dye my hair black as well, and colour my skin brown.* An internal finger wagged at her: *you can't do that! That would be blackface!* But Caroline struck it down immediately. This was India, and all internalised concepts brought as baggage from America collapsed in the face of the immediate reality.

Asha is here. Somewhere in these labyrinthine lanes is my daughter. Somewhere behind those crumbling facades is the most precious person in my life. I have to find her. But how? And when?

Time, that ephemeral concept that in America forced people to race against themselves, that precious commodity constantly in deficit, seemed eternal here in India, and she herself had fallen into a rhythm in which time did not exist; there was no rush, no hurry, for time stretched before them as an endless river and all one had to do was flow along with it. She took a deep breath – acrid with Bombay sweet-and-sour – and told herself: *Caroline, relax. You will find her. Just have faith. Have hope. Asha is here and you will find her. Sooner or later. Take your time. This is India, and all things are possible.*

Chapter Thirty-Five

Asha

The Bengali lived in a very big, grand house with many servants. He was not married. I thought that lady had brought me there to marry him but I was wrong. That was not true. Anyway, she did not have the right to find a husband for me. Only Amma has that right but Amma's soul has left her body. So I was very confused. I was thinking of those films. They filled me with horror.

The Bengali was an elderly man. He was very thickset and had cheeks that hung down next to his mouth and wobbled as he spoke. He was very rich. I could tell because of the house. There were thick carpets on the floor and everything was golden and shiny. A servant opened the door and another servant led us to him.

I was wearing a shiny red sari decorated with many sequins, and that lady had spent hours on my hair and face. She had put all kinds of coloured creams on my face and black colours around my eyes. My face felt clogged and stiff. My lips were red with paste. She put jewels in my hair and in my nose and ears and around my neck. I did not feel as if I were myself at all. I was clothed like a princess in a film but I was not a real princess. Just an artificial one, a doll, a human body dressed up to look like royalty, but inside I was just as wretched as before.

Clothes do not change a person. Just because I was wearing all those shiny red clothes and those jewels and the colours on my lips and eyes, I was not a princess. Inside I was trembling with fear.

The lady too was dressed up in a shiny sari, stiff like paper, that rustled as she walked, and she wore new *chappals*, and perfume so strong I thought I would faint.

The Bengali was horrible. He stared at me with a certain look in his eye. 'Lovely, lovely,' he said. 'Even more beautiful than in her photo. A little too old perhaps but still very lovely.'

He even spoke to me. 'You are very beautiful,' he said. 'You will be my woman.'

When he said those words I almost fainted with shock. I cannot describe the terror that coursed through my body. Truly, I would rather have entered a tiger's cage than to be in that room with the Bengali.

He stretched out his hand to hold my wrist but I flinched and drew it away. That made him angry.

'What!' he said. 'Come! Let me hold you!'

But now I was trembling all over my body, and shrinking away from him. That made him even more furious. He shouted at me.

'What is this!' he yelled. He was yelling not at me but at the woman who called herself Devaki Aunty. 'I thought you said she was trained!'

'I have told her what she is to do,' said the woman I would not name. 'She is just being coy. She knows how to behave.'

'I do not like resistance! I want a feminine girl, a loving soft girl who will be good to me! This girl is not even smiling!'

'She can smile beautifully, Mr Chaudhuri,' said the lady, who was smiling herself and simpering. 'Show him how you can smile, Kamini!'

But I did not smile. I could not. My whole body was trembling. I could not help it.

'She is trembling with fear! I do not want a girl who fears me!'

He was shouting at the lady. His face was red with anger.

'Mr Chaudhuri, little Kamini is an innocent girl. You said you wanted an innocent girl, not a professional. That is why we chose this girl for you. You must understand she is afraid because she is innocent. She is so pure. It is natural for a pure girl to feel fear at first. You must understand that. You must be gentle with her.'

The Bengali stopped shouting then, calmed by her words.

'Yes, yes, you are right. She is fearful out of innocence and purity. I like purity – that is what will cure me of this disease. But I do not want to rape her. I am not a rapist. I am an honourable man. I want her to come to me with joy. You must train her to do this. Even a pure girl can learn. She is not well trained. You must take her away and train her some more. She must be docile and loving, coming to me with joy in her heart. That is what I want. I give you a week to return this girl with better training. I want her but in a compliant and soft loving way. You said she speaks English. I want her to talk to me in English, sing to me beautiful songs of love, in English. My favourite songs: 'The First Time Ever I Saw Your Face', and so on. That is what I want. Otherwise half-price.'

I did not fully understand what he said. I am only repeating the words, as I remember them. I did not know words like rape and rapist. I wished I had a dictionary, or Janiki to explain. Now I know.

But I did understand words like loving, and joy. There was no love and no joy in my heart and in my life. I could not give this Bengali what he wanted. But the lady promised me to him, well trained.

'Give me a week,' she said. 'I will train her some more. I will talk to Mr Rajgopal.'

Another word I understood well was half-price. I am not stupid. I understood well that I was to be sold to the Bengali.

Chapter Thirty-Six

Caroline

By morning's end Caroline was a walking heap of sweaty exhaustion.

'Seen enough?' Gita asked, and when she nodded, continued: 'So, now you know what you're up against.' She looked at her watch. 'It's eleven thirty. Go back to your hotel and rest; but be sure to come to the team meeting at four. We'll have a brainstorming session – if you have any ideas on how to move forward, bring them there. See you!' And she was gone.

'I need a meal and a nap,' said Caroline to Kamal and Gita. 'How about you?' She looked from one to the other.

'I'm going to take a walk,' said Kamal. 'I need to think. I'll see you at the house at about three forty-five, OK?'

Caroline nodded, disappointed. She had hoped to discuss matters with Kamal over a light lunch, but already he was walking away, melting into the crowds on the Bombay sidewalk.

'And you, Janiki? Are you going back to your hotel? Where is it, anyway? I'm staying at the Taj.'

Janiki laughed. 'The Taj is way out of my league,' she said. 'I'm at some cheap digs not too far away. But I don't need a rest. I'm going back to Tulasa House. I want to use the computer.'

Janiki hailed two rickshaws, one for Caroline and one for herself; her Hindi, she found, was good enough to bargain down Caroline's taxi fare a little (the Taj, she found, combined with Caroline's white skin, demanded an inviolate luxury levy) and so they parted company. 'See you later,' she said, stepping into her own vehicle.

* * *

Sleeping during the day always had the effect on Caroline of a heavy drug, knocking her out for hours. She avoided it in America, but here, in India, in combination with jet-lag and the sleeplessness of the previous night, it was like opium. Fortunately she had set the alarm, and it woke her at two thirty; yet she found she could not get up. The lethargy clung to her like a coarse skin; she lay under the slowly rotating ceiling fan, too lazy even to get up to pour herself a glass of cool water from the flask on the sideboard. The drawn blinds kept out the afternoon sun, and the gloom was like a further narcotic.

'Get up,' she scolded herself. 'Take a shower. There are things to be done. A meeting to attend. Asha to be found.'

And so she forced herself out of the soft lavishness of the bed, into the coolness of the shower where she washed her hair and then dried it with the hotel-provided drier. Thank goodness it was so short, cut for convenience just before her flight to India.

Looking at her open suitcase, she remembered her resolve to buy a *shalwar kameez*. She had noticed a boutique down in the hotel foyer; this was a good time to go down and buy herself something. She put on clean trousers and a blouse and made her way down. The boutique attendant was almost obsequious in her desire to sell a matching trio of flowing tunic, wide trousers and shawl, but Caroline could not make up her mind, and eventually left the shop without a purchase. Those suits were all – well, unsuitable, she thought, wincing at her own bad pun. Far too swish, too shiny, too Taj. She needed something simple. Something like what Janiki had worn. Cotton, not silk. She walked out into the heat of the day, onto the pavement, and hailed a rickshaw. In broken English, and fingering her blouse to demonstrate to the driver, she managed to make her intentions known: *Shalwar kameez* shop? Sari shop? He bobbled his head and drove off.

By three thirty Caroline was the proud owner of five brand new simple but pretty *shalwar kameezes*. Too late to go back to the Taj.

'I'll wear one now,' she had told the obsequious shop attendant who had helped her choose. In fact there had been three of them, all male, eager to help her make the right choice, offering her a chair and a cup of tea, which she had gratefully accepted (and when the chai came milked and sugared, she held her breath and drank it all up, because that was the Indian way, the polite way, and she was learning), and bending over backwards to help her choose only the best-quality and most expensive suits. But she had gone with her instincts and chosen for practicality, not for fashion.

'Madam, it is not suitable for wearing right away,' said the attendant. 'The fabric is too stiff. You must wash it once before wearing to remove the starch.'

'No, it doesn't matter if it's a bit stiff. I have to wear it now. I'll wear this one: see, the shawl is soft and flowing. I'll put it back on. Thank you for your help.'

'Thank you, madam, no problem. I will write you a bill; you just take it to the cashier at the front of the shop.'

As she walked away every one of the attendants in the shop – all male – stood back and made *namaste*, smiled at her and bid her farewell and thanked her for her custom. Americans, she thought, could take some lessons in customer service from the Indians. Once again she stepped out into the sweltering Bombay heat. It was now three thirty. She might just make it to Tulasa House in time; she certainly wouldn't make that tentative three-forty-five meeting with Kamal. Once more, time had dropped into a hole and the day was more than half over and Asha was not found.

Basically, she had wasted a day. Wasted a whole day strolling around Kamathipura like some kind of a celebrity diva and then sleeping and then shopping, all while Asha was still in jeopardy, still not found. And time still seemed to be stretching before her, waiting for her to quicken her pace, get back into the rhythm she had once known, that sense of time constantly on the ebb, constantly running away, taking success and achievement and victory with it; and if she did not run with time all would be lost, for ever. In America, time was something to grab, now, here, before it was too late. In India, time was leisurely and eternal. But it held Asha captive, and that was the problem. She needed to inject a little bit of America into India. This dawdling was not for her. And yet, today, she had subscribed to it completely.

'This won't do,' she told herself. 'I've wasted a day and Asha is out there and nobody seems to see the need to make each moment count. We need to change pace. Go full steam ahead. I need to take control. I'll speak up at that team meeting.'

Chapter Thirty-Seven

Asha

She began to slap me the moment we entered the car. Slap, slap, slap, right cheek, left cheek, right cheek again. And all the time shouting at me for being so stubborn.

'You are a silly, stupid girl!' she yelled. 'Do you know what you have done? You have only made matters worse for yourself and for everyone! I told you to be nice to him; that is all you have to do! You are a proud, stupid girl. You think you are so pure but wait and see what happens to stubborn girls! You do not know how lucky you are to be chosen by Mr Chaudhuri! Do you think he takes just any girl? He is very particular and you are so lucky! Do you think he just takes any little girl dragged from Kamathipura? You think so?'

Well I did not think so as I did not know what Kamathipura was. This all happened in my days of ignorance.

Now I know.

She made me watch some more of those terrible videos with women doing dirty things to men. It made me cry.

When I cried she got even more angry.

But then she went away and when she returned she was quiet and her voice was sweet and syrupy.

'Only one thing is going to bring you to your senses,' she said in that quiet sweet voice. 'You must know what the alternative is. You must experience yourself how lucky you are, how very fortunate to be chosen by a man like Mr Chaudhuri. You must see where you will end up if you refuse to be compliant. That will help you to make a decision.'

She moved me that very night.

That is how I ended up in the cages of Kamathipura. It was all my fault, because I was not compliant. Compliant was a word I did not understand at first, because I had never heard it before. But I learned the meaning very quickly, and now I knew it. To be treated well I had to be compliant.

Chapter Thirty-Eight

Janiki

I'm addicted, thought Janiki as she thankfully pressed the *on* button on Dr Ganotra's computer. Away from the screen for too long and I develop withdrawal tendencies.

But it was more than that, she knew. Asha was out there, somewhere, and Janiki believed with all her heart that all the information they needed to know was swirling out there in cyberspace; all she needed was the key to enter that space. Walking through Kamathipura this morning had been a complete waste of time; it had been for Caroline and Kamal's benefit, as she had been there, done that already the day before. The obligatory tourist walk-through that left anyone more ingenuous in tears of distress. Caroline, indeed, had been near tears at the end.

'How will we ever find Asha in that labyrinth?' Caroline had asked her, tears welling in her eyes. 'Janiki, it seems impossible!'

'It's not impossible at all,' Janiki had said, thinking of the computer and her itchy fingers. 'We just need a strategy. Come to the meeting this afternoon – we'll share our ideas there. Go home and have a rest now – you look exhausted.'

Caroline had nodded and stepped into the taxi Janiki hailed and negotiated for her.

Caroline shouldn't have come to Kamathipura, Janiki thought. She should have stayed in the luxury of the Taj and let us Indians find Asha. The shock of Kamathipura's reality was too much for her. Americans are so oversensitive, she thought. They need conditions to be just right, and then they are strong; the moment outer circumstances go against the grain of their personality, they collapse into a heap. Caroline should have stayed in her pristine sheltered world and let us do the work. Kamal and me. Both just as desperate to find Asha as Caroline, but better equipped to deal with the squalor and the poverty and the ugly heaving throngs that is everyday India. We grew up here. We know. We are impervious, better equipped to hold our true inner selves separate from the ugliness without.

And besides, thought Janiki, how on earth could a blonde white amber-eyed American be of any earthly help in the quest before them? Someone who couldn't speak a word of an Indian language, a spoilt rich American who didn't even know it was inappropriate to wear a diamond ring in a slum? Janiki shook her head. She'd have to have a word with Caroline. Persuade her to let her and Kamal do all the searching needed.

Kamal. Janiki smiled as his name once again came to her mind.

Yes, Kamal had changed. But so had she. He no more the older uncle, she no more the child – mature enough to care for his daughter, maybe, but still a child. He had been so austere, at first, so locked within himself, but she had found the key to his armour, and the key was Asha.

It was as if their mutual quest had linked them together in some intangible way, beyond the attraction she had initially felt towards him. They were together, now, together in their desperation to find that lost daughter of India, together in their need to save her from whatever horrors she faced or – touch wood – had already been subjected to.

'Dear God, let it not be too late,' Janiki prayed now as she opened the web browser and tapped in the keyword to Mr Ramcharran's email account. Let there be some clue, some sign, some hint as to her way forward. Hopefully Mr Ramcharran had not closed the account, had not changed the password...

There. The account opened, along with a list of at least thirty unopened mails. That meant that Mr Ramcharran was probably still in jail; hopefully he would stay there and be tried and spend the rest of his days in hell. For what he had done to Janiki, and most likely other girls like her. How could men do this thing? How could they? Did they not have daughters, sisters, mothers, wives? *If I ever have a son,* Janiki swore to herself, *I will teach him this: treat every woman as you would wish your mother, sister, daughter to be treated. Let that be your guideline. Then you can do no wrong. Love and respect women as they deserve to be loved and respected. As human beings with lives of their own, and not as property to be used and abused.* If only every mother would teach her son that golden rule!

She scanned the list of mails, looking for a crumb of a clue. Something to work with. Something that would point her in the direction to be taken next. But the names of the senders, the subject titles all seemed innocuous. Just *Hello!* and *What's up?* and *Can you make it?* Some in Tamil, some in English. Mostly from men, some from women. His sister was one of the first, before she knew of his arrest, apparently; reminding him of his niece's tenth birthday and prompting him to visit, or at least call: *you know how much Indira loves her favourite uncle!* Such words now seemed ominous. Why was Mr Ramcharran a favourite uncle? Had he oozed himself into Indira's favour, but with an ulterior motive? No, surely not. Not his own niece. Yet, to a man without morals, perhaps even a niece was fair play. Janiki shuddered. It didn't bear thinking about.

The personal messages were interspersed with several ads. Spam, it was called, Janiki had learned in America; spam, as in a kind of fake meat. She remembered suddenly that Caroline had craved spam when she had stayed with the Iyengars, when Asha was a baby. Funny, how an irrelevant memory can suddenly pop into the mind. She left the obvious spam messages and worked her way down the list, reading, then marking the messages as unread. Just in case. Covering her tracks. Obviously, she was even ahead of the police investigation in this respect at least. They didn't have his password. One after the other she rejected the messages as useless. There was talk of a Lotus Pond. It sounded interesting. Was it a bar, a brothel? *You need a password to get in,* someone said. *What is the password? I'd like to join.* The first someone replied: *The password is Dhuan. Smoke.*

She did an Internet search for a Lotus Pond bar or club in Bombay, but there seemed not to be one. Maybe it was a secret place where these men met.

The next one down, sent four days ago, was from a Mr Chaudhuri. Janiki read it, sat up straight as a bolt, and read it again. It was curt, but compelling. And, thought Janiki in triumph, crucial:

She is lovely. I want her.

Janiki grinned to herself as she printed out the message. Just a little more fiddling on the computer, a few more of the tricks she had learned over the last few years, a search in the sent folder, a couple more printouts, and she was ready for the team meeting. She looked at her watch. Just after 2 p.m. Enough time for a short nap; the team meeting was at four, and she now had juice for them. Against one wall of the office was a *charpai.* She lay down. Sleep came in an instant.

* * *

'Janiki! Janiki, wake up!'

She stirred, grunted and opened her eyes. A face hovered within the half-mist of wake-up. Grunting again, she sat up on the *charpai*, rubbing her eyes. 'I could have slept for ever!' she complained. 'Why did you – oh!'

Looking at her watch, she sprang to her feet.

'Exactly!' said Gita. 'Half past four. The rest of the team has been at it for a while – we've been discussing the HIV patients. But we're moving on to Asha now, and you need to be there. Come on.'

'I need a shower,' Janiki said, 'but I'll make do with a splash. Where's the bathroom in this place?'

They left the room and Gita pointed to the bathroom door. 'When you've finished, join us in the conference room. It's opposite the kitchen,' she said. 'Caroline and Kamal are both there already.'

Freshened up, Janiki returned to the office and collected the printouts before joining the others in the main room at the front of the house. There were almost twenty people in the room; Caroline and Kamal sat on a wooden bench at the back. Janiki edged her way in and Caroline moved to the side, making space for her. Dr Ganotra seemed to be leading a lively discussion, but when Janiki entered he looked up and changed the subject abruptly.

'Here she is!' he said. 'We can move on to Asha now – we'll get back to the mobile clinic schedule tomorrow. Team – I wanted you all to be here to meet our newcomers. This is Janiki, from Tamil Nadu; Caroline from America, and Kamal. And these...' His arms swept around the room to indicate all the people sitting there, some on chairs, a few on an old sofa, a few on the floor. 'These are the wonderful people working in the field, on the streets, in the brothels, trying to bring a bit of humanity and caring into the profession, a bit of relief into the suffering. Doctors, nurses, social workers... I won't introduce them by name – you won't remember the names. Some are here professionally, many as volunteers, but all fully dedicated. Now, friends: you've all heard the basics: a little girl, Asha, twelve years old, abducted, lost like so many others and the trail has led to Kamathipura. You know the story. Caroline is her mother and has come all the way from America to find her. Kamal – over there – is her father. She grew up in Tamil Nadu with foster-parents and after their death was mistakenly passed on and presumably sold to a pimp and she's here, somewhere.

'Now, all of you are active on the streets, in the houses. I want you to keep a sharp lookout for this girl. Ask questions; follow leads, however slight.'

'A needle in a haystack,' said a man near the back.

'Yes, we all know that. But sometimes a miracle occurs and we find that needle, and we're going to find this one. And now I'd like to know—'

'Any photos?' said a thin girl sitting near the front.

'Yes,' said Caroline, standing up. She passed a manila envelope to Dr Ganotra. 'These are the most recent photos I have of her, taken a year ago, just before her eleventh birthday. I don't have anything more recent, unfortunately. But—'

Janiki interrupted. 'But I do!' she said triumphantly. 'I have this!'

She held up high an A4 sheet of paper. Everyone looked up. The page showed a grainy black-and-white print of a young girl dressed as a woman, a sari wrapped around her, bangles on her arm, dangling hoops hanging from her ears, studs in her nostrils. An ornate necklace lay beneath her throat. On her face an expression of utter confusion. Her eyes, wide open, showed cold, naked fear. Though Caroline had seen the photo before, during the email exchange with Janiki before they came to Bombay, it was still a shock. Asha, all dolled up. A prostitute in the making.

The photo was passed around, and when it came into her hands Caroline couldn't help it: she burst into tears.

'Where did you get hold of this photo?' someone asked.

'I did a bit of searching on the computer,' Janiki explained. 'It was easy, basically. I still have that Madras fellow's email sign-in details. I checked his sent folder. He sent this photo to a Mr Chaudhuri just over a week ago. Mr Chaudhuri replied, saying he wants her. I checked Mr Chaudhuri's IP: he's in Bombay'

'Well done, Janiki!' said Dr Ganotra. 'It's something to go on – not really much, but something.'

'It's a common name,' said the man at the back. 'Do you know how many Chaudhuris are living in Mumbai? Hundreds, probably, if not thousands. Do you want to go through the entire telephone book?'

'It would take days!' said someone.

'What's an IP?' said the same thin girl.

'And how would we go about it?' interjected the man at the back. 'Call them on the phone and ask them if they molested a girl? Oh yes, that would work beautifully!'

Caroline, voice shaking with tears, said: 'Can't we just give this information to the police?' The room exploded into laughter.

'The police? Really?' said someone. 'You really believe the police will help find some girl? How much do you intend to pay them? More than the pimps are surely paying?'

'Police are corrupt,' said someone with finality. 'No help there.'

The discussion swung around to police corruption and how if anything the police were to be avoided. Finding Asha was up to them, the people in this room. Strategies had to be offered, ideas, suggestions.

'What about the American embassy?' asked someone. 'Surely it's their responsibility to step in?'

Caroline, shaking off her emotion, shook her head. She remembered her resolve. She needed wits, and fortitude, not tears.

'No. I already called them yesterday. They won't help because Asha isn't American. She's Indian. So even though her mother is American it's not their job. They said I have to go to the police.'

Everyone in the room groaned or chuckled or shook their heads or rolled their eyes. Holding the printout against her breast, Caroline stood up.

'May I say something, please?' she said, and without waiting for an answer, continued. 'I think we need to step up our game. Put more effort and urgency into it. My daughter is out there, in jeopardy, and I need to find her. I need to find her, like, yesterday—'

'Yesterday?' interjected the thin girl, frowning. 'How can you find her in the past?'

'It's just an expression,' said Caroline impatiently. 'It means we're working against the clock. She's out there, in danger, in someone's hands, and I want her back. It's all so leisurely here in India, people have no sense of time, it's like a go-with-the-flow hippie thing. Lethargic. I'd like to see a bit more dynamism—'

'Why? What's so special about this girl?' said the man at the back.

'She's my daughter and I want her back!'

'Oh, because she's American, white, or half-white, she's special, is she? Actually every little girl out there is special. Asha is no more special than any other girl. Every girl is some mother's daughter. You're not the only mother who—'

Caroline was silent, but Janiki felt her jerk and cast a surreptitious glance at her; that was harsh. She reached out and took Caroline's hand, lying on the bench between them. Caroline squeezed her hand and Janiki squeezed back.

'Enough, Giri!' said Dr Ganotra, pushing his palm towards the speaker. 'This isn't the time for that. Fact is, Caroline's here, now, and we have a lead. There might be hundreds of Chaudhuris in Mumbai, but not so many interested in young girls. I want you all to keep your ears open and your tongue loose. Ask everyone you meet out there if they've heard of this Chaudhuri. Keep asking.'

'What I wanted to say just now, but I didn't get to finish,' said Caroline, 'is that we need a strategy, a plan. We need ideas! I'd like to have a brainstorming session, and—'

'What's a brainstorming session?' asked the thin girl.

'Your ideas. All your ideas. For instance, my idea is to dye my hair black and get my skin darkened somehow. There must be a way to do that. Maybe a beautician would know, and—'

'Nobody makes themselves darker in India,' said the man at the back. 'Now, if you want a skin-bleaching treatment…'

'Caroline, why do you want to make yourself dark? I don't understand!' said Janiki.

'Well, it's obvious, isn't it? You saw what it was like. When I go out into the streets I stick out like a sore thumb. I can't go looking for Asha looking like some tourist. I'm trying to Indianise myself. I even bought a *shalwar kameez*!'

She plucked at the shoulders of her tunic.

'Yes, I saw that,' said Janiki. 'It suits you. But I still don't understand how looking like an Indian is going to help. You don't speak Hindi or even Tamil. How are you going to search if you can't even talk to people?'

Caroline did not immediately answer, and in the gap Gita spoke up.

'My idea actually is that you stay American, but we give you a *legend*. That's what it's called, isn't it, in your spy novels. We say you're a journalist, and one of us goes with you to the brothels where we know they keep young girls and say you are writing an article for an American magazine and want to talk to people about the work.'

'But why would they talk to us? Surely they would be suspicious and tight-lipped?'

'Not if you pay them! Find the right people, the ladies in charge of the younger girls, and offer them money. They'll talk. I bet. Just use your wits.'

'That's an excellent idea,' said Dr Ganotra. 'Anything else? Kamal?'

'I have two ideas,' said Kamal slowly. 'One is to hire a private detective. And the other – well, it's not something I'm keen on doing. But it might work. What if I pose as a client looking for young girls myself? Ask to be put in touch with… girls like Asha?'

He grimaced as he said the last words, and Janiki felt for him. Their eyes locked.

'It's a good idea,' she said, 'if you can do it.'

'I must,' he said. 'It's about the only thing I can do.'

'Sudesh, maybe you can help him there. Introduce him to your contacts, let him infiltrate the trade as a client.'

The man addressed as Sudesh nodded.

Others from Dr Ganotra's team offered their own suggestions and wrote down addresses on pieces of paper; the man at the back threw cold water on every suggestion, and the thin girl asked question after question. The team members were to go out there and keep asking, find a lead to Mr Chaudhuri. Kamal would pose as a client looking for a sweet young virgin, superior quality. Caroline would go with Gita, posing as a journalist writing a story on Kamathipura, bribing her way into the brothels, asking for access to the youngest girls. Money, she said, would be no object; her husband Wayne was behind her all the way and would wire her as much as she needed. There were other suggestions. Each one was thoroughly discussed, considered, and either rejected or accepted as a possibility.

'What will you do, Janiki?' asked Caroline.

'Since I don't think I'll be much use on the streets or in the brothels – I don't even speak Hindi,' said Janiki, 'I'll do what I've always done: surf the Internet, find clues there. I feel a bit cowardly…'

'Janiki, you're the only one here who's made any progress at all, and it's all been at the computer. Don't feel bad; you've been great. Maybe you can crack the code. More and more detectives in America solve problems from the comfort of their own office. You've been great!'

'Thanks,' said Janiki. 'So I guess that's it. When do we start? Tonight?'

Dr Ganotra raised his voice.

'Meeting's over,' he said. 'I'd like to hold a short *puja* before we disperse. That our work may be blessed.'

Several people nodded; Dr Ganotra lit a small oil lamp at a shrine set into an alcove in the brick wall, and some sticks of incense. People stood up and gathered around him for *arati*, flame-waving worship. Dr Ganotra raised his voice, strong and deep, in the *arati* song, 'Jai Jagadisha Hare'. Others joined in as he lit a piece of camphor on a metal plate, slowly waved the flame before the shrine, passed the plate on to the next person. The plate passed from person to person; each one waved it before the shrine. Caroline shook her head as it came to her, so Janiki took it. Waving the flame, she closed her eyes and spoke a silent prayer before passing on the plate.

The *puja* ceremony ended; people from the team began to mill around, checking their watches, saying their goodbyes. Through the open window the sounds of the Mumbai evening were growing louder: horns honking, sirens, the steady growl of traffic. The day was coming to a close. The team member called Sudesh approached Kamal and spoke a few words with him; Kamal said goodbye to Janiki and Caroline and the two men left together.

Gita said to Caroline, 'Now isn't a good time to start. Their work day is just about to begin; no good asking for interviews now. Go back to your hotel; get all the rest you can and we start work tomorrow.'

Caroline looked relieved, as if released from a nasty obligation. Janiki felt more and more respect for her. Clearly out of her depth in Bombay, Caroline was still doing her best to overcome her natural revulsion and sense of alienation. It was touching, how she had bought herself a *shalwar kameez*. And now, Janiki saw with a smile, Caroline had even smeared *vibhuti*, sacred ash, on her forehead, and wore a *bindi*, the red dot made of turmeric paste and lime, on her forehead. She was adjusting, adapting, shedding her American alienation to work with them all. The man at the back had been quite rude, and at times Caroline had seemed ready to either explode in anger or break down in tears. But she had rallied, calmed down, and now she was one of them.

Tomorrow their work would begin.

Their task seemed futile. Impossible. She closed her eyes again. *Let the impossible be possible,* she prayed. Her fingers itched; she flexed them, clawing the air. *Back to the computer.*

Chapter Thirty-Nine

Janiki

An hour later, Janiki shut down the computer and stood up, stretching her arms and legs. It was no good. She was hungry. She hadn't eaten since breakfast time; she had simply forgotten to, but hunger now gnawed at her innards and she could no longer ignore it. She was tired, too. *I'll grab a bite*, she said to herself, a*nd then go home and use the hotel's computer room and do some more research*. It was all getting so interesting…

She had noticed a restaurant near her hotel, Ashaak*;* she'd go there.

Downstairs, the house was silent; but a murmur of sound came from the upper floor. Janiki decided to pay a quick visit to the girls up there, and to Subhadai, before going out. Where was Dr Ganotra? Out working in the field, no doubt. The man never seemed to rest.

The sounds grew louder as she climbed the stairs. The new girl, Sakhi, had been put into the room next to Ratna. The rooms had a connecting door, which was open so they could be together if they so wished. Both rooms were empty. The sounds came from behind the closed door of another room. Janiki knocked on the door, tried the handle, pushed gently. The door opened a crack; she put her head around it and saw what had been making the sounds: a TV set, on a table against the wall, with some kind of a romantic story unfolding across the flickering screen. Across the room, sitting on the floor, the three girls and Subhadai. The latter sprang to her feet as Janiki opened the door wider and stepped inside.

'You want watch TV?' she said. 'Come, come, sit down, I have chair only. Bringing from kitchen.'

'No, no, that's all right. I just wanted to say goodbye, but…' Janiki smiled and gestured to the girls, whose gazes had stayed glued to the screen. 'I won't disturb you. I'm going now; see you tomorrow. Goodbye! Goodbye everyone!'

She waved, but no one waved back; she and Subhadai exchanged *pranaams* and she walked back down the stairs. It was good for the girls to find distraction in videos, she thought, but ultimately what were they going to do with them? They still needed help: some kind of therapy, some kind of healing for the agony they had been through. She'd think of all that once they found Asha.

She opened the front door to step into the street, looking at her watch.

'Hey, Janiki, look where you're going!' said a familiar voice, and she looked up. It was Kamal, standing in the street.

'Oh. Hi!' she said. 'Sorry – I – are you back already? I thought…'

'Tomorrow,' said Kamal. 'The fellow we were supposed to meet is busy tonight. Gives me a bit more time to prepare I suppose.' He grimaced. 'Where are you off to?'

'Going to grab a bite to eat, then back to my hotel, probably. What about you? What are you doing here?'

'I came to get my bag. I stayed at the Taj last night – Caroline insisted – but I want to move out. What's your hotel like? Do they have room? Is it far away?'

'Probably, yes,' said Janiki. 'It's about half an hour from here. I'll take you there, if you like, and you can ask.'

'Fine. Let me just get my stuff.'

He slipped into the hallway and into the kitchen, returning with a small backpack slung over one shoulder.

'Are you hungry? I was just about to go for a meal.'

'Very,' he replied. 'I'll come and eat with you – if you don't mind?'

'Of course not,' she said, and to herself added, *not at all. Quite the contrary.* Their eyes met, and Janiki had the distinct feeling that Kamal read that thought, because he smiled a secret smile, and so she smiled back; but he had already turned away, and was trying to flag down a taxi on the busy street. And so she did the same. It was a while before one stopped, and they both got in.

'Whew,' said Janiki as she slid along the back seat to make room for him. 'Bombay traffic is even worse than in Madras. It sounds impossible but it's true.'

She leaned forward and showed the driver her hotel's card. He nodded and drove off.

'We'd probably be there quicker if we walked,' said Kamal after ten minutes of stop-and-go driving.

'True – I came this morning early and it wasn't so bad. It took half an hour. With this traffic, though, it'll be twice as long.'

'Well – I suggest we find a place to eat nearby, and then go to the hotel later, when the traffic is maybe a bit better.'

'Yes, let's do that. You talk to the driver, ask him to take us somewhere good nearby.'

Kamal leaned forward and exchanged a few words in Hindi with the driver, who nodded and turned on his indicator. This new street was less congested, and after a few more traffic lights, a few more minutes of standstill and crawling, they arrived at a brightly lit restaurant. The taxi stopped, they emerged, Kamal paid and they entered the restaurant, where a waiter in a white jacket showed them to a free table and handed them menu cards.

'Wow – this is a bit fancier than I expected,' said Janiki.

'My treat,' said Kamal. 'I owe you so much. I can't even begin to thank you. Coming all this way to help…'

'Why should you thank me at all? I love Asha. I am her chin-na-amma. I raised her like my own child, even though I was really a child myself. I need to find her as much as you and Caroline. I feel terribly responsible for what happened. I should never have left her with Paruthy Uncle. I need to find her too!' Tears stung her eyes and she raised her menu card so he would not see.

Kamal laid a comforting hand on her wrist.

'We have to. We just have to,' she said, almost sobbing.

'We will.'

They were both silent then, inspecting the menu cards.

Then Janiki looked up and began:

'The thing is, Kamal—' She stopped, chuckled, and said, 'I hope you don't mind me calling you Kamal. Somehow I can't call you Kamal Uncle any more!'

He laughed. And it was the most open, natural, relaxed thing he had done since she'd first seen him here in Bombay, and she couldn't help but laugh out loud too. And in that moment of laughter their eyes met and something surged in her and she could only call it joy – a deliciously warm, utterly satiating sense of completeness; joy, expelling for the moment the gloom and despair that had held her in its grip, banishing the exhausting sense of futility that had nagged at her throughout the day. All that darkness fled in the instant that their eyes met; they were as one, aligned, lifted up together in this one moment of freedom from anguish.

'Don't you ever call me Kamal Uncle again!' said Kamal. His words shattered the spell, and at the same time established a new intimacy that warmed her from tip to toe. They regarded each other with smiling eyes for a moment longer, and then the waiter appeared and took their orders and everything was back to normal; except it wasn't.

Meals ordered, they looked at each other again. Janiki thought it was her turn to speak, but she didn't know what to say and suddenly it felt awkward – how do you deal with such a sudden and silent rapport with someone you don't really know at all? Does one make small talk, or get down to discussing the serious issue that engulfed them both? Should they talk about personal matters: his life, her life? But then Kamal solved the problem by speaking first.

'So what do you do all day on that computer?' he said. 'It's almost like your best friend.'

She chuckled wryly. 'You're sort of right. I can't stay away from a computer for too long. But you have to admit it's been useful. Look where we are! Everything we know about Asha, we found out through a computer and the Internet.'

'Yes, but what are you actually *doing?*'

'Same thing you all are doing: searching for Asha.'

'In a computer?'

She nodded. 'Digging. Following leads. Analysing. It's quite fascinating what you can find.'

'For instance?'

'Well, for instance, I've tried to find some access to online communities that traffic in children in India. I thought maybe I could discreetly ask around for this Mr Chaudhuri. I thought maybe these people know each other and exchange knowledge. So I managed to get into a chat room and I am there right now, just listening at the moment.'

'What's a chat room?'

'Well, it's what it sounds like – a gathering of people talking, just like in real life, except that you don't see each other, and they chat in writing instead of talking. It's called the Lotus Pond. A secret room. It was very hard to find, but I did in the end. Everybody has a secret ID and they discuss whatever they want to discuss. You can pretend to be someone quite different. You basically make up a character and then chat away.'

'What do you chat about?'

'Girls, of course. The younger the better. Occasionally boys. It's pretty disgusting, I can tell you.'

'So you have a secret ID in this chat room?'

'Yes. But I haven't written anything yet. I'm just lurking, as they call it. Eavesdropping. I made myself a male ID. My chat-room name is Foreigner.'

'Why Foreigner?'

She shrugged. 'It's just a stupid ID name, a handle. Everyone has silly handles. One guy calls himself Moviestar, and another is Millionaire. Some just have place-name names like BombayBoy or MrBengal, or even a real name like Ashok. It's play-acting in a way. Foreigner just popped into my head because I feel so foreign here now. This place – what am I doing here? It's not me. But I have to find Asha!'

He nodded. 'I know. I'm a foreigner too, in my own task. It's all so – alien. I'm dreading tomorrow night when I have to do some real life play-acting.'

'What are you going to be doing?'

'Sudesh has discreetly put me in touch with some fellow who deals in young girls – a pimp, I guess, though they didn't use that word. I'm supposed to be a foreign-returned Indian visiting Bombay who's looking for action with very young girls, prefer-ably foreign-looking, fair-skinned. It's grim. Horrible. But this guy, this pimp knows all the networks and I'm hoping that this Mr Chaudhuri is one of his contacts and – well, it's all very vague. I'm going to have to play it by ear.'

'What if they take you to a real girl and it's not Asha?'

Kamal shuddered. 'It turns my stomach.'

They were both silent for a moment, contemplating the hor-ror of it all. A young girl, who wasn't Asha, caught up in a net of iniquity. A girl, every bit as precious, every bit as lost; but not Asha. Kamal would have to walk away...

'And that's not the only problem, Kamal.'

She paused.

'Yes?'

'You'd never convince them. You just don't look like that sort of a man.'

'What sort of a man?'

'You know. Rough. Ruthless. A man who would – rape – a young girl. Anyone could tell at a glance.'

'I'll just have to act really well then. I used to be a good actor, back in the day. As for my looks – there's a profession called make-up artist. Actors use them all the time.'

'Still – you can't change your eyes, Kamal. Your eyes show who you are. They show kindness.'

'You're saying I'm a wimp? A softy-wofty?'

'No. A good man,' she said, almost whispering. 'A caring man. A man who would do anything in the world to save his daughter.'

Again, their eyes met. Again, that sweet warmth washed through her.

'That's not weakness, Kamal,' she added, 'it's strength. A quiet strength, but a strength all the same. The mistake you men make is that you think strength is domination, control, bullying, even. It's not. Compassion is the true strength.'

'I know that, Janiki. I was just teasing. I know that strength. It's why women are the stronger sex after all. That old maligned role of nourisher, carer: it has made them so very strong.'

'And you are like that; and you're going to need every bit of it in the role you've chosen to play. Going into the dragon's den, pretending to be a dragon yourself...' She shuddered.

'A man's got to do what a man's got to do, as they say in America.'

'I guess I have the easy task, sitting at a desk tapping stuff into a computer. But I do think that's the best task for me, Kamal. I'm not trying to avoid the real-life things you and Caroline are doing out there. It's just what I'm good at, and it does bring results.

'Like in this chat room, if I ever decide to come out of hiding – it's called de-lurking – I can do the same thing you're doing: I can say I'm looking for a foreign-looking young girl, fair-skinned, English-speaking. One of the reasons I chose Foreigner as my nickname is that I don't speak Hindi and a lot of the chat is in Hindi, or half-Hindi half-English. So if I ever de-lurk I'm going to say I'm foreign-returned and living in Bombay but my native tongue is Tamil and that's why I can only chat in English. English is the one language that connects us all in India, wherever we live. It's the one good thing the Raj left behind.'

'Supposedly,' said Kamal. 'So, basically, we're doing the same thing, just that you're doing it behind a screen and I have to go out there and face the real horror of Kamathipura.'

Janiki nodded. 'I'm sorry. It sounds so cowardly. But trust me, it works. We wouldn't even be here at all if it wasn't for computers and Internet.'

'I'm not blaming you. You're actually getting results, unlike the rest of us. But—'

'Kamal! I just had an idea! A brilliant one!'

'Yes?'

'Why don't we combine tactics? Why doesn't Foreigner come out of lurking, start talking in the chat room, say that he's a foreign-returned Indian looking for that kind of girl – what if the people behind Asha contact Foreigner, and we set up a date, and then YOU turn up, as Foreigner?'

'But how will we know it's Asha I'm meeting?'

'Trust me, that's how it works. People chat online and make connections and then they connect privately through direct messages and arrange meetings and so on. The things I've seen, Kamal – it would make you sick. One man offered his own daughter! Can you believe it!'

'Believe me, I can. But—'

'Listen, Kamal, it's brilliant. I'll pose as a very rich foreign-returned, OK? Build up a whole identity for Foreigner: back from America, an engineer, mid-thirties – describe the real-life you. And then I describe the kind of young girl I want. And I bet there aren't many girls like her in Bombay. I bet I'll get some offers. I'll then set up direct messaging. If people offer me girls like that, I'll ask for a snapshot. I can always say I don't like the snaps, until Asha turns up. And when she does, I set up the meeting. And you go and get her. Somehow.'

'It sounds good, Janiki. But it'd take days. Weeks, even!'

'None of us has anything that will be any quicker. Looking through the telephone directory for the right Chaudhuri? Posing as a journalist? Pretending to be a customer? All of those tactics could take days or weeks. My method, at least it sorts the wheat from the chaff in advance. You don't know for sure if this guy you're going to meet has Asha, do you? You're just guessing?'

'Well, yes. But…'

'But my idea is quicker, much quicker. People can hide online the way they can't in real life. I'm telling you, the Internet is going to explode in the next few years with all the possibilities. It's connecting the whole world, strangers chatting and getting to know each other without ever leaving their homes. My way, I can maybe dig right down to the centre of things. These people are savvy, Kamal; they work with the latest methods now because that's where the money is. They are all online. It's big business. Everyone keeps saying that finding Asha is like looking for a needle in a haystack; well, I'll tell you this, if anything can find a needle in a haystack, it's a computer!'

'If you say so. But I still need to keep that appointment tomorrow, right?'

'Of course. And tomorrow I'll get up bright and early and get moving as Foreigner.'

By now they had finished their meal. Kamal summoned the waiter, and paid.

'So, what are you doing now?'

'Going back to my hotel, I suppose. And you wanted to check in there, didn't you?'

He nodded. 'And then?'

'Well, I was thinking of the internet shop near the hotel. Do some more research.'

'Can't it wait till tomorrow? Have you been to Juhu Beach yet?'

'No, of course not. I basically went straight to Tulasa House.'

'Shall we go there now? Go for a walk, stretch our legs? You need to get away from that computer, Janiki. Let's do that.'

She nodded. 'OK. And anyway, there's some more things I wanted to talk to you about.'

'Really? Sounds mysterious. What?'

She shook her head. 'Later. Let's go.'

Chapter Forty

Asha

The lady came with me in the car, and it was night. We sat in the back seat. It was a big nice car, but most of the time it was stuck in traffic. Bombay streets are full of cars. Cars everywhere and they move so slowly and always blowing horns. It would be quicker to walk, I thought, but maybe it was too far.

The streets got narrower and narrower and then the driver stopped and the lady said we have to get out. She got out first and grabbed my wrist and almost pulled me out. She did not let go of my wrist. Come with me, she said, and led me into a narrow street. It was too narrow for the car – that was why we had to walk. It was a strange street. The houses loomed over the road and the upstairs windows were lit with red lights. And women sat at these windows, behind bars, looking down at the street. On the street practically everyone was a man. Except in the doorways to the houses. There was a horrible smell everywhere and loud music coming from the doorways. People stared at us as the lady led me down the street, still tightly holding my wrist. I wanted to run away and she must have known that and that was why she held my wrist so tightly.

I will show you what happens to bad girls, she had told me earlier that day. *I will show you. You have a week to reconsider. Mr Chaudhuri is a good man; you are such a fortunate girl, why are you being so stubborn? I will show you what will happen to you if you do not behave. You will live in that place for a week. If you do not learn to behave and obey that is where you will stay for ever.*

I had such a bad feeling about that place, that street, those houses. People kept staring at me and I did not like it. A rat ran across the road and almost ran across my feet. I screamed and the lady shouted at me. *Shut up,* she said. *You asked for this. You think a rat on the street is bad? What about a rat in your room, licking your fingers when you sleep because it smells the food you have been eating with your bare hands, and you did not have enough water to wash? What about the cockroaches scurrying across the floor and you hear their tiny footprints in your dreams? When you have been here just one night you will be begging me to go back to Mr Chaudhuri. It is then you will appreciate how fortunate you are that he wants you.*

But I did not feel fortunate to have the choice between the Bengali and this terrible place. What kind of a choice was that? I did not belong here. I belonged with Janiki. And all the time I screamed for Janiki. But it was a silent scream.

I felt all cold inside and scared. The place seemed to be closing in on me and I could not escape because it was all around and the lady was holding my wrist so tightly. And people were looking at me and pointing and laughing and the smell was so strong I could hardly breathe.

And then we entered a house, a narrow doorway where a woman squatting in the entrance spoke to the lady in Hindi and handed her something, I didn't see what it was, and we went in. We passed by some other women standing or sitting on the floor in that narrow corridor. It was lit by a string of small blinking red lights. At the back there was a staircase leading up. The staircase was very narrow so she walked sideways, in front of me, still grabbing my wrist. Her fingernails were long and they dug into my flesh. It hurt.

And then up another staircase and another. We had to be at the top of the house by now. And then a narrow hallway, and then we stopped at a door. There was a padlock on it. The lady produced a key and unlocked the door and opened it, and pulled me in behind her. The lady pressed a switch on the wall and a bulb hanging from the ceiling lit up the place behind the door.

It was a small narrow room with some old bedding on the floor in a corner, and a pot with a cover on it. That was all there was in the room. The floor was dirty. It had not been swept for months or years. There were piles of dust on the floor and red smears on the floor, which was of old faded lino. There was no window. All the light came from that single light bulb, which was dirty. And the air was close and stinking.

This is your new home, she said. *Isn't it lovely?* And she laughed.

She pointed to the covered pot. *That is your toilet. Someone will bring meals. Now while you sit here pondering your life you can consider whether you prefer to go to Mr Chaudhuri and be nice to him, speak English and just be kind and loving and feminine the way he wants. Think about it. You have seven days. But of course if you want to return to him tomorrow, because you cannot stand this place, you are welcome. Just tell one of your keepers, and I will come and get you. Mr Chaudhuri will be so pleased.*

And she left me there in that room and it was just as she had said with the rats and the cockroaches. But I did not say I wanted to go to Mr Chaudhuri. How could I ever be nice to a man like that?

Chapter Forty-One

Caroline

Despondency clung to her like a shroud as she picked up the receiver and punched in the US number.

'Hi, Wayne.'

'Sweetheart! At last! How are you? Where are you? What's going on? Is she OK?'

'Sorry to call you at the office. The time difference makes things difficult – that's why I didn't call sooner.'

'Honey – you can call me any time. Middle of the night, any time. So tell me? Have you found her? How is she? When are you coming home?'

'Oh Wayne – she's – she's… No, I haven't found her. Wayne, I've lost her. She's lost. I'm in Bombay, trying to find her, but, but… Oh Wayne!' And she burst into tears.

'She's been abducted! Stolen! She's here in Bombay and they want to sell her as a child prostitute! Oh Wayne! What am I going to do!'

'Damn! Honey! Look, we need to talk. You need to tell me but, damn, this is the wrong time – I'm due in court in half an hour and…'

'It's all right. I'll be all right. I'm sorry. I'll call again and tell you everything. Or write an email. Yes, I'll do that. It'll calm me down.'

'Honey – are they demanding a ransom? Listen – you still have your HSBC account in India, right? I'll put some money on there

– a few hundred grand. Whatever they ask, you pay it. I will make arrangements – I have contacts to the US ambassador to India. And Dad knows the CEO of HSBC. We'll work it out. Send me an email to let me know the details. I'll arrange everything. We will get her back. Don't worry. Honey, I have to rush now but I'll get my secretary to wire over the money. Bye honey.'

And he was gone. That was Wayne all over. Always too busy. Never time for her. Thinking that money and contacts and pulling strings were all that was needed to get through life. But it wasn't. If only he would actually come, join her here, help search for Asha… but he never would. Too busy.

And what would happen when this was over? If – no, *when* – they found Asha would Wayne accept her? Would he be a father to her? Did she even *want* Wayne as father to Asha? And what would she and Kamal do? Kamal would also want Asha. She wasn't about to fight for custody. She was far too tired. She couldn't handle it, and it certainly wouldn't be good for Asha, who'd certainly come away from this with a trauma to be healed. But she was a therapist; that was her job. Asha would be fine with her. But what about Kamal? The best thing, Caroline thought, would be for her and Kamal to get back together again. Be a family again, in America.

Caroline went to the bathroom and splashed her face with cold water. She looked in the mirror. She looked terrible, terrible. But no wonder. After today, after this evening, walking the labyrinthine streets of Kamathipura yet again, this time with Gita, the futile interviews, the fake smiles, the wads of money handed out so that the women would talk, seeing those women, those girls, some so young, so very young, so resigned to their fate, the blank stares, the hardened faces, the dull eyes; knowing that Asha was lined up to join their ranks or maybe, maybe – she forced herself to think it – maybe *already was* one of them.

It didn't bear thinking about. She wished she had someone to talk to. Janiki. Kamal. Where were they anyway? Kamal had checked out of the Raj early that morning, to look for a less fancy place, he said. Where was he? The three of them should be together, comforting and supporting each other. This city – it devoured strangers, and that's what they all were. Here she was, facing the greatest challenge of her life, and she was all alone. Even Gita had disappeared, gone back home to her husband and children. There was no one to talk to.

And she needed desperately to talk. To confess her blistering sense of guilt. Because she was guilty. Completely guilty. This was all her fault. She had abandoned Asha when she was still a toddler; rushed back to America and never returned for her daughter. She remembered Kamal's words: we will return to America. I will get a job there, no problem. We'll take Asha and be a real family, anywhere you like. If you prefer to go to work, you can do that and I'll look after her. I know it's hard, but tough it out for a few months more, Caro. Just a few months more. But she had gone back and moved in with her parents and fallen in love with Wayne and had an affair and abandoned Asha. And this was the direct result of that abandonment. Of course she was guilty. And there was no one to confess to. No one to grant absolution. Maybe Kamal was angry with her still, and that's why he had disappeared. Maybe Janiki blamed her. Both of them knew what she had done. Both of them must hate her. Because now the little girl they all adored was lost in the worst hellhole on earth.

Her very clothes stank of Kamathipura. It was in her hair, her skin. She tore the blue *shalwar kameez* from her body, shoved it into the rubbish bin. Maybe a maid would salvage it tomorrow; she didn't care. Naked, she stepped into the shower. She stood under the gushing water for ages. Washed her hair, scrubbed her skin. The shower gel and shampoo on offer from the Taj smelt delicious. If only she could wash away her thoughts, make them smell sweet. Maybe she could. She would try to meditate afterwards. She was hungry, but didn't think she could eat. Her stomach was churning; she'd probably throw up everything. She needed to *talk!*

* * *

After drying her hair and putting on a new *shalwar kameez*, she made her way down to the hotel lobby and asked for the Internet room. Found a computer, found her mail account and began typing. Telling Wayne the whole story might, perhaps, help. She began at the beginning, with the soul-destroying visit to Gingee. By the time she got to the discovery that Asha had been removed from the house in Madras, however, she began to lose control. Tears rolled down her cheek; she wiped them away with her *dupatta* and typed on. Now and then she sniffed as her nose began to run, but still she typed on.

Someone tapped her on her shoulder. She looked up; it was a man, an Indian man, late thirties, smiling at her. He brandished a handkerchief.

'I'm at the next computer,' he said. His accent was British, cut glass. 'I hope I'm not being interfering, but I thought you could use this, instead of that lovely shawl.'

She looked up at him with anguish spilling from her eyes, still immersed in her story, not quite hearing.

'What did you say?'

'I thought you might like a hanky,' he said. 'I couldn't help but hear you crying. I'm sorry if...'

'Oh. Thanks.' She took the handkerchief and snorted loudly into it.

'Keep it,' he said, stepping away, and Caroline turned back to the keyboard and her typing, now crying openly, sniffing and snorting and blowing into the handkerchief, and somehow it all helped, telling Wayne everything and crying and blowing her nose, and she stood up just a little bit unburdened. Maybe she could, after all, eat now. Just a snack.

She left the computer room. The handkerchief man was waiting for her outside, sitting in a chair beside the door and reading a newspaper.

'Hello again,' he said, smiling. 'I was worried about you. You seem so distressed – is there anything I can do to help?'

'No,' she replied. 'Nobody can help me.'

'But it's not good to be alone with one's distress. Would you join me for a drink? A glass of good wine can work wonders.'

'No,' she said again. 'No thank you. I'm heading for the restaurant, for a snack.'

'Well, may I join you there? I don't like the idea of a lady being alone with so much sorrow.'

Caroline thought for a moment. Why not? All that lay in front of her was food and drink and then bed with some novel or other and the anguish gnawing away at her mind preventing her from understanding a word. Maybe a little distraction would help.

'OK,' she said.

She had an omelette and a glass of wine, and then another glass, and learned that his name was Hiran and he was a businessman in Mumbai on business and flying home to London a few days later. And he was nice and ready to listen, so she told him the whole story and he commiserated and comforted and supported her and reassured her that of course she would find Asha, of course she would, and if he could help in any way he would, but in the meantime she needed to take care of herself, seek relief, release the tension. He slipped his business card across the table, gold-rimmed. Hiran Kapur was his full name.

'I have the day off tomorrow, doing some sightseeing,' he said. 'It's my first time in Mumbai. I was born and bred in England. Why don't you come with me, relax a bit?'

'No,' said Caroline. 'I've got to look for Asha.'

'You have to think of yourself as well,' he said. 'Take care of yourself. You're a wreck. You need to relax.'

'It's all my fault. That's why I'm a wreck,' mumbled Caroline, sipping her wine. She told him that part of the story, how she had abandoned Asha. She confessed her guilt. It felt good to talk about it but it wasn't enough. She needed absolution.

'It's not your fault,' said Hiran, but the words sounded hollow, repeated from a thousand pseudo-psychological movies. People could repeat a thousand times that it wasn't your fault, but if you *knew* what you'd done, the words couldn't undo it.

'I need to go to bed,' she said, standing up, swaying slightly.

'Why not come to my room, and enjoy a bit more wine and some music? It will help release the tension.'

'So that's what this was all about,' she said, turned her back and walked off.

Hiram grabbed her elbow. 'Wait!' he cried. 'I didn't mean—'

Caroline shook him off, turned to face him. 'Yes, you did!' she spat. 'Everything else, all that friendliness, was just a run-up to this, wasn't it? Poor needy American lady needs man, right? Easy Western woman, right? Well: not this one!'

She marched off. *Men!* she thought. *That's all they ever think about.* She would have liked to give him a slap, but what remained of her dignity would not allow it.

She went back to her room, stripped again and dived between the sheets. No book. No TV. Just sleep, and forgetting. Tomorrow Gita was picking her up early. Tomorrow she'd be that fake journalist again. She'd have to get some more cash. Bribing those brothel women was expensive. She fell asleep the moment her head touched the pillow.

* * *

The next day dawned. Gita picked her up as promised and, just as Kamathipura began to come to life, they began the same old routine: stopping at the brothels, introducing Caroline as a journalist, talking to the women, Caroline asking the questions in English and Gita translating into Hindi, and then, when the women talked, the same in reverse.

The questions were always the same. First the general introduction and enquiries. How many girls work here? What ages are they? Where do they come from? How long have they been here? And then the specifics. Any Tamil-speaking girls? English-speaking? Educated girls? High-class girls? Could Caroline interview any of them? For more cash, of course.

Always cash. One thing Caroline had learned by the end of the day: money talked. The cliché was quite true. But in this case, the talk was invariably empty.

She returned to her hotel more despondent than ever, and alone as ever. A shower, a meal, a siesta. And then the phone rang. Wayne, perhaps; it would be his lunch break now. He'd have read her email and was calling to commiserate.

But it wasn't Wayne.

It was Janiki, breathless.

Chapter Forty-Two

Janiki

Mumbai traffic being what it was, it was almost ten when their motor-rickshaw reached Juhu Beach. Despite the late hour it was still crowded with people. The vendors were out, briskly selling veg biryani, samosas, Bombay chaats and other local specialties.

'Care for some dessert?' asked Kamal, and when Janiki nodded, bought two ice *golas* and handed her one: a crushed ice lollipop covered with flavoured juices.

All around them, families were out enjoying the night breeze. The beach was well lit, and the women's saris shone in the lamps' glow like bright moving jewels. People sitting, walking, some running; groups of friends, couples canoodling, children playing or sleeping on their mothers' laps. It was hard to believe that this was the same city; that such a relaxed and joyous community could harbour the evil that had swallowed Asha. That's India, thought Janiki; the juxtaposition of extremes. The highest bliss and the deepest misery. Abject poverty next to fabulous wealth. Shining saintliness next to darkest evil. And everything in between.

Licking their *golas*, they walked out towards the sea; black waves touched with ripples of frothing white surf lapping at the sand; a cool breeze playing with her hair and her *dupatta*.

It was perfect. A bubble of delight stolen from the anguish that defined her life right now, and his.

'So what did you want to talk about?' asked Kamal after a while.

'Your grandmother,' said Janiki.

He stiffened, and looked at her abruptly.

'My grandmother? What do you know about my grandmother?'

'I met her,' said Janiki. 'I'm sorry; I haven't had a chance to tell you yet – everything's been about Asha up to now. I was looking for you when Asha first went missing and I had no contact details, nothing at all. But I remembered Amma being so impressed that you were actually a prince, and—'

'I'm not,' said Kamal, cutting in. 'Don't go repeating that nonsense.'

'Kamal, I know you reject—'

'You listened to her lies? Yes, they are all lies. We are not a royal family. Not a drop of our blood is blue. No maharajas and maharanis. It's all a huge big lie. What happened is this: we're a very wealthy family. We're from a long line of silk merchants; we made all kinds of silk, but our speciality was and is patola silk. Patola-weaving is a closely guarded family tradition; only a few families know how to do it. It can take six months to one year to make a single sari; that's how precious the silk is. In the past it was only royalty that wore patola silk; it's still only the fabulously wealthy. Anyway. A few generations back one of the Indian royal families was getting poor and so they married one of my ancestors. That's the whole story. That's our only link to royalty. All this talk of maharajas and the Maharani of Jaipur and her wedding – it's just stupid boasting. Daadi is a fake, Janiki. That's why I cut all ties with her.'

'She said it was because she was trying to arrange your marriage.'

'Nonsense. Why would I be annoyed for that reason? It's normal in India, and all I had to do was ignore her. Which I did. I married Caroline, didn't I? No, Janiki, marriage wasn't the reason. When I was in America I did the research and discovered who we really are. That she had tried to raise me on a pack of lies. Made my childhood miserable. I was so furious – I wrote her a letter and told her not to contact me ever again. And went my own way. I had a trust fund, still have it, for that matter, though I've not needed it for a long time. It's for Asha. No – I just couldn't deal with the lie. She tried to brainwash me with it when I was just a boy, kept me practically imprisoned in the palace – which by the way was never a real palace. Just a huge luxurious home some ancestor built a long time ago. She fed me all that nonsense about being a prince, and by the way, all those women she tried to marry me off to – she fed them the lie as well. Her dishonesty is what enraged me, and she knows it. She just won't admit to anyone, not even to herself, that she isn't royalty. She's crazy.'

'She's just an old woman who's very lonely, Kamal. I mean, why would she make up such a huge fiction? Surely it can only be because she feels insecure? She's desperate for contact with you. Did you know she's been following you around with the help of private detectives, all this time? She knew exactly where to find you. She even called your office in Dubai while I was there. I bet she's got a detective following us right now. That's how obsessed she is. And she's interested in Asha, too, Kamal. That's what I wanted to say. Why don't we get this private detective of hers to help? She's dying for you to make contact. And one day she will die, Kamal. Her health isn't at all good. You should make up with her before she dies. You really should.'

All through Janiki's little speech Kamal had repeatedly tried to interrupt, but she had just ploughed on. She had to have her say. She paused slightly now to take a breath, which she knew would give him a chance to speak up, but he didn't, and so she just continued.

'It's not good to harbour resentment for so many years, Kamal. It's not good for your mental health. It just gnaws away inside you and it's not good. Like a little leech that won't let go. You should contact her. Reconcile. It would do you good. I promise. You know, this might sound strange, but I feel sorry for her. I really do. She's really lonely, stuck in that palace with her Bollywood movies and her luxury and not being able to walk and having to be cared for. She's just a disabled old woman.'

'A fat disabled old woman.'

'She probably got fat because she's so unhappy. And then it becomes a vicious circle; you eat and you get fat and you get unhappy and you eat because you're unhappy and you get fat. It's no reason to hate her.'

'I don't hate her. It was anger, not hate, that caused the rift.'

'Well then. If you don't hate her it's time to cool down the anger. It's high time, Kamal. You shouldn't nurse anger for so many years. It's really unhealthy.'

'You're quite a little guru, aren't you?'

'It's just common sense. That's all it is. Anyone could tell you that.'

'So you take her side, do you?'

There was a smile in his voice now, and Janiki knew she had won. Still, she had to make her point clear.

'It's not a question of taking sides. I'm just telling you what would be good for you.'

'Hmmm. Still, she seems to have won you over. What else did she tell you?'

It was Janiki's turn to smile.

'Promise you won't take this the wrong way?'

'Promise.'

'She thought I should marry you.'

He laughed out loud. 'Typical! So typical. And what did you say to that?'

'I told her you were too old for me.'

'What! Are you out of your mind? Old? Me?'

She chuckled, and shrugged. '*Too* old, not old. I also told her I was already engaged.'

'Really? I didn't know that.'

'Well, I was. He broke it off just after I got to Bombay.'

'He broke it off? Really? Why? Stupid fellow! A lovely woman like you, caring and wise and educated as well? What more could he want?'

'I guess he was more traditional than I thought. His parents weren't keen any more. Not since my parents died. They wanted a big wedding, which my parents would have provided, and also the fact that I was actually an orphan – they thought it was bad luck. They talked him into breaking it off.'

'So it was an arranged marriage? I wouldn't have thought…'

'No – it was a love marriage. I mean, it was going to be a love marriage. But of course our parents discussed it and approved and all that Indian stuff. You can never really get away from it. We did care for each other. We were going to get married when I returned from America.'

'So are you very upset?'

'To be honest, no. He told me via email – what a way to break up with someone! And I was already in the throes of the whole drama of Asha so everything else seemed so minor in comparison. It was like water off a duck's back.'

She paused, and they walked in silence for a while, each lost in their thoughts. Then Janiki said:

'And what about you and Caroline? Amma used to say your heart was so thoroughly broken you would never recover. She admired you so much for that.'

'Oh, nonsense. Of course I was hurt when she dumped me; I loved her, and took my marriage seriously. And I've got that thing called male pride, and that was hurt too. And it was tough for a while. But I'm a realist. I got back on my feet. I went to stay in an ashram for a while, and found my spiritual bearings again, and that helped. And then I simply got on with life. What's the point of nursing a grievance for years and years?'

'But you know, you're so cold towards her. At least, what I've seen of you together. As if you're still mad at her. She's trying so hard to be nice to you and you're like a cold fish. It made me think you're still in love with her.'

'A cold fish, am I? I wasn't aware of it. OK, I'll try to be nicer to her in future. But I'm definitely not still in love with her. Not at all.'

'Rani Abishta also thinks you're clinging to the past, and that's why you never remarried. Or showed any interest in women.'

'Oh really. Rani Abishta said that. What else did Rani Abishta say about my marital prospects?'

'For someone so furious at her, you seem very interested!'

'Of course! I want to know what you women get up to when you discuss my future marriage. Go on – what else did she say?'

'Well – she said she had arranged for you to meet attractive women again and again. But always you refused. She thought maybe you were homosexual. Or you were still grieving for Caroline. Or a would-be monk. Or something.'

He laughed. 'No to all of that. Those beautiful women who kept bumping into me accidentally on purpose – I might have known she was behind it all. But no. I just haven't – hadn't – met the right woman. It's not so easy. Not in India. Not even in the West.'

Especially not in the West. My closest female friend in California, Terri, always used to say I was so lucky to be already engaged. She wanted to find Mr Right but you can't even mention marriage and kids on a first date, she said, when you're trying to suss out the basics, like if the guy is only out for a fun time or if he's serious. And usually it's the former. Just fun. Pleasure. And pleasure isn't enough, is it? It can get really frustrating, Terri said, because you have to avoid the subject for months and even years and then when you finally find out he's commitment-phobic, you've wasted a lot of time and energy and emotional investment, and it all ends in acrimony and leaves you with yet another scar so that you're afraid to trust. But you're a good feminist and so you put on a brave face and pretend to be just as commitment-phobic and you don't need a man, and you try again and it's the same coyness and scars and by the time you're thirty – she's twenty-nine – all you are is one big scar and you can't trust anyone. At least that's how she seems to me, and she admits it too. With us Indians, you know from the very first date that it's all about marriage compatibility.'

She stopped for breath and the silence between them was thick as he absorbed what she'd said, and her last two words seemed to echo up to the stars. And it was suddenly embarrassing. Had she been too open? Too... *something.* She'd spoken the M-word, so taboo in the West. The surf splashed and lapped against the beach in frothy gladness, as if laughing at her silly little speech. So revealing, so unnecessary. So un-feminist. But then, this wasn't really a—

He spoke into her self-recriminations, and it wasn't what she'd expected.

'So, Janiki, does this count as a first date?'

She chuckled. 'Does that count as an expression of interest?'

They both laughed then, and he said, 'I guess it's a *yes* to both questions, then. No coyness.'

His hand closed around hers, and she left hers there. It felt just right.

Chapter Forty-Three

Janiki

Let me introduce myself. I'm not really a foreigner, just foreign-returned and foreign-educated. I've been in the USA studying and working for ten years and now I'm back in Mumbai. I have certain tastes and I would like them to be fulfilled. I've been lurking for one or two days to get the feel of this place and I think you fellows can help me out. I like this group; it seems very open and yet discreet. A trusted friend gave me the password and so I'm here. Obviously no more personal details. In the coming posts I'll tell you more about what I like and what I don't like. I will begin with saying that what I don't like is vulgarity. I want a cultured girl. A virgin if possible but at least inexperienced, as I want to train her myself. I have a nice apartment in Mumbai and she will live with me as my maid and companion until I tire of her. So that's enough for now. I am an educated man and I don't like common girls. I will pay for superior quality.

Janiki read it over, made a few adjustments, copied it, took a deep breath and pasted it into the Lotus Pond forum.

There. It was done. Foreigner was part of the conversation.

Replies came thick and fast. Welcome messages, suggestions, men discussing the perfect age: thirteen? ten? five? Men boasting that they raped babies. Tales of this girl and that. Recommendations. Lewd remarks and jokes. Janiki took a deep breath and joined in. *Lord forgive me,* she whispered. *It is for a good cause.*

She kept it up all morning, pausing only to run out and buy herself a cup of coffee. Foreigner grew in popularity. It was possible, on the forum, to add 'reputation points' to certain messages and his 'reputation' grew stronger and stronger. A few private messages came through, but none of any consequence. Particularly, a MrBengal shared his taste and understood him perfectly. *Such cultured girls like to play hard to get, he wrote, but they are worth it in the end. I have my eye on one myself.*

In the space of a few hours Foreigner became one of a close band of paedophiles. He knew the deal. He was demanding, yes, but, as he had said, he was willing to pay for superior quality. No cheap slut from the streets. Only best quality. Fair-skinned. Young, of course (twelve to thirteen was the ideal age), and beautiful. If she could speak English it was a bonus. He himself was from Tamil Nadu. Madras. That was where he grew up. In a very prosperous family. He himself was very prosperous through hard graft. His family dealt in luxury silk.

Janiki was a little nervous about writing that last; it was a little too close to the truth. Yet, what harm could it do? Nobody had contact with Kamal, the real Foreigner, and they wouldn't know about his background. It was fine.

Around midday a private message notification popped up on the screen. It was from a member named The Vituperator. *I might be able to help you,* said The Vituperator. *How?* asked Foreigner.

Just such a girl. All of your requirements fulfilled. Her native language is Tamil but she speaks English.

Can we take this to email? Can you provide a photo? When can I meet her?

Certainly. If you like the photo I can show you her tomorrow. How much are you willing to pay?

What is the asking price?

She is already being reviewed by someone else. If you can improve on his offer she can be yours tomorrow. Just one thing. She is not compliant. Is that an impediment?

Not at all. So much the better. I will make her compliant. A little discipline and a few slaps never hurt.

Very well. Tell me your email address and I will send photo. Once we agree on price I will take you to view her. Only viewing tomorrow. I will meet you at midday tomorrow and take you there. If you like her same-day delivery to your place.

A minute later an email with an attachment popped into her Yahoo account, on the email address she had created just for this purpose.

It was the very same photo she had printed out yesterday. Asha.

OK OK. Very nice. But tomorrow is no good. I want to see her today.

Unfortunately not possible today. Please understand that there is competition for this girl as she is superior quality. We have other bookings tonight.

If you tell me the address I will go and view myself.

I am not disclosing address. You will have to wait till tomorrow. But please note that tomorrow she might no longer be available.

I am telling you I cannot make tomorrow. You absolutely need to prepone the viewing. If you do not tell me the address the deal is off. I will just go and look. I will pay advance for immediate viewing. Money is no object. And if I am liking then delivery tonight to my place. If I am liking I will make an offer you cannot refuse.

A long pause followed, in which Janiki thought the deal was indeed off, or at least, the immediate viewing. She would have to give in, agree to a meeting tomorrow; but then Asha might be gone for ever, sold to a stranger. A viewing today would mean she had to find Kamal, and quickly, but there was no other option. She wasn't sure she could. Kamal had told her he'd be spending today with Sudesh, the social worker who that coming night would be passing him into the underground, the network that would hopefully lead him to Asha. But now there was no need. Now he could make direct contact; but she had to know the address. Perhaps Kamal could rescue Asha today – delivery to your place! All he had to do was outbid the other suitor. Kamal had money, a lot of it; and so did Caroline. Whatever the price.

The minutes ticked by. Ten. Fifteen. Twenty. Then:

Ping! A new notification from The Vituperator.

Very well. I will give you address now. But you must pay in advance. One lakh of rupees advance only for viewing. You must hand it to the mistress of the house I will send you to. I will inform her that you are coming and of the amount by telephone and she will count it before letting you in. There is a password. It is Blue Lily. If you say the password she will take you to see Kamini. That is the name of the girl. You will view her only through the door, a peephole. No talking and no touching. Tomorrow there will be further price negotiations. As I told you someone has already reserved her for viewing tonight. Whoever offers the better price can have her. If you agree to pay one lakh of rupees for viewing only I will give you address discreetly. This is very special girl, virgin, superior quality. Wheatish complexion. She is worth the price. If deal is off, half of advance will be returned. You must go between three and four. After four, deal is off.

Janiki was shaking as she closed down the computer. She'd done it! Now to find Kamal. She smiled to herself, remembering last night. The walk along the beach, holding hands; the taxi drive back to the hotel, again holding hands. The warmest hug ever at her door, and finally, the kiss that said everything.

She slipped the note with the address into the pocket of her *kameez*. Hopefully, she'd find him in time. Everything in her laughed as she ran out into the street. *Kamal!* she cried silently. *We've done it! We've found Asha!*

Chapter Forty-Four

Caroline

'We've found her!' Janiki's voice was so loud Caroline had to hold the phone away from her ear. 'We've found her, Caroline, I know exactly where she is! We've found her!'

'Where – how…' Caroline could only stutter.

'She's in a house in Kamathipura. Kamal has to go and look at her between three and four; the trouble is I can't find him anywhere. He's gone out with Sudesh – the social worker – and no one knows where they are. I don't think I'll find him in time. God, how I wish he had one of those mobile phones!'

'If you know where she is, if you have an address, can't you just send in the police? Why do you need Kamal?'

'Caroline – you heard what Dr Ganotra said. You can't trust the police! They are paid by those pimps. They're absolutely in their pocket – they're all thugs together. If we run to the police I can guarantee that within five minutes they'll put Asha somewhere else and we'll never find her again. No, I've set up an appointment for Kamal and he's the one who has to go – I'll explain later how, but now I just wanted to ask if you've seen him? If he's been in touch?'

'No,' said Caroline. 'Kamal hasn't been in touch. The only person I've seen since yesterday is Gita. She's coming to pick me up at two. In fact…' She looked at her watch. 'It's nearly two now. She could be here any time.'

'Damn. Damn damn damn. I should have tried to force a night appointment, we'd have had more time to find him.'

'What are you talking about?'

'Just thinking aloud. I need to do something, postpone the appointment. He won't be pleased.'

'Who won't be pleased? What's going on?'

'I'll explain later – it's just that I went to a lot of trouble to get this appointment and Kamal is supposed to go and look at her through a peephole to confirm he wants her and then he can buy her tomorrow. We have to negotiate a final price; but he has to make a down payment today, before he views her. It's complicated. One lakh rupees he has to advance today.'

'How much is that in dollars?'

'A lakh is a hundred thousand. At today's rate it's about one thousand five hundred dollars.'

'I'll pay it. I'll go myself. I'll cash some traveller's cheques and go. Or go to HSBC bank; Wayne told me he'd wire money to my account there.'

'Wait. Let me think this through. Someone has to go but he expects a man. They don't know what Kamal looks like, so any man can go – but the problem is, only Kamal can really identify her. I might be able to get one of Dr Ganotra's team but they're all out working right now. It's too short notice. The money has to be paid to the brothel madam.'

'Make up some story – tell them Kamal can't come so he sent me instead. Tell them anything. As long as I hand over the money – just for looking, that's a crazy amount – they shouldn't mind.'

'An American woman instead of an Indian man? It just sounds fishy. He'd never believe me. He'd know something's up.'

They both fell silent, thinking. Then Caroline said:

'I know someone who might do it. If they don't know what Kamal looks like any man will do, right?'

'What man is this, Caroline? You can't just pick a man off the street—'

'No! Somebody I met. An Indian. Same age as Kamal. I told him the story. He knows. He'll help, I'm sure. I just have to ask him.'

Yes, Hiran would help. She'd apologise for walking away last night. For being so rude after he'd been so gallant, so helpful. She'd beg him to help. He'd been so supportive; of course he'd do it. She'd promise him anything, anything. He'd said he had today free; maybe she'd find him, ask him, offer herself – whatever he wanted. Just let him go and find Asha.

'He'll do it. Janiki. I'm completely sure. He's nice. He's helpful.'

'Well…'

'Janiki! It's our chance! We have to, don't you see? Just give me the address. I'll go and talk to Hiran – that's his name. Get the money, and it's done.'

'Well I guess that's a good enough option. You said he knows the whole story?' 'Yes. I was – I was lonely last night and I told him everything. He really cares, Janiki. He'll help, I'm sure. I'll show him a photo of Asha so he can recognise her. Are you sure it's Asha, by the way?'

'Absolutely certain.'

'Well then. Let me do that. I need to do something, Janiki. I feel so helpless. Let me do this. Let me. Please!'

'Hmmm… well, I suppose it would work. He only has to hand over the money, say the password and look through a peep-hole. That's it, really.'

'See? It's not much. He'll do it.'

'Ok. I'll give you the address and the password. Have you got something to write with?'

'Hold on a minute… yes. Fire away.'

Janiki dictated the address, spelling out the Hindi words as Caroline wrote them down in her diary. 'And you need a password. The password is Blue Lily.'

'Got it,' said Caroline.

'OK then. I guess that's it. Confirm it's her, and tomorrow Kamal buys her back. That part should be simple enough – he's supposed to be buying her as a live-in companion and maid.'

'Ugh. Horrible. Makes me want to puke.'

'I know. But if it works that's all that matters.'

* * *

But Hiran was not in his room. He was not in the dining room either. He had probably gone sightseeing on his own, and now she was stuck with the address: a priceless winning ticket and no one to redeem it.

She had left a note for Gita at reception, and indeed, there was Gita waiting for her, jumping to her feet at her approach.

'Hi,' said Caroline. 'I've got news.'

She gave Gita a quick summary of the situation.

'So either we have to find a man to replace Kamal immediately, or—'

'Or we lose this chance,' Gita finished.

'No. Or I go myself.'

'You must be crazy! It has to be a man!'

'I'll fix that,' said Caroline. She opened her handbag and showed Gita a large wad of banknotes. 'Money speaks. It's just a brothel manager who will show me Asha, not the actual pimp. I'll give her the money for the pimp as arranged – see, there it is in the envelope, all counted out – and pay her extra for letting me in instead of a man and keeping her mouth shut. An extra lakh. It's nothing for me, and a fortune for her. She'll do it. I bet she'll do it.'

'Caroline, you're—'

'Brilliant, right?'

'I was going to say crazy. But brilliant will do. And brave.'

'Maybe all three. But c'mon. Let's roll.'

Chapter Forty-Five

Caroline

It was a squalid grey building in one of Kamathipura's narrowest and busiest lanes. Barred windows in its top storey were flanked by ragged scraps of would-be curtains. Between the two narrow holes of windows hung a washing line sagging with the weight of a few nondescript pieces of clothing. A woman stood at the window, screaming down at another woman who sat cross-legged on a *charpai* outside the doorway, nursing a baby and playing cards with a boy of about thirteen, and yelling what sounded like abuse back at the woman above. Gita took Caroline's hand.

'This is it,' she said.

Sensing their presence, the card-playing woman looked up, quickly assessed Gita and Caroline as irrelevant, and returned to her card game and her screaming match. She pulled the baby away from her breast and laid it on the *charpai* behind her, where it began to squall with rage. The boy had his back to them and did not look around. The door was open, offering a glimpse of a long black passage in whose depths blinked a string of red fairy-lights, perhaps framing a door, perhaps lighting the way upstairs.

'*Namaste*,' said Gita. The woman on the *charpai* looked up. She stared first at Gita, then at Caroline. Everyone here stared at Caroline and she was getting used to it; she met the woman's gaze steadily, nodded in greeting and turned to Gita.

'OK, can you translate, Gita. Tell her that the fellow who was supposed to come couldn't make it and I came instead. Tell her

I have the money for her pimp but also the same again for her if she keeps quiet. Tell her I want to see the girl.'

Gita spoke.

'She says she's not interested,' Gita said after a few sentences. 'I think she wants more. She's taking a risk, after all. It's you being a foreigner, I bet, and a journalist. Word gets around fast; talk of a white female journalist doing research might have reached her already.'

'Tell her I'll pay her more for her silence and her help. We have more to lose than she does; all she has to do is lead me to Asha. That's it. I don't have a camera. She has nothing to lose, and a lot to gain. See if you can bargain with her. Offer her whatever she wants, within reason.'

'What's within reason?'

'I have the equivalent of four thousand dollars with me. One and a half is for the pimp. You can offer her the rest.'

Gita, Caroline could tell, was a hard bargainer, but so was the woman, who sent away the boy and gathered up the cards before getting down to what was obviously hard business. Finally, Gita said, 'She says two lakh to show you the girl and for her silence. But first, the password.' 'Blue Lily,' said Caroline at once. Gita repeated it in Hindi and the woman nodded.

The woman got up from the *charpai,* taking her time doing so, as if moving caused her much pain. Once she was standing she rearranged her sari, tucking in various corners and ends, hawked and spat into the gutter, screamed at a skinny dog that had ventured under the *charpai* foraging for grains of cooked rice, and then gestured to the two women to enter the house behind her.

The corridor, lit only by the red fairy-lights, was so dark that Caroline and Gita were forced to walk slowly. It ended in a staircase so narrow, and a ceiling so low, they were forced to stoop as they ascended. Caroline groped until she felt the wall, cool and dank with what felt like slime. She shuddered, but moved on until she stumbled against something like a plank at ankle level; but by now the blackness had lightened to grey and she could see the shadowed outline of a steep staircase.

The building was narrow but tall – four storeys high. The staircase was, in effect, nothing more than an appropriately adjusted ladder, fitted to slant snugly against the wall and upgraded with a precarious banister. She reached the first landing and edged herself along a dimly lit corridor that was little more than two feet across and interrupted by several narrow doorways, some open, some curtained. Glancing through the open doorways Caroline saw tiny cubicles, each one about the length of a human being and the breadth of a human being with an arm stretched out. A cot occupied half of the space, and on each one lay a filthy mattress and crumpled sheets. There was a rat-like creature scurrying at the far end of the corridor and Caroline glimpsed the shadow of a human being disappearing into a cubicle and heard the *ratch* of a quickly drawn curtain, which still shivered as Gita passed it seconds later.

At the end of the corridor was another flight of stairs. The woman led the way up, Caroline trying her best to keep up.

She reached the second landing, where she stopped for a moment to draw breath and, literally, sniff the air. The smell was acrid, an alloy of rancid body fluids and other unidentifiable rotting waste. Caroline felt her mind like an open satellite dish, receiving signals imperceptible to the senses: thoughts and feelings, heartbeats and heartaches, and a never-ending, silent wail of terror. Up the next flight, to the third storey, the woman panting by now. This corridor was identical to the two beneath it, except that the cubicles here had doors, and all the doors were shut – and bolted, with heavy steel padlocks hanging from the bolts.

The woman, panting still, stopped in front of one of the doors and pointed.

'This is the one,' said Gita. The woman reached up to a small curtain at eye level, drew it back. There was a tiny window, the glass smeared, let into the door. Caroline peered through into a box room, little more than a cubicle, lit dimly by a single bulb dangling from the ceiling. A *charpai* was pushed against the far wall, and on the *charpai* a small girl reclined. There she was, curled up in a foetal position with her back to the door. Her face was not visible. Yet still, Caroline knew. Perhaps it was the colour of her hair – not jet black as an Indian's would be, but a dark chocolate colour, and curly, just as in her photos; a mop.

'Asha,' breathed Caroline. 'Gita, it's her. It's really her.'

'Let me have a look,' said Gita, and she too looked. She shrugged.

'I can't see her face!'

'It's her all right. I know.'

The woman drew back the curtain so that the peephole was covered once more, and turned to go.

'Stop!' cried Caroline. The woman stopped, and looked at her.

'Tell her to open this door,' she said to Gita. She pointed to the bunch of keys dangling from a knot at the end of the woman's sari. 'Those are the keys. They were the first thing I noticed about her. Tell her to open it.' She tapped at the door.

Gita spoke to the woman, who replied sharply in Hindi.

'She says that wasn't the deal. The deal was to look only. No opening of doors, no talking, no touching.'

'Tell her I need to see the girl's face. That was the deal. The girl's back is facing the door. I will tell her boss she did not show me properly so the deal is off. I want her to open that door. I need to see the girl properly. Now. Or else.'

At the 'Or else' Caroline fumbled in her handbag and produced her Swiss Army knife, flicked open the blade. It was a pity to have to threaten a woman, but needs must.

The woman scowled and fumbled with the knot in her sari, muttering and uttering what could only be foul curses. She held the bunch of keys up nearer to the naked ceiling bulb.

The door creaked back, opening into the cubicle.

Caroline entered the room. The girl on the cot sat up, rubbing her eyes.

'Asha? Asha, it's me. It's me, my darling. It's Mom.'

The girl stared for a moment. Terrified eyes focused in recognition, and the brow above them, creased with a frown of puzzlement, smoothed out.

'Mom? Mom!' she cried.

Caroline, arms held out, rushed forward towards Asha. She was halfway across the room when a loud crash made her stop and swing around. The door to the cubicle had been slammed shut; she heard the rasp of the bolt as it crashed into its slot. The clatter of keys and the click of the padlock snapping shut followed, and the vile cackle of their jailer.

The woman shouted something obviously very rude at them from beyond the door. There was shouting: Gita's voice, and the woman's, in Hindi, and 'I'll send help, Caroline!' from Gita. Steps on the stairs, growing fainter by the second, after which there was silence.

She was locked in with Asha.

Chapter Forty-Six

Gita

Once out on the street Gita ran. She ran for her life, zigzagging down the crowded lane, sometimes knocking into people, running without looking back, leaping over a ditch here or a dead dog there. Heads turned as she ran but she tore on until forced to stop for breath, and when she had recovered she ran on until she reached the edge of Kamathipura. There she flagged down an autorickshaw.

'Telephone shop,' she cried. 'Quick!'

They didn't have to drive far; the driver found a small shop with the ubiquitous sign STD International Calls Fax Internet in five minutes. Gita leapt from the rickshaw before it had stopped, thrust a bundle of rupee notes at the driver and plunged into the shop, finally able to stop for breath again.

She nodded to the shop attendant and practically leapt into the telephone cubicle next to the open doorway. She dialled the number of Tulasa House; Subhadai answered. In reply to Gita's breathless demand she said, calmly, 'Doctor is not here. Nobody is here.'

'Damn!' muttered Gita, and fumbled in her shoulder bag for her notebook. Finding the number for Dr Ganotra's office at the hospital, she dialled that, but without much hope. No reply. She dialled a few other numbers of possible contacts, but nobody was available. The person to contact was Kamal; but he was out with Sudesh. Janiki, too, could not be reached. By now she could hardly think. But she had to. She sat herself down on the rusty metal chair in the cubicle and buried her face in her hands and thought. A few deep breaths. *Think, Gita, think.*

There remained, of course, the police. But everyone knew what the police would do: nothing at all. Kamathipura was out of bounds as far as a police rescue mission was concerned. Riddled with crime and prostitutes and pimps, it was beyond redemption and a person lost in there, a person imprisoned or abducted, had only themselves to blame. Even if that person was a foreigner, a white-skinned blonde, an American.

An American! Gita gasped. Of course! Yesterday they had discussed contacting the American embassy for help, and the problem had been that Asha was not American. But Caroline was. The American embassy would be bound to help. They'd send in the CIA, the military, a whole arsenal of gun-toting troopers who would march in there and storm the building and pull out both Caroline and Asha.

She needed the number. There was a fat, dirty, seriously dog-eared Bombay telephone book on a shelf in the cubicle, dated several years ago. Gita leafed through the chunk of A pages. Several had been torn out, including, she realised, the pages beginning with Am.

She burst out of the cubicle. 'Computer!' she cried to the assistant. 'Internet!'

He nodded languidly and pointed to a terminal at the back of the shop. Gita swung herself onto the rickety chair, tapped a button and waited impatiently for the computer to boot and connect. That done, she tapped in 'American embassy'.

There was a number, and opening times. She looked at her watch. They would be closed by now, but there was an emergency number. She scribbled it into her notebook, returned to the cubicle and dialled.

'How may I help you, ma'am?'

'My friend, an American citizen, has been imprisoned! She's in danger! She needs immediate help.'

'Very well, ma'am. Please describe the circumstances of the emergency. Where is your friend? How did this happen? Have you notified the police?'

Gita gave a quick run-down of the situation. The woman at the other end of the line asked questions, but the more Gita spoke and the more the woman asked the more Gita became aware of the scepticism and the doubt, even the reluctance, in the voice.

'So you're saying this friend of yours went voluntarily into a brothel in Kamathipura? And she is locked up in there?'

'Yes, yes, she went to rescue her daughter—'

'Her daughter is a prostitute?'

'Yes – no – her daughter is a child, imprisoned there, she...'

'Is the daughter an American citizen?'

'No, she's Indian, but the mother, my friend, is American, and—'

'Ma'am, Kamathipura is an extremely dangerous area. A high-crime area. Was your friend aware of this when she entered? Was she aware of the risk involved?'

'Yes – listen. Could you just write down the address and send someone to rescue her, right now?'

'Have you reported this to the police? You must submit a FIR – a First Information Report. And then—'

'But the police won't bother. They're all bribed! Can't you do it? Please – you have to send someone with authority! The Consul himself – or – or...'

'Just give me the address, ma'am, and I'll see what we can do.'

'You'll help, won't you? You'll send someone around right away?'

'I will ensure that the information gets to the Regional Security Officer, ma'am, and we will see what we can do. Now just give me the address, please. Better yet, come yourself to the Consulate tomorrow and speak to him in person.'

Gita was weeping as she dictated the address. She left the cubicle and the shop, slumped into herself, physically and mentally. She had to find someone, someone who understood. She flagged down a rickshaw. Where would Janiki be? At a computer somewhere, no doubt. She had said there was an Internet shop across the road from her hotel. Gita looked at her watch. It was almost six o'clock; dusk was approaching. Kamathipura would be coming to life for business. Would Caroline even be there, still? Wouldn't they have removed her straight away? She had to talk to someone, if only to relieve her own distress. She gave Janiki's hotel address to the driver, and he chugged off.

Chapter Forty-Seven

Caroline

Caroline turned back to Asha, to complete her embrace; but Asha, it seemed, had had a change of heart since the door slammed shut and now, instead of coming forward, shrank away, back to the *charpai,* folding her limbs into a huddle.

'Honey, oh honey! Don't be scared – I'm here, and I'll never leave you again. Never. I'm so happy I've found you. You're happy too, aren't you?'

Caroline waited for Asha to nod, but the girl did not react. She simply sat there, staring straight ahead as before.

'Oh honey, say you're happy I found you! I love you so much. I'm sorry, so sorry, you're here and I'll do my very best to get us out. I promise. I really promise.'

But Asha continued to cower and, far from showing happiness, the spark of animation she had shown on hearing her name, on calling out to her mother, her expression now reflected trepidation and distrust. Caroline noticed a tightening of the grasp that held her legs hugged tightly to her body.

Watching her, for the first time Caroline took in Asha's physical appearance. And for the first time she acknowledged Asha's almost ethereal beauty, which managed to shine through in spite of the veneer of abject misery that coated her both physically and mentally. The girl was the personification of distress, and yet instead of distorting her features that distress itself seemed somehow uplifted by resting on this girl; it glowed with a pain so exquisite and poignant Caroline could feel it almost physically, echoed in her own heart. Asha's eyes were amber, like her own, but opaque; saying nothing, yet eloquent in their very lifelessness. Her features had a symmetrical swing; her skin, so fair for an Indian, was translucent; her cheekbones too prominent. Her clothing was ragged and dirty; her hair unkempt. Yet all of this seemed to accentuate her beauty rather than diminish it.

'That hag!' said Caroline. 'The awful woman! Listen, Asha! I came here to rescue you, and I will. We've all been looking for you. Not just me: your daddy too, and Janiki. We've been looking for you for ages and now I've found you I won't let you go again.' Caroline couldn't be sure, but she thought she saw a flicker of something in the staring eyes at the name 'Janiki'. Certainly, Asha was closest to Janiki, and the fact that Janiki was also nearby must have given her… Hope? Longing? Or simply the absence of terror, a drawing back of shadows? Whatever it was, Caroline was encouraged, and continued.

'Oh, Asha!' she sighed. 'Maybe you think I abandoned you. Maybe you think I didn't love you, and that's why I left you behind. It's not true, my darling. I always loved you. There hasn't been a day, a minute, a second, that I haven't thought of you in all these years. I left you because – because…'

Because what? Caroline thought. *What reason can I give, that she would understand?* She stumbled on. 'Because I was ill, Asha. I was lost, just like you are now, just not in a physical sense. I was lost in my mind, lost in a darkness I could not banish. I wish it wasn't so. I wish it had been different, that we could have been together, that I could have been your mom all your life. But I can't turn back the clock. I can't change the past. But I can change the future, Asha, and I will. I promise. I will be a proper mom from now on.'

She talked. She talked to Asha as the shadows lengthened and the noises outside the room grew louder: female chattering and buckets clanging. She talked when the door opened about six inches, and a blackened aluminium pot was pushed through the opening at floor level – Caroline got a glimpse of a tiny hand, the hand of a child, pushing it in, the fingers flicking it forward, and then quickly jerking back to safety. The door was slammed shut again, the latch rasped, the lock snapped.

The pot contained rice soaked in a yellowish liquid. There were neither plates nor cutlery. By now Caroline was ravenous, and she supposed Asha was too. She forced herself to take three mouthfuls – scooping up the rice with her fingers – before giving up and turning away in disgust. Asha ate even less. No wonder she was so thin. So Caroline continued to talk.

Asha meanwhile huddled in her corner; now and again she fell asleep, her head lolling to one side, her body leaning abjectly against the wall. Even in her sleep she shifted several times, as if unable to find a comfortable position

Caroline kept on talking, in a voice that she hoped was calm and soothing and trust-evoking. She spoke about her life before coming to India, about her family, her dreams, her plans for Asha. Asha seemed not to be listening, but still Caroline talked, because she knew that somewhere, at some level of her consciousness, Asha heard and understood.

While talking Caroline tried to stay calm, but that calmness was filtering away with every passing minute. The endless waiting with no sign that it would ever end. Her ramblings for Asha's benefit now seemed more banal even than the silences they broke; her ears constantly strained to pick up noises from beyond the door. Occasionally she heard voices or footsteps from the bowels of the house but they never came up to this floor. Her sense of frustration was like a rising tide of boiling water within her; she wanted to get up, move around, stretch her limbs, aching from so much sitting. Occasionally she did; but the cubicle was too small to bring any relief and every time she simply flung herself back onto the mattress. Only Asha seemed resigned to this infinity of waiting; or rather, she didn't wait at all, but simply existed, as if her mind had lost the capacity to measure time, to even conceive of a better future, to hope for change. As if she had given up.

Near the door was a rusty pail, which obviously served as a toilet and also had obviously not been changed for a day or two. Caroline had grown used to the stench by now; occasionally she stood up and walked to the opening that served as a window to sniff the fresh air that seeped in through the wooden slats. She looked through the windowpane, but it was so smudged that not much could be seen except the vague outline of the opposite building, an almost black tenement with barred windows just like this one. Caroline inspected the window more closely, to see if there was any chance of opening it, but it was nailed securely shut, and the bars outside it were obviously solid, so that even if she broke a pane of the glass there could be no escape that way; nor would shouting down to the street be of any use, for who would hear them? And who would care?

Asha was asleep again, huddled against the wall, and Caroline took the liberty of touching her again, helping her down into a lying position and covering her with one of the torn sheets. Asha did not wake. Caroline longed to partly undress her, to check her for wounds; she longed to stroke her hair. If there was one thought that made this predicament bearable it was the thought of Asha. She may have been impulsive, reckless, headstrong, giddy – but she had been right. She was with Asha. Better that she should be with Asha, than that Asha should be alone.

The night seemed even more endless than the day; the sounds filtering in from the street, muffled though they were, helped keep Caroline awake. The street had been quiet during the day; now, at night, it seemed to wake up and the melange of loud-speaker music, raucous laughter, shouting and a thousand other noises conspired to ensure she could not escape from her carousel of thoughts for even half an hour at a time.

She hugged Asha to her, kissed the top of her head. She smelt; she had obviously not had a bath or washed her hair for days. Caroline pulled her closer yet, and closed her eyes, and somehow, perhaps through sheer exhaustion, dozed off.

It seemed only seconds had passed when she was abruptly shaken out of her restless nap. The light bulb glared overhead; there were voices in the cubicle, loud male voices, and, as she saw on rubbing the sleep from her eyes, the men to go with them. Beefy Indian men, clones of each other, and of every Bollywood villain who ever scowled on an oversized hoarding on a Bombay street corner: the thick moustaches, the slicked-back greasy hair, the sideburns, the puffy jowls, the hooded long-lashed eyes. Caroline would have laughed at the cliché if she did not feel more like crying.

The woman was there too, chattering loudly and coarsely, pointing and glaring at her. She bent over and snatched Caroline's handbag, which was lying on the floor. She opened it, found the purse and took out the knife and the rest of the paper money. She threw the bag back onto the floor, counted and folded the hundred-rupee notes and stuck the wad into the neckline of her blouse.

'Don't try any trick, we got knife! We got gun!' said one of the men, and 'Who are you?' said the other. 'Why you come here?'

'I'm her mother,' said Caroline, 'and I'm staying with her.'

At that moment, Asha woke up. Rubbing her eyes, she squeaked, 'Mom? Mom? I'm scared!'

'Don't be scared, honey. I'm with you.'

'She talking?' said the first man.

'Of course she's talking. She's my daughter.'

'You going. We not needing you here. She is ours.'

'She's not. She's my daughter and I'm not leaving her any-where.'

'Mom, Mom!' Asha kept crying, clinging to Caroline.

'Don't worry, sweetheart. I won't let them take you away.'

There followed a conversation in Hindi, of which Caroline understood not a word; except, now and then, the word 'foreigner', and 'English' and, occasionally, the name Chaudhuri. Chaudhuri, that rang a bell. Wasn't it the name that Janiki had found on one of her Internet searches? The name they'd all grasped like drowning people grasped at a lifebuoy, only to discard as useless?

One of the men pulled out a black brick-like gadget, which Caroline recognised as a mobile phone. He pulled out an antenna, punched one of the keys and spoke some sharp words in Hindi, eyes fixed on her all the time. Caroline could only recognise the word 'Kamini' every now and then. The man listened, nodded, then put away the phone. He spoke to his companion who, abruptly, spat on the floor and, with quick shooing gestures towards the door, said in English:

'You can go. We don't want you. Only girl. You free.'

'No! You're not taking her anywhere!'

Asha clung to Caroline.

'Mom! Mom! Stay with me!' she cried.

'I'm staying with you, honey. They're not taking you away.' To the men, she repeated: 'I'm staying with her. You can't take her away.'

One of the men tried to pull Asha away, but she screamed and clung to Caroline. 'Mom! Mom! I'm scared!'

There was a struggle; Caroline holding onto Asha and pulling her away, Asha screaming and clinging. The other man pulled out the phone again and made another quick call.

Putting the phone away, he spoke sharply to his friend, who let go of Asha.

'OK OK. You can come. Both of you can come. You come with girl. But you come quietly otherwise I shoot you. I got gun.' He tapped his pocket, where indeed a gun-shaped bulge was visible.

'Where are you taking us to?'

'You will see. Better place than this, to be sure. We take her, with or without you. But better with you.'

The man strode over to the *charpai* and made as if to grab Asha again, but she shrieked and clung to her mother. Caroline laid a protective arm around her, hugged Asha against her.

'Don't touch her. We'll come. We can talk. I can pay for her, buy her off you. We are wealthy foreigners. Take me to whoever is your boss and I'll talk to him.'

Chapter Forty-Eight

Caroline

They reached the front door and then were out in the street, Asha clinging to Caroline's arm. Caroline felt a tight grip on her other arm; one of the men had taken hold of her and was urging her forward, up the lane. Glancing to her left, she saw that Asha was being held on her other side by the second man. She looked over her shoulder; The street was half deserted. She saw a few women in bright saris standing in doorways as they passed. Late male stragglers made their way to the end of the lane, where the main thoroughfare, in the daytime a roaring, fuming chaos of motor vehicles, lay quiet and forsaken.

A black car crouched at the roadside. Its back door opened silently at their approach, as if by the hand of a ghost. Caroline and Asha were summarily bundled into the back seat; the car door slammed and they were enclosed in the black, musty interior.

There was a third man already waiting in the driver's seat, reeking of some heavy aftershave and smiling in a manner that made Caroline cringe and draw back in disgust. Their two male escorts slid into the back seat with her and Asha, one on either side, next to the doors. The motor coughed once, twice, then relaxed into a quiet purring. They drove off.

It seemed an endless drive all through the night and into the dawn. But it could have been one hour, and it could have been three. Caroline dozed off now and then, only to be startled into wakefulness by a dream or a memory or a sound, then to drift back into sleep. Sometimes when she was awake she heard the men talking; sometimes she heard nothing but the hum of the engine. When she woke up for the last time the car had stopped and she felt fresh air on her cheeks and heard raised male voices. She blinked, and could make out only the silhouettes of houses and a few male figures. Were they still in Mumbai? She could not tell.

Someone pushed her out of the car. Loose gravel crunched beneath her bare feet. She reached for Asha's hand and held it tightly.

'It's OK, honey. I'm here,' she whispered. Yes, she was afraid. But how much more afraid must Asha be? It was her job to calm that fear, and doing so helped calm her own. She could see nothing but those dark silhouettes, and here and there a dim light against a building. The tight hold on her arm did not relax for a fraction of a second. They entered a door beneath one of the outside lights; behind it was a dim passageway leading to a steep flight of stairs. She walked up, still clinging to Asha's hand. Asha's bare feet padded beside her own. The voices around her were loud and rude, the grip on her arm tight and uncompromising. All that could be seen were walls.

They reached the top of the stairs and then there was a woman's voice, speaking three or four sharp words, and uncouth hands tugged at her and pushed her inside a brightly lit room. Caroline blinked at the harsh light, then looked around. The men from the brothel had been joined by a woman. She did not look at Asha, for the woman was staring at her with such intensity she could not look away.

The woman could have been anything between thirty and fifty. She wore a faded beauty with the dignity of a queen, though she was not dressed to fit that role. She had obviously been roused from her bed, for she wore a long neck-to-ankle cylinder of a nightgown in pink seersucker, slightly gathered around a buttoned bib that rose above a generously loose bosom. She had skin the colour of dark honey, high cheekbones and long heavy-lidded eyes that seemed to have slid slightly lower down her cheeks than was originally intended. Her hair hung in a long plait over her right shoulder. She wore several gold rings on her fingers and a small gold stud at the flare of her nostril. She was speaking to one of the men, but her gaze flitted now and again from Caroline to Asha, summing them up with cunning expertise. Caroline felt like a collector's doll being offered for sale.

The woman had obviously been unprepared for their coming; she was also obviously of higher rank than the men who had brought Caroline and Asha. She was arguing with them, but Caroline, of course, could not understand a word. Finally the woman addressed her directly. She shrugged. One of the men spoke, and she understood the one word: English. The woman addressed her again, this time in her own language.

'Your native tongue is English?' Caroline nodded. Asha neither nodded nor spoke. The girl was edging behind her, trying to hide. The hand in her own trembled like a small captured bird. The woman addressed Asha now; she reached for her, gripped her by the upper arm and pulled her out from behind Caroline.

'Let me look at you,' she said, and turned Asha around, forcing her to let go of Caroline's hand. 'You have grown so thin, Kamini. What have they done to you? Did they starve you at that place? Well now perhaps you can appreciate how lucky you were before.'

Asha did not answer. The woman spoke to the man who appeared to be the senior, the taller, darker, bulkier one of the two.

There followed a long conversation in Hindi, in which the man spoke the most, the woman merely shaking her head and saying '*acha, acha*' at intervals. Then the woman took over. Finally they seemed to reach a sort of agreement, for the tone of voice changed; it became friendly, almost. The man and his crony turned and clattered down the stairs. The woman gestured for Caroline and Asha to follow her, and led them a short way down the corridor and through a door. They were in a fairly large room now, sparsely furnished with a double bed, a chest of drawers and a wardrobe; frugal, but, compared to the room they had just left, a queen's chamber, for it was clean, the bed had a sparkling white sheet, and both the windows were open, though barred by wrought-iron patterned grids.

'It's late,' the woman said to Caroline. 'You should get in the bed and sleep now and we'll talk in the morning. You are Kamini's mother I understand, and you have caused her to speak again. That is a good thing for Kamini. We only have to decide what to do with you. It is not my decision. If Kamini is speaking it is very good for her. I will explain all in the morning. Now take rest. You will be fine here but don't try any tricks. I'm kind but I don't stand for any nonsense. Don't give me any trouble and I won't give you any. Are you hungry? Shall I bring you some food? There's water in the jug over there.' Another flick of her thumb, this time towards the flask and two glasses on a tray. 'Look, I'm tired and I have to go and finish the business with those men so I'm leaving now. I'll talk to you in the morning. You'll find night garments in the top drawer.' She pointed to the chest of drawers.

Then she was gone, and Caroline's reply, that indeed she was hungry, they were both hungry, and could she have something to eat, died on her lips. They key turned in the lock.

Caroline sighed and, assuming there would be a breakfast within a few hours, helped a passive Asha out of her sari and into one of the nightdresses the woman had indicated. While doing so she had the perfect opportunity to see, for the first time, the three bloodied welts across Asha's thin back.

The vicious witch, Caroline thought angrily. It must be that hag at the brothel. People like her ought to be publicly flogged. One of the wounds seemed to be infected; it ought to be dressed properly, but Caroline knew there would be no help tonight. Tomorrow would have to do.

Caroline then pulled on the other nightdress. It was white, starched and ironed, and smelt strongly of washing powder. Whatever the future held, at least their conditions had drastically improved since yesterday. She thought of her friends. Kamal, and Janiki, and Gita. Gita would not know where to find her. Why, oh why, had she not let Janiki arrange things her own way? Why had she leapt in where angels fear to tread? I did it for Asha, she said to herself. At least Asha is no longer alone. The words that had been, and would be, her single comfort throughout the ordeal. She thought of Wayne. They cannot keep me imprisoned for long, she thought. I am an American citizen. This time, they will have to act. Have to set the police on me to avoid an international incident. Wayne had influential friends in government. They would put pressure on – whomever it was necessary to put pressure on. Wayne would help. She touched the rings on the chain around her neck. What was she thinking of, to even contemplate getting back together with Kamal? Wayne was her husband. She loved Wayne. When this was over it would be her and Wayne and Asha.

Kamal might want Asha too, said a little voice inside, but she brushed it away impatiently. Kamal's chances of getting custody were exactly nil. She was Asha's mother; she was married, and she and her husband could provide a happy family for Asha. A single man like Kamal – not a chance.

It was 3 a.m. when she glanced at her watch before turning off the light. She walked to the bed where Asha had lain down and now, as far as Caroline could gather, was already fast asleep. A minute later Caroline, too, was sunk in sleep.

* * *

Caroline awoke to the sound of a key turning, and sat up, still groggy but immediately aware as soon as she saw the woman from last night crossing the room. Behind her followed a maid with a tray, on which were some slices of toast, butter and jam, as well as cups, plates and a steaming pot. The delicious aroma of coffee drifted in Caroline's direction, stimulating the accumulated hunger of the previous day. The maid set the tray down on the table and silently left the room. The woman stayed.

'All right. Take food. I want to have a few words with you. What is your good name?'

Caroline told her as she sat down at the table and poured herself a cup of coffee. Asha was still asleep. Let her sleep as long as she can, Caroline thought.

'This girl has been very naughty,' said the woman. 'She refused to speak. Her only chance of a good future is if she is nice and pleasant to our customer. That's why we sent her to that other place. To teach her a lesson. Our customer is a good man. He will treat her well. I want you to encourage this girl to be pleasant towards him.'

'You must be out of your fucking mind,' said Caroline. 'Who do you think I am, a monster like you lot?'

'Don't be rude,' said the woman sharply. 'I told you: don't give me any trouble and I won't give you any trouble. I only know she was speechless and thus useless. I hope you can change that.'

'I'm not changing anything,' Caroline said. 'My daughter will speak if she wants to and be silent if she wants to.' She wanted to continue but stopped herself. She did not want to provoke the woman more than necessary.

'How can you do this to young girls,' Caroline asked, 'don't you have a heart? She's terrified. Of course she doesn't speak.'

'Pah! She'll just have to put armour around herself and get on with it. It's survival of the fittest in this trade. Otherwise she won't last very long.'

'Not the way she's been whipped, she won't!' Caroline retorted. 'I need something to dress her back with. It's covered in welts.'

'What?' cried the woman, and hurried over to the bed where Asha still lay in deep sleep. Clearly not worried about waking the girl, she turned her over onto her stomach and pulled at the nightie till Asha's back was exposed. She inspected the welts, running her fingers lightly along them.

'Those scoundrels! They never said… Well, anyway, she's very beautiful and with a bit of care she will get more beautiful, fill out again and so on. A doctor is coming today to look at both of you. But first you have to be bathed and deloused. Both of you stink to high heaven. This is a respectable house, not like that place you came from. We never beat our girls here. If a girl is so recalcitrant she needs to be beaten she is simply passed on to such houses where beatings take place; Mr Rajgopal doesn't stand for any corporal punishment in his houses. He believes in treating his girls kindly, then they will work willingly, for they know they are in a good position. You are very lucky to come here.'

'My daughter is not Mr Rajgopal's girl, whoever he is,' Caroline protested loudly. 'And neither am I.'

'Ha!' the woman cackled. 'Tell that to Mr Rajgopal. I paid for you both and you both belong to me – that is, to Mr Rajgopal. He bought this girl for Mr Chaudhuri, who is very attached to her. I am only doing my job. I have nothing to do with you – what do I care? I only make sure he gets good quality for the price. He trusts me completely, you see. I'm good at my job. But it's only a job. Mr Rajgopal is kind though, or at least as kind as any man. I've seen much worse but not many better. Thank your deity you were brought here. But I'm glad Kamini has been returned, given another chance. She was wasted in Kamathipura. A girl like this needs special care and now she will get it – they don't call me Devaki the Blameless for nothing! Maybe you can help her find her tongue. Mind you, if she doesn't find it within the week it's out she goes again, back to Kamathipura, this time for good! We can't have stubborn girls here. All our girls work willingly. It's good you speak English, I can do with some girls speaking English. You sound educated as well, that's a good thing.

I can get you some excellent escort work. But Kamini now, she's the real prize. You don't realise how...'

Devaki chattered on as if she hadn't noticed that Caroline had stopped eating long ago, and was only fiddling with her food. She had stopped listening too, ever since the words: 'I paid for you both.'

It couldn't be. It just couldn't be. It wasn't possible that she had been sold. She had volunteered to come with Asha, for goodness' sake. She had been set free; she could have gone but had insisted on coming. She knew for a fact that the men had not bought her. She could have left at any time before getting into the car with Asha. She had not been bought; so how then could she have been *sold*?

But perhaps such logic did not exist in this business.

Slowly, slowly, it dawned on Caroline that at some point during the drive between the house in Kamathipura and this house she had changed status. She had been transformed from the self-determined, free individual she had been into a commodity, a marketable ware to be bought and sold at the whim of strangers. Janiki was perfectly right: she had rushed in like a fool where angels fear to tread. She now belonged to Devaki.

Chapter Forty-Nine

Kamal

'So this is it,' said Sudesh to Kamal, stepping out of the phone cubicle. Kamal stood up from the rickety chair he'd been sitting on in the Internet shop during what seemed an endless wait while Sudesh made his calls. The two of them left the shop and returned to the crowded pavement. Kamal felt lost, disoriented in this behemoth of a city, a city teeming with strangers. Disheartened. How could anyone find anyone here? Where was Caroline, where was Janiki, where was Dr Ganotra, where was Gita? Most of all: *where was Asha?*

He wished he could talk to the others, somehow make contact; but each one was isolated, each on a separate mission; no way to find out if any one of them, Caroline, or Janiki, or Gita, or someone from Dr Ganotra's team, was any closer to the goal, or had any news to report. *What we all need,* thought Kamal, *is a mobile phone.* A few people had them already; maybe the day would dawn when such a gadget would be as commonplace as a wallet, and everyone would have one. But this was now; and this was Mumbai, India's most crowded city, and there was no contact, no collaboration. It was each man, each woman, on his or her own.

'This evening, six o'clock,' Sudesh continued, steering him around a dead dog lying on the pavement, 'we are meeting a fellow called Ramsingh in a coffee shop. Ramsingh has contacts in the business. He will introduce us to another fellow. I don't know his name but he's the real thing. A real pimp. He's the one who will take you to the girl believed to be Asha.'

'How certain are you that it's her?'

'Not absolutely, but it sounds like her. Seventy-five per cent certain. In the description it sounds like her.'

'And what then?'

'Then he will take you to a special hotel. After that it's up to you. I cannot plan the rest in advance. If it's her you can negotiate to buy her. Then she is yours.'

'And if it's not her?'

'If it's not her just say you don't like her and it's done. No problem. Then you return home and we try again the next night.'

'And keep trying, I suppose. Until the right girl turns up. It could take weeks! I actually think my friend's plan is better. She is going to try and connect me through some Internet chat room.'

'That's nonsense,' said Sudesh with a dismissive hand gesture. 'Those chat rooms – I know them. People boast a lot and pretend to be who they aren't. Just a lot of overblown egos. I wouldn't trust anyone I met in a chat room.'

'Well, I guess I'll meet this Ramsingh and see what he has to offer. Did he show you a photograph?'

'No. But the description is fairly accurate.'

'What does fairly mean?'

'It means it could very well be her and you need to take a chance.'

'OK then. And till then?'

'Till then I want to show you the inner workings of the trade. Just come around with me today while I work, see what I do. I don't want you to send you in there as a total innocent. You look too innocent already.'

'So I've been told.'

'Yes. You need toughening up so you can play the role correctly. You need to change your looks too. You look too clean.'

'So you're going to dirty me up?'

'Right. Not literally. But you'd be surprised what make-up can do. You need to look a little more rough. Haggard. Tough.'

Kamal shrugged. 'I'll do as you say.'

* * *

'Kapoor is my name. Happy to meet you. My task is to ensure your full satisfaction or money back. What languages do you speak?'

'Hindi, Gujarati and English only.'

'My native tongues are Marathi and Hindi but I also speak English. What language do you prefer to converse in?'

'Either Hindi or English; no Marathi.'

The man bobbed his head in agreement. 'You have the money? I need everything in advance. Ramsingh must have told you the price. Cash of course.'

Kamal handed over the cloth bag he held. Kapoor looked inside; it was filled with wads of banknotes, all bundled together with rubber bands, a slip of paper with the rupee amount tucked into the band. Indian banks did not provide banknotes larger than a thousand rupees. The bag was almost full.

'We are going there in a car. While we are driving I will count the money to make sure everything is correct. We will pick up the girl in about half an hour. She will be delivered to the car and then we will take her to a certain hotel. I will wait outside until you are finished and pick her up afterwards. Agreed?'

'Agreed,' said Kamal.

'Very well. Let's go.'

A slick white car with a driver was waiting at the kerb. Kapoor got into the front seat and gestured for Kamal to get in the back, which he did.

'Excuse me while I count this money. It seems correct though. The bag is nice and heavy.' Kapoor, turning to speak to Kamal in the back seat, grinned, bouncing the bag up and down to demonstrate its weight. He then turned around again and started counting. He was halfway through when a phone rang. Kapoor fished a mobile phone out of his pocket, held it up to show Kamal.

'These things are so convenient. You must get one.'

He pulled out an antenna and the phone stopped ringing. He listened for a minute and then let out a word that could only be an expletive. After which a cascade of words fell, but in Marathi so that Kamal could not understand what was spoken. This went on for quite a while; Kapoor was obviously agitated, but after a while seemed to calm down somewhat, bobbed his head, saying *acha, acha.* He put away the phone.

'Is there a problem?'

'No problem, sah. No problem at all. Everything fine.'

He spoke to the driver in Marathi, then picked up the phone again and punched in a number.

'Excuse me, I need to make another call.' A few seconds later he was chattering away again in Marathi, excitedly, urgently. Once again he put away the phone, once again he conversed with the driver. The driver reacted by swivelling his head back and forth to assess the traffic, blaring his horn and barging his way through a slight gap in the traffic ahead before making a sudden and swift right turn.

'Just a slight detour,' said Kapoor, turning to grin at Kamal.

'What's wrong?'

'Nothing, nothing at all. Just a slight change in pick-up destination. No problem at all.'

He grinned another white-toothed grin. Kapoor, Kamal thought, could have stepped off a Bollywood hoarding as either a villain or a hero. He was clean-shaven except for a full moustache, his hair slicked back; he wore a chequered long-sleeved shirt with the sleeves rolled up and open at the neck down to the third button, revealing an extremely hairy chest. Around his neck a gold chain, and on his wrist a gold watch.

They had driven for a further half-hour when the phone rang again and he answered it. He seemed happy with this conversation, which was very short. But afterwards he turned to Kamal.

'We are nearly there. Just five minutes more. But there has been a slight change of plan. Unfortunately the girl is not available tonight. We have arranged for a replacement, in a slightly younger age group. I am certain you will be completely satisfied with this new arrangement. A very lovely girl.'

'Wait a minute! I don't want a replacement! I gave you the specifications!'

'Yes, sir, calm down. This girl meets your specifications exactly but is slightly younger. No problem. We aim to provide complete satisfaction, your money's worth.'

'Look, I don't want a slightly younger replacement. I want my money back. Give it back, now, and let me out. The deal is off.'

'No sir, you have paid your money and there is no refund. Ramsingh surely made that clear to you. Now we will provide our side of the deal. We are almost there. A very nice girl. You will be absolutely two hundred per cent satisfied.'

'Don't you understand? I said I don't want another girl! Come on, give me back the money!' He leaned against the front seat, reaching out for the bag. Kapoor, however, dropped the bag into the footwell of the passenger seat.

'I said no refund! You will take this girl. One girl is the same as the next and this one is even better because she is younger. A virgin. She is ideal for you. Look, here she comes now.'

They were on a quieter street now. The car slid to a stop beside the kerb. A man was walking towards them along the pavement, holding a child on his hip. The car stopped; the man grinned into the front window. Kapoor opened it and slid a packet of banknotes through. The man glanced at the bundle, grinned and nodded, after which he opened the back door and thrust the child into the rear seat. She was a girl of, at the most, five years old.

She was snivelling. 'Bapu, Bapu!' she cried to the man who had shoved her in; he patted her on the head, and said, in Hindi, 'Be a good girl, little one, you will be back soon,' and turned away. A moment later he had vanished from sight.

The girl was now sobbing silently, face hidden in her hands. Kapoor turned around again.

'You see? A lovely girl. You will have a lovely time.'

'Are you out of your mind? This is a child! I didn't ask for a child! That man was her father?'

Kapoor, still twisted around, shrugged. 'Yes, her father. Her mother died a year ago and he lost his job. What can a man do. Life is a struggle.'

'This is insane! She can't be more than six years old!'

'Five, I think. You are being unreasonable, sir. Many men prefer them at this age. It's a very good replacement, much more valuable. You will definitely be getting your money's worth. Her name is Ragi.'

Kamal fell back against the seat. He had no answer. He had no words. The girl was bent forward with her face still buried in her hands, her shoulders shaking as she wept. His heart went out to her.

If it is not me it would be someone else, he thought. *So it is better that it is me.*

After a moment's thought he spoke again.

'Very well. I've changed my mind. I will take her.'

'Ah, very wise. Very wise,' said Kapoor. 'You will be a very happy man tonight.'

'Indeed,' said Kamal. He wanted to comfort the child but was wary of touching her. Yet he would have to touch her. Scare her. He looked up, at the traffic. They were approaching a traffic light, red. The car stopped. Kamal waited. He waited and waited until he believed the lights were about to change to green, and that's when he grabbed the girl, opened the passenger door, leapt out of the car with the girl in his arms and ran, leaving the passenger door dangling open. All around him horns blared. The lights changed and the traffic began to move forward. Clutching the child tightly, he dashed between the cars, the girl bouncing on his hip and wailing. From the car he had left came a shout; he didn't look back but the sound of a car door slamming indicated that Kapoor had leapt out after him. He reached the pavement and ran. He ran and ran. Behind him the traffic was moving on, swifter now. He dared to look behind; Kapoor was stuck now between bumper-to-bumper ranks of traffic: a sea of metal, cars, rickshaws, lorries and motorcycles now moving forward, the car he had vacated standing still as other cars swerved around it, horns blaring, a madness of metal. Kapoor leapt Bollywood-style onto the bonnet of the next car and made to jump to the next: but that driver jerked forward at the last moment and he stumbled and fell. Slipped between the cars – right into the path of a motorcycle zipping forward between the lines of traffic. There was a loud crash. Kamal stopped, turned and stared; but he could not see much. Just that the motorcycle was no longer zipping and Kapoor was no longer running.

Horns and klaxons blared louder yet; somebody yelled, maybe Kapoor himself, maybe the motorcyclist. Cars stopped and doors opened and people gathered, shouting and gesticulating. *May you rot in hell*, he said aloud, *may you never harm another child. May you be reborn as a cockroach.*

Then he strolled away and looked for a taxi, the girl riding on his hip and crying on his shoulder.

* * *

Kamal's taxi took him back to the hotel. The child was still weeping silently, her fists dug into her eyes. It was now past ten; Janiki would be in bed. He knocked on her door.

'Janiki – it's me – Kamal!' he said, not too loud, because it was so late. He heard bare feet running across the room to the door, which flew open.

'Kamal! Thank goodness! I've been—'

Janiki, standing in the open doorway in a nightdress, stopped suddenly, and stared.

Kamal thrust the little girl at her.

'Take her. She's scared. Of me and probably all men. I told her I won't hurt her but she doesn't believe me – yet. It wasn't Asha, it was her. Her name is Ragi.'

'Oh darling. My sweet. Come to me, *beti*.'

Speaking in Hindi, Janiki held out her arms and immediately the little girl leaned forward and swung into her embrace. Hugging her close, Janiki turned away from Kamal. 'Leave me alone with her for a while. She's terrified. You can tell me what happened later. And… oh, I'll tell you tomorrow.'

He nodded and, gently, she closed the door in his face.

Chapter Fifty

Janiki

They breakfasted together, all three, at a restaurant down the road, and Janiki filled Kamal up on yesterday's events and Caroline's plight.

'So the good news is that she found Asha, the bad news is that now they're *both* captured.'

'For goodness' sake!' Kamal spluttered. 'Why didn't you tell me that last night when I came? I would have gone round there right away and—'

'Kamal, if you remember, we had other problems last night,' said Janiki, glancing at the girl. She was, astonishingly, tucking into her breakfast with appetite. She had calmed down almost as soon as Kamal had left last night, and fallen asleep curled up in Janiki's arms. Though she had refused to speak a word, she had this morning seemed to have recovered from the shock of last night's events and allowed Janiki to wash and dress her. Her clothes seemed reasonably clean and in good condition. She and Kamal had to decide what to do next; but first Kamal needed to know the news about Asha.

'Why didn't you send round the police right away? Why—'

'Kamal, you keep forgetting we're in India, not America. I keep forgetting it too. When Gita came around and told me what had happened that was also my first thought, and she just laughed it off. She'd already thought of everything, called the American embassy, who aren't being at all helpful. Kamathipura is the problem. The police don't care, Kamal. They're completely in the pockets of those pimps, and the fact that Caroline is white isn't any help. They'd either stroll around there in two or three days' time and enjoy a cup of coffee with the madam, or not bother at all.'

'Caroline's American. This time the American embassy *has* to help.'

'I told you – Gita already tried them. And again, Kamathipura is the problem. Try explaining why they should rescue an American woman who voluntarily went into the worst area of Bombay, into a brothel, and see how eager they are to help.'

Kamal said: 'I'm going to call Wayne. He'll know what to do. Caroline said he has good contacts; he knows the ambassador. We need to pull some strings.'

Janiki nodded. 'Yes, do that, call Wayne. But: do you really think Caroline and Asha are in the same room still? Surely they have been removed by now? All we can do is hope that Caroline is astute enough to free them both. I don't think wild horses could separate her from Asha now, and unless—'

'My God, Janiki, how can you be so sanguine about all this? Caroline can't deal with being locked up in Kamathipura by a bunch of goons! Caroline can't deal with India at all, much less handle a situation like this! I have to go…'

He leapt to his feet as if to rush off to help Caroline.

'Wait, Kamal, wait… listen: you unloaded another problem on us last night and we really, really need to deal with this little girl as well. What do you want me to do with her?'

They both glanced again at the child, who continued to shovel food into her mouth as if she hadn't eaten in a year.

'She's so thin!' said Janiki. 'So now tell me – what happened? How did you get her?'

'It's grim,' said Kamal, sitting down again. 'They offered me her as a substitute for the girl I was supposed to get, shoved her in the car. I escaped with her. That's it, basically. All I know is that her own father sells her. I saw it with my own eyes. Her mother is dead, apparently.'

'Gruesome.' Janiki shuddered. 'We should take her to Dr Ganotra, so he can take her into his programme. And she needs to go to hospital, Kamal. She needs to be examined and we need to get social services looking into it. If she's being trafficked by her own father she can't go back to him.'

'I agree, absolutely. But, Janiki – can you do that alone? She's terrified of men, and no wonder. And yesterday I kind of grabbed her and ran – must have been scary for her. Look – I'll deal with Caroline and Asha, and you take her to Dr Ganotra, OK?'

'You'll be needed, though, Kamal. You'll have to make a police statement at some point, describe what happened.'

'I thought the police didn't care?'

'They don't. But with a child as young as this – well, they can't send her back to her dad and there must be some system set up and they'll have to investigate. Dr Ganotra will want to know.'

'Right. Well, when they need me, I'll come. Right now, I need to go and look for Asha and Caroline. Are you finished? I am. Why don't you stay here while I run off. What's the address again?'

Janiki handed Kamal a slip of paper with the address of Asha's tentative whereabouts on it. 'But she won't be there any longer. I guarantee it.'

'I'm going to the embassy and then I'll call Wayne. He'll pull some strings if they aren't helpful. Caroline told me Wayne's uncle is a senator. That'll do the trick.'

Kamal paid the cashier next to the door and loped out into the morning sunshine. Janiki shook her head. His eagerness and sense of urgency was understandable, but going back to that house was nothing less than futile. Janiki had plans of her own. She'd deliver the child to Dr Ganotra and then return to the computer at Tulasa House. Talk to The Vituperator – who had been unavailable yesterday afternoon – and somehow bargain with him. Maybe he was the key to rescuing Caroline and Asha. She had an idea how to do that. But first things first. The child.

* * *

'They tried to sell her to Kamal,' said Janiki to Dr Ganotra. 'He managed to rescue her.'

'Well done,' said Dr Ganotra, squatting down to the girl's level, holding out a hand. '*Namaste*, little one. What is your name?'

But the girl recoiled, hid behind Janiki's back, covered her face with the hem of Janiki's *kameez*.

'She's like that with Kamal too,' said Janiki. 'She's scared of all men. Her name is Ragi.'

Dr Ganotra stood up. 'Right. We see that a lot with children this young. Can you come with her to hospital? Stay with her while she's being examined? She seems to trust you.'

Janiki thought of the computer, but only for a second.

'Of course I'll come. She does seem to like me. Come on, *beti*. Come with Janiki Aunty.'

She held out her hand and the little girl took it and walked with her out of the house. Dr Ganotra flagged down a taxi and they all three entered. Janiki laid an arm around Ragi and pulled her close. The girl stuck a thumb in her mouth and nuzzled into Janiki's side. Janiki pulled her even closer, and stroked her hair.

* * *

Janiki was sitting at Ragi's bedside – she had now been transferred to a ward – when a nurse approached and said, 'There's someone outside to see you, ma'am. Are you able to come?'

Janiki glanced at the girl. She was asleep. She could go. She rose from her chair and walked out of the ward. Kamal was waiting for her.

'So?' she asked. 'How did it go? Did you go to the embassy? Talk to Wayne?'

Kamal looked drained, haggard. 'I went to the police station first and it was like talking to the Great Wall of China. Then I went to the American embassy, and just as I was going in Gita came out and we had lunch together. They're not too interested: seems they think Caroline put herself deliberately into harm's way and it's a high-crime area. They said the American embassy isn't a nanny. And you know Bombay. Sluggish, indifferent. So...' He shrugged. 'But I managed to get hold of Wayne on the phone and spoke to him. He's going to ask this senator uncle to intervene, and he's getting the next plane out. He's frantic. We've not only not found Asha, we've lost Caroline as well.'

'I *told* her not to go,' said Janiki. 'If she'd only waited I could somehow have sent you or some other man instead and you could have officially bought Asha the next day. It was all perfectly arranged; she had to go and mess it all up. So now we have to wait for the Americans to act? But you know, they could both just disappear into a black hole now. You know that, right?'

'I know. So what now?'

'What now? Nothing. It's all a waiting game. It seems that all we ever do in Bombay is wait.'

Chapter Fifty-One

Caroline

Up until this point Caroline had successfully kept her fear at bay. It was as if she had worn an armour of invulnerability. She tried to speak, but the words would not come. Devaki, on the other hand, was still talking away, her back to Caroline, while sorting the clothing from one of the drawers into two piles.

'These are some of the best *shalwars* you can find in Bombay. I still call this place Bombay; old people like me can't suddenly change like that. I think you would look good in a rich emerald green. Kamini would look beautiful in any colour, any style. Look, I have found something suitable for you. I want you both to wash your hair now. Afterwards I will put some ointment on it to get rid of the lice. The best thing is shaving off all the hair but that is too extreme in this case. The bathroom is through that door. Here's a nice red *shalwar* for her, but don't get dressed properly until after the lice treatment.'

'Devaki, listen.' Caroline found her voice, and though it seemed, to her, to be little more than a croak, it was determined. 'I told you – I'm not for sale. If those men sold me it was a mistake. I stayed with this girl voluntarily in order to look after her. I don't know what's going on but I'm glad you speak English and maybe you can explain to me—'

'I have no time for explanations! It's quite simple. I work for Mr Rajgopal and this girl had been selected by Mr Chaudhuri who is his customer. That's all there is to it. You are an older white woman. Mr Rajgopal will decide what to do with you. He might not have any use for you if you say you are unwilling. I don't know. You were cheap so I don't care. Mr Rajgopal will make the decision. There are several options but I would strongly suggest that you behave and look your best for him because then you will have a good life in a very good house.'

'You can't keep me. I am an American citizen. My husband has important contacts. They will come after me as soon as they know and there will be big trouble for you. You should let us both go, now!'

But Devaki only shrugged. 'How will they find you? People don't talk here. This is a huge city. Just behave yourself and you will be fine.'

'You can't honestly expect me to suddenly become a – a *prostitute*? I'm an American! I have rights! Important contacts! My husband will raise hell when he finds out. You will get into big trouble.'

Devaki chuckled. 'Oh, so high and mighty! You think you are better than ladies of the night because you never had to sell yourself? Better than me? You privileged white people think you are gods or something. You think you have *rights*? Who gave you those rights? You think anyone here cares about your rights? Well let me tell you this, there are people out there who would pay a good price to bring down a white god like you with all your rights. You are valuable even though you are too old really. Willing or not. Unwilling is even better, but easier for you if you are willing. And—'

'They will find you! My husband will find you! I'll make sure that you go to prison for life! I—'

'And *how* will he find me? You don't even know where you are. This is a city of almost twenty million. Nobody knows where you are. They cannot find you. And you'd better explain to Kamini that she needs to be talking. I expect you to encourage her, then she can return to Mr Chaudhuri soon. She will have an excellent career. As for you, you're not bad-looking but you don't have her class – I know of a good place for you but you can't expect luxury. I'll have to separate you, of course. Now look… No, don't interrupt me. I haven't much time. I have to see to some other girls upstairs. You get her bathed and put on your nighties again for delousing. I am sending a maid with the bottle. You just massage it into the hair and leave it there for ten minutes. It's a special ointment we import from Germany, very efficient; all the lice and nits are gone afterwards, I call it Devil Juice. When you have done that you are to wash it out properly again, then dry your hair and hers and get dressed. I'll be back in an hour to see how things are. I want you looking lovely for Mr Rajgopal, it's all to your advantage. If I were you I would persuade her to speak now. He has a bad temper sometimes and if he thinks she is still being stubborn he might just send her into one of the cheap houses back in Kamathipura. You don't want that. You've been there, you know what the houses are like. Both of you could have a better life but you have to behave sensibly. Then all will be well. So I have to go now. Do what I said and get yourselves cleaned up. You'll have to wake her, she can't sleep all day. I'll be back in an hour.'

When Devaki had left the room Caroline walked to the window and looked out; she was trying to assess their chances of escape. Her heart sank as she saw that the house was in the middle of a garden, and that garden was surrounded by a high fence of wire netting. There was an iron gate, obviously very securely locked, and two sentries in khaki uniforms sitting on metal folding chairs just inside it, to the side of the gravel driveway, smoking and chatting. Though they weren't very alert at the moment, Caroline knew that they would be armed, and that they would be vigilant should she ever manage to leave the house. From this window, at least, there was no escape. It was firmly barred.

Her panic on realising that she had, in Devaki's eyes at least, been sold into prostitution had settled into a quiet dread and stimulated a wary, high frequency of thought. She had plunged into this predicament without thinking, following only her instinct. The moment Asha had clung to her in fear she had known she could not leave her, never again. There had been no premeditation. It was that maternal instinct, the one she thought she had lacked, springing up in full force.

Since there could be no escape for the moment, it seemed to Caroline prudent to do as Devaki said. It did not seem as if she and Asha were expected to begin 'work' immediately; in that case going along with Devaki was a play for time. Sooner or later a situation would turn up that would make flight possible; until then it would be best to keep Devaki's guard down. And as far as flight was concerned, she would play it by ear. She would wait for the right moment, trusting that at that moment the right means of escape would present itself. More than that she could not do. And anyway, she was dying for a shower.

Her mind firmly made up, she walked over to the bed, gently placed her hand on Asha's shoulder and shook it.

'Asha,' she said softly. 'Wake up.'

* * *

Her head was still tingling from the delousing liquid. The instructions on the bottle had been in German, but she had done what Devaki said and doused first Asha's, then her own hair generously, left the liquid to soak in and then washed it out. In Asha's rinse water there had been several dead lice, in her own none, but it had felt good to know that if any had been hiding there, they were now well and truly wiped out. And she had to admit it – the emerald *shalwar kameez* suited her well. Asha looked simply stunning – if one did not look at her eyes. She wore crimson silk, the *kameez* embroidered all the way up a front seam, with a pattern of tiny sequins sewn into the neckline. She looked like a princess.

Asha had submitted willingly to Caroline's handling of her. On awakening, she had followed the bathing, shampooing and delousing routine without a word. Afterwards she had allowed herself to be fed, and had drunk from the cup held to her lips. She had stepped into the *shalwar* Caroline had held out for her, right foot, left foot, holding onto Caroline's shoulders for balance, and allowed the drawstring to be tied; she had raised her arms and let Caroline pull the *kameez* over her head and fasten the hooks and eyes at the shoulder. Her hair had been blow-dried and brushed, so that it fell in a thick black curtain halfway down her back. Now she sat in the chair with her hands in her lap and stared at the wall, and her eyes, large almond eyes that should have been like brilliant amber sequins shining with spirit, were dead.

All this time, Caroline talked to her. Told her again and again she was sorry, so sorry, for leaving her behind as a small child. Sorry, so sorry, for not coming to visit more often. So very sorry for not coming to get her, taking her to live with her in America, being her mother. So sorry for not knowing that Sundari and Viram had died and Asha had no one to care for her, for not protecting her against Paruthy Uncle, for not writing or calling each and every day to tell her how much she loved her.

'But now I'm here, Asha. Now I'm with you and I'll never, ever again let you go until you are ready to go, all grown up and not needing me any more. I will protect you. I will keep you safe. I promise.'

Asha seemed not to listen, not to hear. But Caroline knew that deep inside, Asha was hearing every word and absorbing every promise, and that deep inside Asha also knew that this time she, Caroline, was here for keeps. And though all of Caroline's efforts to catch those eyes and fan a little spark into them simply failed, like flies hitting a pane of glass and falling stunned, somewhere, she knew, somewhere deep inside her daughter's heart a tiny spark was still alight; and it was that spark she spoke to, believed in. It would grow. She knew it.

Caroline now tried to keep up a lively, cheerful banter.

'Asha, I think it's going to be all right. We're much better off here, and if I keep my wits about me I'm sure we'll be able to get out soon. Don't worry. And look how clean it is here, and we get fed properly. I think your luck has turned, Asha. But I don't know how long it will take. We have to meet the owner of this place in a while, and somehow impress him. I don't want to push you, you can take your own time, but it would be much better if you would speak a word or two – just to keep him from shunting us back into Kamathipura. I'm sure you can do that. Say good morning, and try to smile. Just to let him know you speak English; it's a play for time because I don't know when and I don't know how I'm going to get us out, but I will. That's a promise!'

But all Asha did was stare, and her lips did not so much as twitch.

Caroline was beginning to despair of ever coaxing a reaction from Asha when once again the key turned in the lock and Devaki entered, followed by the same maid who had brought their breakfast.

'Oh, you look lovely! Very lovely, both of you! Who would have guessed it – though I certainly knew that beneath all the grime there were two little jewels hiding! Mr Rajgopal will be extremely pleased with you – this girl is simply delightful. She has a very rare beauty! Have you persuaded her to speak?'

'Not yet,' Caroline admitted, 'but I'm sure I will.'

Everything in her rebelled against the role she knew it was necessary to play. She wanted to lash out at Devaki; to dig at her eyes, scratch at her face, bite and kick her before taking flight; but she knew she had only one trump card, and had to play it carefully. The time would come; and the means would not be violent ones, but wily ones. She would not lose this battle, even if it meant, for a while, playing the mild meek pussycat while a tiger crouched within, waiting to attack... But no. There would be no attack. The situation called for cunning.

Devaki impatiently beckoned the maid forward and said something to her in another language.

'What you both need is some jewellery. I will have some costume jewellery sent up. What's that?' She reached out and fingered the rings around Caroline's neck.

'They're my rings. Wedding ring and engagement ring.' As an afterthought she lied: 'They are of sentimental value only.'

'Well, if they are of any value at all I would take them off and hide them if I were you – that's my tip. Because Mr Rajgopal will want them – you need to pay him back the price he paid for you, you know. He is rather greedy. I am sure they are worth a lakh or two. Even that he would want.'

'Do you think I could buy my freedom with it? And Asha's?'

'With that?' Devaki laughed. 'A lakh or two is peanuts to Mr Rajgopal. I know a little about jewellery and I can tell he won't be impressed – it's certainly not enough to offset the amount he intends to make with you. If you like, you can give them to me. I will keep them safe for you.'

'Why should I trust you?'

'Oh, I am very trustworthy. Don't think because I am working in this trade I am a thief. You won't find a more honest person than me working in the trade. In fact, I am a very decent woman, my origins are extremely respectable. I used to be a maid for a very high-class English lady. I have a good education, my parents sent me to an English-medium school! And I am a very kind woman; I have never hit any girl working for me in all my life. I only happened into this trade through bad luck.'

Caroline realised that if there was anything Devaki liked doing, it was talking. The woman seemed under a compulsion to talk, talk, talk, and Caroline realised that the more she kept her talking, the more information she would get out of her, and the better she would be able to figure out an escape.

'What happened?' she asked boldly.

'Well, it was that dastardly son of the Englishwoman – James was his name. Very good-looking! I was a young woman of seventeen at the time, very impressionable. He coaxed me into acting against my conscience – I was a very innocent girl, what did I know of the ways of men? What could I do to repulse the advances of a young Englishman? He was younger than me, fifteen, sixteen. Well, all went well for a time but what did I know about the facts of life? Before I knew it I was expecting a child and that woman threw me out. What could I do? I could not return to my village – what a disgrace for my parents! I found a Catholic home where I could stay till my daughter was born. They wanted me to give her up for adoption but I would never do that – give up my own flesh and blood! Never. So I put her in the orphanage and went to look for work. Well, what work could I find after that disgrace – me, a woman on her own in such a big city? I was a fallen woman, and I fell still further – how could I not? What a terrible life I was forced to lead! But the worst of it was losing my daughter. Ay! Those nuns found out what I was doing and wouldn't let me near her. They wanted me to sign some papers to take her away from me permanently – in fact they stole her from me. But I wasn't doing that! And when she was six I stole her back.'

Devaki opened a plastic box. It was brimful of hairstyling apparatus: brushes, combs, ribbons, grips, everything one could possibly need.

'I shall make this hair really beautiful,' she said. 'You won't believe what magic my hands can perform!'

'So how old is your daughter now?' Caroline prompted. She had to keep the woman chatting.

'About the age of this girl, or a year or two older,' said Devaki. 'Perhaps not as lovely but to a mother her daughter is always beautiful! She is fair too, of course – her father was an English-man, after all. You must tell me your daughter's story one of these days. I like to hear all your stories – I am like a mother, I really care about my girls.'

'If you really cared about them you'd let them go. You wouldn't be doing this at all!'

'But my girls are happy! I can tell you're new at this trade – any girl who's lived for a time in Kamathipura would give her eyes to work for me! You are very ungrateful. I can tell Kamini here thinks differently – she can appreciate the difference now.' Devaki was now vigorously brushing Asha's hair, and obviously taking great pleasure in it.

'But would you let your own daughter work like this? If she's Asha's age, do you also have her doing this kind of work?'

The woman glanced at Caroline and scowled. 'Of course she isn't working like this! Don't even suggest it! That's one of the reasons I used all my cunning to advance in my profession, so I could move out of that place I was living in and find a more respectable lodging for me and my daughter. But rents are so expensive in Bombay – all I have is a small room and it's quite near Kamathipura. The nuns would not tell me where she is but I found out. She is now in another home for young girls. She goes to a normal school.'

'But if – say she lived with you. Would you allow her to…?'

'Never! Of course not! I would never let her work this way! My daughter is very lovely. She is also educated, and in a year's time she will have finished school.'

'What will she do then?'

'Well, I have to try and find a proper husband for her but it is difficult – I want her to marry decently but how can I prevent the boy's parents from finding out what I do for a living? That is my great sorrow. It is hard enough raising a child alone, but finding a husband for a daughter is near to impossible for a single mother and especially trying for me. But everybody has their dream.'

Devaki twisted a strand of Asha's hair into a long curl and clipped it to the top of her head. She picked up a second strand and did the same again, over and over, till only one strand was left. This she began to plait with quick, deft fingers. Every now and then she stopped to push the bangles up her arm. Why doesn't she just take them off, Caroline wondered vaguely, since they all keep falling down anyway?

'What is your dream?' she asked.

'My dream? Well, I don't usually tell this to my girls but between you and me, for my daughter's sake it would be necessary to start all over again, in some other city where I can be anonymous. Lucknow: that is my dream! My native village is in the vicinity of Lucknow and I know the city well. A nice clean little flat for me and my daughter. It doesn't have to be big, but respectable. I don't even mind working as a housekeeper for some rich family – I would not earn as much as I do here but I would make good contacts that way. My daughter could also find work as a maid – I would train her myself. But hairdressing is my real dream. I have a gift for hairstyling. I would like to style the hair of brides – I'm sure I could make a business out of it! And my final dream is to see my daughter as a bride herself, and style her hair for her own wedding! But it is only a dream. How can I start anew? I am trying to save every *paise* I have but life is costly here – money just fritters away and I am struggling even to survive. How can I save anything? You see, we all have our problems, and everyone's problem is a mountain to that person, so you shouldn't complain. Now please don't talk to me any more, I have to concentrate. When I'm finished you will see why.'

And Caroline did see why. Asha's hair, when finished, was truly fit for a bride: smooth and sleek around her face, and at the back a sculpture of interwoven plaits. It managed to be sophisticated and simple at once, every strand placed in exactly the right position, not a single hair out of place.

Pleased with herself, Devaki pushed the bangles up her arms again and turned to Janiki with a smile. 'See! That's how Mr Rajgopal likes hair to be styled. Now it's your turn.'

* * *

After Caroline's hair was finished Devaki said it was time to go, to visit this mysterious Mr Rajgopal.

'Usually he would come here but he has a tight schedule so we are going to his place. A car is coming to pick us up. It will be here in ten minutes.'

Caroline had not spoken a word since hearing Devaki's story. She had let Devaki style her hair without comment, murmuring only an 'um' in answer to questions, or nodding when asked for approval. She'd been thinking, planning, plotting. Now it was time to speak up.

'Devaki,' she said, quietly. 'I'm going to make you an offer. Come; look at me.'

'Yes? What is it?' Devaki was touching up Asha's face; a little bit more rouge, and a touch more kajal. Asha now looked more like eighteen than thirteen, and Caroline wondered in passing why, if young girls were so coveted in this trade, so much effort was made to make them look older. But other things were on her mind and so she said now, 'Come, Devaki. Leave her and come.'

'Just a little bit more – close your eyes, darling – I'm coming. What is it? We have to hurry. The car will be here soon—'

'Never mind the car, Devaki. Listen: how would you like to fulfil your dream now? Right now – next week, maybe? I can make your dream come true.'

Devaki's eyes narrowed. 'What do you mean?'

'I mean I have money. I have money here in my bank in Mumbai. I have my own savings, but my husband is also a very rich man. Only yesterday I was talking to him and he said he is going to wire over some money to my bank account in India. I have a bank account that I use to pay for Asha's maintenance. Well, now it is full of money. I will give you enough to buy a little house in Lucknow and set you up independently there. You are so good with hairstyling. You can start your hairstyling business right away. I will help you. I promise. I can write you a cheque right away. I have my chequebook in my handbag.'

'No cheque. Cash. We go to bank and you give cash.'

'I won't be able to withdraw a large amount in cash. I know this from when I was living in India. But I can get them to issue a bank draft. That is just like cash. Then you can deposit it in your own bank and in a few days the money will be yours.'

Devaki frowned, thinking. 'But if I do that and you report me maybe you send police to put me in jail. When I collect money from bank.'

'No, Devaki. I would never do that. I promise. You can trust me.'

'Why I should trust you? No. It is a trick.'

Why, indeed? Caroline, the panic rising within her, had to think quickly. It was now or never. She closed her eyes, took a deep breath. Cleared her mind. And in that moment, inspiration came to her. She reached up, behind her neck.

'Look, Devaki. These rings. They are my engagement ring and my wedding ring. I lied to you. They are worth a lot of money. More than a crore. It is a real diamond on the engagement ring. It was very expensive. But I will give both to you as a deposit. Because I trust you. If I can trust you, you can trust me. Listen: we will go to my bank now together. I will instruct them to write a draft, which I will give you, along with the two rings. In a few days' time you call me at my hotel and we go together to your bank, to collect the cash. And once you have the cash, you return the rings to me. So the rings are a deposit. I trust you, and you trust me. The rings are very precious to me but I trust you. You could sell them for a lot of money, but it would take time, and it is risky as it would be theft. The bank draft would be easier for you. You could be in Lucknow in a week's time. All you have to do is give me back my Asha. I am a mother too, Devaki. As mothers together, let us help each other. Here. Take the rings.'

As she spoke, unclasping the chain, she looked Devaki in the eye, trying to hold the other woman's fickle, flickering gaze. She slid the two rings off their chain and held them out to Devaki. Devaki held out her open palm, her eyes still hesitant, dithering, doubtful. Outside, a car blew its horn. Devaki snapped back her hand as if bitten, wiped it on her *dupatta* as if it were stained.

'No,' she said. 'The driver has come. We have to go. Mr Rajgopal is waiting.'

She turned as if to walk away, but Caroline reached for her, grabbed her shoulder, cried out in desperation: 'Devaki, no! Please, let us go! You will be free and your daughter too. Let's do this! Don't let those men win! Free my daughter. Build a life with *your* daughter. Please, Devaki, please!'

Her eyes filled with tears, and that was the moment Devaki could finally look into them, feel their depth and their pain, feel her own pain, her own needs, her own longing for freedom. Devaki's own eyes grew moist, and she reached out and closed her palm over Caroline's hand that still held the rings. And finally, their gazes met, connected.

'I do not need your rings. Keep them. I trust you. We will do it. We will go to the bank.'

* * *

The car slid through the open gate, Devaki in the passenger seat, Asha and Caroline in the back. Caroline held her breath. Would Devaki change her mind? Would she rethink her decision, get cold feet, fear that she would be caught, mistrust her, Caroline, again? The silence was unnerving – but what could she say to break it?

They drove in that unnerving silence for half an hour through stop-and-go traffic. Then Devaki turned to the driver, and spoke a few words. He bobbed his head in acquiescence.

'The doors lock automatically,' she said. 'He has to unlock them for you. I told him we are going for a meal at a restaurant at the next corner. He's a stupid man, and I'm his superior – he will obey me, though it's an unusual request. But he knows I don't fool around. So he'll let you out. When he has driven off we will get another taxi and go to your bank.'

The car stopped in front of a restaurant. There was a click as the locks were released. Caroline opened her door, and she and Asha stepped out onto the pavement. Devaki's door opened too, and she climbed out to stand beside them.

'Now we all walk calmly towards the restaurant. Driver will have to drive away, he's going to park somewhere nearby and I told him to pick us up in half an hour. When he comes he won't find anybody!' Devaki could hardly hide her mirth at this thought; she placed a hand over her mouth to suppress a giggle. 'He's very faithful to Mr Rajgopal but he has to obey me. Come on, let's go. Walk in front of me as if I'm the boss!'

They made their way towards the restaurant; the car slid past them.

'All right. He's gone. Now a taxi!' Devaki flagged down an empty motor-rickshaw, which stopped immediately. The two women and Asha climbed in. Caroline checked the address of her bank's Mumbai branch.

'Central Avenue Road, Chembur,' she said, and Devaki repeated the instructions to the driver. The rickshaw scooted off.

It took an hour to get to the bank, and another half-hour before the cashier slid the bank draft over the counter to Caroline.

They left the bank together, and Caroline placed the draft in Devaki's hands.

'Here you are. Two crores of rupees. Take it to your own bank. It is yours. It is your new life.'

Devaki placed the draft between her two palms, raised her hand to her forehead, closed her eyes.

'It's the grace of God,' she said. 'You are God in human form.' Caroline laughed, and *namasted* in return.

'No, Devaki, I'm just a mother doing what is right for her child!' she said. 'I wish you well. And your daughter. I think the trade is losing a little piece of humanity today.'

They *namasted* again; then, simultaneously, they turned around, parting company. Devaki walked in one direction; Caroline took Asha's hand and walked in another.

She had no idea where she was. Traffic snorted and screeched around her, exhaust fumes belched, the pavement heaved with a stream of humanity that parted at their coming and closed again behind them. She decided to take a taxi. Devaki had let her keep her little shoulder bag; she rummaged inside it. The brothel-keeper in Kamathipura had taken her purse, but her credit card was still there, stored separately in a zippered pocket. She had been warned to keep only cash in her purse, in case of pickpockets.

'Come, Asha. Let's find a bank, and a cash machine. And then we'll take a taxi and go home. We're free. For ever! And I'll never let you go again.'

She took Asha's hand and walked on. And then she could no longer walk. She ran, and as she ran she laughed, and Asha ran beside her and she laughed too.

Chapter Fifty-Two

Janiki

'Have you had lunch?' asked Janiki.

'Yes. Well, I went to a restaurant with Gita and had a bite but I couldn't eat much. I feel sick. But you must be starving – I take it you haven't eaten? It's nearly three. Let's go.'

They walked down the stairs to the hospital's entrance lobby. Kamal stopped, and stared. And then he rushed forward.

'Caroline!' he cried. 'And, oh my God, Asha! Asha, my sweet, there you are! You're safe!' He gathered his daughter into his arms. But Asha pushed him away. She rushed forward, and practically leapt into Janiki's arms. 'Janiki, Janiki, Janiki!'

And they were both laughing and hugging and kissing. Caroline looked at Kamal, rather shyly. 'Don't take it personally, Kamal. She needs time. Remember how close she was to Janiki.'

Kamal nodded, but said nothing.

Janiki and Asha stopped hugging and Janiki said, 'Asha, that was very rude of you not to greet your daddy. Come on now and say hello. He's been so worried about you all this time.'

And she led Asha back to her father and Kamal held out his arms and Asha, very slowly, smiled at him and said 'Hello Daddy.' And they hugged, not in the wild and overjoyed way Kamal had wanted but in a reserved and polite way. And Janiki stroked Kamal's arm and said, 'It's all right, Kamal. It will be all right.'

And Kamal nodded, though his heart was breaking. And then it was Caroline's turn to hug everyone.

'Yes,' she said tiredly. 'She's safe. We're both safe. I'll tell you the whole story later. Right now I'd like a doctor to see her; she's got wounds all over her back.'

'You should take her to Dr Ganotra first to be registered for the Safe Haven programme,' said Janiki. 'That's the way it's done. He has an office here. I'll take you there. He's here right now. Come on.'

* * *

A while later, she and Kamal left Caroline and Asha in Dr Ganotra's office and set out once again for the lobby, heading for the postponed meal. On their way down the corridor they passed a woman in a white coat, a stethoscope around her neck. 'Doctor! Doctor, stop a moment,' cried Janiki, 'I'd like you to meet Kamal. He's the fellow who rescued Ragi. Kamal – this is Dr Pratima Nath-Willard. She's the one who examined Ragi! She's fantastic! Got her to talk a little!'

Dr Nath-Willard was a woman in her late fifties; huge brown eyes assessed Kamal and reflected the warmth of her smile.

'Pleased to meet you, Kamal. You're quite the hero, you know. That girl – she's been terribly abused. But she's recovering well, and slowly telling us about her wretched life. You will have to talk to social services, tell them what happened, describe the father and so on – they'll try and find him to raise charges of child trafficking but most likely nothing will come of it: they won't find him. She'll go into care. We have a few good orphanages in Mumbai.'

'What if – what if someone came forward, and wanted to adopt her,' said Janiki tentatively. 'Wouldn't she be better off in a family?'

'Oh, definitely. In particular, she needs to regain her trust in men. She needs a loving father. Desperately. Someone who—'

Suddenly grasping the subtlety of Janiki's words, she stopped speaking and looked from her to Kamal.

'Is this' – nodding at Kamal – 'Is this your…'

Kamal and Janiki locked eyes in the pause. Kamal's eyes asked a question, Janiki's eyes gave the answer, accompanied by a very slight, almost imperceptible, bobble of her head.

'Fiancé,' said Kamal. 'That's right. And we'd like to submit an expression of interest. Where do we do that?'

Dr Nath-Willard smiled. 'The social worker dealing with her case will take down your particulars and she will do the needful,' she said. 'Congratulations.'

Epilogue

Asha

So Mom saved me in the end. It all happened so quickly. Suddenly they were all there, all the people I loved: Mom and Dad and Janiki, and even people I didn't know, but who already seemed to love me, a man I called Wayne Uncle but Mom said he was to be my new dad so I mustn't call him Uncle. So he said I could call him Wayne, but it's rude to call an adult by their first name so I called him Wayne Uncle in my mind and just never said it out loud. I didn't want to be rude. But he was nice. He came from America. He is Mom's husband. He only stayed a few days then he had to go back to America, to work. But he said he would come back for the wedding, and he did.

And there was a little girl called Ragi who they said was to be my little sister, and she loved me too; she was a bit scared of everyone except Janiki and she clung to me so I took care of her, and Janiki laughed and said I could be her chinna-amma. And then there was a very big lady who never got up because she can't walk, and she is called Rani Abishta. I was scared of her but they said she is my great-grandmother. That means she is Dad's grandmother, and I should call her Daadi. She was scary but very kind to me, feeding me sweets all day, but Mom said I wasn't to eat so many sweets; it wasn't healthy. But Daadi still fed me sweets and called me to sit on her lap but I didn't want to, so she just laughed and fed me some more sweets. Those were the most delicious sweets I ever ate in my whole life. I couldn't stop eating them. So whenever I could I sneaked away and went to Daadi for sweets, and I took Ragi with me because Ragi liked being with me, and she liked the sweets too.

We left Bombay soon after my rescue to go to this place where Rani Abishta lived. It was like a palace in the *Mahabharata*, like Indraprastha, with beautiful gardens and marble buildings and carpets and tapestries and wonderful paintings everywhere. It is Daadi's home and she said it is my home too. We could all stay there as long as we wanted. And she and Dad spent a lot of time together talking so I was mostly with Mom and Janiki and Ragi. We went for long walks in the gardens and there were mango trees and we could eat mangoes straight from the tree. I took good care of Ragi. She held my hand all the time and Mom and Janiki laughed and said, 'We cannot separate them. They are sisters.'

And then there was a wedding in that place. Dad and Janiki got married. It was the most beautiful wedding in the world. Janiki looked so gorgeous in her red sari. She and Dad love each other very much. They walked around the holy fire together and vowed to always love each other. That's what marriage means, Janiki told me. Janiki said I didn't have to call her Amma now; she would always be my chinna-amma but I could still call her Janiki because she is my sister as well as my chinna-amma. Wayne Uncle came for the wedding but left again. He works hard.

After the wedding we came to another place and that is even more beautiful than Daadi's palace. It is in the Nilgiri Hills in South India, and it is just like living in heaven with lakes and hills and trees and flowers. The place belongs to Dad. It is part of the silk business that Dad owns, a resort for the staff.

Mom is working with Ragi and me in that heavenly place. She is doing a thing called Therapy, which sounds scary, but it isn't at all. It's fun. We paint a lot and make figures out of clay, and we play musical instruments and sing and dance, and act in plays. Doing all these things makes me happy, and it makes Ragi happy too.

Ragi has a lot of problems, Janiki said. She had an evil dad who did mean things to her and she was very sad inside so we all had to love her very much and that will cure her. Our love will gradually wash away the bad feelings inside her. Our love will make the ugliness she has known melt into the past, so she can have a future. Our love will make her life beautiful. So we all love her as much as we can, and Ragi has learned to smile and love back. And she has even learned to love Dad too, because Dad did Therapy with her. She used to be scared of Dad, but Dad played with her and me and we swam together in the lake, and we sang and made music together. And I no longer think Dad is a god; he's just Dad and I love him like you're supposed to love a dad.

And another good thing happened. Mom has a friend in America who is a journalist. And when Mom told her my story, and about Ragi, that friend wrote an article and it was published in a big foreign newspaper with photos of me and Ragi. And all the foreigners in America and England and all over the world got all angry and made a huge fuss and so the Indian newspapers also made a big fuss and everyone in America and Europe was outraged. And we were even on American TV! And English and German and Italian TV!

And then Indians also got outraged and the Indian politicians and lawmakers and police also got outraged and they came to talk to me and Ragi and Daddy and Mom and Gita and Janiki. And everything came to light and they arrested all kinds of people and even Mr Chaudhuri and Mr Rajgopal, and they will go to jail. But not Devaki Aunty because she went to live in Lucknow, Mom said, to start a new life, and Mom didn't tell the police about her. Because Devaki Aunty helped, and trusted us, and she has a daughter too, Mom said.

And people sent donations from all over the world to help little girls like Ragi, and in the space of a month Dr Ganotra was able to rescue five more of them. And so many donations came in that he was able to buy another house in the country so that they have a place to go when they are rescued, because Tulasa House is not enough. So you see: even when terrible things happen, good things can result. And now I understand why I never gave up hope.

We have been here for months now. Because Therapy takes a long time. But sooner or later, Janiki said, the adults have to decide what they want to do and where they want to live.

'We all want to stay together,' Janiki said. 'Kamal and I are adopting Ragi so she is our daughter, but you are everyone's daughter, Caroline's and Kamal's and mine, and so we all have to live together, and Wayne too. It's a bit of a problem, baby, but not a big one. We can buy a big house for us all in America or here in India. A house where two families can live, with a lovely garden, or two houses next to each other. Wayne already has a job in America so probably it will be there. All the rest of us are more flexible and we don't care; we just want to be with you.'

So it looks as if we are all going to move to America. To a place called Massachoosits. It's a lovely place, Mom said, and we'll have a lovely big house, big enough for all of us, with a porch all around it, and Ragi and I will go to school. But first Ragi has to learn English, but she already can say some words. I am teaching her.

Janiki loves computers, but she does not have one here. She says she is taking a computer break. But when the break is over she is going to work as a detective. Just like in the stories we used to read together, except she will be a computer detective. She found me through detective work on the computer. She wants to find other stolen girls with the computer. She is going to work with Doctor G, who is the doctor who helped find me. He said I can call him Doctor G because I can't remember his name; I just remember it starts with G. And Gita's name also starts with G. She is Janiki's and Mom's friend. She showed us some nice places in Bombay – but still we were in a hurry to leave, because of the bad things that happened there. 'We must put the past behind us,' Janiki said, and that's what we're going to do.

So now I have two mothers and two fathers and a little sister, and maybe one day some more brothers and sisters, Janiki said. But it just shows that I was wrong when I said I was lost for ever. Bad times are never for ever. Bad times come and bad times go, and when they are with us, we must remember that all will be well by the power of all harmony. And that is the simple truth. And that is why my name is Asha: Hope.

Letter from Sharon

First of all, I want to say a huge thank you for choosing *The Lost Daughter of India*. I hope you enjoyed reading Asha's story just as much as I loved writing it.

If you did enjoy it, I would be forever grateful if you'd do two things; firstly, tell others: readers in your family, friends and social media circles. Nothing helps a book as much as word of mouth: simply telling others 'I loved this book.' The more the word spreads, the more people will look it up, read the reviews, feel encouraged to buy it. Secondly: write a review. I'd love to hear what you think, and it will also help other readers discover one of my books for the first time.

On a more personal level, there's nothing that makes my day as much as a reader's letter so do please drop me a line, either on my social media pages or through the contact form on my website. I promise to reply!

This particular book is close to my heart, since it addresses a heartbreaking situation that unfortunately is still alive in today's world. At this moment, there are children such as Asha and Ragi who are sold into prostitution like pieces of property. They need our awareness; awareness leads to help. Please go on to read my author notes following this letter.

Last of all, if you'd like to keep up to date with all my latest releases, just sign up here:

www.bookouture.com/sharonmaas/

Thank you so much for your support – until next time.

Sharon Maas

Find me on:

www.bookouture.com/sharonmaas

 @sharon_maas

sharonmaasauthor

www.sharonmaas.com

Author Notes

Asha, Ragi and the other 'lost' girls who appear in The Lost Daughter of *India* might be fictitious, but they are nevertheless real. I first came into contact with the horrendous plight of such girls in the year 2000, during the research for one of my early novels; like Janiki and Caroline, I walked the streets of Kamathipura, and was able to visit a few brothels and talk to young girls who had been stolen from their homes for the trade.

In my research I was aided by Dr Gilada, the founder of the People's Health Organisation in Mumbai. Dr Ganotra of *The Lost Girl of India* is based on Dr Gilada, and the story he tells of the Nepalese girl Tulasa is taken directly from an interview I did with him back in 2000. Tulasa's story is true. There are still many Tulasas in Mumbai and other Indian and Asian cities today. Her story is shocking; but sometimes we need to be shocked. However, there is at last some good news. Here is that interview, with an update:

Saving Tulasa, child sex worker from Nepal

An Interview with Dr Gilada

Dr Ishwarprasad Gilada, founder, General-Secretary and driving force behind the People's Health Organisation in India, has been fighting against the horrors of the Bombay sex trade for the last two decades.

Sharon: Your crusade against child prostitution in India began with the rescue of Tulasa in 1982; back then, the story made front page headlines in India and Nepal, and opened a viper's nest of horrors. Who was Tulasa?

Dr I.G.: Tulasa Thalpa was a twelve-year-old Nepali girl who in 1982 was kidnapped from her village and sold into prostitution in Bombay. She was systematically raped to make her fit for the trade and then forced to entertain an average of eight clients a day. I met her ten months later in the Bombay hospital where I was working at the time. Her tiny body – the body of a child – was completely broken. She was suffering from three types of sexually transmitted diseases (STDs), genital warts and brain tuberculosis, which left her disabled and wheelchair-bound, and finally killed her. The story she told was horrific. The People's Health Organisation embarked on a full-fledged 'Save Tulasa' campaign, and with the support of the media managed to rescue her. We located her father – her mother had died shortly after her disappearance – and sent her home.

Sharon: You say with the support of the media. Didn't the police help in the rescue campaign?

Dr. I.G.: Police collusion with the flesh trade was a crucial point in Tulasa's revelations. Even today the police and the politicians are in collaboration with the pimps – the profit is huge. Back then, the uproar generated by her story forced the police into action, and in no time thirty-two persons involved were arrested, including the three brothel owners Tulasa had worked for. The police knew exactly what was going on, but only stepped in when forced to do so. It took them eighteen months to ascertain her age and three years to file a charge. And only last January, eighteen years later, did the case finally to come to trial. The police were given a month to produce her in court. Only then did we receive a message that Tulasa had died two years previously. Meanwhile, her abusers have been running free.

Sharon: After her rescue didn't she find peace in Nepal?

Dr I.G.: No. At first there had been an outpouring of sympathy for her – offers of adoption and marriage, an invitation to Switzerland, gifts of money and medicine. None of it came to much. Tulasa was rejected by her father's second wife, and moved into a home. Her father avoided her to keep the family peace. She was in constant pain, but worst of all was the feeling that nobody loved her, that she had been used and abused and finally discarded like a piece of rubbish.

Sharon: Is Tulasa's story typical of child prostitutes in India's megacities?

Dr I.G.: Yes. Soon after Tulasa's rescue the air was abuzz with innumerable stories of girls who were caged and treated like animals in Kamathipura, Bombay's infamous red light district. They narrated harrowing tales of torture and abuse. The PHO has to date directly rescued more than 130 girls, and more than 3,000 indirectly. The youngest girl we rescued was only eight years old.

Sharon: Has trafficking of children in Bombay improved since Tulasa's rescue?

Dr I.G.: Horrifying as it is, Tulasa's case has had some positive fallout. The episode threw the spotlight on the appalling practice of child prostitution – the public outcry was tremendous. As a result, the governments of India and Nepal signed a treaty for the rescue and repatriation of Nepali girls from Indian brothels. In India the sentence for trafficking minors has been hiked from seven to thirteen years. Child prostitution has been reduced by about 40 per cent.

Sharon: How do children end up as prostitutes in India?

Dr I.G.: About 40 per cent of all child prostitutes have been abducted from villages all over India and Nepal. They are lured away on some pretext or other: going to movies, cities, temples, making them film stars, lucrative job opportunities, marriage. Another major source of child prostitutes is the Devadasi system. Every year thousands of girls are ceremoniously dedicated to the goddess Yellamma. They are sold to the highest bidder and after a brief period of concubinage turned over to the urban brothels. The system is officially banned but continues to operate clandestinely, contributing up to 20 per cent of urban child prostitutes.

A small proportion of child prostitutes come to the trade after being raped. Others run away from incestuous relationships with family members. Yet others are daughters of prostitutes, who have no other option than to follow their mothers' profession.

Sharon: What are their living conditions in the brothels?

Dr I.G.: The girls live in unimaginable squalor, usually about ten–twelve girls in a small room. The brothels are foul, stinking holes, often overrun with rats and vermin. They eat from filthy cafeterias or vendors, and have to pay twice the price for their food and other necessary commodities. Most of them are forced to abuse drugs, alcohol and nicotine. 75 to 80 per cent of the girls suffer from STDs. More than half of the girls are HIV infected.

Sharon: What is the PHO doing to deal with the situation?

Dr I.G.: The prevention of child prostitution and the containment of AIDS are two of our main aims. We have a mobile clinic – donated by a German organisation – and go out into red light districts several times a week with a team consisting of health workers, social workers and ex-sex workers. We distribute free condoms, and provide medical check-ups and counselling on specific health or social problems. In many of the brothels there are prostitutes working for us, helping to educate others so as to prevent the spread of AIDS. We have had considerable success in this area.

Sharon: What success have you had with your other main aim, the prevention of child prostitution? Is it possible to rehabilitate the children you rescue from the brothels?

Dr I.G.: At the moment, the emphasis is on prevention rather than rescue. The problem is, where can they go after they have been rescued, or when they contract AIDS and are thrown out of the brothels? They are often rejected by their communities and families and cannot return home, and we simply do not have the facilities to look after these girls. We have a twenty-five-acre plot of land on the Bombay–Goa highway, where we had planned to build a home for rescued children, a training centre and a school – but we simply don't have the funds to carry on. The PHO operates on a shoestring.

UPDATE 2016

Sharon: Dr Gilada, it's good to talk to you again! It's been sixteen years since our first interview took place. I'd like to know if anything has changed in that time, and especially, if things in Mumbai have improved.

Dr Gilada: Things have indeed changed. Street and brothel prostitution has decreased a great deal, by almost 80 per cent, thanks to the HIV awareness, and HIV affliction among sex workers. New recruitment is less, as their trade/business has taken a beating. Child prostitution, though not extinct, is much reduced.

Sharon: Did the home for rescued children ever materialise?

Dr Gilada: The planned home for rescued sex workers could not come to fruition due to legal tangles and opposition from the villagers surrounding the land.

Sharon: So that's good and bad news at the same time. It's good to know that there are now fewer recruits to the trade, but it's sad that it still continues at all, and that the home could not be established. What does your work consist of now?

Dr Gilada: Most of my time is dedicated to working for HIV/AIDS patients at my clinic. I deal with several young children/adolescents, who have been infected at birth, now at marriageable age. They have their own challenges.

Sharon: Dr Gilada, I thank you for this interview, and wish you all the best for your important work.

Acknowledgments

The work for this book goes back over a decade: the basic research was done for another, similar, book way back in the year 2000, and my greatest debt is to Dr Ishwarprasad Gilada, who so kindly explained the Mumbai situation to me, answered my questions, accompanied me into Kamathipura, and basically gave me the background for Asha's story. So to him go my first thanks.

For me, writing a new novel is a demanding time, especially as I am also in full-time employment, and have a disabled husband. Friends, both in real life and virtual, help me to relax. So thanks go to Gisela Oess-Langford, Helen Zettler, Ann Claypole, Angelika Frank in Germany; my cousin Rod Westmaas and his wonderful wife Juanita Cox Westmaas in the UK; my fellow Bookouture authors Rebecca Stonehill, Renita D'Silva and Debbie Rix; and of course my children-friends, Saskia and Miro. It's so easy to fly off into a fictional world and never return; thanks to you all for helping to keep me grounded!

Last but not least, thanks to my super-editor Lydia Vassar-Smith for her help in moulding this book into its proper shape; and to Kim Nash, Lauren Finger, Molly Crawford and everyone else on the Bookouture team. Again: Thanks!

Sharon